Acknowledgements

The Angel of Justice: Vatican would not be possible without the hope and faith of the lovely bunch of people who read the original stories I had written.

Thank you to Sarah Barnes, Matthew Brown, Emma Wilson, Nina Parkin and Randy Belaire your love for the character has kept him alive all these years.

Also thanks to the talented artists that have fought side by side with Vatican as we battled to bring it to life as a comic. Thank you Aidan Mountford, Dody Eka, Lee Ciasullo.

VATICAN

ANGEL OF JUSTICE

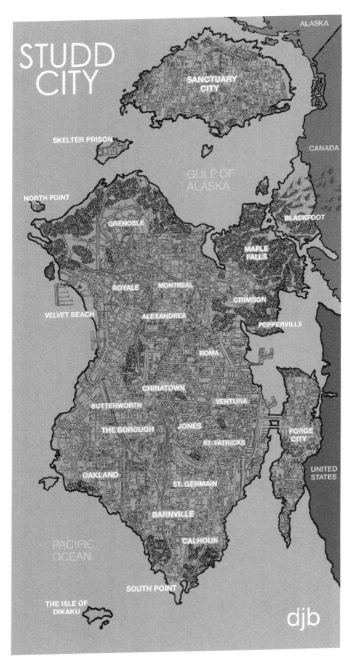

STUDD CITY

ALASKA

SANCTUARY CITY

SKELTER PRISON

CANADA

GULF OF ALASKA

NORTH POINT

GRENOBLE

BLACKFOOT

MAPLE FALLS

ROYALE   MONTREAL

CRIMSON

VELVET BEACH   ALEXANDREA

PEPPERVILLE

ROMA

CHINATOWN

BUTTERWORTH   VENTURA

THE BOROUGH   JONES

FORGE CITY

ST. PATRICKS

UNITED STATES

OAKLAND   ST. GERMAIN

BARNVILLE

PACIFIC OCEAN   CALHOUN

SOUTH POINT

THE ISLE OF DIKAKU

djb

For everyone that still believes in heroes.

Chapter 1

GENESIS

The Creation of the World

In the Beginning, God created the heaven and the earth. And the spirit of God moved upon the face of the waters. And God said, "Let there be light" and there was light.

And God said, "Let there be a firmament in the midst of the waters and let it divide the waters from the waters." And God said, "Let the dry land appear." And God said, "Let earth bring forth grass, and herb yielding seed and the fruit tree." And God made two great lights, he made the stars also. God created great whales and every living creature, which the waters brought forth abundantly and every winged fowl and made the beasts of the earth and God said, "Let us make man in our image." And God saw everything that he had made and behold. It was very good.

Holy Bible

Thomas Gabriel sarcastically chortled to himself as he sees the irony scribed into the worn pages of the thick leather backed bible, which was safely nestled on his lap. He closes the book, the heavy mass of pages thump together sweeping the tiniest puff of air into his face, bringing forth with it all the fabulous aromas that this ancient tome possesses. The kind of smells that only seem to dwell in the oldest of books. Thomas smiles again seeing the bold calligraphic lettering shimmering in worn gold, showing the words 'The Holy Bible'. He pushes the bridge of his glasses back up his slender nose with his index finger where his dark rectangular framed glasses settle back into place. He looks around the Boeing 747 as passengers clamber for their coats and their carry-ons that have been hidden away in the darkness of the overhead storage units. Thomas shakes his head in wonderment, *why don't people just be patient and wait* he thought to himself. A disgruntled looking stewardess appears from behind the curtain and snatches the tannoy receiver from its holster. She blares into the receiver "Ladies and Gentlemen!" her screeching voice crackles through the static and feedback as it bursts from the speakers scattered all around the aircraft. The sound is so irritating it stops everyone in their tracks. The stewardess's demeanour mellows and she returns to her normal tone.

"May I remind you that the Captain has turned on the fasten seatbelt sign! We will be landing shortly. Please make sure that your seat belt is securely fastened!" and through a grin as large as a Cheshire cat's (and through gritted teeth) she says, "Thank you." The Stewardess disappears back behind the curtain accompanied by (probably) an array of obscenities under her breath. Thomas turns to look out of the cabin's window and through a thin layer of congested condensation, he glances for the first time in many years to the place of his birth, Studd City. He chuckles to himself again as he remembers the irony that grabbed his attention from the last line of the first paragraph of Genesis. *And it was very good...* but Studd City wasn't. It was not very good at all.

Chapter 2

From a few thousand feet framed by masses of doughy clouds and set on an exquisite tranquil vanilla sky, Studd City could be mistaken for a pleasant place to live. Stunning in fact, especially with a setting fall sun catching its own breathtaking reflection in the gigantic glass structures. Structures that are so gargantuan that they have only the birds for company to share their lonely days with. These grand structural designs stand firm and strong, arrogantly showing off their architectural beauty, flaunting it in fact like an enthusiastic peacock does with its plumage prior to copulating. However these buildings are very new and they cast a dominating and intimidating shadow over the rest of the city. Dismissing anything beneath their supercilious gaze as they ignore what dwells below, the downtrodden roots of Studd City. The real Studd City. If you dig down deep through the overbearing silhouette of the modern assembly, you'll find a desolate place, frigid and desperate. A place where crime runs amuck like an unruly brat with a loaded catapult. The innocents that live there carry on with their daily routines. They try their best to turn a blind eye and try to forget the things they see, erasing the sights and sounds from memory. They exist in a constant pattern of pretence. They sink further and further into a mire of denial every passing day. No, local shopkeeper, Mr. M. Brown of Montreal Square didn't just see those two degenerates drag a young woman into a secluded dark alley. No, he didn't hear the distressing squeals and muffled blubbering of yet another rape victim. No, Miguel Sanchez, the driver of the night bus from Race Street to Icarus Lane didn't notice in his rear view mirror a group of thugs hammering a defenceless homeless man into a quivering pile of pulp on the backseat. And no, yoga instructor Charlotte Skinner, didn't leave the YMCA in Ventura one evening and witness a man selling illegal substance to a cluster of crater faced school children. No, her pace just quickened and she kept on walking. The twelve hit and runs in numerous areas leaving eight dead - two of those just children, three left with broken bones and severe injuries and one man currently in St. Vincent's Hospital fighting for his very existence on life support was witnessed by no one. Yes, Studd City has poison running through its very veins, and there is no vaccine. Thomas Gabriel looks down at the city below, squinting in the glare of the sun. The plane circles the dormant city like a hungry vulture stalking some half-starved and dehydrated pitiful creature with nothing left to do but let the scavengers take it. Thomas brushes his floppy hazel hair back into place and sighs the heaviest of sighs, the sort of prolonged sigh one emits that seems to go on forever. That kind of nervous exhale one releases when one is on the verge of a life changing escapade. A mixture of fear and adrenaline is unleashed as one struggles to get control of one's conscious. The side of your brain that produces uncertainty and trepidation. It's a battle that doesn't always bring victory, the war between mind and matter is an ongoing one. *Should I just stay on the plane and go back to Rome?* But Thomas has come an extremely long way and this time his drive is the victor.

No. Of course not! I have a job to do and I will see it through. I have to.

He looks down again surveying Studd City through a concentrative squint, investigating what he can see like a detective does a murder scene. Thomas begins to softly rub his fingertips over a small embossed scar shaped like a crescent moon, which slices through his right eyebrow, no longer allowing the growth of hair to sprout from the blemished skin. He does this for several minutes, fixated on what lies beneath. A habit he has had for a long time that he doesn't realise he does. *Those are new.* He thinks to himself as he focusses on the enormous skyscrapers that pierce the sky like regimental pipes that rise from a cathedral organ. This part of the city has had a tremendous amount of capital spent on it, but curiously not in any other part of the city can any new builds be seen.

It's like night and day down there. Fantastical new improvements to one area and then none to any of the others? Curiouser and curiouser thinks Thomas as he caresses his now heavily stubbled chin.

I desperately need to shave.

The travelling regime has taken its toll on Thomas. A couple of hours from Rome to Zurich and then the long haul across the pond to the United States, that has taken just under ten hours. And obviously his daily skincare routine has also suffered because of this. For one that likes to stay clean-shaven all the time for his job, a daily shave is a must.

That five o'clock shadow soon comes around.

However at this moment in time there is nothing he can do about that. The bulbous Boeing 747 from Liberty 3 airlines gradually starts to descend. Thomas' ears immediately become congested and it takes his attention away from his 15" x 10" pane. His hearing now impaired with everything sounding slightly muffled as if his head has been submerged in a fish bowl.

I hate that.

Thomas rapidly manipulates his lower jaw into several peculiar positions to unblock his ears. His ears pop just as the Stewardess can be heard once again over the tannoy.

"Ladies & Gentlemen, we're now approaching Studd City where the local time is 18:16. At this stage, you should be in your seat with your seatbelt firmly fastened. Personal television screens, footrests and tables must be stowed away and all hand luggage stored either in the overhead lockers or under the seat in front. Please ensure all electronic devices including laptop computers and computer games are turned off." The Stewardess's eye brows rise into her heavily made up forehead to emphasise the importance of her next statement.

"Please! remain seated until the aircraft comes to a complete stop!" the erratic eyebrows are immediately replaced by that pearl grin once again.

"Thank you again for choosing Liberty 3 Airlines." The Stewardess quickly holsters her handset like some seasoned gunslinger in an old western. Her face drops again out of tiredness and annoyance before disappearing back behind the curtains to the mysterious land of First Class. Thomas smiles at the fleeing stewardess and her false faces.

I guess she's had a long day, we all have. Can't really blame her for what they put up with though, the general public can grate on the most patient of us. A smile costs nothing but a false one... well it isn't really worth it is it? Two faces. Yes, most of us wear two faces.

Thomas looks down at Studd City as the aircraft heads for the airport.

Yin and Yang. Just like Studd City, it wears two faces, but which one is the Yin, and which one is the Yang? The beautiful buildings that have been constructed to glamorise the city by the rich, the powerful and the no doubt corrupt. Or the downtrodden and overlooked, struggling to stay alive from day to day, treading water in the murky pool of crime and poverty. Who really knows for sure. But I will know. I have made it my mission to know.

Thomas fidgets with the collar on his shirt, stuffing two of his slender fingers down deeply past his Adam's apple and adjusting the uncomfortable stiff collar of his clerical shirt.

I guess I'll never get used to this thing, but it comes with the territory.

Thomas gazes out of the window again.

But, that is the least of my worries. I know what is really going on down there and if nobody else is going to do anything about it, then I guess I will.

Chapter 3

Thomas stands patiently in the baggage claim area of Studd City Airport. He is swamped by a gaggle of other passengers from flight L3 2510, tired and bitter after such a long flight. Now they must wait for their luggage at the empty carousel fizzing like a box of pissed off puff adders. Thomas looks around patiently, people watching, something that he has found he always does and in a perverse kind of way, a pass time he enjoys immensely. He tries to block out the seething profanity that hisses through their gritted teeth like poisonous gas.

"For God's sake!" comes an aggressive growl through the crowd, followed by a "Jesus Christ" and then (what he considered uncalled for) the legendary "Fucking Hell!"

Thomas shakes his head, *why does the big man and JC always get the blame?*

Then came the extremely loud "C'mon you whore fucking douchebags!" in a gruff Brooklyn accent.

That's a new one on me thought Thomas with an uncontrollable smirk caressing his lips. When he looked around and nobody batted an eyelid, that is when Thomas realised he was back in Studd City. Soon after the douchebag declaration the worn rubber conveyor belt starts up and slowly begins chicaning, like a sidewinder does through the thick dunes of the hot desert sand. Finally, the luggage starts to appear through the black rubber flaps that conceal the douchebags in their natural habitat. No doubt taking a cigarette break and watching the unbeknownst angry passengers boiling in their own aggravation, waiting until the very moment the Vesuvius explodes. You can just imagine the baggage handlers sitting there, taking bets on who will break first. Everyone pushes forward in a chaotic mess to get as close as they possibly can to the sluggish carousel that carries on its back an abundance of various types of suitcases. So many colours spew onto the belt, vivid bright coloured cases making it easier for its owners to find them like a moving rainbow. It's almost as if a small child had purposely emptied the contents of their *M&M's* packet, to survey what vibrant shades lay hidden within. Mass hysteria takes over and then it is a free for all. Like a scene from a zombie movie, grabbing arms stretching to their fullest, all of them trying to grasp their cases through a relentless wall of bodies that are unwilling to move for anyone. Thomas watches this closely. He does not move a muscle, he just observes. To him they appear as if they are in slow motion and then he can really witness the carnage playing out before his eyes.

If the people of Studd City are like this at baggage claim, then what chance do I have of helping them?

The rabble descend on the luggage like uncontrollable rabid animals. Thomas remains upright and still waits patiently. Finally, he spots his suitcase slowly meandering towards him. In a strange way the suitcase seems to mirror his posture, standing upright in all the pandemonium around them, the case is small indicating that its owner travels light. The tan leather is worn and stifled with several stickers that have started to corrode, indicating the places they have visited. Amongst these decals that act like a photo album of their travels together, are countries such as France, Italy, Germany, Russia, Japan, Thailand and China, all of them proudly showing off national monuments or landmarks. The case arrives and is immediately intercepted by Thomas with surprising feline reflexes, as he grabs the handles and snatches it away from the carousel. With the two reunited they make their way towards the exit. Thomas walks through the busy airport, his finely cut Italian leather shoes gleam in the strobe lighting and tap out an almost rhythmical ditty on the hard floor below, like a pair of vigorous woodpeckers jackhammering away at some redwood. His dark suit and a clerical shirt is shrouded by a dark woollen double breasted peacoat. As Thomas approaches the exit of the airport, the doors slide open as if it was some long-lost relative welcoming him with open arms. He steps through back into the place he once called home. He stops and looks out at the skyline in the distance. A lot has changed but in a strange way it looks the same to him, even with an increased mass of large buildings to the southwest side of the island. The fall sunset is a captivating array of oranges and pinks. Thomas stands on the sidewalk adjacent to the drop off zone which is filled with all manner of different coloured Taxi cabs of various firms. Thomas has zoned out and is fixated at the skyline that glitters seductively with winking lights of fabulous blues, yellows and reds. Suddenly the cool fall breeze caresses his face and with it, carries all the familiar odours that he left behind all those years ago. The over baked doughnuts near Ventura, the congested fumes from the constant traffic, even the sickening aroma of dead fish from the docks brings a smile to his lips in a moment of surreal nostalgia. The wind blows again, this time chillier as if to persuade Thomas to return from his trip down memory lane and move on. He shivers, and his skin is coated with a layer of goose bumps which sends that tender shock all over his body in an uncontrollable domino effect. Thomas lowers his case to the sidewalk below and buttons up his coat. He delves into his coat's deep pocket and retrieves a beautifully vibrant red scarf which he quickly whips around his neck, like a boa constricts around a tree branch. The scarf flaps uncontrollably in the evening breeze as if it was looking for an escape route. Thomas quickly grabs a hold of the flaying piece and packs it tightly inside his coat. With the wind playing havoc with his hair, Thomas fights to brush it back into place but to no avail and immediately gives up, sighing with a little hint of annoyance. As he pushes his glasses back up the bridge of his nose where they belong, a gruff voice gets his attention like someone chewing on rocks it makes its way through the wind.

"Hey, Guy!" says the voice.

Thomas looks startled and replies uncharacteristically "Huh?".

He glances over to see a large boar like face hanging from a yellow taxi cab window.

"You need a ride guy or what?" Asks the driver.

"Oh, erm... yes! Yes, I do." replies Thomas.

"Hop on in, Guy!"

For a split-second, Thomas asks himself whether he wants to climb into a cab with this disgusting looking sow of a creature who sits there filling the window with his bloated frame. It wasn't that the driver was morbidly obese that put him off riding with him, but the fact that he was probing the contents of his right nostril with his index finger digging up there so deeply, it's as if there was a gold rush at mount snout and he was the prospector. But Thomas wasn't that shallow and he climbs into the back seat of the cab closing the door behind him. He is immediately struck with a very unpleasant scent, the unholy union of flatulence, sweat and cigar smoke.

Lovely thought Thomas sarcastically as the offensive trifecta viciously attacked his twitching nostrils, causing the centre of his face to contort the same way it would if a slice of lemon had been wedged into his mouth. Thomas makes eye contact with the driver in the rear-view mirror and promptly amends his misshapen appearance and smiles as to not offend the driver. The driver smiles back flashing an unfinished smile, several of his teeth are missing giving him the appearance of used piano keys.

"Where you goin' to?" Asks the driver, followed by several coughs and splutters to which at one-point, Thomas did indeed think that a lung would be hacked up to join his ornamental Buddha on the dashboard.

"Royal Street, please."

"No problem!" snorts the driver as they pull away. Thomas soon becomes somewhat used to the unpleasant odour and starts to lose himself in thought, as darkness starts to consume the sky above and he is absorbed by the alluring lights outside as they move deeper into the city.

Well, it's good to be back...I guess?! It's been a long time since I've found myself penned in by the impenetrable walls of this concrete jungle. Years. Yes, it's been years. Heck, I was only a kid when I left and after living on these streets for a few months, I thought I knew everything there was to know about the world. Boy was I wrong!

Thomas gazes out of the window, caught in between the limbo of the Studd City of his past, the one he remembers and the one he sees on the other side of the taxi cab window now.

But some thing's never change, in some cases they get a lot worse.

Thomas slowly shakes his head in disbelief as blatant acts of crime go on all around him, while he sits helpless in the back of the pungent taxi. They are halted for a moment at the traffic lights and Thomas witnesses an elderly gentleman hobbling along on his cane at a snail's pace. If ever anybody looked more out of place, it was this silver haired senior citizen enclosed by the endless array of vibrant graffiti that congests the walls behind him. Thomas wondered if this old fellow would ever reach his destination in such leaden-footed motion.

What are you doing around these parts of the city after dark anyway? You should be safely nestled away in your apartment by now. Slippers, hot mug of cocoa, watching reruns of M*A*S*H while you drift in and out of dreamland in your cosy armchair. Instead you're shuffling around Patera, one of the most dangerous places in this city.

Just then, a young-looking guy dressed in an all grey sweat suit topped off by a hood to cover any disguising features he might have, strolls up to the elderly man. With a ridiculous swagger that these modern-day wannabe gangsters do, almost as if the one leg is on a coiled spring. The hooded youth kicks the old man's cane out of his hand and the poor elderly gentleman collapses in a heap on the sidewalk. The youth punches the guy square in the face and then rummages around in the man's coat pocket and retrieves what appears to be a wallet. He removes the money that lay within and then throws the wallet back down on the poor defenceless old man, before bouncing off down the street. Thomas' face is consumed with colour out of sheer vexation and he tries to open the door, but the handle is not cooperating due to it being locked by the driver, obviously to stop his fares leaving without paying.

"Hey, Guy! I ain't letting you out in this neighbourhood!" Grunts the driver.

"But, the old man, he was..." Pleads Thomas.

"Sorry, but it ain't our problem."

Thomas' beseeching is to no avail as the lights turn green and they're on their way again. All Thomas can do is woefully watch on as the old man tries to get to his feet all alone.

I wish I could have helped him. Damn it! He sighs. *The most disappointing part of that whole performance was that nobody lifted a finger to help him or even batted an eyelid at what occurred. This has become the norm. This is what I have come to put a stop to.*

A look of determination etched itself across the brow of Thomas, who was trying to calm himself down after the despicable act he had the misfortune of spectating. As they enter the area known as Roma, the ambience changes to that of illuminating lights of seductive shades of red, enticing and inviting. This was the city's red-light district.

"I don't mind letting you out here, Guy." Chuckles the driver.

"No thanks!" comes the immediate reply from Thomas.

"You sure? Some of these girls are fucking hot, I tell ya! And they'll do anything, and I mean anything for the right price." The driver and Thomas make eye contact in the rear-view mirror, with an awkward wink from the driver to his passenger. Thomas answers with a look of disgust that he was unable to conceal, the driver gets the idea.

"Sorry I asked." He shrugs and focusses back on the safari of whoredom outside. Gentlemen's clubs queue up next to each other, congesting the strip with one after another. Each trying to out do their competitor with more flamboyant lights and signs and each name more elaborate than the next. *Masquerades* and *The Cat's Whiskers* appear to be the venues of choice on this particular evening. As you move down the strip, lesser clubs and businesses can be made out by smaller signs. The majority just settling for the three X's emblazoned on the side of most buildings, with most of the bulbs either flickering wildly or defunct. A group of prostitutes huddled together under the strobe of a streetlight shout obscene remarks towards passers-by and the slow-moving traffic that rolls past. A large breasted black woman with a blonde wig and wearing some kind of cerise leather catsuit, makes eye contact with Thomas. She blows him a kiss and purrs like an aroused feline.

"Hey, sugar! Wanna slice of this pie?!"

Thomas just gawks at her like a fawn staring down the barrel of a hunter's rifle. She quickly slides down the zipper of her catsuit with her long slender fingers that are topped with serrated golden nails, all uniform and identical. She pulls it open with both her hands, exposing her voluptuous ebony breasts for all to see. Her nipple protrudes, and she caresses it with her thumb and index finger, squeezing it slightly.

"How about a suck on these big bad titties, mister?" Embarrassment rains down on Thomas like a monsoon and his face glows a blaring red that mimics the neon signs that flicker at him from outside. The car moves on and Thomas tugs at his collar emitting air like a boiling pressure cooker.

Well, that sums up just how bad this city has got. I can almost smell the fear in the air. Time has not been kind to this city and the people who inhabit it. These streets are filled with evil...pure evil! I hope and I pray that I can make a difference to this place, but before I start on my journey I have one stop to make.

"Here ya go. Royal Street!" scoffs the driver.

"Thank you."

"That'll be $22.50!" Thomas hands over three ten-dollar bills.

"Keep the change."

Thomas steps out the cab and it drives away, leaving Thomas standing on the corner of Royal Street looking up at an old derelict building.

23

Chapter 4

Standing on the corner of Royal Street is a dilapidated building. It is easy to see that once upon a time this structure would have been majestic in its appearance, with several exquisite designs hand carved into the stone. However, weather damage and damp have double teamed it so much it is now too difficult to tell what the design was originally meant to be. Amazingly plant life has started to sprout out of various cracks in the buildings face and soft moist moss hangs off ledges and drainpipes as if clinging on for dear life. Yes, this tall once slender structure now appears almost lifeless and crooked, giving the impression of an elderly person holding one's self up with the use of a crutch, fearing that at any moment it could come tumbling down. Thomas stands at the foot of the building and looks up at it, the roof disappearing into the dark night sky. *The old place seems a lot smaller now.*

He surveys the building, glancing at the broken panes in the windows, some of them boarded up by various rogue pieces of wood that look as useless as the building does. Thomas approaches the building and slowly steps up the small flight of steps that lead to the two large wooden doors. The once thick magnificent mahogany doors are now sadly riddled with thousands of tiny holes, manufactured by every type of wood's arch nemesis, woodworm. A bronze plaque can be seen bolted to the wall adjacent to the entrance. The words etched into it cannot be seen due to a thick layer of dirt and dust, driving home the fact that this place has been closed down for a very long time, years in fact. Thomas wipes away the grime with the sleeve of his coat to unveil the words 'The Studd City Orphanage for Boys' and then underneath in smaller letters 'Established in 1888'. Thomas tries the door and to his astonishment it opens. A backdraft of nostalgia is carried on a cloud of disrupted dust, becoming the harbinger of recollection immediately effecting Thomas' emotional state. Sorrow is the first sensation he experiences.

I forget how this place made me feel.

He steps in through the doorway and finds himself in the large entrance hall. He loosens his grip on his suitcase and allows it to drop to the bare floorboards below. A cloud of dust erupts and engulfs the case like a sandstorm, before seemingly disintegrating into nothingness. Thomas stands there taking in all the memories that overwhelm him, so much so he is unaware of even dropping the suitcase.

All the familiar smells are back again. It's like I have never been away. I can still smell that vile concoction of the weeks leftovers we used to receive on Saturday evenings. Repulsive stuff. It's safe to say the chef, Ms McIntyre was not an expert in the culinary arts and received no Michelin stars for her efforts at Studd City's Orphanage for Boys. But then there is the pain I feel. That is the emotion I can no longer suppress. So much pain. So much sadness confined by these walls.

Thomas looks around and surveys the hallway. A thick layer of dust blankets everything. On his left is the library, its doors open wide but nothing of any interest can be seen. No furniture, no books, just wall to wall mahogany shelving peppered in woodworm holes. In front of him is a bifurcated staircase that splits off midway and joins the 1st floor with twin stairwells. Apart from a few broken spindles, the staircase looked in good condition but with closer inspection, one would soon recognise that our old friend the dreaded woodworm had struck again. The walls of the building are no longer dressed in such luxuries as wallpaper and bare brick is dominant throughout.

I am amazed that this place hasn't been used for a crack den or bed and breakfast for some down and outers. Not even a glimpse of graffiti. Very odd. Or maybe all the lowlifes in this city once dwelled here and want nothing more to do with the place. I can't say I blame them.

Thomas steps forward further into the hallway approaching the stairs. He places his hand on the sphere like newel post disturbing yet more dust, but he stops and looks to his left and sees a closed door with the simple word 'Boys' stencilled onto it in golden lettering. Thomas stares at it and swallows hard.

Pull yourself together Thomas. You're a grown man now for goodness sake. He can't hurt you now.

The pep talk seemed to work and he span on the spot and moved towards the door, but still Thomas had to mentally convince himself that the experiences that he once encountered on the other side of this door were not lying in wait for him, ready to ambush him. He pushes the door which demolishes several cobwebs as it sluggishly opens. The tight hinges screech like a ravenous buzzard that hangs in the wind before plummeting down on its prey. Thomas steps into the room and just like Dorothy stepping into Oz, he was in a different world or different time. In his head he was back there again and he could see it all taking place as clear as day, remembering when he was twelve years of age. Six sparkly white porcelain basins stand regimentally in a line each paired with a small mirror screwed above it. The chrome taps glisten in the fluorescent strobes that clings to the ceiling. No urinals like in most male lavatories, but adjacent to the sinks in mirroring fashion were six cubicles, all with cobalt blue doors hanging in place.

A young Thomas enters the restroom and approaches the sinks. He turns the hot tap on, it spits and splutters before flowing into a constant stream. He takes the bar of soap that sits in a damp icky nest of residue on the ledge where the bar spends its lonely existence. Thomas vigorously rubs his hands around the bar of soap which immediately lathers up and bubbles away under the heat of the hot tap, steam rising from the water. Suddenly he hears sniggering seep from one of the cubicles. He investigates the mirror and the reflection shows that the one of the cubicles behind him is indeed closed and soft clouds of smoke rise out of it like a peculiar shaped chimney. Thomas goes back to washing his hands and ignores the chortling that he can hear. As the rapid flow washes off the froth from his hands, he hears the cubicle door unlocking looking in the mirror to see who is in the cubicle, the steam has all but consumed the mirror and obscures his view. Thomas turns around to see three large boys standing in the cubicle, all of them a few years older than him and much bigger than him. All of them with lit cigarettes clenched between their lips, the embers burning away mimicking their eyes that do the same as they stare at the unwanted visitor.

"Hey, Fuck face!" calls the boy in the centre of the trio.
Ricky. Ricky Landell. I thought I would never set eyes on you again.

"Hey! I'm talking to you, A hole!" Ricky says raising his voice, which is much to the pleasure of Tweedle Dee and Tweedle Dum that hang back and snort at everything that comes out of Ricky's mouth. Thomas slowly turns the tap off and walks towards the paper towel dispenser situated on the wall at the other side of the wall.

"I'm leaving now." squeaks Thomas.
Ricky's eyes double in size and he throws his cigarette on the gleaming tilled flooring.

"Oh, are you?!" Thomas pulls out a paper towel and quickly tries to dry his shaking hands. The trio move in on Thomas like a pack of hyenas.

"Nobody uses this restroom without paying a price!" Ricky says in a matter of fact tone, as he treads on the discarded cigarette and trounces it into the tiles with the sole of his shoe, his two disciples follow suit.

"I only came in to wash my hands, that's all!" stutters Thomas.

"That's all?!" barks Ricky sarcastically and is immediately joined by the others parroting him.

"That's all, that's all!" and then bursting into fits of

28

laughter.

"Well fuck face, I'm afraid we charge double for hand washing." Ricky snarls as he towers over a helpless Thomas.

"But, I haven't got any money!"

Thomas' eyes become glazed with the consummation of a tear.

"Well I guess we will have to teach you a lesson then, hadn't we?"

"No! Please!" Thomas snivels as he attempts to make his getaway through the door but his route is cut off by Tweedle Dee smiling sadistically.

"I don't think so squirt!" he chuckles.

Thomas turns around and is met by a fist straight in his left eye. His vision becomes blurred and the tears that were teetering on his eyelids fall rapidly. He sobs as his head throbs and his ears ring like the constant wail of a fire alarm. Ricky clenches his fist up tightly again, so tight that his skin turns pale. He hits him again, this time in his left temple so rapidly that the young defenceless Thomas loses count, like the tears that fall from his eyes, too many to count.

Thomas falls to the hard, cold unforgiving tile as Ricky stands over him breathing heavily brushing back the greasy blonde hair that hangs over his crater faced appearance.

"I told you...you have to...pay the...price." Puffs Ricky almost out of breath. Thomas lies on the floor his left eye closing concealing his innocent soft green iris. A trickle of blood emerges from his nostrils as he becomes immersed in a puddle of tears and now urine, as he slowly wets himself.

"He's pissed himself!" laughs one of the disciples.

"You dirty little shit!" snarls Ricky, "You know where piss goes don't ya?" he asks.

"Please!" sobs Thomas, mucus bubbling from his weeping nostrils as he pleads for no more.

"Pick him up!" sneers Ricky, and his acolytes grab poor Thomas and follow their leader to the cubicle from where they came.

"This is where piss goes, fuck face!" and points to the toilet bowl that is filled with used cigarette butts and un-flushed urine.

"No, no please don't!" cries Thomas struggling to no avail in the grip of Ricky's followers.

"Dunk him!" demands Ricky and they oblige, driving him headfirst into the contents of the toilet bowl. In the fishbowl of other people's waste, Thomas hears muted laughter as tears mix with blood which in turn mixes with urine, stinging his eyes and tests his gag reflex. He retches, but is then pulled out as he tries to catch his breath but before he can, he hears the order again.

"Dunk him!" shouts Ricky again and immediately Thomas finds himself back in there. This time it isn't for long and he is pulled out again. Thomas' gag reflex can withstand no more and he vomits. The two let go of him and drop him into a heap on the cubicle floor. Thomas' bruised face hits the puddle of vomit. Ricky laughs at him as he curls up on the floor, taking the form of an impotent foetus.

"So, it's like I said, Fuck Face..." Ricky sneers as he unzips his fly and removes his penis as he starts to urinate on

Thomas.

"You want to go tinkle then you pay the price." Thomas emerges from his wicked reverie and drops to his knees in floods of tears.

Those boys were so cruel. So, so cruel. Why did they have to do that? The humiliation of it all.

Thomas removes his glasses and wipes his tears away with the back of his hand.

But, are they really to blame?

He looks around the deserted restroom which looks the same as it did back when he was child, apart from the grime that had been built up over years of being unused and just darker, like his memories there, dark. Nothing to illuminate them or the room now. Thomas rises from the dirty floor, the knees of his dark trousers now stained with a layer of dust that he tries to brush away with a sweeping hand. He walks towards the sinks and instinctively uses the same one he did all those years ago, he turns the tap but nothing. He wipes the dust and cobwebs from the mirror, which causes an unsuspecting spider to scurry for safety up the wall.

Thomas stares at himself and puts his glasses back on.

It was all they knew I guess. It was how they've been brought up.

"No, Thomas!" he says out loud his voice echoing around the empty room.

He talks to his reflection in the mirror and asks, "Why do you always have to see the good in people?" He sighs obviously knowing the answer, as he cannot win an argument with himself as he'll always know the answer. He turns and leaves the room. Thomas looks saddened as he leaves the room and returns to the hallway before moving towards the staircase. He puts his hand on the handrail and looks up the stairs. He takes several steps up in quick succession, which are accompanied by an aggravating screech each time the old wooden steps slumber is disturbed. Thomas' hand ploughs through the dust that blankets the handrail exposing the smooth mahogany beneath. His hand slides up the rail and then comes to a stop and he grips it tightly. He halts as he reaches the half landing. Another memory. Another painful souvenir from Studd City's Orphanage for Boys. A young Thomas saunters down the staircase towards the half landing where unfortunately for him, Ricky and a selection of his horde had settled, clustered together like the way Emperor Penguins huddle to shield themselves from the cold. Obviously up to no good. Thomas looks up and slows down when he sees them, his eye as black as an eight ball, bulbous and polished. He slows down as to try and pass them unnoticed but to no avail, one of Ricky's lackeys nudges Ricky and whispers something in his ear. Ricky looks up and makes eye contact with Thomas and grins callously.

"Hey fuck face, what happened to your eye?" Ricky asks sarcastically. Thomas ignores him and continues his way downstairs, but suddenly his way down is blocked by a barricade of bootlickers. Thomas stops dead in his tracks.

"Hey! He asked what happened to your eye?" growls one of the bricks from the wall of intimidation.

"Yeah! Answer the question, Asshole!" squeals another

shoving him in the chest. Young Thomas can now feel movement in his bladder and clenches his shaking thighs together tightly, fighting the urge not to wet himself again.

"Leave him." Says Ricky nonchalantly.

The unmovable mountain that stands in front of him sags and cracks begin to show as it starts to disband.

"But…" One of the minions attempts to ask but is cut off mid-sentence by Ricky who snaps like bear trap.

"I said leave him!" They part, and the way is clear. Thomas turns to face Ricky and manages a meek "Thank you."

Ricky nods at him in acknowledgement but as soon as Thomas goes to take the next flight of stairs down, Ricky kicks him in the backside causing Thomas to violently fall down the stairs. The sound of his feeble bones cracking as they strike the solid mahogany steps was sickening. He lands in a heap in the hallway like a bison that has been brought down by a band of native American arrows. He lies floored and motionless when he is quickly approached by Ms Blanchard, who comes to the fallen Thomas' aid.

"Are you okay, Thomas? What happened?" She asked in frantic concern. He looks at her through his one open eye with all the innocence of a child.

"I tripped… It was an accident." Ms Blanchard knew this wasn't the case and looks up the stairs wearing a scowl on slender face, just in time to see Ricky and his band disperse from the crime scene.

"What happened here?" she roars, but there was no answer in return only the sound of several pairs of feet stomping

33

up the first floor. Thomas returns to present day again, another unpleasant daydream, his fingers gripping the rail so tightly in anger.

Broke my arm that day.

He sighs again and with that his grip loosens and he carries on with his journey to the first floor. His pace now a little slower as he attempts to evade the apparitions that continue to plague him. Thomas reaches the top of the stairs and walks along a corridor, his nice shoes now scuffed by the blanket of dust that settles everywhere like freshly fallen snow.

They were bullies and I should have fought back, but I wasn't strong enough then. But I'm strong enough now. Yes, I'm strong enough that I won't let that happen again. Not to me and not to anyone else. I have no time for bullies. And there is no room for bullies in Studd City. In my city.

Thomas walks along a narrow corridor, becoming sandwiched either side by an abundance of doors. Some closed, some open but all of them homing old forgotten dormitories. He glances in as he passes them. The rooms still hoard decrepit metal frame beds, positioned in the same way they were left, in rows like forgotten tombstones in a cemetery.

They made my life here a living hell. I hated them but I have no room for hate in my life now. It is not healthy to hold on to such feelings.

Thomas passes room after room and it is obvious he has no emotional connection to any of the rooms on this floor, or surely he would stop and reminisce a while. He reaches another flight of stairs and continues to climb upward through the building, passing by several other dorm rooms and offices but ignores them completely.

All the boys lived and slept in these dorms. All of them except for me and one other kid. We didn't have the luxury of so much space, but we had something more precious in a place like this. Privacy.

It is not until he reaches the eighth floor that he stops, maybe to catch his breath. Now he stares at a small ladder that leads up to the attic room and suddenly again he is intercepted by the powers of recall. This time the musing is not unpleasant and a smile caresses his lips as he envisions a dumpy middle-aged woman, with greyish permed hair.

Mrs Jess!

"Now come along, Thomas. This is where you will be staying." She says softly.

Mrs Jess was Thomas' care worker and she was always so nice to him, he remembers her fondly.

What a lovely woman, Mrs Jess was. Homely and wholesome. She made me feel calm after what had happened to have me end up here. I needed her. She was my shoulder to cry on, and I did a lot of that back then. She had one of those faces that some old women have, like a Cabbage Patch doll, with those plump cheeks that seem to dominate her face, giving her those creases either side of her mouth. It made her look like a ventriloquist's puppet, but she was just so nice to me, so warm. She made me feel...well, normal.

Thomas stood there beaming at the thought of this ray of sunshine that beamed through his dark and cloudy past.

Just the thought of her rotund backside trying to climb up those steps was enough to set me at ease back then. Oh, what a sight. Still makes me smile now.

Thomas enters the attic room through a trapdoor and comes up like a gopher bursting from its hole in the ground. Two beds lie on the damp floorboards beneath a constant trickle of rainwater, which comes from a hole in the roof.

Yes, it's a shame that dear old Mrs Jess couldn't have stayed on. My life there might have been easier if I'd have had that sanctuary to go to share my problems and vent my frustrations. But, if I would have had that, then my whole life could have been different. Thank you for everything Mrs Jess. Dear old Mrs Jess.

He rises to his feet and stands in the small attic room surrounded by what appears to be rotting wood. The shattered roof above appears that its days at the top are numbered and is looking to join the circular window that is somehow hanging on in its decaying frame. He hears the echoing voice of Mrs Jess one more time.

"It'll be okay, Thomas. You are sharing with young Lewis here." As the sweet voice disappears for the last time to be locked away in the back of Thomas' mind, he sees a small black boy sitting crossed legged on one of the beds. He smiles at Thomas. One of those smiles that makes you feel comfortable, ear to ear in a way that presents his flawless pearly whites in all their glory. A genuine smile. A genuine person.

"Hey, Thomas. C'mon in!" Lewis says enthusiastically. A young Thomas looks up at Mrs Jess for reassurance and she gazes back at his puppy dog eyes and smiles and gives him a little nod. In that nod was all the trust that Thomas needed. Lewis sat on his bed surrounded by several old torn and tarnished boxing magazines.

"Hey Tom, you wanna look at my boxing magazines?" he asks Thomas excitedly.

"Sure!" comes the reply and young Thomas joins him on his bed as they look at his magazines together.

Lewis Johnson. My only childhood friend. We shared a common bond. We were both bullied. Lewis was bullied because of the colour of his skin but he was much tougher than me. Mentally stronger. He fought back. He was adamant he would one day become Heavyweight Boxing Champion of the world.

Thomas sits on the bed, the old dirty mattress that lies on it is wet through but he doesn't seem to notice.

He always had my back and looked out for me like a big brother. Even though I was two years his senior. One day he got jumped by an unknown gang. Yeah, unknown, sure! Well, he ended up in hospital.

Thomas rises from his squelching resting place and casually walks over to the window to look out at Studd City. All of it is lit up in an array of coloured lights like a Christmas tree, welcoming like butter wouldn't melt.

Lewis was one of the lucky ones. He made it out. One of the nurses that looked after him apparently took him into foster care. I never saw him again.

Just then, there is a huge smash which startles Thomas from his reminiscing and he sees a hole in the wall where the circular window once sat.

It's time I moved on before the whole place comes down.

Chapter 5

The dockyards of Studd City are situated in the southeast of the island and is the first district that one encounters when entering the city from the Ventura Bridge. This bridge connects Studd City to Forge City over the Hennig River. The history between Studd City and Forge City is not pleasant, since both cities have rival gangs that refuse to let go of a war that has been raging for decades. Ventura is home to one of the largest gangs in the United States of America, known as The Doomsday Gang. This particular gang was first introduced by its patriarch Salvatore Valentine AKA 'The Father of Crime' back during prohibition in the 1920's. Valentine controlled all the distribution of alcohol in Studd City, Forge City and further afield into small towns such as Barnville, Robertsville and Crimson. Valentine ran the city old school, through fear. Offering up protection to the small businesses in Studd City in exchange for money and goods. With Valentine's passing due to a lengthy battle with lung cancer his son, Vinnie 'The Thunder' Valentine took the reins and took The Doomsday gang in a new direction, the distribution of illegal substances throughout the city. Many look to catch him in the act but his hands are always clean and he has several legitimate businesses and restaurants throughout the city. All his dealings appear to be on the level, on paper anyway. You could say Vinnie Valentine is untouchable. Forge City homes the Hispanic gang known as La Familia and is run by a very aggressive and violent individual known as Eduardo Gonzalez, AKA 'The Coyote'. He still holds a grudge against The Doomsday Gang for allegedly leaving La Familia to take the wrap for some drug trafficking. This later saw all its members serve long stints in Skelter Prison situated on Skelter Island which has become known to all as Limbo as it sits between both cities on a piece of rock they call an island. While Gonzalez and his gang were away there was no one to watch over Forge City and The Doomsday Gang took it for their own. La Familia later took it back and forced The Doomsdayers back to Studd City and so the hatred has remained bubbling away like a cauldron of loathing and hostility. On this particular night in Ventura an area homing several abandoned warehouses was unusually active. Three large slender cranes stand upright and dormant, like a trio of scarecrows overseeing the evenings proceedings.

Various types of vehicles surround one warehouse in general and light illuminates through the countless shattered windows.

From the shelter of an undercover doorway, concealed in the gloom is a double doored emergency exit that is standing in for the main entrance this evening for all the venues visitors. Clouds of smoke emerge from out of the dark nook and dance together into the night sky before evaporating into the damp air of the neighbouring docks. The smoke rises out again and two men walk out from the darkness grasping cigarettes between their lips. Smoke continues to be emitted from the doorway and the figure of a man concealed by a red hooded sweatshirt, can be seen seated on the floor with his back up against the wall. One of the men paces back and forth the way that a would-be father anticipates the birth of his child. His hair is long and mousey and tied neatly and tort into a ponytail. His features are chiselled and ruggedly handsome which is framed by a short covering of stubble. He frantically looks at his fake watch with the word Bolex etched on its gunmetal face, displaying the time with its hands at precisely 9:23pm. The man is clad in a worn leather biker jacket and stonewash jeans tucked neatly into a pair of tan leather cowboy boots, with an intricate pattern woven into them. One item of special interest, is his large bulky belt buckle that depicts the skull of a bull draped in the controversial confederate flag.

"Where the hell is he?" He asks impatiently, taking yet another anxious drag on his receding cigarette.

The man standing next to him looks less anxious while he casually puffs on his cigarette as he looks out at the Hennig River. He is a larger man and wears a viridian shade of tracksuit that's trimmed with a thick white line that runs down the arm and leg. His skin is very pale and his hair is jet black and slicked back into a greasy looking pompadour style. He could almost be mistaken for a Vampire or maybe even Count Dracula himself, if it wasn't for his sturdy chin and square features.

"Dallas, are you sure you told him the right time?" He asks in a thick Eastern European accent. Dallas blasts another stream of cigarette smoke out of the corner of his mouth before answering.

"Yeah. 9 o'clock sharp!" Says Dallas before cutting him a confused look, "Boris, you were fucking there when I told him man!"

"Oh yeah!" comes the nonchalant response as he continues to watch the ripples in the Hennig River, caused by the gentle fall breeze. The man seated in the doorway leans out from the dimness, shrouded in a mass of marijuana smoke. Most of his face is concealed in shadow from his drooping hood, but his gaunt features can be made out on his long face. With pointed features, his nose slicing through the shadow looking like bird's beak.

"You know what he's like!" comes the rasp of the seated man.

"Yeah, Sniff is right. He's always fucking late!" agrees Boris.

"I know, I know! But this shit is important. We could all end up in a pair of concrete shoes if he carries on like this." Replies an anxiously pacing Dallas. Suddenly the distant rumble of a car engine can be made out, the sound rapidly becoming louder as a red car approaches in post-haste. The car is a 1992 Corvette ZR-1, coated in a luscious candy apple red and the nostalgic pop-up headlight beam slices through the night, illuminating the driver's welcoming committee.

"He's here!" says Sniff, before tucking himself back into the safety of his doorway. Boris and Dallas simultaneously turn to the sound of the oncoming muscle car, snarling away like an irritable panther. Both immediately forced to squint and shield their eyes by the dazzling headlights.

"Damn it, Spider!" grunts an annoyed Dallas, blocking the beams of light by raising his arm up to his face. The hard rubber tyres carve through the gravel as the Corvette skids to a halt in front of them. The headlights slowly sink back into the sanctuary of the hood and takes with them the twin beams. The engine dies.

"Finally! Where the hell have you been man?" calls Dallas stretching his arms out wide.

The door opens and out glides Spider, a black man with shoulder length dark hair, roped into a dreadlocked style.

"Yo, Mudder Fuckers! What's the haps?" grins Spider. The handsome Spider oozes charisma and it is immediately apparent that he is in charge and likes to play by his own rules. He slams the door shut and approaches Dallas stretching his arms open too.

"Dallas! My main man!" He hugs him, while Dallas remains standing arms out horizontally like an aircraft marshal, wearing an annoyed grimace on his stubbled face.

"Where have you been?" scoffs Dallas.

"Been cruising man! Got myself some sick new wheels!" He pulls away from Dallas and points to his new Corvette.

"That's a nice car!" Nods Boris in agreement. Dallas cuts Boris an irritated look.

"Don't encourage him, Boris!"

"But it is a nice car!" shrugs Boris.

"I know!" Snaps Dallas, who is then ganged up on by Sniff in the doorway, who doesn't move a muscle from the shroud of the doorway, but offers his thoughts on the matter.

43

"He's right, Dal. It is a nice car."

"I fucking know it's a nice Goddamn car!" shouts Dallas in aggravation. He looks at Spider who is just grinning profusely at him, his several gold teeth sparkling like nuggets sunk into the wall of a mine. Dallas sighs and shakes his head. "I don't know why I bother!" he says before fist bumping Spider who just laughs.

"C'mon, Webheads! We'd better get inside before Dal gets his panties all twisted."

Spider leads the way with an arrogant swagger, his pristine white trainers shuffling through the stones and gravel. He fist bumps Boris too, the golden chunk of bracelets clangs together as the two meaty paws connect, his forearm and triceps tense up with the impact. His white vest helps show of his athletic physique which is covered in tattoos, most noticeable in the designs are spiders, cobwebs and skulls.

"So where did you find the car?" Dallas asks, disposing of his cigarette after one final drag.

"Over in Butterworth, was left unattended outside Pinewood High. The asshole left the keys in with the engine running and everything." Brags Spider.

"What a dick! Must not be from round here." Chuckles Dallas.

"For sure!" Laughs Spider.

"Seriously though, you know the boss is gonna go apeshit cus we're late again man!" Dallas says, trying to get his point across. Spider stops in mid stride which halts Boris and Dallas in their tracks, obviously hammering home that Spider does indeed call the shots within this group. He looks at Dallas with a sincere look of seriousness on his youthful face, a face you can't quite put an age on but you know he looks younger than he is.

"Look, Dal, you're my boy, yeah?" he asks.

"Yeah, you know that." Dallas replies.

"Then trust me, yeah?" Smiles Spider, softly tapping Dallas' cheek with the palm of his hand.

"Okay, okay. Enough of this gooey shit!" Dallas replies smiling.

"Well, as long as you know. I ain't scared of the old pompous asshole! And he ain't no boss of me, got it?"

"Okay, man. Whatever you say, we are with you."

"Good!" Spider turns and moves on again towards the entrance. Sniff remains seated in the doorway as they approach, still sucking on his joint like some homeless chimney.

"You're late!" Spurts Sniff

"Fuck off, Sniff!" Replies Spider as he nonchalantly steps over him like he doesn't even exist and walks in through the doors.

Chapter 6

The broken down Ventura warehouse was illuminated by several long-chorded bulbs hanging from its metal girder rafters. The bulbs surrounded by rusty metal shades light up the cold hard concreted flooring, homing nothing of interest but empty wooden crates. The lights sway slightly in the evening breeze that is circulating in through the broken windows of the derelict building. The large roof of the structure is made up of corrugated metal sheets split up occasionally by long narrow skylights. The warehouse is swarming with Doomsday Gang members, all shapes, sizes and all races but all with the same despicable grimace etched on their faces. A kind of visage worn by the dastardly villainous bandits of the silent era, as they all appear to be planning some heinous act. A grumbling sound works its way around the warehouse as the gang members talk amongst themselves. There must be at least one hundred low life degenerates congregated in a half circle around three large individuals. Spider and his band enter with Sniff casually letting the door slam behind him. The noise echoes around the vast warehouse, reverberating through its corrugated roof panels causing an immediate turning of heads. Silence descends on the crowd as Spider and his troop are greeted by a sea of eyes, all of them fixated on the late arrivals, who have tried to sneak in and failed miserably. An awkward silence sets in, the fall breeze is all that can be heard now and Spider's group all seem to have shrunk in stature and appear sheepish and would love for the ground to open to swallow them whole. But not Spider, his heavily ringed fingers clench into tight fists, his arms tensing, mirroring the sneer that as formed on his face.

"What the fuck are they looking at?" Spider growls quietly. Dallas grabs his wrist and intervenes before Spider erupts like a volcano.

"Take it easy man." Dallas whispers. This seemingly calms the beast and Spider's posture loosens.

"So glad you finally blessed us with your presence, Spider!" A gravelly voice booms through the quietness. The voice is loud, and it is apparent with the swivelling of a hundred heads that it is the voice of the man in charge. He has such presence and respect that he has everyone's undivided attention with just one sentence.

The booming voice belongs to Vinnie 'The Thunder' Valentine, The undisputed leader of The Doomsday Gang. Spider can't help himself and as they join the rest of the group, he makes a snide comment.

"Hey man, just out there making your money for ya!"

Valentine smiles a crooked smile as his lips grasp a large bulbous Cuban cigar that burns away in his grip. He inhales before removing the chunky cigar from his lips and blows a large cloud of thick smoke into the air.

"I like that, and I'm going to let your lateness and disobedience slide just this once. I have more important matters to address than to waste time talking about you kid!" Valentine's smile turns into a sneer as he burns a hole straight through Spider's face. Valentine is a very large individual, his broad shoulders form his frame giving him a square like appearance to his huge upper body. He doesn't appear muscular or even fat for that matter, just big. Genetically gifted as if he were half man, half grizzly bear. The only thing bigger than his form is his presence. He stands with his rapidly receding cigar in-between his sausage like fingers, with a roomful of people silent in anticipation of what he is about to say. He is the conductor and these followers are his orchestra. Valentine looks out at his disciples waiting with bated breath for him to say something, anything. He knows that he could tell them anything and they would do it for him. He could tell them to all jump into the freezing cold Hennig River and fetch him the hidden treasure chest. He knows that and even some of his disciples know that, but it wouldn't stop them from looking. That is the amount of respect that he has with his gang. His Doomsday Gang. He brushes back his slick jet black hair that has grey flashes either side around his ears and takes another drag on his cigar. His piercing grey eyes, twinkle through the cigar smoke, eyes that look like they hold secrets, information and knowledge not to be shared with anyone else. He struts around surveying his flock, his Italian black leather shoes tapping on the concrete floor which echoes with every step. Valentine's style is impeccable, clad in a tailor made three-piece suit, in an elephant skin shade of grey, accompanied with a faint light pinstripe running throughout. A pristine white shirt is tightly fastened around his thick neck which is completed by a dynamic violet tie fixed in a chunky Windsor knot.

"My boys..." is all Valentine has to say and the place erupts in cheers and then deafening chants of 'Doomsday! Doomsday!' fills the empty building. Valentine turns and winks at the two figures that preside over him just a few yards back, The Chapman Twins. Two large looking individuals, bigger than Valentine himself but bulkier, and more rotund. They share identical features as they shared the womb, twins. 'Big' Ben and 'Little' Ben, ironically 'Little' Ben is taller than his brother by an inch. Both their egg like shaped heads gleam in the warehouse lighting, causing twin shimmers on each of their domes. Even their grooming is identical with both favouring a goatee moustache in an auburn nest of hair surrounding prised lips. Matching black sunglasses and black suits make up their uniform, complemented by the most lavish of accessorises, the HK MP5KA4 submachine gun.

"Boys! Boys... please!" Valentine holds his hands up in the air and the thundering bellows stops.

"Thank you all for coming. I understand it was short notice, but obviously I didn't get to discuss with you all the main reason for our last meeting. Due to the obvious interruption from the SCPD!" The mob start booing and showing their disapproval at the mention of Studd City's finest boys and girls in blue. Valentine raises his hand in the air again and they immediately stop their cries.

"But, they couldn't stop us, could they?" Cheers rise from mass and Valentine nods his gigantic head in agreement.

"No! No, they could not!"

The cheers grow louder, accompanied now by stomping of feet.

"We lost several good men last week and I'm sure it's obvious to you all that they did not die in vain. We will continue to push forward in the memory of our fallen brothers!" Valentine's voice grows in volume and so do his disciples.

"The Doomsday Gang is like a hydra! If you cut off our limbs we will grow stronger! We will grow hungrier! We will grow deadlier!" Intensity grows in the words that Valentine now speaks, helping to rile up his flock into a frenzy.

"They cannot kill The Doomsday Gang! Doomsday is forever!" He shouts, and the exuberant crowd eat it up like hungry crows picking at roadkill. They believe him. They love him. They think he is untouchable and for the most part, he is. As a youth he was like a rollercoaster that had no rails, a runaway train without a driver. He was irresponsible and disregarded the consequences of his actions, he believed his own hype and he paid for it. He spent a total of eight years in Skelter Prison on numerous visits to the island. His police record was as long as his arm. Everything from Grand theft auto, GBH, ABH, possession of illegal substance with the intent to sell as well as money laundering, robbery and firearm offences. But that was in the past and now he is a legitimate businessman. He has kept his nose squeaky clean for the last several years, overseeing the running of many popular Italian cuisine restaurants throughout Studd City, known simple as 'Valentines'. Now he is the puppet master and controls all the crime in the city, there is nothing that doesn't go through him and the SCPD are finding it very difficult to ever pin him to any wrong doing. Vinnie Valentine is as clean as a bar of soap.

"Obviously..." Valentine continues as the crowd simmers down again "...I don't have to tell you to all stay away from our old meeting place in Solo, the SCPD will have eyes on that place now. So, until you hear different from me or your generals this place will be the venue for all upcoming meetings"

Valentine takes a moment to survey the crowd, obviously looking for a particular person or persons in the captivated crowd. He locates who he was looking for and nods at four individuals standing together in the crowd. His Generals.

"Ah there you are. My boys, you all know who your General's are, but I want you to familiarise yourself with the other groups Generals. They will be taking a more hands on approach in my absence as I tackle those boring day to day problems of running a franchise. So, for all of you who don't know all the Generals, I would like to introduce you to firstly, my right-hand man and longest confidant... Jack 'Twitch' Thompson!" A middle aged pale man, with greying hair with flicks of white in it like some grizzled old badger, steps forward. His face is haggard and filled with wrinkles and lines, giving his skin the texture of an old mistreated treasure map. He wears a dark pair of trousers and an ugly olive coloured bomber jacket that has seen better days. His only real distinct characteristic is that he suffers from an uncontrollable nervous spasm and randomly convulses from time to time, but his right eye twitches the most and rapidly at that.

51

"Next up is the owner of 'The Cats Whiskers' Gentleman's Club, which I'm sure you're all familiar with. 'Cheshire' Charles Samuels!"

'Cheshire' Charles grins like the cat who got the cream as he raises his hand and waves it like a member of the royal family. He got his name for his remarkable resemblance to the Cheshire Cat from Lewis Carroll's, *Alice's Adventures in Wonderland*. Charles is a small black man of around 5 feet 5 inches, but he seemed bigger with his larger than life personality and flamboyant dress sense. This evening's choice was a shiny gold suit, leopard print tie, draped in a humongous white fur coat, like a lifeless polar bear carcass just left hanging from his shoulders.

"Hey, hey players! Hope to see you all at the club later. I got some top-notch booty working tonight! Hot Damn!" He squeals in his annoying high pitch voice, but with him saying this, excitement is stirred in the crowd. He laughs like some dying hyena as he arrogantly rubs his index finger across his moustache, like some prima donna.

"Okay, settle down you bunch of horny bastards!" Chuckles Valentine.

"I've got a feeling business is going to booming tonight, baby!" Laughs Charles clapping his hands before rubbing them together vigorously, the way you'd envision Ebenezer Scrooge to react on seeing the toppling piles of coins he has in his possession.

"Then my next General probably needs no introduction, but I'm going to give him one anyway." Smiles Valentine clamping the now half worn cigar into the corner on his mouth and pointing out towards the crowd.

"The former Defensive Tackle for our very own Studd City Sharks none other than Desmond Zachariah Reed!" Valentine pauses as he takes another drag on his stubby cigar before continuing, "Or more affectionately known as..." and before he can finish the warehouse is filled with chants of "DEE ZEE, DEE ZEE!" the nickname of the once famous American Football Player.

A large black male steps forward with his arms stretched out wide soaking in the adulation from his fellow gang members. A large afro sits on his head, swaying with the motion of his nodding head. He is big, like a powerful armoured rhinoceros standing upright looking impenetrable and intimidating, but he's overweight and out of shape. 'Dee Zee' Reed is no longer the majestic beast that he once was and now covers his bulbous protruding gut with an oversized football jersey in Emerald green, the number 32 (his old number) emblazoned on the front and back in a bold white collegiate font. A gold medallion swings from around his neck like some heavy anchor being weighed by some gigantic departing vessel. The gold is not just displayed around his thick neck but on his fingers three large *Premier Bowl* championship winners' rings, that he proudly displays like an arrogant peacock. While everyone is lost in a haze of 'Dee Zee' Reed gratification, Dallas whispers to Spider "Yeah, he shows off those championship rings but, forgets he was stripped of them all for testing positive!"

Spider smirks.

"Yeah, I know right!" his smirk turns sour like he's just licked a piece of freshly cut lemon "Stupid fat bastard lost me a lot of money!"

"You bet on him?" Dallas enquires

"Yeah, his last game. Bookies wouldn't pay out when he got banned!"

"Lesson learnt. Don't bet on sports."

"It's my only vice." Chuckles Spider.

The noise dies down again as they linger like hummingbirds waiting for Valentine's sweet nectar.

"And finally..." He yells "They call him 'The Terror of Tenth Street', Grill!"A tall but muscular Caucasian male, his hair blonde and tied back tightly into a cornrow style, and a soul patch style of facial hair comes into view. His real name George Ramsbottom is a given name he attempts to live down, instead he is known to all as 'Grill'. He smiles widely showing off the reason for his given nickname and two rows, top and bottom of gold plated dentures, each tooth intricately decorated in dozens of minuscule diamanté's, all of them twinkling each time the light collides with them.

"Yeah, baby!" Grill shouts at the top of his voice, as he bangs his fists on his chest like the aggressive domineering gesture of a silverback gorilla. The crowd fall silent and there is no reaction, only the sound of a few coughs in the distance. Someone hacks the word "Wannabe!" under their breath and sniggers start to circulate through the crowd as Grill starts to look disheartened. Someone in the crowd calls, "Step back Sheep's Ass!" and everyone erupts into laughter. Even Valentine sniggers as he turns to look at The Chapman Twins who are doubled over laughing. Grill looks like a sulking child as he folds his arms abruptly and stands pouting. 'The Terror of Tenth Street' is obviously a joke and to the majority, he himself is a joke, but he is loyal to Valentine and that is why he is one of his Generals.

"Settle down, settle down!" Valentine again takes control of his boisterous herd.

"We have built this empire up from nothing. The Doomsday Gang is the most powerful force in Studd City!" His gravelly voice booms throughout the warehouse and cheers start to rise again in support of their leader.

"It's only a matter of time now my boys, and we will own Studd City!" The volume swells into a gigantic rhythmic passionate chant of "Doomsday, Doomsday!"

Deep in the crowd of the Doomsday chorus Spider doesn't share his fellow gang members enthusiasm and lets it be known to his band.

"Bullshit!" he sneers. Obviously not buying what Valentine is trying to sell.

"He means he will own Studd City!"

Boris and Dallas sandwich him and hold his now rigid arms to try and calm him down.

"Spider, shh!" Whispers Boris

"How stupid are these assholes?" Spider continues.

"You need to calm down or you're gonna get us killed!" adds Dallas trying his upmost to calm down this living, breathing, ticking time bomb.

"I just don't see how they can buy this shit!" growls Spider, slowly calming down.

During all this, Sniff remains uninterested by anything going on in the warehouse, whether it is coming from Vinnie Valentine or his fellow horde, he simply goes on as if he is in his own world and rolls up another joint between his flaxen tinted fingertips.

"I'm very proud of you all!" Valentine continues, strutting around again. This time with one hand casually tucked into his trouser pocket and the other grasping his cigar.

"Yes, proud! Like a father is proud of his own children. If you all keep moving the goods like you have been, it will make us all filthy rich!" He smiles a sadistic grin and yet again he has them all eating out of his hand as cheers rise again for their beloved leader. Spider shakes his head in disbelief of what he is hearing and that everyone else in the room believes what is coming out of Valentine's mouth.

"The lying bastard!"

"Dude, please!" pleads Dallas, not wanting to end up in the bottom of The Hennig River.

"How can these idiots..." Dallas grips his forearm tightly which gets Spider's attention and he looks at Dallas.

"Look, man! I know how you feel bro, but this is not the time or place for this. If he hears you, we're dead. Plain and simple!"

Spider nods in agreement.

Valentine starts to laugh as he makes an announcement.

"And I tell you my boys we are doing a lot better than our neighbours in Forge City. The La Familia!" He scowls with the mere mention of his rival's name and removing his cigar, he spits a large amount of phlegm onto the concrete floor as a mark of utter disrespect for the gang from their sister city. The crowd also show distain at the mention of Eduardo Gonzalez's gang, with monstrous growls and boos of displeasure.

"But, yet again your leader Vinnie 'The Thunder' Valentine shows his superior intellect by intercepting their latest delivery from our friends in Venezuela."
With Valentine's last statement the daydreaming Sniff suddenly stops rolling his joint as if he has had epiphany.

"Isn't that the job we pulled yesterday?" He asks, a look of puzzlement on his droopy face.

"Yeah!" Spider scowls, "The bastards a hypocrite! Taking all the glory for the job we did, he never gets his fucking hands dirty!"

"I guess that is why he is untouchable." Adds Boris innocently and immediately regrets it when he is cut a look by Spider that slices through Boris' harmlessness.

"Nobody is untouchable!" Says Spider.
Valentine signals to one of the twins who nods back at him and leaves the warehouse.

"Leaders of each section, meet 'Big Ben' outside and he will give you your monthly supplies. Again, I can't put into words how proud I am of you all. But I am afraid this meeting has come to an end so until next time my Doomsday brothers!" The crowd cheers and then start to disperse through the exit. As Spider and his crew turn to leave, the booming voice of Valentine stops them dead in their tracks.

"Spider! You wait! I want to see you!"

For a moment they all stand frozen in time like ivory statues. Spider stares at Valentine who grins back at him a grin that lets you know he knows something that you don't.

"What does he want?" Boris whispers.

"I got this, no worries!" scoffs Spider and he fist bumps his crew.

"We will get the gear and meet you back at the apartment." says Dallas

"Yeah, safe!" adds Spider as he swaggers over towards Valentine. As the last of the degenerates leave, Spider tries to act cool even though his heart rate has just doubled in pace and the anticipation of what could happen to him sets in. He knows that people have died for less with this guy. Could he stop him if he pulled out a gun and plugged him in the head? Probably not! Would anyone mourn him, would anyone care when he is fished out of the Hennig River? Probably not.

"Yo, what's this about? I've got shit of yours to sell!" Spiders says, already regretting how that came across. Valentine snorts at his comment as if it was as significant and signals 'Little Ben' with a slight flick of his index finger. Little Ben arrives and stands before Spider towering over him.

"So, which one are you again?" Spider says arrogantly, knowing all too well that something unpleasant is on the horizon, but he just can't help himself. It is quite apparent by now that Spider does not have a filter. Little Ben curls up his large meaty paw into a pulsating fist and ploughs it into Spider's torso. Spider immediately drops to his knees in agony, gritting his teeth in an unattractive grimace. Valentine stands over him sucking away at his cigar and blowing smoke into the fallen Spider's vicinity. The thick transparent smoke circulates around him, almost mocking him as he remains hunched over on his knees, coughing and spluttering something that once dwelled in the pit of his stomach but has freed himself and is heading northwards.

"Thank you, Little Ben!" says Valentine.

Valentine then joins the circulating and now dispersing smoke as he saunters around Spider.

"Don't you ever disrespect me again kid. Listen, you're good at what you do I'll give you that and you make me a lot of money!" He starts to laugh to himself as Spider looks up spurting blood into his hand violently.

"That's probably the only thing that has saved your scrawny ass. I mean maybe one day you could wind up being a General!" Valentine crouches down so they are at eye level. For several seconds nothing is said, they just stare at each other. Spider is screaming inside to shout 'Fuck you!' in his face and add an exclamation point onto the end of it by spitting the bile into his face, but that would be suicide. He will live to fight another day. Valentine takes out his purple handkerchief from his blazer pocket that matches his tie identically in a luscious silk and wipes away the blood from the corner of Spider's mouth.

"I know you think you're a big shot, but just remember this kid! No one is untouchable in this group! Especially not you!" Valentine rises and drops the blood-stained handkerchief in his lap before leaving with Little Ben, leaving a trail of smoke in his wake like some tremendous locomotive leaving a station.

With Spider left all alone, he collapses into a heap on the floor and clutches his stomach. He rolls onto his back and looks up at the sky lights, the gentle fall breeze is there again flowing over him and the smell of Hennig River caresses his nostrils. He is alone with his thoughts.

"No one is untouchable!" Spider turns his head and vomits.

Chapter 7

The distant sound of a police siren can be heard echoing through a forest of long slender buildings. The siren grows louder and louder accompanied by the deafening shrieking of tyres. The smell of smouldering rubber now whisks into the air and around the corner of Crosby Lane as an old beaten up Ford Country Squire charges to its destination. The emerging car has somehow managed to drag itself out of the 1980's, held together by its dated wood panel exterior, giving it the appearance of a coffin on wheels. With how it was struggling to move combined with the exasperating gasps escaping from its engine, made it just that. A death trap. The whole area is immediately illuminated by the two bright vanilla headlights that slice through the darkness of Studd City's streets. The car swerves and skids wildly which almost causes the driver to lose control at the corner of McQueen Street. Somehow the driver manages to not crash up onto the sidewalk but merely brush the lip of its edge and then levels off, managing to power on through.

The Irish district known as St. Patricks is lit up by the car's cherry that rotates constantly, painting all it touches in a streak of vibrant red. The dilapidated vehicle carries on and ploughs down some narrow back streets, only just wide enough to home the car itself. As it emerges through onto Alexandria Lane, it skids again straight into busy traffic and is met by several angry blasts from car horns. The car levels off again and rages on, dodging any surrounding cars like a seasoned professional of Nascar. Straight on through Roma and suddenly the cherry's beam is lost in a shroud of neon red lights. But the stay is short and another short cut off the main road and into another back street sees the car plough straight into some overflowing trashcans that explodes with garbage, sending it rising into the air like a grotesque firework display. Rats run for cover and head for the safety of the shadows that hug the graffitied walls of this back street. The car glides onto another road, this one less busy and is not met by too many aggravated horn blowers, maybe three in total, short and sweet and again the Ford Squire is on its way zooming down Muraco Street and headed for Ventura.

Inside the car there are two males, two police detectives. It's so obvious that they are police not only made apparent by the obvious flashing red cherry stuck on their roof but by their look. The crumpled and creased shirts they wear, sleeves scrunched up and homed above the elbows. The collar unbuttoned around their necks and the loose noose of dangling ties, which are stained with coffee and the sugar from an early evening doughnut. Their eyes are also a huge give away, as they are dragged down by bags, the heavy kind that are worn by those that work long hours and have short sleep patterns. The eyes of the stakeout cop. The maniac behind the wheel is Detective Sidney Graham. With an intense look of somewhere between determination and irritation, he grips the glossy wood finish of the Ford Squire's steering wheel tightly. So tightly that his fingers and knuckles are now the palest white. Beads of sweat seep from his auburn hairline, cascading down the crevices of his worn middle-aged face and disappear into his goatee style beard that frames his gritted teeth perfectly. His left hand leaves the wheel for only a second to wipe his brow with his exposed hairy forearm. As he grips the wheel again, his wedding ring clanks on the now moist steering wheel.

"Jesus Christ, Sid!" shudders the voice from the passenger seat, his partner and best friend, Detective Richard Freeman. Graham cuts him a look as if to say, 'Don't fuck with me right now'. Freeman reads the signs and turns back to face the road ahead. Detective Freeman is a handsome black male in his late thirties, short black hair is tapered to perfection and a slender elegant moustache bridges over his plump lips. With a worried frown brandished on his forehead, the sweat doesn't drip like a leaky tap like his partner's, but instead gushes like a cascading waterfall. The Ford Squire swerves around the vehicles in front, too close for comfort if you ask Freeman, who covers his eyes with his forearms as they clip the wing mirror of an unsuspecting 1998 Plymouth Voyager, that immediately screeches to a halt in a cloud of burnt rubber. The horn is hit hard and continuous by the angry driver. Detective Graham ignores it and keeps on going.

"Sid!" calls Freeman in shock.

"He can bill me for it!" comes the reply from a focused a determined Detective Graham, who is like a bloodhound on the trail of a fox now, he's on the hunt and there is no turning back or in this case no slowing down.

63

C'mon Richard, you should get this by now! You know how it works. You know how long we've been on Valentine's tail. You know I must nail this bastard! You know how... "Get out of the fucking way you moron!" *...how I feel about this guy. I should be saying all this to him, but I don't want to sound like a broken record, he knows. Plus, I'm still pissed at him for making us go three blocks out of our way to get those damn doughnuts. If we hadn't of stopped off at Perfect Java we'd have been there ages ago.*

Graham looks over at Freeman who is twitching in his seat like he's having a seizure, suffering from random convulsions every time they breeze past the traffic. Graham smirks to himself.

That will teach him, always thinking with his stomach. I'll let him stew in his own poop filled Calvin's for a while. This time I will catch them in the act. I won't let what happened last time happen again. I owe that much to the families of the fallen officers of last months failed attempt at catching The Doomsday Gang.

The screeching of the tyres and the shrill of the siren join forces to startle several pedestrians at the corner of Hoth and Urban as they surge on into Solo, a small part of Studd City that borders Ventura. Nearly there now so close. It's a short stay in Solo and suddenly they hit Ventura. The Ventura Bridge can now be seen in all its cobalt coloured steel. The police radio fizzes and crackles and the sound of a female's voice comes through, a little distorted but it can be made out.

"...in Graham, Come in Graham... do you copy...over... over?" Graham knows he needs to focus on the task in hand and glances at Detective Freeman.

"Can you get that, Richard?" He asks his partner. Freeman plucks the receiver from the safety of it holster.

"This is Freeman. Go ahead!"

"...is your location?...over...over!"

"Just entered Ventura, heading towards the warehouses along the docks, over!"

"...is...reason of your change of... location, over...over!"

"Anonymous tip off that Doomsday Gang are in attendance. They're having another little get together. Over!"

"..."

There is a moment of radio silence.

"...stand down until... up can join... over!"

Graham's face glows as red as the cherry sitting on top of the Squire's roof.

"Fuck you!" He blasts at the top of his voice.

"That's a negative. Freeman and Graham continuing as planned!" Graham holds the grimace on his face but looks at Freeman with an intense nod of the head.

"...await back up...please Detectives...over!" Graham grabs the receiver from his partner with his right hand, the car wriggles for a moment but Freeman instinctively clutches the wheel and helps steady it.

"Cut the crap, Rhonda! You know what's riding on this!" Graham bellows.

"...too dangerous, Sid...please wait for..."

"No can do, Rhonda. We're almost there!"

"..."

Again the detectives are met by silence.

"Look, get me all available officers in the vicinity to the docks in Ventura ASAP!" Continues Graham.

"...ETA six minutes for back up. Proceed with caution!"

"You're a wonderful lady, Rhonda!" Smirks Graham.

"Screw you, Sid! Over!"

"Received." Laughs Graham.

Graham takes the wheel again and puts his foot down on the gas again, pushing the rickety worn Ford Squire to its max.

"One of these days the Commissioner is going to nail your balls to wall Sid. You know that right?" Says Freeman, matter-of-factly as he wipes his seeping brow with a napkin left over from his earlier purchase at Perfect Java.

"Yeah, I know." Graham answers with a defiant grin, like the insolent look of a shrewd guttersnipe that is up to no good.

"You're one gutsy bastard, Sid." Freeman laughs shaking his head.

"That's why you love me partner!" grins Graham and accompanies it with a little wink.

Suddenly they are overshadowed by the steel construction of the elevated train track, it's sturdy girders patched with an amalgamation of rust and graffiti. The word 'Doomsday' is emblazoned across the construction in bright red spray paint, indicating to all that you are now in The Doomsday Gang's territory. The laughter dies down and Graham kills the cherry and slows his speed down to a normal pace, blending in with the other traffic as to not draw attention to themselves. There will be eyes everywhere. There is a moment of silence in the front of the car as it trundles along, and Graham turns to Freeman and in a quiet solemn tone asks him.

"This time we'll get them won't we, Richard?" His eyes appear anxious, opening the real Sidney Graham up to his partner, his friend.

"I hope so Sid, for your sake!" answers Freeman. Maybe not the answer Graham wanted, but he knows it's the right one. Months and months on this case to bring down The Doomsday Gang is breaking him. It's starting to affect his home life too and cracks are starting to show in marriage of sixteen years. Making matters worse, if he can't bring in this supposedly untouchable force then he will be out of a job.

The Ford Squire indicates and turns off Adonis Street and onto the gravelly track of the industrial estate that sits on the dockyards of Ventura. The moon reflects on the dark waters of the river, that fall breeze rears its head again and the moons reflection twitches. The Ford Squire quietly drives towards their destination and headlights appear from behind. Graham checks the rear-view and is met by a sudden flash of the headlights.

"Well, at least we have some back up!" Graham says as he pulls over next to a large crane about two hundred yards away from the abandoned warehouse that they believe is hosting Valentine's get-together.

"Ready?" Graham asks turning to Freeman who gestures with a nod. They exit the car quietly and walk around to the rear. Popping the trunk of the car, they retrieve bulletproof vests and slip into them, effortlessly like they've done this a thousand times before, which of course they have. But there is always that doubt in their minds that this could be the last time they ever do this. A thought that surely every police officer goes through from time to time and this was one of those times. They remain in complete silence as they strap themselves in, each adjusting the versatile Velcro straps to each's personal specifications. They check their police issue Glock 22's in their tan leather shoulder holsters, checking that they are packed with ammunition. They safely slide them back into the holsters again and instead reach into the boot of the Ford Squire and retrieve a Remington 870 shotgun each, which they cock in unison.

"A big job calls for the big guns!" says Graham.
The Chevrolet Impala squad car that signalled with its headlights just moments ago, pulls ups behind them and two officers exit the vehicle. They are both clad in their dark navy SCPD uniforms and both apply their dark peaked caps. One of the officer's is female, petit and pretty with jet black hair tied up neatly into a tightly packed bun. She approaches the two detectives with confidence.

"What are we dealing with here, detectives?" She says looking at both as she approaches, but then just focussing her attention towards Detective Graham.

"Nash. Good to see you. We have received a tip off..." Graham is interrupted by Nash's partner tripping over and eating the gravelled floor. The young male looks up at them, now with a subtle shade of red pulsating in his cheeks.

"Sorry, Sir!" he stutters.

"Get up Wilson, Goddamn it!" snaps Graham. Wilson pulls his long gangly limbs from the floor and brushing the dirt from his once immaculate uniform joins them, straightening his cap on the way.

"I don't know why the hell I've got stuck with the rookie!" Nash griped, rolling her eyes as Wilson saunters over to join them.

"We have reason to believe that inside that warehouse, Vinnie Valentine is having a meeting with his cronies. This could get nasty." says Graham.

"Don't worry, Sir. You can count on me." Nash smiles.

"Me too, Sir!" stutters Officer Wilson.

Another squad car pulls up and two male officers get out of the car.

"It's Stone and Mountford, Sid!" Says Freeman, seemingly relieved that they at least have someone to watch their backs in this suicidal mission.

"Good! Richard, go and fill them in and take the rear of the building."

"Gotcha, Sid!"

"All being well, we'll meet you inside."

Freeman jogs towards Stone and Mountford to fill them in and with their guns drawn, they disappear around the side of the warehouse.

"Right, you two come with me!" Graham says to Nash and Wilson, who nod in unison.

What the hell am I doing?! This is potentially suicide! Call it off, Sid. Call if off right now. These guys don't need you leading them on some crazy crusade that could end up seeing them on a slab at the morgue.

Detective Graham leads them to the entrance and skulk either side of the door, waiting patiently in complete silence.

What is going through their heads? Why is this old buffoon dragging us into this? Behind this door could be a roomful of unsavoury individuals loaded up to the gills with deadly firearms. But this is what we sign on for. They all know the dangers that come with the job. Yeah, granted Sid, but not like this. You don't even have a plan do you? ... You don't do you? ...

He glances from Nash and then to Wilson, scanning their faces like some scrutinising customs officer, suspicious but looking to acquire much needed information. Nash wears a mask of gritty determination, unfazed and focussed, how a cop should look like in this type of situation.

The chick's got balls, I'll give her that much. Yes sir, little Valerie who was top of her class in everything at the academy, she has a bright future ahead of her and the peachiest ass in the precinct... focus Sid.

Wilson clenches his firearm with both hands in a vice like grip. Several beads of sweat tumbling down his forehead and his police issue Beretta Model 92 firearm slithering around in his moist quivering grip.

And then there's this guy. Straight out of diapers, probably never even fired that Beretta he's juggling. How can I drag him into this? Look at him shaking like a shitting dog. Damn it, Sid... Look he's a cop now and this is his job.

"You ready?" He whispers to his officers. Nash gives a slow nod with almost a sparkle of anticipation in her delightful indigo eyes, framed by soft flickering dark eye lashes. Graham wonders for a moment whether that lingering look was meant to come across like it did but brushes the thought aside. Wilson nods which is accompanied with a side order of deep gulp, the nod says 'yes, I am ready' the look on his face says something completely different.

"Let's do it!" Exhales Detective Graham and slams his size 12 into the middle of the double doors, shards of splintering wood explode around his worn old brown leather dress shoes. They burst into the large warehouse and the anticipation dies like a deflating balloon. The building is completely empty. A strange amalgamation of relief and annoyance is exhaled and fills the air. The pulses settle and the rush of adrenaline slowly subsides as handguns are safely nestled back in their homes. Detective Graham rests his shotgun on his left shoulder like one of the seven dwarves hauling a pickaxe.

"Well, shit!" sighs an annoyed Detective Graham as his partner and his crew appear on the other side of the warehouse almost mirror imaging Graham and his band.

"Looks like they did us again, Sid!" echoes Detective Freeman's voice from across the desolate concreted landscape.

"Good and proper! Either this anonymous caller likes fucking with me or I'm just getting too slow in my old age!" says Graham scratching his head with his nicotine stained finger tips.

"C'mon, you're not that old." Laughs his approaching partner.

"Well either way, Vinnie Valentine is laughing at us again. And guess who now has the unfortunate task of informing Commissioner Hayes that he screwed up again?"

"I will let you have that pleasure, my friend." Smiles Freeman with a reassuring and playful arm around his shoulder and softly squeezing his arm.

"What's new! You just want to see him nail my balls to the wall don't ya?" answers Graham sarcastically.

"C'mon Sid, they went a long time ago." Laughs Freeman, the officers in the background wear an anxious look on their faces, wanting to laugh but not sure whether they should.

"Yeah, that's true. Last time I saw them they were in my Mae's purse!" He answers as straight faced as a veteran comedian delivering the punchline to his best joke. Immediately the warehouse is filled with laughter as Freeman leads the attack and is joined by the other officers, who could not physically hold onto that chuckle that scratched away at the back of their throats. Freeman pats his partner on the back and Graham joins in with the laughter. The young rookie, Officer Wilson gazes around the warehouse. His nose and eyes scrunched up, as he surveys the room.

"D'you know what, Sir. I don't think they were even here!" say Wilson matter of fact.
Detective Graham stops laughing and turns to face him.

"To the untrained eye kid, maybe!" Graham approaches him and hands the shotgun to him. He unconfidently takes it, grasping it in both hands the way that someone unexperienced with children might hold a baby.

"What's that on the floor?" He asks the young rookie.

"Where, Sir?" Answers Wilson, looking around without a clue, like some new born doughy eyed fawn.

"There!" States Detective Graham pointing straight in front of them on the floor where a small puddle of blood has seeped into the hard concrete and has started to dry up appearing almost black in colour.

"Oh, wow! I never even saw that!" Comes the response from shocked looking face of the bewildered greenhorn, which immediately turns beetroot, flourishing with embarrassment.

"Gotta keep those eyes peeled, Kid." Sighs Detective Graham, patting him on the shoulder, the action oozing with pity for SCPD's newbie.

"And then there is the overpowering aroma of Cuban cigar smoke. Gran Manzana brand. Valentine's brand!" Continues Detective Graham, as he watches the officer's nostrils twitch as they try to pick up the same scent as the veteran sniffer dog.

"We saw some tyre tracks outside, Sir!" pipes up Officer Mountford, who was one of the officers who arrived later. A tall, gaunt looking individual, a reddish beard framing his face with a domed head homed under his hat.

"Enough to take a print?" Asks Graham.

"I'd say so, Sir!" replies Mountford

"Great! Mountford get me a cast team down here right away!"

"Yes, Sir!" answers Officer Mountford as he leaves to run his errand.

"Nash, get onto HQ and tell them I want forensics down here asap! I want to know who that blood belongs to."

"Sir!" comes the regimental response by the petite little

73

pocket rocket.

"Oh, and Nash! Take Sherlock Holmes with you please." Mocks Detective Graham.

"Yes, Sir! Come on, Wilson!" Nash, grabs Wilson by the elbow and leads him out of the warehouse. Wilson still grasping the shotgun like it's going to explode any minute. The remaining officer, Officer Eric Stone, a good-looking young guy with chiselled facial features and by the look of his build, has the body to match, walks off surveying the room for any other hidden clues. Detective Freeman smiles at his partner and shakes his head.

"How the hell do you do that?"

"Do what?" Answers a confused Detective Graham.

"Make chicken salad out of chicken shit!" comes the reply through a snigger. They both laugh and Graham takes out a box of cigarettes from his trouser pocket. He flips the lid of the Freebird brand cigarettes exposing the four, no five cigarettes that are rattling around inside, as if they are excitedly calling 'pick me, pick me', he pulls one out and nestles it between his parted lips and then offers his partner one, who takes it sliding it out and then resting it in-between his plump lips.

"I mean five minutes ago you had nothing but an empty warehouse!" squawks Freeman out of the corner of his mouth, cigarette dangling out of the other side. Graham flicks his silver plated lighter; engraved with the words 'Happy Birthday Daddy, Love from Billy and Todd' on the side of it. Flames rise and engulf the end of Freeman's cigarette.

"Thanks!" Says Freeman as he puffs a few times on the

cigarette like some native American does a peace pipe. Then he continues as he watches Graham light his cigarette.

"Where was I? Oh, yeah one minute you have nothing and then you have the cast team on their way, Forensics coming..."

"Don't forget the cigar smoke!" Chuckles Graham.

"I'm serious, you are a marvel, Sid!"

"Saving my ass is what I'm doing, Richard."

"Well, seriously I want to say thank you for always teaching me something new every day!"

"Oh, enough with the Hallmark shit, Richard!" Laughs Graham, puffing on his cigarette, "You're telling me you didn't notice any of that?"

"I saw the blood on the floor, but, I thought it was just an oil stain or something." Answers Freeman, the words exploding out of a cloud of cigarette smoke as they leave his mouth "And I genuinely didn't notice the cigar smoke until you mentioned it!"

"Well, that's why they pay me the pitiful inadequate salary!" Graham snorts as the two are entwined by a cloud of smoke and laughter. The laughter dies down to silence. The breeze pushes its way through the building again and in the distance the sound of more police sirens can be heard.

"Why do we always miss them, Richard?" Sighs Graham quietly.

"Just bad luck I guess." Shrugs Freeman

"Well, I must be the unluckiest bastard in Studd City!"

"There is always somebody worse off than you, Sid!"

Graham just looks at him, not knowing whether to burst out laughing or strangle his partner.

"You are so damn positive, Richard. I hate it!" Then the two laugh again.

"It's like chasing Houdini or something. Always too late! Or when we do turn up on time, shit hits the fan and people die! And still never any sign of Valentine." Growls Graham flicking his half-worn cigarette away.

"Erm, won't that infect the crime scene, Sid!"

"My crime scene, my rules!" He winks "Maybe they will test it and find my DNA on it and think I'm in cahoots with Mr Valentine!"

"Okay, no need to get sarcastic!" Freeman answers with a smile.

Officer Stone approaches. "There is a small trace of cocaine by the back door." says Stone, with a tone of familiarity with the two Detectives.

"Good find, Eric! Get them to take a sample of it when they get here." Says Graham.

"Sure! Are you guys leaving?" Answers Stone.

"Yeah, we have some unfinished business at Perfect Java." Graham informs Stone.

"Hell yeah, there is a custard filled doughnut with my name on it!" adds an overly excited Detective Freeman as he takes one final drag on his cigarette, before discarding it nonchalantly.

"Yeah, and it's your turn to pick up the bill, Richard!"

Freeman's face drops, as Graham leaves and Freeman follows.

"Oh, before I forget, some of us are having a get together at Lionhearts later for my last day at the precinct. I just wondered if you guys could make it?" Asks Stone with a beaming smile that you would find hard to say no to.

"Oh, it's your last day! I totally forgot! Eric, I'm so sorry!" Graham gripes halted in his tracks.

"It's cool, you guys have had a lot on your plate. Just be nice to have you guys there you know?" Stone adds.

"I'll be there." smiles Freeman

"I don't know, I should probably get home..." Graham looks at his watch and scratches his head, wearing a look of a man in two minds. It's almost as though one could see his brain trying to calculate a way he can go and still be back in time to spend time with his loving wife.

"Don't forget the big fight is on tonight. Johnson vs Bundy!" Appeals Stone, trying to entice Detective Graham through his love of Boxing.

"Okay, you've twisted my arm. I'll stop by for one drink!" Concedes Graham.

"Great! See you there in an hour or so."
The two Detectives leave as Stone stands guard over the crime scene and Graham calls back.

"Oh and Eric?"

"Yeah?"

"Tell forensics to ignore any cigarette butts. They were Richard's." Smirks Graham as he leaves with Freeman quickly following him.

"Bastard!" Laughs Freeman.

Chapter 8

Thomas strolls down the dark lonely streets of Royale (Queen Street to be precise) or in Thomas' head it could probably be renamed Memory Lane. All the old haunts are still there, all of them illuminated by the soft buttermilk beams that gush from the long slender streetlights that stand upright in unison and almost regimental along the sidewalk. He almost doesn't notice that he has stopped and is now teetering on the edge of the curb like a reluctant diver on the lip of a diving board, swaying slightly back and forth in the gentle breeze. It is the sight of the places he visited as a boy that has captured his attention. Places that he hadn't visited in what seemed to him to be a lifetime. Places that have sat silently in the very back of his mind, covered in dust and forgotten like the contents of an old attic. But now they are there, right in front of him, over the street like they had always been there and of course they have always been there. When Thomas left Studd City all those years ago they didn't just shut up shop and cease to exist, no, nothing stopped just because Thomas Gabriel left Studd City. These places are the cogs in the machine and they just went right on turning.

I don't believe it! There they are.

A sweet smile caresses Thomas' lips, like the innocent smile of a child, but that is what Thomas was the last time he glanced at these places and the heart felt memories came pouring back into his mind.

I guess this place wasn't all bad. All my old haunts are still here... Nunzio's Italian Restaurant... I can't believe it looks exactly the same! It's like time has stood still.

And it was true of this part of the city you could say that time hasn't changed it. Most of it has been neglected, abandoned like some weary old glasshouse found in the overgrown backyard of some surplus property out in the country, consumed by thick intertwined vines that refuse to let it leave its boa constrictor like grasp. Most of Studd City has been developed and improved with money from the conglomerate, Devine Inc. But, the North part of the city has been left to fester and scab over. Thomas' eyes scan across the stores that are blocked together in a long line, like a group of protestors that have linked arms and refuse to leave.

Yeah, Nunzio's I wonder if the old man is still running it? Surely he must be dead by now though? He was ancient when I was a kid! But, I guess we see things differently as children, he was probably 50 or something like, that but when you're young, all adults appear old to such young eyes.

It had an all glass front, sunk into the old red brick of the building. The word 'Nunzio's' expensively engraved into the panes of the colours of the Italian flag. The long waterproof material canopy that is now slightly worn, tops off the ensemble in a fading emerald green tone, again with the word 'Nunzio's' emblazoned across it in peeling white letters, identically matching the font used on the window.

Best meatballs in town I can tell you, 'That's Momma's secret recipe' Nunzio used to say...

Again, Thomas' mind wanders as he rummages in the back of his mind, like one would rifle through an old trunk, looking for that mislaid item. This time the memory is a good one, a nice one and it makes him smile.

I remember when I first came to the city and in the custody of my social worker, Miss Fosdick... She was a very attractive woman, I guess she would have been early twenties and new to the job. I know that because she told me that I was her first case since graduating. It was her job to make sure that my transition into the orphanage went smoothly. She brought me here for lunch so we could chat and she could get to know me a little. I don't remember much of the conversation, back then I was still hugely affected by what had happened, but boy do I remember those meatballs! I also remember Nunzio flirting with Miss Fosdick outrageously without any thought for his large rotund wife Rosa, who was stood at the bar burning a hole into his wide back. Ha, probably chewed him up and spat him out later in the kitchen with all the Italian curse words you could think of.

Thomas strolls across the quiet road, and luckily for him it is a quiet road because in his dazed saunter he paid no attention to any of the cars. He stood outside Nunzio's and looked in, the set up was the same as he remembered, the layout of the chairs and tables, the light fittings, everything even down to the wall of fame. The walls that were inside were all covered with framed 8x10's of all manner of famous people. All the black and white photographs of their headshots looked back at him. Fred Astaire, Lou Costello, Phil Silvers, Dom DeLuise and more, much more.

There has been a lot more added to his wall of fame now. He always said it was the only place to dine for these Hollywood A-listers when they came to town. To be honest I think most of them were fake as all the autographs shared a suspicious resemblance to each other.

He got closer and peered into the window. An autumn gust blows through and the canopy above his head rippled violently, but it refused to be moved, the material gripping on for dear life. The wind died down and the canopy settled back into place. Thomas was happy to see that there were a bunch of people scattered throughout the restaurant all enjoying meals.

Business looks good. I am glad. Maybe...

For a moment Thomas ponders and is tempted to go in, but then decides not to and backs away from the window.

Maybe when I'm settled in I can come back and see if those meatballs are still the best in town.

Thomas turns away and just as he is about to leave, he hears a voice bellowing in a deep Italian accent come from inside the restaurant.

"Hey, it's Momma's secret recipe!"

Thomas' head turns quickly as if it was on a turntable and he sees Nunzio.

Well I'll be...

Obviously much older now, most of his hair gone and what is left is a dark smokey grey, the colour of wrought iron, slicked back from bald to receding to greasy hair in the rear of his head. He

81

laughs loudly as he playfully pats the customer on the back, who in turn nearly chokes on the large meatball that is stuffed in his mouth.

And there he is. Looks like he has been eating a few too many of those meatballs himself, bless him.

Nunzio's large sphere like physique turns slowly and he waddles towards the kitchen. A walk as if he needs the use of a cane, but stubbornly refuses to use it. Thomas retrieves his case and then moves on and passes the next few buildings. The next store is in darkness but the bright candy pink and bubble-gum blue combination on the store's sign above it makes it come to life.

Oh, boy! Pringle's Parlour! It's still here!

Thomas immediately drops his case onto the sidewalk and presses his nose up against the glass, like an over exuberant child looking to get a glimpse of the treasures that await inside. But, it is in total darkness. Thomas peels his face from the glass with a disgruntled look on his face. These places are really making him feel like a child again.

What am I doing?

He laughs as he shakes his head and adjusts his glasses back into place. The door sign is turned to closed and inside chairs are neatly stacked onto circular tables on the tiled floor. The ice cream display refrigerator lies dormant and empty, eerily like a show casket in a funeral parlour. Thomas imagines the refrigerator filled with ice cream, all the tubs each homing a different flavour, all in an array of vibrant and tantalising colours. Thomas recalls his favourites... *Pralines and Cream, Mississippi Mud, Chocolate Eruption...* Thomas' mouth waters

82

and that childlike grin caresses his lips again. Thomas walks on surveying the next stores that are all closed for the day. Sprig's Hardware, Vanda's Records, Leslie's Barber Shop and then as he reaches the corner of the street, he can see Perfect Java. An old fifties style diner lit up in the darkness like a Christmas tree, the blue neon calling to him like a beacon.

Well, well! There's a sign I haven't seen in a long time. 'Perfect Java' the best coffee and doughnuts in the world! Still standing strong on the corner of Royale and Quebec, of course it's missing an 'F' but it's still here.

Thomas quickly crosses two lanes of traffic and stands outside the diner. The letter F comes on and illuminates in a splendid neon turquoise like the others but then flickers and goes off again. Thomas stares at the flickering letter and drifts off again into the past.

Thomas as a boy, looks up at the diner licking his lips. His clothes are tattered and torn, and are splattered with several unknown stains. His face is gaunt and you would be hard pressed to pinch an inch of flesh on his fragile frame.

Living on the streets was tough. Anybody that must do that has my complete sympathy. That is why now if I pass a homeless person on the street I don't keep on walking with a tight grip on my change in my pocket so it doesn't jangle, no I don't ignore these people, I always give them what I have. Not because of my religious calling and as a priest I should but, because I have been there, I have lived it, and let me tell you it is not pretty. Those few dollars you have in your pocket could be enough to save that person's life. You have no way of knowing how long they have gone without food. I always give.

A large bulging police officer wobbles out of the entrance of the diner with a long rectangular box, filled with various doughnuts, glazed ring, maple iced, chocolate iced glazed, cruller, chocolate & custard filled and chocolate with sprinkles. There may have only been six doughnuts in that box but to a young starving Thomas it might as well have been sixty, to him this was heaven, this was a banquet.

I never wanted to steal anything. But when you're living on the streets and haven't eaten in days, and you're scraping the contents out of trashcans every morning, it's survival. I knew this cop, he always walked the beat through Royale, Hope and Montreal, his name was...What was it again? Jaworski! Charles Jaworski, but everyone called him 'Chuck'.

Officer Jaworski was severely obese, how he was still able to keep his job with SCPD was a mystery. His dark navy uniform clung to every lump that rolled from his bloated torso, the buttons on his shirt stretched to the maximum allowing windows to open and reveal his gross hairy paunch. Maybe one day he became a pencil pusher, who knows.

Officer Chuck was a little overweight... Okay he was morbidly obese. And I didn't think he would miss one doughnut. I knew he wouldn't chase me, and if he did he couldn't catch me, right? I'd seen other boys on the street knock his cap off or kick him and run away. He never gave chase just stood there waving his clenched fist in the air as he shouted obscenities at them. Yeah, there was no way he was giving chase over one stolen doughnut.

As he trudged out the diner he stood on the sidewalk swiping at his plump lips with his thick pink tongue, like some gluttonous monitor lizard. His tubby mitt hovered over the box, like the claw in a teddy picker machine, surveying what was below and what would be chosen first. Thomas had focused his sights on the Chocolate & Custard filled doughnut.

"Please, don't have the custard one." He whispered to himself. He gazed at it, he became infatuated with it, the small blob of custard that hung out of the piping hole, the sunlight bouncing off the chocolate glazed topping. Thomas' mouth began to water and without even knowing it, he began to dribble. He was suddenly entranced by his hunger and a gurgling noise began in the very pit of his stomach and grew ever louder as it made its way through his gut. It's as if the sound echoed through the walls of his stomach it was that empty.

Empty. As empty as one of your Daddy's promises. Where did that come from? I haven't thought of that for an age. Mama used to say that all the time. Before she...before she died...

For a moment it's as if his return to the past had halted and he thought about his Mother. He could still see Chuck holding the doughnut box, but it was like he was on pause and the image quivered. Thomas was somewhere else for a second but moments later he was back. Chuck began to move in for the kill and lunged at the helpless doughnut box, snatching up the glazed ring, forcing the 45 grams of sugary, doughy goodness into his gaping hole. With three bites it was gone.

It was definitely a sight to behold. Even David Copperfield couldn't make things disappear that fast.

85

Chuck stood chewing like a gurning camel, only not as attractive, with the sticky frosty glaze gripping to the stubble that surrounded this unrelenting chewing machine. His mouth might have been busy chomping away but his eyes had already found their next victim.

"Please, please not the custard one!" Thomas whispered again. Chuck's tongue protruded out of its cave and attempted (but failed) to remove the glaze that had clung to his face. His hazel eyes darted back and forth around the box at the remaining five doughnuts, like he was following the random light sequence of some TV game show. Then as quick as a viper he struck again, this time seizing the unsuspecting sprinkled covered chocolate doughnut. As he squeezed it in his unescapable grip, the sprinkles exploded and started to fall to the ground. The various coloured pieces showered the vicinity as if they were trying to escape, frivolously launching themselves into the air to take their chances with the fall rather than finish up in Chuck's gnawing maw. Again, with three bites the tasty morsel had been devoured and the sound of Chuck sucking his porky fingers was too much for Young Thomas to take, he made his move.

I made my way towards him and slunk down next to a bulky fire hydrant. He didn't see me, why would he? He was too busy slapping his tongue against his sticky fingertips. I eyed up that exquisite looking chocolate and custard doughnut and with a lick of my lips I was away.

Young Thomas sprang into action and with all the finesse of a bulldozer, flung himself at the unsuspecting Officer.

I meant to grab the chocolate and custard doughnut and then run but, in my overzealousness I knocked the entire box into the air.

The weather had changed, a forecast that had not been predicted. It began to rain doughnuts.

It seemed to happen in slow motion and I can still see the look of surprise and absolute horror on Chuck's face as those doughnuts rose into the air and then fell to the ground. As they all hit the sidewalk, there was a moment of stunned silence and everything froze. I looked at the doughnuts then up at Chuck. Chuck looked down in distress before looking at me. We stared at each other for what seemed like an eternity. Then I spotted the chocolate and custard doughnut just sitting there on the sidewalk luscious yellow custard escaping from the doughy bun. I didn't care that it was on the floor, on the sidewalk, where thousands of people walk every day, where dogs have done their business, where stray cats have chased filthy sewer rats. It didn't matter to me. I was that hungry.

Thomas stooped down and grabbed the doughnut of his choice and ran.

Little did I know that on this particular day, Officer Chuck was feeling rather energetic, either that or extremely pissed off.

"You little bastard!" Shouted Chuck and with that, he gave chase. It was the last thing that Thomas expected and as he turned his head to see if he was safely out of sight, his eyes doubled in size and his mouth dropped in astonishment to see Officer Chuck stampeding towards him at full pace. Thomas turned back to face the direction he was running and ran straight into Harry Hawtrey's newspaper stand. At that precise moment, Harry had just had a delivery of magazines and he had just finished unloading the last bundle onto the sidewalk next to his newsstand. Thomas couldn't stop, it was too late and he ran straight into them, knocking poor Harry on his backside and falling over all the bundles of magazines which in turn, sent them flying all over the sidewalk.

"What the hell are you doing, Kid?" yelled an angry Harry, who was trying to get to his feet.

Thomas looked up and saw Officer Chuck getting ever closer. He took a quick glance at the contents of his hand and safely secured in his vice like grip was the doughnut. It wasn't going anywhere, not if Thomas had anything to do about it.

"Sorry, Mister H!" Thomas yelled as he scrambled across the magazines that had blanketed the sidewalk and then he darted again.

I was running as fast as I could, but I was low on fuel. Three weeks of eating whatever you could find in the alleyway restaurant and trashcan café, doesn't tend to leave you very full.

Thomas continued to run in and out of pedestrians that filled the sidewalk, but he was tired and he was slowing.

"Stop that punk!" He heard Officer Chuck bellow, but he didn't glance over his shoulder, he daren't. Nobody tried to stop him, whenever anybody calls that, even a police officer, nobody ever does do they? Nobody ever wants to get involved.

"I'll get you for this you little shit!" Called Chuck again, this time sounding closer than before. Thomas continued to bolt

88

down through Montreal, down Titan Lane and turned into St. Davids. Still Officer Chuck gave chase panting and puffing like some old locomotive, sweat dripping down his bloated red face as it jiggled up and down like bowl of jello. Thomas took a sharp turn and down a back alley. It was dark, damp and dingy covered in all manner of obscene street art, gigantic penis' mostly and the classic 'call such and such for a good time on 888-LAY-ME'. Thomas kept on going, there was a huge clattering sound from behind him but he didn't turn around. The sound was a bunch of trashcans erupting as the Jaworski express collided with them at full force, which was immediately followed up by "Shit!" and then "Damn, little bastard!" but to his credit he pulled himself up (now covered in all manner of grime and filth) and kept on going. Thomas turned again and onto Race Street where he stopped to catch his breath for the first time since this marathon had taken place. Another clatter of trashcans from the alley indicated to Thomas that he should move again. He did.

I knew he was still on my tail and then I spotted The King's Dockyards. I headed towards it with all I had. I knew there would be lots of places for me to hide there.

The docks were in full swing loading up large cargo ships with all manner of crates, storage boxes and fruit and vegetables. None of the workers batted an eyelid at Thomas scampering passed them as they continued with their strenuous work. Then suddenly an outrageous smell of fish sucker punched Thomas in his face, it stopped him dead in his tracks and suddenly Thomas felt nauseous. Thomas hated fish with a passion, its odour had always turned his stomach as long as he could remember and he could never bring himself to eat any. In front of him was a small fishing boat in the midst of unloading tonnes of sardines in large tubs onto the dock. Thomas somehow held his stomach in place and slowly made his way passed them, cupping his mouth with his dirty mitt just in case. He took two steps and threw up over the side of the docks into the calm waters below.

Just the thought of all those sardines piled on top of each other with their beady black eyes all staring at me. Yuck! No, thank you, Sir!

Meanwhile on the corner of Race and Victoria, Chuck emerged out of the alley covered in yet more filth and trash than before. He resembled a badly made up monster from some B-movie horror flick. Panting like some thirsty bloodhound, Chuck looked around left to right. He looked over at the dockyards and knew that he had lost him, there was no way he was going to find him in there. He dropped to his knees and placed his hands on his thighs, breathing in and out ever so heavily. An SCPD squad car pulled up next to him and an officer wound down the window with a huge grin on his face. He was accompanied by another officer riding shotgun who peered over the driver's shoulder to get a glimpse of the fallen Chuck.

"What the fuck are you doing Chuck?" chortled the officer. Chuck couldn't speak he was breathing so heavily.

"Bad day at the office, Chucky?" sniggered the other officer.

"You look like shit!" the driver added.

"Kid...doughnut...lost..." Chuck managed

But the officers just looked at him bemused. The driver turned to his passenger his face contorted with confusion and was met with a shrug of the shoulders from his partner.

"Do you want a lift back to the precinct?" he enquired. Chuck nodded his head and rose very meekly and slowly to his feet and opened the door to the back. Chuck calmly slunk into the rear of the vehicle and closed the door behind before collapsing onto the backseat. The squad car rolled away slowly to a siren of wailing laughter. Back at the docks, Thomas shuffled away from the edge of the docks wiping his weeping mouth with the sleeve of his sweatshirt. When suddenly, he heard someone shout and he instinctively thought it was Officer Jaworski. Thomas ran again and came to the end of the line. All that was waiting for him was a huge cargo ship, emblazoned with Chinese symbols. The ship was being loaded up with huge cargo containers of all various colours by large cranes.

Thomas looked around and noticed a bunch of wooden crates all herded together, all of them stamped with Chinese symbols. Did the symbols match those on the side of the gargantuan cargo ship? Thomas didn't know, he didn't know Chinese and at the precise moment, he didn't care. One of the crates lids were still open so he scrambled inside and secured the top back into place.

I had no idea of knowing whether Officer Chuck was still looking for me, so I thought the best thing I could do was stay exactly where I was.

The interior of the crate was filled with thousands of soft white Styrofoam pieces, all over them whittled into letter S shapes. Thomas sank down into them and underneath the barrage of foam pieces he heard something crack, like the sound of breaking ceramics. Thomas didn't even look to see what lay beneath him that he had broken, could it have been some ancient Chinese porcelain on its way home to its motherland? Thomas didn't care, he was exhausted. Horizontal beams of sunlight sliced through the crate, gaps unveiling themselves between each nailed in blank that made up the crate.

I glanced through a gap between the blanks of wood. I could see all the dockers working hard and loading up the cargo ship, but no sign of Officer Chuck. However, I couldn't take any chances, so I stayed put.

Thomas then remembered what this whole ordeal had been about, he investigated his hand where the remains of a chocolate and custard Perfect Java special had collapsed in his sweaty grip. He opened his hand to reveal the squashed doughnut, the glazed chocolate topping had now become one with the palm of his hand and the gooey moist custard clung to his fingertips. Thomas smiled and without a second thought he slammed his face into the demolished dessert. He did not care that the doughnut no longer resembled the succulent dessert it once had, after everything he'd been through to get it he was damn well going to finish it. He stuffed it into his mouth as quickly as he could, chomping vigorously and obnoxiously loud. The look on his face told the story, a euphoric satisfaction, as he closed his eyes tightly and enjoyed every rhythmic movement of his jaw, his taste buds on his tongue fizzed with excitement. Chocolate, sugar and custard giving him such a delightful high. Thomas lay back into the soft foam and happily licked the remains of the doughnut from his fingers the way a bear would slap his tongue against its paw after it has raided a beehive. Each movement was accompanied by a crack of porcelain, which remain ignored by Thomas. Thomas smiled and fell fast asleep.

Several police cars bolt past the almost mannequin like stance of Thomas. The shrieking of the sirens wakes him from his daze and his head moves in a series of convulsive shakes as he follows each car as it charges past him heading into the heart of Studd City. As quick as they were there they are gone and a hush falls over the breezy corner of Royale and Quebec. Thomas looks back at the diner and smiles.

"It would be rude not too!" and with that he walks inside. The diner is relatively quiet on this night but it is bright and inviting. The colour scheme very much white and pale blue, in the familiar fifties style that has become accustomed with these sorts of restaurants, appealing to nostalgia with various fifties style posters and signs dotted around the place. A chunky jukebox sits in the corner lying dormant at this time. The normal sound of fifties classics that are usually commonplace in such an establishment is replaced by the evenings basketball game that echoes around the diner, informing all those that are in earshot that The Angels are behind by 13 to 26. Thomas looks around two tired looking police detectives sit in a window booth devouring doughnuts and black coffee and sharing laughter. On the opposite side of the diner, a woman sits in window booth, her head buried in a book while her coffee that sits on the table in front of her continues to get ever colder. He approaches the long slender bar that runs almost the entire diner and waits to be served. To his left are a number of middle-aged men all huddled together on the pale blue and white leather bar stools, looking up at a wall mounted television that is broadcasting Studd City Angels against Pepperville Pandas, the score now 15 to 30. Amongst the gaggle of silver haired Angels fans, is an ageing bald man with a chunky white moustache. He is situated on the other side of the counter but leaning on it with his exposed elbows, paying no attention to Thomas and only to the game, the score now 15-32. The man's brow is wearing the familiar contours of annoyance that is often seen on the sports lovers faces when their team is not performing as they would like. The man constantly pushes his bottom lip across the bristles of his moustache, obviously a trait of his while concentrating. Thomas doesn't want to appear rude but would obviously like some service.

"Excuse me!" Thomas meekly asks but isn't heard.

"Erm...Excuse me!" He asks again but is suddenly drowned out by moans and groans.

Angels 15, Pandas 35.

Thomas places his case down on the pristine white tiled floor and unravels his woollen red scarf that has been wrapped around his neck and shoulders. He stuffs it into his pocket and now his dog collar can be seen.

This usually gets me noticed. Not wanting to use his occupation as a way to get attention but needs must and Thomas needed coffee.

"Hello. Excuse me!" He tries again, raising his voice a little but is still met by nothing. Just when Thomas is about to give up and reluctantly go somewhere else for a hot cup of Joe, he is noticed by one of the detectives in the window booth. He makes eye contact with Thomas and nods.

"Keith!" Shouts the detective.

"Yeah? What do you want Sid?" Comes the almost annoyed reply.

"You've got a customer if you can drag yourself away for a moment!" Keith looks over at Thomas, obviously annoyed sighs a heavy sigh and hollers,

"Jess! Get out here and serve this gentleman." Keith turns back to the television grumbling as he has missed a resurgence in his team.

Angels 22, Pandas 37.

Thomas smiles over at the detective who smiles back, gesturing a 'No problem' kind of nod response.

"What the hell, Dad!" Growls a young lady who bursts out of the kitchen wiping suds from her hands with a damp towel.

"Customer!" Keith fires back without turning away from the scream.

"Why can't you serve people? I'm up to my neck in it back there!" She is met by no response and growls with aggravation. "Goddamn it! I have to do everything around here!" and with that she throws the damp towel down on the counter, and looks up at Thomas. She notices his collar and then realisation sinks in at what she has just said.

"Oh, I am so sorry Father!" apologises Jess, her pretty blue eyes doubling in size at the mere glimpse of the collar.

"It's okay, Miss." replies Thomas making her feel a little

less embarrassed with a friendly smile.

"Well, what can I get ya?" She asks, smiling back and pulling a small worn-down pencil from behind her heavily pierced ear and a notepad from out the concealment of her white pocket apron that is tied tightly around her slender waist.

"Can I get a cup of coffee. Black?"

"Sure!" comes the bubbly responses as she scribbles the words 'B Coff' onto her notepad.

Thomas surveys the doughnuts that are displayed behind glass on the counter adjacent to him but cannot spot the flavour that he desires.

"And I don't suppose you have any chocolate and custard doughnuts, do you?" Thomas enquires hopefully. Jess smiles nodding as she scribbles 'C & C Doh' onto her pad,

"I can get you one out of the back!" Jess slides the pencil back into place, safely nestled back behind her ear. Her bleach blonde hair cut so short at the sides that the pencil just slid back into place without any hinderance.

"That'll be $5.00 please, Father." Thomas hands over a battered and crumpled up five-dollar bill which Jess takes, flattens it out and slides it into the cash register with bundles of other notes of the same value, before driving the drawer shut.

"Take a seat and I will bring it over to you!" Jess says with the sweetest of smiles. Thomas returns the smile and picks up his case as he scours the diner for somewhere he would like to rest his weary rump. He walks over to the right side of the diner where it is quieter, away from the laughing detectives and the mewling Angels fans.

Angels 28, Pandas 47.

The lady hiding behind her book (which happens to be *Dracula* by *Bram Stoker*) averts her eyes from the pages for a second and looks at Thomas.

Wow!

All that he can see are two pools of blue that is shrouded by long hazel hair hovering over the top of the book. He smiles at her, but he can't tell whether she has returned the pleasantry and those beautiful pips of blue focus their attentions back on the pages in front of her. Thomas sat down in the window booth in front of the lady's booth with his back to her.

I best not face her. The last thing I want to be known as is the creepy priest that stares at attractive women...Did I say attractive? You can hardly see her! But what beautiful eyes she has... I mean... For goodness sake Thomas you're a priest you're not dead from the waist down.

To make matters worse, Jess saunters over with Thomas' coffee and doughnut. Her petite frame hugged perfectly by the tight pale blue waitress dress, her hips flicking out from side to side with each movement.

"There you go!" says Jess as she places them in front of Thomas. However the gentleman averts his eyes to the window when she bends down in front of him to deliver his order.

"Anything else you need, just holla!" and with that she turns and returns to the kitchen, her little motor vigorously moving from side to side like a pendulum. Immediately Thomas is reminded of one of his favourite movies, *Some Like It Hot* and in his head even says the line in Jack Lemmon's voice... *It's just like jello on springs.*

"Thank you!" Thomas says, but it's too late she's already out of ear shot.

Thomas ignores the coffee and picks up the doughnut staring at it with all the love and devotion a parent would show a new born baby. And for the first time in 15 years, Thomas sinks his teeth into a chocolate and custard doughnut.

Chapter 9

Another straight flush for Dallas and Boris is beginning to get a little annoyed, well he's more than annoyed, he is damn right pissed.

"What the fuck!" Bawls the irate Ukrainian, slamming his now useless hand of playing cards onto the turned over wooden crate, which is being used to hold this evenings Ventura poker night. Dallas can't help but smirk as he rakes in dozens of screwed up bills of various values.

"If you can't take the heat, get outta the kitchen big man" he boasts in his heavy Texan drawl.

"Fuck you!" Spits Boris like a bad tempered Llama.

"And fuck this game!"

"Jesus, you are one sore loser." Dallas replies, trying so hard to suppress the laughter that is eminent.

"Fuck you!" Comes the reply once more as Boris folds his arms in a juvenile like sulk and turns on his battered swivel chair. It's stuffing spewing out of the seat and backrest making it resemble some poorly made scarecrow.

"I not play this game no more!" growls Boris in his gritty eastern European accent.

Dallas leans back in a creaky wooden chair, counting his winnings with a smug smile across his face.

"Hey, that's your call man!" Dallas flicks through the crisp notes very slowly not looking at them but at Boris, waiting for him to turn around and make eye contact with him, lying in wait like some hungry Jaguar ready to pounce on its unsuspecting prey. He waits. Boris does not move but carries on muttering in his native Slavic, like the sound of distant rumbling thunder. Dallas props up his fine leather cowboy boots onto the crate and tucks his greasy shoulder length hair behind one of his ears, as he then starts to fan himself with the money. Baiting and casting the line to catch himself a rare Ukrainian fish.

"It sure is hot in here tonight." Smirks Dallas. Boris doesn't take the bait and continues to stare in the other direction. Dallas looks around the dingy abandoned apartment. The only light is that rising from an old gas lamp, that is situated on a woodworm infested coffee table. Dallas tries again, raising his voice a little louder this time.

"Yeah, boy is it hot!" which is accompanied by a puff of air from his mouth and then a vigorous shake of the bills again. But nothing. Boris isn't biting. Dallas looks over at Sniff who as always, is paying little to no attention to what is going on around him and yet again escaping to, what he refers to as The Magical Kingdom, while puffing on the magic dragon.

"Don't you think it's hot in here, Sniff?"
Sniff who is lying on a defeated sofa which resembles an old dilapidated jalopy rotting in a scrapyard, looks over at Dallas as his joint dances between his fingertips. He opens his mouth to unleash an outpouring of sickly smelling smoke, and pauses for the longest time. His sunken bloodshot eyes working overtime to

focus, he blinks several times like a waking grizzly from hibernation and answers.

"No!"

Dallas rolls his eyes and points over at the grumbling Boris, who is still gazing at nothingness. The penny finally drops and Sniff speaks again in an unconvincing stoned drawl.

"Oh! I mean yeah. Yeah, it's hot man!" He slowly pinches the smouldering joint between his stained fingertips and drains it of its seemingly magical power.

"Yeah, it sure is hot, hot, hot fucking hot, man!" smoke rises out of his mouth again. "Hot, hot, hot, fucking hot, hot to trot, the hotspot, the hottest of the hot!"

Dallas sneers at Sniff who has obviously returned to kingdom. "Alright Sniff! Don't fucking milk it!"

Boris turns around, a look of confusion etched into his furrowed brow.

"What are you two talking about?"

"It's real hot. Don't you think, Boris?" Dallas explains again accompanying his statement with a fan of dollar bills being shook vigorously from side to side.

"Fuckin' Idiot! It's October and it's colder than a goat's ass!" Yells Boris, still not noticing the money fan.

Dallas stops waving the money and stares at him blankly before howling with laughter.

"What are you laughing at?" Boris asks, becoming even more annoyed with Dallas with every passing second. Dallas finally stops laughing wiping a tear from his eye with the back of his hand "Oh, man! Oh Boris, how do you know that a..." Dallas bursts into another fit of hysterics before he could even get his sentence out.

"Fuck you!" Boris seethes and attempts to turn back around away from Dallas. Dallas sees that he may lose his prize catch if he turns away again and forces himself to stop laughing.

"Okay, Okay... Boris, I'm sorry man!" Dallas calms himself, clears his throat with a few little coughs and tries again.

"How do you know a goat has a cold ass?" Dallas' face contorts hearing such a ridiculous statement leave his lips. He balls up his hand to a fist and brings it up to his heavily stubbled chin, half concealing his mouth, resting it on his quivering lips, trying so hard to shield his amusement. Boris looks at Dallas and in total seriousness says, "You try standing around with no pants on and see how cold your ass gets!"

That's it, and Dallas has gone again. Uncontrollable laughter erupts, spitting saliva into the air like an unstoppable geyser. He becomes bent over double grabbing at his stomach.

"Oh it hurts, it hurts!" he chuckles, with a constant flowing of tears mirrored on each side of his face, he bangs his fist on the crate a few times, which causes a couple of empty Bobby Light beer bottles to topple and roll around on the crate and on top of the discarded playing cards.

"Cold goat ass." Mutters Sniff.

"That's some funny shit, man!" he continues.

"It wasn't supposed to be funny!" states Boris but starts to chortle himself before joining Dallas in an uproarious duet.

"You should maybe think of going on *Slavs Got Talent*. Do they have that over there?" Sniff enquires in a now heavily baked condition.

Boris stops laughing and looks at Sniff with a look of stern seriousness.

"Most of our families don't even have TV." A blanket of silence falls over the room as if there is remorse and the trio are sharing a moment of contemplation, but then all make eye contact which acts as the detonator to unleash a powder keg of laughter. Even Sniff joins in with the merriment with his slow gravelling sounding honks.

"Fuck this bullshit! Let's play cards, yes?" Boris asks

"You got it partner!" grins Dallas, winking at Sniff who turns away to take another drag, accompanying this act with the immortal words "Cold goat ass!" before returning to the magical kingdom. The prize Ukrainian fish has been hooked and reeled in. As Sniff's almost lifeless carcass disappears into a thick Marijuana mist, Dallas retrieves the discarded playing cards and shuffles them back and forth while grinning profusely at Boris.

"Maybe your luck will change, big man!" says Dallas as he starts to deal the cards to Boris and himself.

"Ha! It can't get much worse!" Scoffs Boris. With the cards dealt, they're simultaneously fanned out in each players hand like they're holding a pair of miniature displaying peacocks. They eyeball each other over the tops of the cards, both sharing an arrogant look, expressing to the other that they have the winning hand. Who is bluffing? Could it be a double bluff? Could both really think they have the winning hand? Or are both trying to play mind games with the other? They could both have complete shit grasped between their sweaty fingers.

"Oh, yeah!" Dallas boasts

"That good?" Boris enquires

"Unbelievable, big Man!" Dallas winks as he repositions his cards in his hands presumably to match up the suits. Boris also does this, toying with each other like boxers feeling out their opponent at the beginning of a bout.

"Me too!" grins Boris. Unveiling two rows of unsightly crooked teeth.

"Good! Are you in?" Asks Dallas.

"Yeah! Yeah I'm in." As Boris frivolously tosses a one-dollar bill into the centre of the crate made table.

"Ooh Big spender. I'll see your Washington and raise you a Lincoln!" as Dallas drops a one-dollar bill and a five-dollar bill onto the pile.

Sniff suddenly bolts up right on the sofa and shrieks.

"Cold goat ass!"

Dallas and Boris almost jump out of their skins in unison.

"Jesus Christ, Sniff! What the fuck, man?" Dallas shouts clutching his chest, mimicking a heart attack but the shock had increased his heart rate tenfold.

"He's late again!" Sniff groans as he swivels his feet around to touch the bare wooden floor and pulls a broken down rickety coffee table towards him. An unsightly sound accompanies the table as it is dragged across the floor. Boris winces at this horrid noise.

"What are you talking about, numb nuts?" Dallas asks. Sniff delves into his oversized, worn red hoody pocket and pulls out a baggie topped with a twist tie filled with around 20g of cocaine. He dumps it on the table that now resides adjacent to him. This cocaine is known on the streets as 'Stardust'. It is from Mexico and it gets its name because there are tiny pieces of gold and silver glitter mixed in, adds nothing to the buzz and is purely there as a gimmick, but the punters are lapping it up and from Hollywood A-listers to kids on the street, it's the IN drug. Stardust is distributed by Elizabeth Martel AKA 'The Vixen', owner of The Martel Circus, she travels the country using the circus as a front to smuggle in Stardust over the border where she then liaises with local dealers to distribute it from coast to coast. Vinnie Valentine and his Doomsday Gang do not deal this type of cocaine, their supply always comes from Venezuela and Valentine's good friend Eduardo Colón. The big boss would not be happy if he knew Sniff was using another dealer and distributing the drugs for his own personal gain. If this became common knowledge this whole little group would be spending their next vacation snorkelling in The Hennig River wearing concrete flippers.

"He's late. Spider is late... he's always late." Sniff stutters as he slowly unties the twist tie to the large bag of cocaine. He does this slowly, not because he is careful but because in his head everything is moving at a snail's pace. Boris looks at his watch and agrees.

"Yeah, I guess he is pretty late. I wonder what Valentine wanted with him?"

"Who knows!" adds Dallas "But I know what I do know, I have this game won!"

"Fuck you!" Chuckles Boris, "Let me see?"

"You want to see me, it's gonna cost ya... let's see... another two Lincolns."

Boris drops another two five-dollar bills onto the small pile.

"Show me!" He demands.

Dallas fans out his hand onto the crate, revealing a straight flush, all embellished with solid black spades.

"Read'em, comrade!" scoffs Dallas.

"Bullshit!" Boris slams his hand down onto the crate again, this time the beer bottles roll off the table and onto the safety of the wooden floorboards below. They roll away from the scene like cockroaches scuttling away from the sole of someone's boot. Dallas laughs again as he scoops up yet more of Boris' money.

"You must be cheating?" Boris complains, "There is no way anyone can be this good at cards"

"We go again!" Demands Boris, determined to end this unfortunate losing streak he seems to be on. Sniff finally manages to untie the baggie and unceremoniously empties almost the entire bag onto the table.

"Oops!" He sniggers as he rummages again into his seemingly bottomless pit of a pocket. Several seconds go by and out comes a flick knife. He immediately triggers the mechanism and the four inches of cold steel explodes from its refuge and stands majestic and erect, the subtle lamplight dancing on the blade. Sniff looks closely at the blade. It sways loosely in his jittery grip and his sunken bloodshot eyes fixate on the blade as it moves, all most hypnotising him. His heavy eyelids begin to slide downwards concealing his doughy eyeballs and for a time he appears to be asleep, still swaying the blade still loosely cradled in his hand. There is a loud Slavic yell of "Shit!" and Sniff is back. From where? Who knows, but he has returned nonetheless. He looks at the shimmering white pyramid in front of him and he smiles a horrid smile, the smile of an addict. The teeth he is blessed to have left are lacking enamel and are the colour of Christmas eggnog with the texture of jagged slate. He leans forward letting his blade lead him, he accompanies this motion with a childlike babble like the noise of an aeroplane. The blade dives straight into the pile point first, disrupting its structure and causing it to cascade onto the table like sand gushing from a broken hourglass. Sniff then stabs at the Stardust randomly and almost violently, the tip of the blade chipping small chunks out of the table. In the back of Sniff's mind somewhere he hears a voice, but the sound is muffled.

"Cut that shit out, man!" Sniff stops, still swaying in his seat. "Cut it out...That shit...Cold...Hot...Goat...ass...goat...ass... He's late...He's always late..." It is impossible to know just what Sniff has taken throughout the day, but by the random incoherent nonsense that he is spouting, it is obvious he's probably had too much. Dallas and Boris don't bat an eyelid, they have seen Sniff like this many times. They carry on with their game of cards and with a huge cry of "YES!" Boris has finally won a hand, four of a kind, Queens. Sniff stares hard at his crooked reflection in the blade which is now plastered with Stardust, the glitter pieces catching the light, sparkling and captivating. He smiles again that atrocious looking smile and whispers "Pretty!" then without any second thought, his damp hairy tongue departs from its serrated cavern and caresses the blade, cocaine immediately drawn to the moisture of it. He licks the blade clean and doesn't even seem to flinch when the blade slices a section of his tongue and blood seeps across its gnarled surface mixing with the glittery substance. Like a wounded creature, it submits lathered in a mixture of cocaine and blood, now resembling a pinkish paste and with the numerous dots of glitter gave it the illusion that it was fizzing. It returns to its chamber, maybe even into the hole that has appeared in the roof of his mouth, something that has come to his attention lately and like any addict ignores it completely. He dives towards the table again and hangs there hovering over the table like a buzzard does surveying the vicinity for its next unsuspecting snack. Several greasy strands of hair hang over his face as he slowly delves in again like a physician about to embark on surgery, blade in hand ready to cut.

"Cold Goat Ass!"

Murmurs of voices again echoing through his head, but he does not hear what is being said or at this point even care. He slices through the thick blinking powder into a hefty line, thick and bulging like the body of a fat slug, but this slug isn't going anywhere it sits and waits, waits for its destiny to ride the infamous Sniff's nasal log flume, where many have been before and many more will no doubt carry on the tradition. Quickly Sniff rolls up a grimy dollar bill, its shape already turned up either end indicating that it has been in a tubular shape before and is happy to roll straight back into the desired position. Pressing a yellowing fingertip to his one nostril, he positions the rolled-up dollar near the gape of his other nostril and swoops forward. He inhales and within seconds the bulky pile has gone, now enjoying the ride on Sniff's nasal log flume, next stop the brain where this ride terminates in a euphoric climax. Sniff slowly leans back into the torn and flat cushions on the sofa, in absolute ecstasy. His cragged smile freezes on his face like a plastic anarchy mask. The red blood vessels dance an exotic dance together as they make their way across the sand coloured sclera and gently kiss the steel blue iris causing his dark pupils to immediately double in size. He tips his head back as far back as it will go over the back of the sofa and lets out a satisfying puff of air.

"Perhaps they killed him" Sniff says, still grinning profusely as his tongue vigorously penetrates the sleek crevice that has formed at the roof of his mouth, stretching with all its might to taste any traces of Stardust that may have fallen in transit riding the flume. Dallas and Boris stop focusing on their card game and both stare at Sniff.

"Who?" Dallas asks, confused at Sniff's statement.

"Why old Spiderino, that's who!" Sniff answers.

"Why would they do that?" Boris adds.

"Because of the dust, man! Because of the dust!"

"Don't be ridiculous!" Dallas shakes his head and looks back at his cards.

"Okay, if you say so." Sniff reluctantly agrees.

"Besides, you're the one going against the boss dealing Stardust, not us. Not Spider!" Boris scoffs, seemingly crushing Sniff's comments.

"True, true! But, he'd kill us all you know. Big Vin would kill us all if he found out you know."

"You're a fucking prick, Sniff!" seethes Boris, who shoots a contorted look of contempt towards his fellow Webhead.

"Yeah I guess I am a prick. A fucking prick! But, that makes you guys pricks too."

"Fuck you!" Boris slams his cards down on the crate again, this time the rage is real.

"Calm down, big man!" pleads Dallas who suddenly finds himself playing peacekeeper.

"Yep, you're all huge fucking pricks!" Sniff stirs.
Boris leaps from his chair which falls to the floor with a thud. His face now clenched as tight as his fists.

"I'm gonna beat your ass you little maggot!" Yells Boris. Dallas rises to intervene and stand between them, Sniff remains slouched over the sofa like a lifeless throw.

"You guys are to blame. You guys sit idly by and watch me do shitloads, and I mean shitloads of this stuff. You know where I get it from, you know that I deal it and you do nothing. So, you gotta ask yourself, who is the real prick here?" Dallas sighs nodding his head in agreement.

"He's right, Boris!"

"What?" A wide-eyed Boris replies in shock, his body loosening.

"Sniff is right. We're all fucked if Valentine finds out. All of us!" says Dallas.

"Told ya!" Sniff squeaks before randomly rattles his teeth together like they'd just been wound up.

"I can't believe we have to babysit this asshole." Boris sighs, knowing now that what his fellow Webheads are saying is the truth.

"You love me really." Sniff smiles that horrid smile again and then makes kissing sounds at Boris. Unexpectedly the conversation is halted by an almighty slam of the front door downstairs and then a burst of hefty footfall on the staircase, growing increasingly louder which each stride. Dallas and Boris retrieve their firearms. Boris, a Jericho 941 from a hidden shoulder holster under his tracksuit jacket and Dallas a Ruler 9mm Luger from the waistband of the rear of his jeans. Sniff doesn't move.

"It's the cops!" Boris blasts and the two of them cock and aim their guns at the door and wait.

The door is blasted in by the foot of an irate Spider, who stands in the doorway seething, his breathing heavy and his shoulders rising in time with each aggravated breath.

"Jesus fucking Christ, Spider! We could have blown your fucking head off!" Says Dallas wheezing with relief. Both lower their weapons.

"That fucking son of a bitch!" Spits Spider, slamming what's left of the door behind him. He wipes blood that stains his lips with the back of his hand, smearing most of it up his face.

"I'm going to kill that fat fuck!" Spider continues looking down in disdain at his designer label t-shirt, now decorated with a one of a kind motif of vibrant blood speckles that is rapidly soaking into the material and starting to dry.

"What the hell happened?" Asks Dallas.

Spider again surveys his once beloved shirt, the splotches of red coughed up blood begin to seep into each other like a gory inkblot test.

"One of Valentine's apes gave me a love tap! That's what happened!" Sneers Spider spitting yet more of his own internal blood out.

"That fucking fat fuck!"

"Ben?" Boris enquires and Spider nods back, as he winches in pain but tries hard to hide the fact that he is hurt from his fellow Webhead comrades.

"Which one?" Grunts Sniff, exiting his dazed state to join the conversation.

"I don't fucking know! They're identical twins, you dip-shit! I don't have a fucking clue which one it was... I don't care either! I'll fucking shoot them both! Pair of inbred fucks!" He growls as he winces again. Spider grabs the collar of his now grimy, blood sodden shirt and tears away at it with aggressive intensity, like a bloodhound ripping through a cornered fox.

"Fucking bastard!" Spider growls again, spitting blood and bile onto the floor once more.

Dallas and Boris look on speechless. They have never seen Spider this irate before as he discards the torn material into a dark corner of the apartment. He holds his torso and he flinches with pain, his eyes closing for a second as he wears foul grimace on his face. He spits again, machine gunning the floorboards with blood and saliva. With each grimace his body constricts, his lean but muscular physique ripples. The skull, cobwebs and various arachnid themed tattoos move with each tort

112

contraction, giving the illusion that each piece is dancing on his ebony skin.

"So, what was it all about?" Dallas asks, making eye contact with Boris, who then both simultaneously glance over at the disinterested Sniff, who is still sprawled over the deformed sofa, like some abandoned pile of laundry plonked there to be taken care off at a more convenient time. Both expecting Spider's drubbing to be something to do with Sniff's moonlighting as a Stardust dealer.

"Same old bullshit. My attitude and my lack of respect... blah, blah, blah!" He winces again and Dallas hands him a lukewarm bottle of Bobbys.

"I don't mind a beating if I've done wrong, you get me?" He states, Dallas and Boris nod in agreement.

"But, when we're out there selling his shit for him, lining his pockets... man, it just fucking pisses me off!" Spider grasps the ridged cap that tops the brown glass bottle and with a snug grip, twist and jerk sequence, the cap succumbs to this well practiced exercise and it tumbles to the floor. The room temperature beer bubbles and ascends up the slender neck before overflowing and dripping down over Spiders hand. Spider seems unfazed by this and continues his tirade.

"I mean, we are the ones taking all the risks! None of the other Doomsdayers can see that, but we are. They're all too fucking stupid to see it!" Spider shakes his head and sits down on the arm of the sofa.

"He's fucking untouchable for some reason. He doesn't get his greasy Sicilian hands dirty, it's the stupid motherfuckers like us that keeps him squeaky clean to any FED's that come looking for his scalp. I'm gonna change that."

"So, what do we do now, Boss?" Enquires Boris. Spider pauses and takes a swig of his beer, a long shallow gulp, his Adams apple pulsating up and down with each deep swallow. He lowers the bottle and wipes the bubbling suds from around his mouth with his hand.

"Fuck! I needed that. Tastes like piss but, anything to wash the taste of blood away" He takes another quick, deep swig before lowering it again, examining the bottle. He swills the remains around in the bottle before sneering at it like he'd trodden in something unsightly.

"Still... Shit suds though."

"Spider!" Dallas interrupts Spider's unenthusiastic review of Bobby's Light Beer.

"What?" Spider grunts

"What are we going to do?" Dallas asks anxiously. Spider empties the rest of the bottle and launches it across the room. It explodes as soon as it makes contact with the exposed brick wall, brown tinted moist glass raining down the wall to the floorboards.

"This is what we are going to do..." Spider begins but is distracted by something.

"...What is that shit?" He growls through his gold platted teeth that glisten in the dim lamplight, producing a horrifying supernatural looking grimace. Spider stares at the dilapidated coffee table buried under a barren wasteland of glistening cocaine.

"Is that Stardust!" He barks. Beer, blood and saliva spraying through the golden snarl like an uncontrollable garden sprinkler. Spider's eyes double in size and he turns to Boris and Dallas who slowly nod. They're wearing identical worried looks on their faces as they know that Sniff is in for it and there is nothing they can do. Spider glares at Sniff, who obviously grins that disdainfully ugly grin at Spider. Spider screams at the top of his lungs and backhands Sniff in his moronic gape knocking him onto the floor.

"You fucking stupid bastard!" Spider screams at him as Sniff scuttles off like a dung beetle for the sanctuary of the corner, which offers no sanctuary for him at all. All he has done is cornered himself. Spider stalks him, almost foaming at the mouth like a rabid dog. He paintbrushes Sniff across his face relentlessly. Blood spurts from somewhere on Sniff's face. It may be his nose or lip,or even a cut caused by one of Spider's many gold rings that cling tightly to his fingers. Boris and Dallas plead with Spider to stop but he does not hear them. Like Sniff earlier, he is in his own world but it is not a world of euphoric joy and merriment, no, it is a place of anger and content. Sniff's latest error in judgement has unleashed Spider's rage and the onslaught continues as he drives his fists into his face. Sniff the cowardly and defenceless runt of a man, cowers on the floor as Spider thrashes through him like an uncontrollable human wrecking ball.

"You stupid fucking bastard!" Continues Spider, chanting it almost rhythmically with every shot. Something cracks in Sniff's face, most likely his nasal bone.

115

"You've broken his nose!" Yells Boris.

"Spider, Stop! He's had enough, man!" Dallas calls and Spider halts the attack. He breathes heavily, every muscle in his torso pulsing as adrenaline flows through his system. He looks at his fists, clenched and covered in Sniff's blood, flesh and skin hanging from a large golden ingot ring on his middle finger.

"You're a fucking idiot, Sniff!" Spider pants like a weary greyhound. Sniff leans up against the brick wall, his face a bloody pulp, unrecognisable as his face oozes from several wounds.

"I don't know why we even have you around! You're a waste of fucking space! Idiot! Fucking idiot!" Spider continues, now pacing back and forth like a confined tiger.

"Do you even realise what you have done?" He yells, but all that comes from Sniff's mouth are several bubbles of blood that burst as soon as they arrive.

"Fuck's sake! We could all be killed for this, do you get that?" Still nothing but blood bubbles in reply. Spider looks as if he's going to attack again, but then stops himself somehow and turns his attentions to the table that homes the unwanted stash. With a cry as deafening as a banshee he flips the table into the air. It almost does a full rotation before meeting the card table crate sitting in-between the unsuspecting pair of Boris and Dallas who just watch it explode right next to them. Stardust is jettisoned into the air, almost hanging there for a moment before softly falling like sparkling flakes of snow. Spider storms out of the apartment quickly followed by Boris shaking his head at Sniff as he leaves. Dallas sighs a long sigh and ties his shoulder length hair back into a messy ponytail.

"You best get rid of that shit and get yourself checked out!" He grabs his worn leather jacket from the back of his chair and wipes off the layer of cocaine now covering the shoulders of it.

"I'll call you when he's calmed down."

And with that Dallas leaves too.

Sniff sits in the dark corner of the apartment alone as he watches a coin blizzard whisper around his head, before cascading on his quivering carcass. Disturbingly, Sniff starts to snigger, bubbles of blood again bursting from his mouth as it dribbles down his chin.

"Cold...Goat...Ass..." he murmurs quietly before bursting into a fit of uncontrollable hysterics. His skeletal hand reaching up as if to try and retrieve the glittery treasure that descends all around him.

Chapter 10

Detective Graham sifts through the stacks of files, binders and paperwork that has accumulated on his thick mahogany desk. Some of them teetering back and forth as if one more sheet of paper could cause an avalanche. Graham sighs a tired and defeatist sigh.

"So much to do and so little time."

He leans back in his chair. It creaks, high in pitch like nails being etched into a chalkboard. Out of boredom he rhythmically taps out a tune on the edge of the desk, seemingly the only part of his desk that isn't consumed by paperwork.

"Now, where did I leave my coffee?" He asks himself, leaning forward again and delving into the never-ending jungle of paper and card. Lifting several folders, he finds his mug of coffee now lukewarm at best.

"Ah, there you are!" he says to himself as he discards the files to another pile and grips the once white mug, that has the words 'BEST DAD EVER' stamped onto it. He hoists up the mug and takes a swig before recoiling with displeasure from the cheap cold java that now fills his maw like tide water trapped in a beach cavern. After several seconds of deliberation (spit or swallow), Graham succumbs and lets the coffee slide down his gullet, much to the displeasure of his innards that grumble and groan as if out of annoyance. He slams the mug back down from where it was found. Remaining drops of coffee sweep up the sides of the mug and land on the wood of the desk and a little speckles some files and paperwork. He stops, noticing a photograph fitted into a golden frame. A family portraits himself and his wife Mae, their two sons Billy and Todd and of course their pet American water spaniel, Charlie. He smiles and remembers that specific day two years ago, taken at Christmas all wearing matching red woollen jumpers, complete with a large snowman painstakingly knitted on to the front by my Mae's mother (*God, rest her soul*). Its large bulbous nose drooping down with the amount of cotton wool stuffed inside them.

Mae told her there was too much in there. But the stubborn old bird wouldn't listen.

He beams with pride at his boys, Todd now aged 10 and Billy now aged 8, both wearing excited addictive smiles as Charlie climbs over them both licking poor Billy's face, but he doesn't seem to care one iota.

What good looking kids! Obviously take after their mother.

A rye smirk caresses his lips as he looks at Todd's short, almost military style haircut in burnish copper.

Looks so much like Grandpops when he was a boy and the sweet freckled face of little Billy, small for his age having been very premature, but that hair... *Oh, that gorgeous mop of auburn hair*. His eyes then stop on his wife. Middle aged but very attractive, many would find it hard to believe she was a Mother of two, her hourglass figure does not seem to be affected by such an undertaking. Graham grasps the frame in his hand

and pulls it closer.

Sweet Mae, I do love you so much. How do you find the time to look after the boys and me? How the hell do you do it? I struggle to even take care of myself. We've been together for such a long time and I still love you now as much as I did the first day we met. Time...time...

"Shit! What's the time?" Graham yelps looking up at the clock that hangs on his wall, surrounded by plaques and awards that he has received over the years of service at the SCPD. The roman numeral faced clock indicates it has just turned 10:30. Graham places the photograph back from where it came and starts to rise from his chair in an obvious panic.

"Oh shit! Shit! Shit! Shit!" He curses rummaging in his trouser pocket for his cell phone.

"Mae is going to kill me!" In his anxious excitement he doesn't hear the tap on the glass door to his office and carries on vigorously trying to retrieve his phone. The door opens, and Officer Valerie Nash is standing in the doorway, her arms wrapped around yet another file resting it on her ample bosom. She looks at Graham wide eyed and then a playful smirk touches her plump grape tinted lips.

"Am I interrupting something, Sir?" She asks.
Graham stops rummaging in his pocket and slowly looks up to see the petite dark-haired Officer standing before him.

"Oh, Nash...erm, it's not what it looks like! I was just..." He squirms but Nash interrupts him.

"It's okay by me, Sir... Really it is!" She looks at him coyly and her long dark eyelashes flutter like two swallowtail butterflies, her piercing blue eyes staring at him through each bouncing flitter.

"No, really I was trying to get my..." Graham tries again in vain to get his story across to her so that she doesn't think that he's some old pervert just sitting in his office jacking off. Nash knows there is a simple explanation for this, but she can't help but tease Graham to watch him squirm and for her to feel so empowered, turns her on. It's no secret that Nash has a crush on Graham and Nash lets him know every chance she gets. Even if a lot of the time it is wasted on Graham who doesn't realise that she is flirting with him most of the time. Nash approaches the desk. Her black heels clicking on the laminate panel flooring. Graham's Adam's apple rising and falling with each step, like a high striker at the state fair. She stops at the edge of the desk and slowly bends forward offering the file. Her upper arms tightly pushing her breasts together causing the shirt buttons that are slightly hidden behind her black tie to gape, revealing an enticing curve of olive flesh.

"Here is that file you asked for, Sir!" Nash says lowering her voice to an almost purring rasp. Graham's eyes grow wider and his gaping mouth joins it in unison. As well as a flushed complexion as he stands behind his desk with his hand awkwardly stuffed into his trouser pocket.

"T-Thank you!" He stutters, captivated and hypnotised by her alluring ways.

"Would you like it on the desk?" She asks slightly gnawing on her bottom lip.

"W-What?" Graham whimpers, sweat starting to trickle

down his forehead. Nash suddenly changes her demeanour and pops up smiling.

"The file, Detective. Shall I just leave it on your desk?" Bubbly and beaming, she offers the file again.

"Erm...yes, yes please, erm... Valerie, erm Nash!" He manages, stumbling over each word.

"Okay!" Nash chirps placing the file on the desk and turning towards the exit.

"See you later, Sir!" she says before almost skipping through the door. Graham finds himself just staring at her backside as it ticks back and forth like the pendulum of a grandfather clock, tightly hugged by her black pencil skirt. Graham literally falls back into his chair and exhales long and hard before shaking his head in utter disbelief.

"Did that really just happen?" He asks himself, now replaying the sensual scene back through his head storing the mental images in the back of his mind for another occasion perhaps. Forgotten is the cell phone in his pocket, forgotten is the need to call his wife and tell her he will be late, his mind has well and truly wandered. He smiles to himself while starting to duel with his conscience about what has just transpired.

Nash has a thing for me? A... you know, sexual thing! Of course she doesn't, she was only playing. Yeah playing with your ding dong! You're lying if you say your loins ain't twitching round about now...Officer Nash is a professional, all she wants is...She wants to fuck you, that's what she wants. Don't be ridiculous, I'm old enough to be her... Sugar Daddy. He bursts out laughing again shaking his head in disbelief.

"Sugar Daddy!" he laughs.

"Say what?" Asks a bemused Detective Freeman entering the office wearing an expression of astonishment with a side order of disgust.

Graham looks up at Freeman and shakes his head.

"It doesn't matter."

"Don't you go falling apart on me old man!" Freeman jibes sitting down on the chair adjacent to Graham on the other side of the desk.

"I'll tell you all about it when it actually sinks in."

"Intriguing!"

"Anything on tonight's findings yet?" Enquires Graham, immediately changing the subject. Freeman leans back in the chair and grasping the back of his head with both hands yawns a very long yawn.

"Oh, excuse me Sid. Been a long fucking day!"

"I know. I've been right there with ya, buddy!" Graham chortles.

The two of them laugh a little.

"To answer your question..." says Freeman, digging at something in the corner of his eye.

"The lab is running tests on the blood found at the scene and Rogers said that he should have a match on the tyre tomorrow. So, I'm afraid there's nothing more we can do until then. Might as well go out and get drunk!" Freeman smiles a gigantic cheesy grin.

"Maybe you can, but I should really get home to Mae. She'll be wondering where I've got to."

"Sid, she'll know exactly where you've got to! Still fucking here as usual!"

"Man, that was uncanny Rich! You sounded just like her!" The two partners share another moment of laughter before Freeman rises from his seat and stretches.

"But, you my friend, are not going home just yet. You have a prior engagement for this evening." Freeman states grabbing Graham's tan coloured leather jacket from the lopsided hat stand that is planted like a misshapen old withering tree behind his door.

"What do you mean?" Graham asks perplexed at Freeman's statement.

"The small get together at Lionheart's for Eric?"

"Oh Shit! Mae is seriously going to kill me!" Freeman launches the coat towards Graham hitting him square in the face with it. The jacket smothers his head giving him the appearance of a celebrity trying to conceal his identity from the mass of awaiting paparazzi.

"C'mon, get your old ass up and let's get out of here!" Freeman says heading for the door.

"I'll get my coat and meet you by the elevator."
Graham pulls the jacket off his head smiling.

"I guess I'm going to the bar then." He smiles. Graham leaves the vicinity of the desk and flicks off the lights and closes the door behind him. The words DETECTIVE S. GRAHAM can be seen engraved in the frosted glass panel of his office door behind him. Now in the main office area of the precinct several officers can be seen rushing around, like tropical fish in a tank flitting back and forth from room to room, desk to desk. The space itself is consumed with desks, all situated in row upon row of each other, all sitting rigid and regimental like headstones in a cemetery. Even at this late hour the phones continue to ring. Crime doesn't sleep, not in Studd City.

"Detective Graham!" Bellows a voice that ambushes him as he exits his office.

"Jesus!" Graham shrieks clasping a hand to his chest, his jolted heart thumps rapidly almost rattling around in the safety of its ribcage.

"Oh, sorry, Detective! Did I startle you?"

"No, whatever gave you that idea Richards?" Graham answers sarcastically as he tries to walk away.

"I have some information for you Detective." Richards says trying to keep up with Graham.

"Can't it wait until tomorrow? I'm about to head out!" Graham continues walking across the hub of the police station.

"I think it may be connected to The Doomsday Gang case, Detective!" comes the whiney voice from a now almost out of breath, Staff Sergeant Richards. Graham stops and sighs as he starts to put on his jacket.

"You've got thirty seconds, Richards. Make it count!"

"Well..." Sergeant Richards begins pushing his thick rimmed glasses back into place, atop his beak like nose.

"...We have received a phone call from a Mister..." Richards stops for a moment and looks down at his note pad (that he is never without) which is accompanied by the annoying clicking of his tongue that hides behind his protruding goofy teeth. This is a regular trait of his that has earned him the unwanted nickname of Bugs around the precinct. Obviously named after the looney toon, Bugs Bunny. He reads the name scribbled on the pad that is filled with a number of other messages.

"Lennox. Bret Lennox!"

"Bret Lennox the movie star?" Graham asks with a raise of his eyebrows.

"No idea!" Shrugs Sgt Richards.

"C'mon, Richards! You've gotta know who Bret Lennox is?"

"No!" He replies "But he..." Sgt Richards attempts to deliver his message, but detective Graham refuses to let the matter drop and tries again.

"He was in all those B movie horrors as a kid, years ago!"

"No, sorry I don't watch horror films." Sgt Richards sneers turning his nose up like he'd just smelt the inside of dumpster.

"You've never seen... Now let me see, what was he in?" Graham questions himself. He ponders for a moment as Sgt Richards still tries to deliver his message.

"Please, Detective, Mr Lennox called about..." but Graham interrupts again.

"Maple Falls Massacre!"

"Excuse me?" Comes the response form a perplexed Sgt Richards.

"Yeah, Maple Falls Massacre and Maple Falls Massacre

Part II and Maple Falls Massacre Part III..." He continues counting them out on his fingers "and..." then Richards interrupts sarcastically.

"Let me guess, Maple Falls Massacre Part IV perhaps?" he scoffs rolling his eyes back in a condescending manner.

"No, he wasn't in that one. That was Corey Feldman."

"Corey Feldman?" Says Detective Freeman arriving at a pivotal part of the discussion.

"He was in Maple Falls Massacre 4." says Graham

"Oh, yeah! What are you talking about?" Freeman enquires

"Well, Richards here has a famous friend."

"Really? Who is it Bugs?" Freeman asks.

"Don't call me that!" Snaps Sgt Richards losing his patience "I'm trying to inform Detective Graham that this evening a Mr Bret Lennox contacted us and..."

"No way! Bret Lennox! He was in..." Freeman is interrupted by Richards.

"Maple Falls Massacre. We know!" He drones.

"Oh yeah those, but I was going to say White Cliffs, The Lighthouse Keeper, ooh, ooh and that new one he's in..." Spurts an excited Detective Freeman.

"Love, Sex and Laughter!" intervenes Graham.

"That's the one!"

"Will you two please let me tell you this so I can go about my business?" Yells the annoyed Sgt Richards.

"Okay, okay calm down, Jesus!" Says Freeman. Sgt Richards rubs his large forehead before scratching his head, under his dark curls the consistency of candy floss, then sighs an irrupted sigh.

"Around twenty hundred hours this evening a Mr Bret Lennox called to inform us that his car had been stolen." There was a long pause and the two Detectives look at each other bemused at what this has to do with them.

"And? What's that got to do with The Doomsday Gang case?" Graham complains.

"Well, the car was a..." Again, he looks down at his scribble pad, tongue clicking away like a little woodpecker, poking away at a redwood.

"A red 92 Corvette... ZR-1. The vehicle was taken from outside Pinewood High School, in Butterworth."

"I still don't know what this has to do with the case, Richards." Answers Graham, turning and heading towards the elevator, immediately followed by Freeman.

"The car was seen in Ventura this evening and Rogers told me he was running a cast for you? Tyre tracks found at the scene?" The pair slow down a little and Freeman whispers to Graham.

"He could be right you know, it could be a connection, Sid."

"Yeah, it could well be, but if we don't keep moving we'll be here all damn night!" the two walk on towards the elevator.

"It could be a match, Detective!" Calls Sgt Richards.

"It's noted, Richards. Thanks!" Graham calls back.

"What would you like me to do, Detective?"

"There's nothing we can do until morning." Graham answers reaching the elevator and pushing the button to call it.

Graham remains fixated at the shiny metal doors. He daren't turn around and make eye contact with Richards again or else that could spawn another longwinded conversation he didn't particularly want. Sgt Richards awkwardly ponders on the spot for a moment, hovering like some agitated moth, jots something down on his notepad and then scurries on.

"Has he gone?" He asks Freeman from out of the corner of his mouth. Detective Freeman slyly looks over his shoulder.

"Yeah. He's gone now."

"Thank God for that!" Graham answers rolling his eyes and adjusting his jacket, preparing it to be zipped up into place.

"Why didn't you want to investigate Lennox's stolen car?"

"Well, 1, Like I said, there is nothing we can do until morning anyway as Roger's cast and report won't be available until then... 2, I couldn't stand another conversation with Bugs, the guy really grates on me."

"And 3?" Freeman asks.

"And 3, I want to go to the bar! I need a damn drink!"

"You could have just skipped to 3, Sid. That answer would have been good enough for me!" Chuckles Freeman.

"Imagine not knowing who Bret Lennox was!" Freeman adds shaking his head in disbelief. There is a high pitch ping and the doors to the elevator shuffle open slowly and cumbersome, and the two detectives step inside.

"Oh, Richard I have to tell you something about Officer Nash." The doors to the elevator close, and the detectives start their descent.

Chapter 11

Thomas leaves the Perfect Java diner, now with a brown paper bag clenched in his hand.

I don't tend to have doughnuts very often these days, what with calorie counting and sticking to a strict diet. I'm at my physical peak now. It's taken me a long time to get to where I want to be. Where I need to be. But, I can treat myself from time to time. So that is why I had to get another one of those doughnuts. One for the road...

As he steps onto the sidewalk, a hooded youth whizzes past him like a greyhound snatching the brown bag from his grasp. Thomas is frozen to the spot, dumbfounded.

"Hey!" He calls out of instinct, taken by such a surprise that that was the best verbal retort he could muster. The youth darts down the sidewalk, dirty baseball sneakers slapping on the flat concrete underfoot.

"Why the little..." Thomas almost chortles with a wry little smile itching his lips. For a split second he thinks about giving chase...*No, I know how that story ends.*

"Yeah, you better run, guy!" He finally calls in jest. Only to then eat his words when the youth's hood falls and he sees a long dark ponytail flop out down the thief's back. There is a slight turn of the youth's head revealing the face of a pretty but mucky Asian girl make eye contact with dark scared eyes, before turning the same corner Thomas did all those years ago. Thomas stands there laughing to himself, several passers-by look at him with dubious gaze and steering clear of the strange man laughing on the corner of Royale and Quebec. He shakes his head and moves along at a slow methodical pace taking in what has just happened.

You will have to up your game Thomas, if a little girl just robbed you and then took off down the street like Roadrunner, leaving you standing in your own puddle of stupid. He laughs to himself again, accompanied by yet another shake of the head. *How are you meant to fulfil your crusade if a little mite like her just made a fool of you? You knew it wasn't going to be easy but come on! She must have only been around 12-13 years old? Gotta be on your toes from now on Thomas.*

He carries on through Royale, walking down Queen Street taking in all the old sights. The old gothic looking buildings that stand dark and slender, all caressed with carefully decorated architecture, along window ledges and over doorways. Beautiful designs that would have been painstakingly shaped by one man using just a hammer and chisel no doubt. Now forgotten about by the regular Studd City locals, their eyes now used to the sights no longer rise above what lies in front of them, as they go about their day to day lives. Either glued to the new arrivals in the shop windows or inspecting the 5 inches of technology that spasmodically chimes in their talon like grip, informing them that Victoria is now in a relationship or Timothy tagged you in a picture. If they took the time to look up at these splendid structures they could see the forgotten wonders of this city. Perched granite gargoyles draped with bat like wings, linger from ledges and corners of the dark majestic buildings, still striving to protect their city below. Even if people have forgotten about them they stick to their end of the bargain, they stay and protect as best they can, it's all they know. One of the gargoyles catches Thomas' eye and he stops gazing up at it. He stares at the gargoyle, its bulging eyes, hog like nostrils and gaping maw that holds one and a half large tusks in place. Its fractured body crouches worn and tired, clawed limbs gripping the parapet tightly but weary.

Your eyes look tired my friend. They stare at each other for the longest time. *Your back can no longer take the strain can it? The burden you have been carrying for all these years is now too much isn't it? The pressure and stress of protecting these people shows, manifesting itself as the green moss that has moulded to your back. Impossible to shake off, it's too late isn't it my friend.*

The Gargoyle just stares back at Thomas with those vulnerable eyes. *Let go.*

A crack makes its way across the gargoyles face, like a strike of fork lightning.

Let me take the burden.

Another crack parts its wing from its torso.

I am here now, I will protect them now. Its moss smothered spine splinters and several chunks of granite fall. *The responsibility has fallen to me now, let me take it from you.*

The full tusk snaps and falls. Thomas watches it hurtle to the ground and fragments with the sudden impact. He looks up again, staring into its hollow eyes, debris flickering down like thick embers.

"Let go" He whispers. The exhausted gargoyle concedes and breaks away, granite crunching on granite as it slips away from itself and falls to the sidewalk below. The whole ordeal lasts a couple of minutes. Thomas stands there until all the debris has fallen before walking on. Thomas remains silent in thought for most of his journey now, he knows that what has just transpired is a sign, a sign to tell him that it is time. A changing of the guards and Thomas will lead the charge. Thomas will be the one to bring peace back to this downtrodden place. It's in his hands now. Thomas stops at the end of Queen Street and glances left to see a vibrant array of amber lights bursting from Chinatown. He looks up to see a two humongous red tower cranes planted over it slowly moving across Chinatown, each with a winking red light, pulsing as they move so very slowly above. A large billboard can be seen near the entrance of Chinatown that is trying to go about its normal routine, with stalls and restaurants still open underneath a prison of scaffolding, that rises into the night sky. The billboard shows what the construction hopes to look like, a glance into the future. Triangular golden buildings all mounted with a slender Chinese dragon makes the finished article look cliché and outlandish. Thomas shakes his head and sighs.

Another traditional part of the city lost to the conglomerates. The name DEVINE Inc. is present on the billboard in bold red letters for all to see who is responsible, arrogantly flaunting who technically owns Studd City now.

"Devine Incorporated?" He turns and looks behind him at the splendid colourful dazzling lights on the gigantic futuristic buildings that sprout in the rich quarter of Studd City. In the middle of all these new structures is The Devine Tower. A gargantuan slender shard like erection that bursts through a forest of metal and glass to stand majestically over all. Egotistically crowned with the word DEVINE illuminated with hundreds of blood red bulbs and if that wasn't enough, it slowly rotates for the entire city to see. But to see what exactly? To let everyone know who is in charge.

Yes, we see you Mr Devine. We know that you are in control. But what happens to this side of the City? You'll destroy it that's what. I can try to save the city from the vile and unjust one way and you will deal with it by gathering the support of the people that live here and don't want to see change. Change is good but destroying this city's history is not.

Thomas quickly hurries across the road and into Montreal. He makes it to the other side in good speed before the next flurry of traffic whizzes by behind him. He looks at his watch, 22:32.

It's getting late. I'd Best look for somewhere to settle down for the night. But one glimpse of my new home first.

Thomas walks on through Montreal and enters St. Vincent's Street. He is pleased to see that the beautiful architecture has not been touched or is not in bad condition. He is also pleased to see rows of small pin oak trees leading the way up the street towards St. Vincent's Square. He saunters underneath the cover of foliage that shrouds the sidewalk, causing eerie shadows on the ground as it blocks the streetlights above. The leaves that cling to the trees are kissed with vibrant yellows and oranges and Thomas enjoys kicking his feet through the fallen brown ones that are now accompanying the sidewalk. They crackle and crunch under the hard sole of his fine leather shoes. He exits the cover of trees and into St. Vincent's Square. An exquisite fountain can be seen in its centre. Statues of several winged cherubs can be seen throughout, as water bursts from the centre and trickles down into the pool below.

Thomas approaches it and gazes into the water, past his quivering reflexion and at the bottom it glistens with a bed of coins, peoples wishes, peoples dreams. Thomas takes out some loose change from his pocket. He sieves through the now useless euros and launches them all into the fountain. After the sound of several splashing sounds, calm is restored and then all that can be heard is the tranquil relaxing sound of the water cascading down into the pool.

"I'm going to need all the help I can get." He smiles, knowing he has religion on his side but hoping that a few well-placed wishes can tip the balance in his favour. Thomas walks away from the fountain and then cranes his head back, where standing before him, is his new home St. Vincent's church.

Chapter 12

Lionhearts is an obscure English bar situated just off the corner of Jones and Monroe, in a little side street, or an alleyway to be precise. It's only a stone's throw from SCPD's Central Precinct in Jones, which comes in very handy as it has become a cop bar and is frequently visited by law enforcement officers from all three of Studd City's precincts. North Precinct has the furthest to travel as it is situated in Grenoble near to SCU (Studd City University) and South Precinct is on the corner of Finkle and Hepburn, not far from the Ventura Bridge that joins Studs City to its neighbouring city of Forge. The Lionhearts has a thick wooden hanging sign, with a colourful design of a majestic golden lion raising up on its hind legs, grasping to a white shield that has the St. George's cross emblazoned on it, the kind of badge you find in any book about heraldry. The sign swings back and forth with each slender gust of fall wind. The several links of metal chain connect the sign to a wall bracket and creaks an unpleasant metallic howl each time it feels the gentle breath of fall. Through the long oblong glass block window, it is apparent that Eric Stone's leaving party is in full force, wall to wall with off duty police officers. The interior of the small bar is smothered with olde world English trinkets, paintings and signs, as well as a splendid oil painting of St. George standing over the dead carcass of the slain dragon. A bloodied sword in hand and his shimmering armour framing a tattered crusader's tabard and a crimson gothic looking crucifix decorating the white cotton of the tabard. The dragon's head is almost severed and blood seeps out onto the dirty floor, where the victorious St. George stands in all his glory. A soft caress of smoke leaves the freshly slaughtered beasts nostrils and seems to surround the knight, capturing this illustrious moment perfectly in a frame of transparent vapour. It truly is a sight to behold and that is why it takes centre stage between all the other paraphernalia on the crowded walls. Also clung to the walls is various English football memorabilia. Signed international caps, deflated pig skin footballs and an array of signed photographs of past masters. The Lionhearts owner (who is obviously English) is Thomas Atkinson, or Fat Tommy to his friends and regular punters. He stands behind the bar cleaning a large glass tankard with a cloth, chatting away to several of his regulars that gather at the long slender mahogany bar, like greedy pigs congregating at a trough. Most of the male officers are gathered around a wall mounted television for the evenings boxing extravaganza. The other side of the bar, where a few tables are situated, is mostly taken up by the female contingent of SCPD, most of them sipping wine and reliving the tales of their day on duty. Officer Nash sits with her best friend, Officer Suzanne Carruthers. A bubbly plump little bookworm with an aggravating laugh, like a neighing mare, all teeth and gums. Nash just nods in agreement at whatever Carruthers is saying, even though she isn't paying attention to anything she is saying. Nash's beautiful blue pools are fixated at the bar and at one man, Detective Graham. He leans on the bar with a tankard of beer grasped in his hand laughing merrily away with Stone and Freeman, totally unaware that his every move is being examined by a very smitten Officer Nash.

"...And he's left standing there, jerking his hand around in his pocket..." chuckles Freeman with tears trickling from his eyes, as he retells Graham's story from earlier in the evening.

"Oh man, that is too much!" laughs Stone.

The two of them doubled over at Graham's expense, who takes it all in good jest.

"You boys are easily pleased." Says Graham shaking his head but wearing a grin on his face.

"Oh, Come on, Sid! Don't be like that!" sympathises Freeman patting him on the back.

"It's not every day you get caught playing punish Percy by a hot little Twinkie like Nash."

As they continue to laugh they are joined by Wilson, with a bottle of orange juice clasped in his hand topped with a straw. He begins to laugh too, trying to join in with the merriment. They look at Wilson all wearing a blank expression, all suppressing the same thought.

Oh Great.

It's not that the trio don't like Wilson, he's a pleasant enough kid, he's just a square peg in a gathering of triangular holes.

"Who's Percy?" Wilson asks innocently and immediately Freeman spits out a mouthful of beer, spraying it out with all the force and velocity of a bursting humpback.

"Oh man, oh man I need the bathroom!" laughs

Freeman, patting Wilson on the shoulder as he leaves, attempting to hold his bladder in check. Graham and Stone snigger profusely as a bewildered Wilson stands there with his orange juice.

"Is Percy in our precinct?" He questions with all sincerity. In the distance Freeman can be heard erupting into a hysterical fit of laughter again, obviously catching what Wilson said as he walked away.

"I hope he makes it in time." Stone chuckles.

"What did I say?" Wilson asks.

"Nothing kid. Let me get you a drink." Graham gestures to Fat Tommy who is at the end of the bar with the TV remote in hand, increasing the volume as the main event of the evening is about to start.

"No, Thank you, Sir!" Wilson intervenes shaking his head.   "I'm fine, thank you."

"Suit yourself." Graham replies taking a big swig of beer. A frothy foam of white latches on to his goatee beard before he removes it with his tongue.

"Are you coming to watch the fight?" Wilson asks them both, obviously bubbling with excitement.

"Didn't take you for a boxing fan?" Stone asks, his eyebrows raised in surprise.

"Oh, yeah! I've always been a big fan. Used to watch it all the time back home in Barnville with my grandpa." A huge grin illuminates across his young innocent face and Graham can't help but smile.

"That's nice, kid. It's good to have those memories.

Cherish them."

"Oh, I will! Well, are you coming? It's just about to start!" Bounces Wilson, taking a slurp of his orange drink.

"Who's your money on, Rob?" Stone enquires to Wilson.

"Oh, definitely has to be Bundy. He's got the age and experience."

"Yeah maybe, but I've seen that Johnson kid, he's impressive and man he's as quick as a cat." replies Graham

"Oh, for sure but Bundy's seen off many an out-fighter in the past..." dismisses Wilson.

"...He's an old school slugger, soon as you get in tight with Bundy, it's lights out!" States Wilson arrogantly. He slurps his orange juice again.

"Johnson is undefeated though." Graham adds.

"Doesn't matter. Bundy ended Logan, Powell and Green's streaks. Bundy's got his number."

"What about that patented 'Left Hook' of his? The kid packs one hell of a punch."

"Bundy will ride it."

"Well, I guess we will have to have a little wager on the matter?" Says Graham.

"Oh, my Mother doesn't like me to gamble." Wilson meekly answers, shrinking back to the unconfident rookie he was about three minutes ago.

"Your Mother here?" Enquires Graham, again taking a big gulp of his beer.

"Erm... well, no..."

"Then why not? She'll never know...and hey, you seem to

know your boxing so what you got to lose, kid?" Graham persuades, winking at Stone over his glass tankard.

"The bell rings and we're underway. I'm Gene Hoolohan and with me as always is Teddy Armstrong."

"Hi folks! This is going to be an epic encounter!"

"Sure is, Teddy. Coming at you live from The Forge City Arena... Johnson is out of the gates like a hot rod! He has blistering pace!"

"Sounds like its started, kid. I have ten bucks says Johnson will beat Bundy in the third round." offers Graham. Wilson dances back and forth on the spot, not knowing what to do. He doesn't want to miss the fight, he knows that his Mother doesn't approve of gambling and doesn't want to go against her wishes, but he wants so desperately to fit in.

"Times ticking!" Graham taunts

"Nice jab by Johnson!"

"But the big man is just taking it, he's leaving that chin out there to entice Johnson, Gene."

"Oh, you betcha, Teddy. Bundy is gonna dangle that carrot all night!"

"Okay! You're on!" Wilson shakes Grahams hand and quickly scuttles off into the crowd and becomes lost in a forest of navy blue uniforms that are gathered around the screen. Graham and Stone turn to each other laughing.

"Oh, that Rob! What a character he is." chuckles Stone

"He sure is. And how's things with you? Sorry it slipped my mind that you were moving on, just had a lot on my plate lately."

"Vinnie Valentine, huh?"

"Bingo!"

"You'll nail him. One day you'll nail him, I'm sure of that."

"I'll drink to that!" Graham laughs finishing off his beer.

"Let me get you another?" Asks Stone, gesturing to Fat Tommy who smiles and comes trundling over like an overweight penguin.

"No, Eric! I really must be getting home." Graham pleads.

"I insist! For everything you've done for me while I've been here." asserts Stone.

"Yes, Eric, what can I get you?" Fat Tommy enquires with a large jolly smile.

"Another two of those, please, Tommy."

Fat Tommy pours the beer into one glass tankard and passes it over to Graham.

"Thanks!" Another is poured and slid gently over to Stone, and Fat Tommy waddles back over towards the television.

"*Oh, and what a right that was by 'The Big Bully'. Johnson will be left checking his fillings after that one!*"

"*He's definitely living up to his moniker, Gene. Bundy is just bullying him!*"

"*So, a*re you looking forward to starting with SWAT?" Graham asks, tipping his glass towards Stone.

"Oh yeah! I guess I'm a little nervous but..."

"Pah! You will be fine, you're a damn good cop and I'll be sad to see you leave the precinct."

"Thanks, Sid. I really appreciate that!" Stone smiles and holds out his glass and with a nod of Graham's head, the two of them clank the heavy glass tankards together. Froth and beer surging up and out of the glass like a wave striking an immovable wall of vertebrates, before spilling onto the thick mahogany bar.

"And that's the bell signalling the end of round one. We'll be right back with Johnson vs. Bundy Round 2, after a word from our sponsors."

"Do you have a Monstrous appetite? Are other fast food joints leaving you howling for more? Then Franken-Burger is the place for you..."

Officer Wilson joins them again at the bar, excitement flickering in his eyes with the look of a small child on Christmas Day.

"What a great round!" Boasts Wilson shaking his head in disbelief. He delves into the bowl of salted peanuts that are loitering on the bar. With his fist now cocooning a cluster of peanuts he excitedly reiterates what he has just witnessed on the 50 inches of plasma.

"I tell you what, Bundy is solid. Best shape I've seen him in. But, I have to admit Johnson is looking good!" Says Wilson in between crunches of peanuts.

"If Johnson is looking good, then my money is safe." Winks Detective Graham.

"Still early days in this one, Sir!"

"It will only take that 'Left Hook' of his to connect and it's lights out for Bundy." Graham winks again this time at Stone who smirks back at him. Graham can be really good at winding people up and he's on the verge of reeling Wilson in. Just as it looked like Wilson was going to sing the praises of Bundy again...

DING, DING.

"And there is the bell for Round 2 for this epic clash between the grizzled veteran, 'Big Bully' Bill Bundy from Boston, Massachusetts and the undefeated young stallion, 'Left Hook' Lewis Johnson from right here in Forge City!"

"I certainly think Johnson is making use of this hometown advantage here, Gene."

"He's definitely playing up to them, Teddy."

"You've gotta give the people what they want!" Wilson's head spins back to face the screen and mumbles something which was undetectable through a mouthful of peanuts. He makes his way back over to the crowd of people who have also been joined by Detective Freeman on his return from the bathroom.

"Jab, jab, jab! Some rapid shots in quick succession from Johnson!"

"I think those blows woke Bundy up, Gene."

"Those right hands reminiscent of his trainer the Wiley old Joe Fox from back in the 70's, Teddy!"

"Don't let him hear you calling him old, Gene! I'm sure Fox still has some force behind those mitts of his." There is a moment of silence between Stone and Graham, as they just sip their beer. Graham takes the time to look around and while his tired eyes scan the room, he makes eye contact with Nash who is still gazing at him like a loved-up school girl and in a way, this is

what this was. Infatuation, a crush, call it what you will but, Graham could almost feel her seductive glare burning into him. She smiled at him, so cute, so inviting as Carruthers continued to talk her ear off. Part of Graham felt a little uncomfortable by it all and the other part of him, his ego, was feeling well and truly stroked. He could almost feel his chest expanding like a titillated peacock.

Oh, please don't look at me like that, Valerie.

Graham smiles back at her trying not to send any false signals but just being polite. Even though part of him would very much like for Nash to take him into a bathroom cubicle and show him what he's been missing. An altercation that could be on the cards if Graham snapped his fingers. The power of something like that was ridiculous, to have someone do your bidding or fulfil a sexual fantasy at the drop of a hat. But, Graham wouldn't do that... He couldn't do that... not to Mae, not to his wife.

But who would know, Sid? Oh, Don't start. No, I'm being serious, who would know? You're so tempted right now aren't you? Yes. Do it then. No! Who would know? I would know.

Graham turns back to face the bar and is so thankful to hear Stone speak.

"So, how's the family doing, Sid?"

"Mae is good, but hates me taking on all these extra hours I've been doing. Can't say I blame her."

"She'd hate it even more if she knew you were down at the bar." chuckles Stone.

"You're not wrong, Eric!" He chuckles back.

"Hey, I'm only here for you anyway, so it's your fault!"

"Okay, blame me! The hours are long and the earache is longer." The two snigger as they take another hefty swig from the tankard.

"And what about the boys? They good?"

"Yeah they're doing great! I have a photo here somewhere." Graham rummages around in his back pocket and pulls out his brown leather wallet. He opens it up, it's filled with the usual various dollars bills, credit cards, library card and a pouch secured by a press stud concealing his change. From behind a hidden section amongst the many cards, Graham retrieves a well-worn photograph, obviously cut down from its original size to fit in its nook in the wallet. The picture shows Mae and the boys smiling at the camera as they are feeding the geese at the local park. A goose's head can just be seen in the shot, but the rest had been cut out to fit into the wallet.

"Good looking kids." Eric smiled.

"Thanks. Obviously take after their Mother. And how about you? Is Crystal doing well? How far is she gone now? Three, four months?"

"Six actually!"

"Six! Wow! Time is definitely moving too fast!"

"Tell me about it. She's doing really well though, she still looks like a million bucks."

"I'll drink to that. I saw her last shoot for Über Bra!" Says Graham whistling in jest.

"Hey, man! That's my wife you're leering over!" Laughs Eric.

"But, yeah I'm a very lucky man."

"I'll say! Job promotion, baby on the way, incredibly hot model wife. What more do you need?"

"A Mustang! Yeah, I really want a Mustang." They both laugh again. Graham looks over and sees that Nash is still looking at him.

Okay, this is getting a little too Fatal Attraction for me now. Who you trying to kid? Go and Fuck her!

There is a ruckus of cheering and jarring from the TV area that gets Graham's attention.

"*Bundy is down!*"

"*But is he out?*"

"*The count is up to six...seven...and no, he's up!*"

"*But he's looking like he's on spaghetti legs, Gene.*"

"*Referee says he is good to go and...*"

DING, DING!

"*Oh, talk about being saved by the bell, Gene!*"

"*That's Round 3 in the bag! We will return right after this.*"

"*Do you suffer from pesky Haemorrhoids?*"

"Barkeeper!" Shouts Detective Freeman as he saunters over to the bar.

"Another beer for me and my friends!"

"No, Richard, I'm going to have to go after this one. It's getting late." pleads Graham.

"I insist!" Smiles a merry Freeman, patting them both on the back and with that, three more tankards are slid out in front of them on the moist gleaming surface.

"We thought you'd gotten lost." Stone asks Freeman.

"Well, I thought it was a number one, but turned out to be a two!" They all burst out laughing again. Then Freeman notices Graham's family photograph starting to submerge into a spill of beer and he starts to shake his head.

"No! No, no, Sid! Not the family album! Put it away." They laugh as Graham flicks of the beer seeping into his photograph with a succession of rapid swipes of his wrist before sliding it back into its dwelling place. Freeman puts his hand over his eyes and holds his hand into the air making a spectacle of himself.

"Tell me you two haven't been sitting here discussing forming a carpool?" Everyone laughs.

"You guys make me sick! With your beautiful American dream lives! You with your white picket fence and you with your hot ass wife... Sorry, Sid! I'm sure Mae has all the junk up in the trunk too, but shit!" The bar erupts into laughter. "

We are full bloodied men!" Shouts Freeman with his tankard hoisted into the air, froth and beer showering the three of them as everyone looks on.

"Yes! My brothers and sisters! Full bloodied men and we want to get fucked up!" There is a cheer from the bar and Graham again makes eye contact with Nash who is wooing along with everyone listening to Freeman's motivational drunken speech, but still just looking at him.

"You just need to get laid, Rich." Says Stone and everyone erupts into laughter along with Freeman who pretends to hump Stone from behind. In all the ruckus round 3 gets underway.

"And here we go with round 3. Bundy comes staggering

148

out of the corner."

"He's trying to shake off those cobwebs, Gene."

"But, look at Johnson! He's practically skipping around the ring!"

"He's floating like a Butter..."

"Oh! That's it! Bundy is down! Bundy is down!"

"What a left hook from Johnson!"

"It's over and Bundy is out. Bundy is out!"

Graham looks over at Wilson who slowly turns away from the screen Graham winks at him and holds up his tankard.

That's ten bucks you owe me, kid.

Chapter 13

Proverbs 3:5-6

Trust in the LORD with all thine heart,
and lean not unto thine own understanding.
In all thy ways acknowledge him,
and he shall direct thy paths.

Thomas gently closes his thick old bible. Even gently closing it makes a thudding sound due to the weight of over a thousand pages falling together at once and being topped by the thick leathered cover.

"And what a path I have chosen!" Lying on an uncomfortable looking bed in a broken down dingy hotel room, Thomas removes his glasses and rubs his eyes. Jet lag is creeping in now. He knows he should try and sleep now else he will miss his important meeting in the morning. He places the bible on the bedside table that homes a lamp that is crowned with an ugly looking frayed shade. Swinging his feet around into a seated position on the edge of the bed, he looks around the compact room that cost him $30. Damp seeping up the walls causing the depressing Pantone wallpaper to crease and ripple and in some places, just give up and start to come away from the wall. He places his bare feet onto the worn carpet below, the texture hard and coarse, more like sandpaper than carpet. He stands up and stretches out his back, his spine creates a symphony of creaks, one after another. It's not his age that is the factor, but the gruelling flight from Switzerland to the United States, with no stop offs is what causes his backbone to sing so dismally.

"I guess I've stopped in worse places." He looks around not really convinced by his own statement.

"But what do you expect for 30 bucks?" He places his glasses on top of his bible and stretches again and yawns, long and loud.

"But it's only for one night." He yawns again, and he rubs his eyes.

"I really should get my head down." Restlessly he saunters over to the window. Clad in his white cotton underwear that clings to his body keeping everything where it should be, along with a white vest which shows off his muscular toned frame. He is not broad or over muscular, but lean and every muscle protrudes and looks firm. Not the physique of your usual priest. His skin is touched with a beautiful and glowing Mediterranean tan, which after a few months in Studd City will soon fade.

"Fifteen years! What a journey to come full circle and to end up back here!" He shakes his head as he approaches the small window that is cramped into the wall. Several slender cracks in the panes and the window sill, practically a swimming pool for the dead flies and other insects that bob up and down in the thick layer of moisture caused by the building's rising damp.

151

He looks out of the window and past the unsightly fire escape that clings to the building for dear life, like a gigantic metallic arachnid latched to its web to protect its eggs.

"Yes, it's taken me fifteen years to find my purpose in this world. Ironically ending up back where I first began." He glances out at the street several stories below. The streets are still filled with commotion, even at such a late hour. Gone are the 'normal' people of Studd City, the citizen, the taxpayer, the voter. Retreating into their homes terrified to venture out after dark, dead bolts and door chains in force to keep them safe and closing the curtains so they don't have to witness the sordid proceedings that go on, right on their doorsteps. If you don't see it, it doesn't happen. If you don't see it you don't have to deal with it. Televisions are put on maybe a little louder than it needs to be, but just loud enough to block out the sirens, the screams, the gunshots. Dinner on lap trays, reruns of *Golden Girls*, *Gilligan's Island* and *Cheers* and then bed. Ear plugs in and gripping each other tightly, praying that they are not slaughtered in their sleep. Joe public just hoping they don't become just another crime statistic on an ever-increasing histogram. Down on the corner of St. David's and North Street, prostitution is rife. Ladies of the night congregate on the sidewalk like they are meant to be there. Trash can, fire hydrant, streetlight, hooker. Nonchalantly standing around in next to nothing with laddered silk stockings rising from their stilettos that are visibly grasped and held in place by suspender clips. Almost hidden by buttock hugging animal print or garish patterned skirts, topped off by short imitation fur coats or throws snaked around their

152

shoulders. With all the animal print and fur it is reminiscent of an African waterhole where prancing zebra and frolicking gazelle graze, innocent and vulnerable but always vigilant of predators lurking in the long grass. Thomas is amazed how many men and women approach these good time girls and after a few seconds of conversation, are on their way to a car, in a hotel or disappearing out of sight into one of the many dark crevices in the city. A confrontation between rival gangs erupts. It starts with a rally of vulgar insults, then a punch is thrown and a ruckus breaks out spilling onto the road. A gunshot echoes through the city and a speeding car turns up like the cavalry and pulls their men out of the war zone. They drive away down the street in a cloud of exhaust fumes and the ear splitting shriek of tyres. From Thomas' vantage point it is unclear whether anyone was hurt. Many of the prostitutes didn't even flinch, just another Thursday night.

Looks like I will have my work cut out for me here. To clean up the filth on these streets, it'll be like cutting the grass of a football pitch with a pair of toenail clippers.

He sighs, and catches his reflection in the broken pane, rubbing at the scar on his eyebrow again. A habit he has done it seems, forever, well since the day it happened...

It's a fine spring afternoon and Thomas' fifth birthday party is in full swing. All the children of the Barnville trailer park community are gathered around the foldout trestle table, crowned with cone shaped party hats. Mouths watered with a silent willingness for Thomas to hurry up and blow out the

153

candles on his *Kermit the Frog* birthday cake so they can gobble down the luscious combination of cream, sponge, marzipan and icing. Thomas remembers looking around the table and seeing all the children, forgotten are their names now but the faces remain hanging in the back of his mind like processing photographs in a darkroom. He looks up and sees his mother's silhouette framed by the dazzling sun. The sun was so bright that day. His mother leans forward and he sees her face, how he remembered her face, smiling. A rare toothy grin, she never had much to smile about but today she did, it was her little boy's fifth birthday and she was also with child.

"Blow the candles out, Tommy!" she says, softly her hay coloured hair falls from behind her ears where it had been safely nestled. He smiled back and nodded. His mother sinks her hands into her lower back and stands back up very slowly, unveiling a large bulbous belly. A lovely floral print cotton dress (her best, for special occasions) clung to her firm tummy. Thomas smiled at the sight, he knew that safely cocooned inside was his future brother or sister. That was the best present he could ask for.

"Goddamn, Tommy! Hurry the hell up will you!" Came the gnawing southern drawl, in an ugly impatient gravel. Thomas' gaze switches to the family trailer. Clean enough but nothing to write home about, it was never going to make it into an issue of *Perfect Homes*. His father stood in the doorway, five o'clock shadow hugging his paunchy mug, a can of beer rising to his lips as his scratched his genitalia. It was if the sun disappeared the second he heard that voice. Thomas looked at his father with fear contorting his smooth unblemished face, his father just grimaced at him while continuing to chug his beer. Thomas looks back at his mother for reassurance, she smiles and that look is all he needs.

"You take your time, Tommy. Pay no attention to him!" Thomas' father crunches the can up in his large mitt before discarding it onto the downtrodden grass outside their trailer home.

"Shut your damn mouth woman!" he growls before turning around and going back into the trailer.

"Go and put your head in a bucket, Dwayne!" comes the reply from his mother and the children begin to snigger. Thomas smiles too and inhales heavily until his face turns a deep red and almost purple before exhaling and blowing all the candles out, leaving a trail of grey smoke snaking off each one.

Thomas returns, still standing at the window in the hotel. He spins on the spot and walks over to his coat that hangs lifelessly on the back of the door, accompanied by his red woollen scarf. He delves into the pocket and pulls out his fine Italian leather wallet. The golden initials TG protruding from it catch the dim light and shimmers. Thomas opens the wallet and hidden behind credit cards, the edge of an old photograph peeks out. He slides it out to reveal a photograph of that day, just him and his pregnant mother smiling. She didn't smile much. Thomas with a hefty piece of birthday cake in his hand, but most of the cream smothered over and around his lips, a little even attached to the end of his button nose, hanging like a trembling icicle.

"I miss you every day, Mama, every single day!" Tears rise and teeter on his lower eyelid before he pulls himself back together and manages to get his emotions in check, the tears dispersing back from where they came. He rubs his fingertips softly over the picture of his mother's face.

"Everyday!" he whimpers softly struggling to hold back his emotions. His right hand again rises up slowly and he skims his fingers over the scar on his eyebrow and his face turns sour, an uncharacteristic sneer wriggles across his face "And everyday I'm reminded what he did. What he did to me, what he did to us!" He wants to scream and release a torrent of abuse into the air, aimed at his absent father, but would it really do him any good? No, not really! He closes his eyes and slows his breathing, slowing his heart rate down. A technique he had mastered in China, to help him control his emotions when things got too much for him, almost self-hypnotism and in less than twenty seconds, he was in a deep meditational trance. Free to go to the places in his mind, but sometimes the doors are locked to the happy memories and he is forced to walk through the open doors that lead back to distressing times. This was yet another technique that he had been taught, to face one's fears. We all have some demon or another tucked away in the dark cavities of our psyche. We can ignore them and they may become forgotten for long periods but it is only lying dormant, waiting, waiting for the right time when you are at your most vulnerable to raise its hideous corpse and with a cruel leer it whispers to you. It knows your anxieties, your worries, your fears and your secrets, the ones that clatter together in the closet, bone on bone. The demon will use its spiteful tongue like an addict's syringe to administer its poison, which will proceed to traverse around your body, poking burning holes of doubt and self-pity into your very soul. It is up to you to exorcise those demons and to do that, you must face said demon head on and look it in its pitch black eyes.

Thomas walks through the door and again it's his fifth birthday, but it is later in the day and the remains of the party lay scattered on the patchy grass. Party hats, scrunched up wrapping paper, paper plates and cups float around in the subtle spring breeze like tumbleweeds. But the area is empty, the sun is slowly bidding an adieu and painting the sky like an artist's canvas with vibrant violets and sultry oranges blending beautifully together.

"I can't take any more of your shit, Dwayne!" Thomas' mother's voice shrieks through the trailer.

"My shit?" Comes the gravelled reply from a worn and stained *lazyboy* currently pointed at the television, watching the 3rd down of Cowboys versus Dolphins. Thomas cowers behind his mother's leg grasping his robot gorilla toy (from the then very popular Beast Borgs TV series) which he had acquired for his birthday.

"Yeah, Dwayne! Your shit! Your fucking shit!"

"Fuck you!"

"I'm sick of this! When are you going to get off your fat ass and get a Goddamn job?"

Dwayne turns in his *lazyboy*, on its rickety swivel and scowls at her as he empties yet another can and squashes it and throws it on the floor where it reunites with its brothers and sisters that it

157

used to share a six-pack ring with.

"Don't start with that shit, Vicky! You know there ain't nothin' out there for me!"

"Pah! So you say." Hisses Vicky, Thomas still gripping her leg as he quivers knowing that something bad is going to happen, something always happened when they argued like this.

"I'm warning you, woman!"

"Oh, screw you, Dwayne! You're a useless fucking bastard and I should never have married you!" The words echo around the small two berth trailer home and seem to hang in the air for the longest time. Thomas had an ice-cold shiver creep up his spine, he knew things were about to get ugly.

The heavyset Dwayne rose quickly from his *lazyboy*. It rocked to and fro on its swivel base with his rapid departure, but quickly settled back into place.

"Well, you shouldn't have fuckin' married me then you fuckin' dirty whore!" He sneered approaching her with pace and a balled-up fist.

Thomas continued to quiver, amazingly the pregnant Vicky stood her ground, defiant with a huge dollop of stupid on the side.

Why didn't you just leave him, Mama? Why did you stay? If you had left, you would still be here.

"Fuck you, Dwayne!" Was the last thing that Thomas' mother said on the matter as Dwayne's clenched fist, which resembled the head of a sledgehammer, was driven into her face. The nauseating sound of bones splintering still haunts Thomas to this very day. All Thomas could do was watch his pregnant

158

mother crumble into a heap onto the threadbare biscuit coloured carpet.

"That'll teach ya! That's what happens when you keep talking shit!" Dwayne glances at Thomas who stands knee high to a grasshopper, perfectly still on the spot, as motionless as an ivory statue, frightened to even breathe out.

"You want to grow up and stop being a pussy, boy!" He snarled before returning to his game. He slumps back into his *lazyboy* with a thump, the chair wheezing under the sudden impact and then positions it back in front of the television.

"Fucking generation of faggots we're raising in this country!" he churns picking up a can from the battered coffee table situated to his right-hand side, it's empty.

"Fuck it! Tommy?" He yells which sends another one of those bitter icicles stabbing into his spinal cord, causing him to convulse with fear.

"Get me a beer!" He yells which is accompanied by a large boar like belch. He looks at the television which indicates to him that the Cowboys are down by 12.

"Ah! Fuck you, Marino!" He growls launching the empty can at the screen. It bounces off the top corner of the jumbo set and spirals into the air, completing several rotations before hitting the floor. Thomas glances down at his unconscious mother, flat out on her back. Her arm draped over the large bun that has been cooking for 7 months. Her face unrecognisable as it now wears a thick crimson mask, which seeps into all the crevices it can find, her sunken eye sockets, her nostrils, her lips. He shuffles away, moving almost robotic, half of his brain struggling to come to terms with what he has just witnessed and the other half trying its utmost to block the traumatic episode from memory. But the latter is never going to happen. Another scar carved into the soul of poor little Tommy Gabriel. Thomas opens the refrigerator, the coldness immediately hitting him and his pale lifeless face is bathed in a   subtle yellowish light. He stares inside looking at the cold bottle of *Bobby's* and then peers around the open refrigerator door to look back at his mother, still lying on the floor of their trailer home, like an uneven bear rug.

"Where's that beer?" Bellows his father growing impatient. Thomas quickly grasps the bottle. The coldness of the glass immediately numbs his small digits that struggle to wrap themselves around it, he closes the door and again takes a moment to check on his mother. Still she remains motionless in an uncomfortable painful dream no doubt. He stretches up to the breakfast bar and places the bottle on the edge, before dragging the bar stool into position. He shuffles over to the kitchen utility drawer and slides it open, gazing at all the cutlery and implements. He doesn't think about seizing the clunky meat tenderiser and caving his father's skull in with it or plucking out the long slender kitchen knife and sliding it between his father's ribcage and sinking it deep into his cold black heart. No, he doesn't think of any of these things because he is five. Five year olds are as innocent as the day is long. He finds what he has been looking for, a bottle opener. He stretches up again on tippy toes like a tiny ballerina performing a relevé. After sliding the bottle-opener on the breakfast bar next to the bottle of *Bobby's* that now appears to sweat with moist desperation, he ascends the stool and kneels on the torn leather seat, chunks of sponge vomiting out of the numerous tears. He grasps the bottle in one hand while the other one digs at the sealed bottled top with the opener. Finally using all his might, he manages to decapitate the bottle sending the cap flying to the surface of the bar, spinning several rotations before coming to a stop, brand side up. He quickly slides down the bar stool, clasping the moist bottle in his hand that slips and slides in his loose grip, but amazingly doesn't spill a drop. There is an impression given that young Thomas has done this numerous times before. He quickly totters over to where his father sits, slowing only once as he passes his grounded mother, but then hurries on.

"Here you go, Daddy." He whispers as meek as a mouse.

His father does not answer, nor give him the courtesy of a thank you, he just grabs at the bottle but in doing so, knocks the bottle out of Thomas' slippery grip and it falls to the floor, spilling out onto the carpet. A lake of cold beer seeps out and merges with the carpet to be one.

"You stupid little shit!" Growls the beast once more and with a swipe of his meaty hand, be strikes the defenceless boy in the face. Thomas is propelled backwards into a heap. His father spins on the swivel chair adjusting the large sovereign that fits snuggly on his middle finger.

"Idiot!" He rises from his *lazyboy* adjusting his bulging genitalia and then scratching it vigorously and looking down at him with an annoyed expression set on his face. Thomas shivers but not because of the climate but through fear. A trickle of blood hangs from his right eyebrow, a loose fold of skin flaps from the wound like a flag on a mast, as the trickling stream rolls down his face. Dwayne storms past him towards the kitchen, Thomas daren't turn around so he stays motionless. The refrigerator doors slams which makes Thomas jump out of his skin and wet himself. The urine fanning out from underneath him as it consumed the carpet.

"I might as well do everything myself in this fucking place!" bellowed his father returning from the kitchen with a new bottle in his hand. He stopped and looked down at his poor son, sitting in his own urine, blood smeared on his face and grunted at him before taking a swig and returning to his seat.

"Your mama can clean up that piss when she gets up. I'm damned if I'm scrubbing it off the floor." Thomas sat in his own filth for an hour before his mother began to stir.
The musing had finished and Thomas lay fast asleep on his lumpy mattress, the photograph still clutched to his chest.

Chapter 14

On the outskirts of city life is Saint Germain, tranquil suburbia, the complete opposite to what Studd City has to offer. An obliging community of genuinely nice people, everybody knows everybody. Good people live in Saint Germain. Great schools too but the next generation that will be spawned from Reeves High have a rude awakening ahead. Wrapped in a protective layer of cotton wool and fairy dust in this *Disney* tale upbringing, not even aware of the hideousness that awaits for them in the big city. Will our children be prepared for what lies ahead? The answer is no. There is no possible way that they will be equipped for such a culture shock. It's extremely late and the geriatric Ford Country Squire trundles quietly through the quaint streets of Saint Germain. Passing Richards Elementary and on Raven Close and then turning left into Willows Lane. The thick bulk of the maple tree trunks burst from the sidewalk, their roots causing waves underneath the swelling slabs that form the pathway. Strong and sturdy they are reflected almost correspondently on both sides of the street and with fall in full affect, are all crowned with a luscious riot of autumn colours. All shades from the brightest Canary yellow to luscious butterscotch that ripples into a warming orange, the colour of candied yams. Some are kissed in a succulent red, like the colour of the stickiest candy apple and some lie dormant in a weary brown, resting peacefully on the ground below. The Squire shuffles along crunching the fallen leaves under its weary tyres. In the silent night the sound seems to be amplified sounding like the first footfalls on deep freshly fallen snow. Detective Sidney Graham yawns as he makes his way along the street where he lives. There is nothing but the sound of the tyres meeting the leaves and the occasional howl from a dog, who is up way past his bed time and maybe trying to sing himself to sleep. Graham rubs his tired eyes with his thumb and index finger, working together like the pinchers of a crab to somehow keep his sleepy lids from closing too early. He passes row upon row of white picket fence, almost every house on the street is enclosed by them, various shapes in panel and thickness but the premise the same, the American dream. He passes by quickly and the white fences become hypnotic to him and he almost dozes off at the wheel. A clip of the curb is enough to startle Graham back into action and after a short tussle with the steering wheel, he wins and manages to level out once again and is back on his way down Willows Lane. He knows he has had a little too much to drink and is just trying to make it home unscathed. He blasts himself for having those two extra pints. His first thought isn't even the dangerousness of what he is doing, the fact that he could possibly crash while heavily influenced by the alcohol or cause an accident hurting someone or even himself. No, his first thought is how embarrassing it would be to be pulled over and breathalysed by one of his peers. No, that wouldn't do at all would it. He squints through the windscreen and spots the Graham family mailbox. A red tin box with the word 'GRAHAM' stencilled in white, held up by a thick 2x4 thickly covered in white paint to match the trilateral topped picket fence at the bottom of his drive.

"Home sweet home!" he mumbles as he turns a tight left and rolls up the drive within touching distance of the garage door. A sequence he had done thousands of times before and no doubt will do a thousand more times, hence the ease in which he did it, even in such an intoxicated state. He staggered out of the car and instinctively slammed the door behind him, immediately wincing with unease knowing that he could have just woken up the whole neighbourhood. He approaches the front door and after several attempts through blurred vision to find the keyhole, the key slides in the lock and with a twist of his wrist it was open. The hallway was dark and as quiet as a cemetery. Gently he closed the door behind him, if he screwed up now and woke the household there would be hell to pay and he would have to deal with a tongue lashing from Mae and deservedly so. He placed his keys in the bowl that all the keys were kept, not surprisingly it was known as 'The Key Bowl'. It was green but transparent, green tinted glass and dotted with various fruits, a gift from Mae's Aunt. Sid always thought it looked ugly as sin but it served its purpose. The metallic keys caressed the ceramic bowl causing a high-pitched song, but it didn't last long. The ear of any sleeping being would never have been able to pick that up, especially when one was settled into a deep sleep. Sid took off his jacket and hung it on the Mahogany newel post and kicked off his shoes. He walked down the hall towards the kitchen, looking into the lounge as he passed, deserted of course, just Mae's knitting lay dispersed on the armchair. Obviously, she had waited up as long as she possibly could and spent the time wisely in trying to finish that scarf for little Billy. He walked on and was met by Charlie, who came shuffling out of the kitchen, looking sleepy and droopy in his movements. The key and bowl duet had aroused the spaniel from his slumber.

"Did I wake you, Charlie?" Whispered Sid as he knelt to greet him, his arthritis ridden knees crunching like a dog gnawing a bone. Charlie whined a drowsy groan and licked Sid's hand, who in turn gave him a caring stroke and a fuss.

"We've got to be really quiet, boy. We don't want to wake everyone up now do we?" Said Sid continuing to keep his voice low. Charlie replied chuntering something in dog before ending it in a long yawn. His jaws gaping like a bear trap, protruding incisors smothered in saliva and his slender pinkish tongue stretching out like a moist ballet slipper, almost touching Sid's nose. Sid's face contorted at the stench that drifted from Charlie's widening gape.

"Jesus, Charlie! What the hell have you been eating?" He sighs palming his snout away from his face and standing back up.

"If that doesn't sober me up, nothing will." Charlie totters back into the kitchen, the sound of his paws slapping on the tiled floor with each sloth like movement. He steps into his wicker basket, circles several times like an aeroplane awaiting the all clear to land, then suddenly he comes to a halt and collapses into a heap.

"Goodnight little fella." says Sid who had followed him

into the kitchen. Sid opened the refrigerator, the glowing vanilla light sprays across the entire kitchen like a lighthouse tiptoeing on the end of the coast. Sid softly hummed to himself, no tune of any merit but the kind that you make up when you are looking for something, but you can't quite remember what. Sid's weary sunken eyes scan the contents of the fridge and with a raise of his eyebrows which was accompanied by a "Ha!", He retrieves what he was looking for. A carton of cold, freshly squeezed orange juice, well that's what it says under the large pair of vibrant oranges printed on the clammy carton. He unscrews the lid and downs almost all the remaining juice in several long slow swallows. He lowers the carton and exhales in a satisfied manner while wiping the pulping leftovers from his goatee beard. It was then that he starred directly at the kitchen table and there lit up by the refrigerator's searchlight, was Sid's evening meal concealed under a plate, that he should have been sitting down to enjoy about 4 or 5 hours ago. He winced "Oh shit!" He knew he had screwed up, again.

Why didn't you call her you idiot! He thought as he closed the refrigerator door, extinguishing the light and plunging the kitchen into murk once more.

I'll tell you why, because you were too busy thinking about Little Miss Tight Tush that's why!

He sighed and looked at the plate-dinner-plate sandwich sitting on top of a floral placemat and guarded closely both sides by silver plated cutlery. Stuck on the top plate (which would have been once used to keep the heat in) was a small post-it note with Mae's handwriting scribbled on, which read *'Nuke it for about 5 mins - Mae x'.*

He lifted the plate and underneath was a bulging pork chop dinner, with all the trimmings and Sid's favourite, mash potatoes. Heaps and heaps of cloudy mash, caressed with a thick onion gravy. Sid sighed knowing that it would all go to waste now.

Damn you, Sid! You could have left after one drink. Heck, you could have come straight home from the station.

He picked up the pork chops and dropped them into Charlie's ceramic half empty food bowl, which had dried dog food stuck to its sides and rim. Charlie didn't even stir as his rear left leg was rampantly kicking out, dreaming, chasing.

You're an ass, Sid. A complete ass!

He then reluctantly picked up the bottom plate that held in place his stone cold dinner and with a push of his foot, up popped the lid of the kitchen bin and he tipped the plate with a quick flick of his wrist. The food slid right off the plate and into the trash leaving behind a thick moist gravy trail, like guck that would be emitted by a departing slug.

A complete and utter asshole!

He placed the plates into the sink and made his way back to the hallway. He had never felt so guilty. Sure, he'd been late home from work so many times he couldn't count, it obviously came with the territory, especially working in a City like Studd. But this guilt was different. He was not only ridiculously late home, but he'd spent the evening drinking an obscene amount which was stupid because he knew he had work in the morning too.

It's not the lateness and the drinking that you're guilty about

168

though is it Sid? "Fuck you" he whispered back as he began to quietly climb the stairs. Each stair seemingly creaking louder than normal, he lent on the hand rail as if to distribute his weight and continue the rest of his climb on tiptoes. On the wall as he ascended, the family portraits stared at him, the faces looking on disapprovingly at him. Sid turned away from them and continued. *How do you plead, Detective? Guilty your honour. Guilty! I'm Goddamn guilty!*

He reaches the top of the stairs and sighed again. He crept over to the boys room and pushed open the door. It grazed the carpet as the door moved slowly along. The room is dark but with the moonlight cascading through the window things can be made out, like the gigantic poster of professional wrestler Randy Rogan flexing and pointing, draped in old glory while his oiled-up physique glistens. His massive biceps bulging, almost giving the illusion that they could pop at any minute, all the while his veins rise up and snake down his arm like ringworm burrowing under his bronzed flesh. He stares back at the poster, at the pointing finger and in his head he hears the gruff growling of his son's favourite wrestler bellowing at him.

You're nothing but a lowlife, good for nothing cockroach, chump! A degenerate that couldn't even lace my boots on his best day! Now get your guilty drunken ass outta here before I take this ham hawk and wallop you over the head with it. Chump! Sid just stares back at the poster. He walks over to Todd's bed, shuffling through wrestling figures and transformers that lay dormant on the floor, like fallen warriors on a battlefield. He leans over and kisses him on the head.

169

"Goodnight champ" he softly whispers, as he pulls the covers up around his neck. Standing back up he looks at the poster and again hears the wrathful rant from the poster.

I said get the hell outta here, chump! Todd doesn't want you breathing your boozy stink all over him!

"Man, how much did I actually have to drink tonight?" Whispered Sid, rubbing his head.

Too much, Mother fucker!

Sid points at the poster.

"Now come one, Rogan! Don't use that kind of language around the kids!" He looks at the boys who both stirred in their sleep and realising how stupid he looks lowers his pointing finger.

"What am I saying?" He says, lowering it to a whisper, almost laughing at himself. He kisses Billy, who grips his stuffed black cat called Pepe like a boa constrictor would with his latest catch. As he leaves, he turns to the poster and sticks out a tongue in its direction but not looking where he is going he treads on one of the action figures.

"Oh Fu..." He almost blurts out while grasping his foot and rubbing at it vigorously while bouncing up and down on one foot. He places his injured foot back on the floor and happens to glance at the figure that caused all the bother. Staring back at him with a huge pearly grin is the spring coiled action figure of Randy Rogan. Sid scowled at him and kicked him under Billy's bed.

"Screw you Randy Rogan!" He murmurs under his breath, only to hear yet another reply in his drunken tired haze.

Don't you ever kick me again, chump!

Sid slowly closes the door behind him and hears the words, *don't forget to say your prayers and take your vitamins…* before the door closed. He entered his and Mae's bedroom. The curtains closed so darkness was all that there was, he could make out the curvaceous shape of Mae on her side of the large queen, wrapped up in the thick duck feather filled duvet. He thought about waking her up, to talk, to apologise but he could hear the rhythmic pattern of her breathing, heavy, deep in slumber.

That would only make matters worse, Sid.

He wrenched at his tie enough that it tightened the knot, which became small and clenched, but he could now take it off over his head. He knew he would be pissed tomorrow morning when he had to unpick that knot but at 2am he didn't care. The tie hit the floor at the foot of the bed, then came his pants, the jangle of the metal clasp on his belt sang a short song before joining the tie. He slides the police issue Glock 22 from the safety of its shoulder holster and as quietly as he can, he checks the load by detaching it from the bottom of the handle. He then jolts it back into place and switches on the safety, sliding it under the mattress for either safety or paranoia. The shoulder holster fell and was followed by a creased white shirt, falling on top of the laundry like a swath of snow. Now clad in just his Y-fronts and grey collar socks he snuck into the ensuite. He closed the door behind him and pulled the light cord which hung from the ceiling. Several spotlights flashed on and caused Sid's tired eyelids to blink rapidly as he tried in vain to fight back the brightness. Sid's eyes finally adjusted, and he walked over to the toilet. He lifted the white porcelain lid and seat combination and started to urinate. There was a constant flow for what seemed like at least 5 minutes but in reality, it was probably closer to a minute. He thought about flushing the toilet then went against the idea as the noise could wake up Mae.

If it's yellow, let it mellow.

He walked across to the sink and looked into the mirror attached to a cabinet that hung over it. He gazed at his reflection and didn't like what he saw.

"You have nothing to be guilty about. You had a few drinks and you were home late, yes. But... You didn't... and wouldn't do anything with Val... Nash. Officer Nash!" He washed his hands quickly, the water was cold as he didn't give the water enough time to warm up, then turned the tap off. He scratched his backside, a damp handprint appearing on his underwear and then moving up, scratched the back of his head. With the deepest of sighs, he faced his reflection once more as he leaned on the sink as he wrestles with his conscious.

"I'll tell her tomorrow."

Do you think that's wise?

"Probably not! But I can't live with this guilt."

Why are you guilty? You haven't done anything with the girl?

"I know that..."

But?

"But... I think I..."

You like her don't you?

He paused and stared at his reflection, almost tearing up.

"Yes."

Now, don't be silly now Sid. You have a lot to jeopardise here.

"I know!"

There is a 13-year marriage to consider...

"I know!"

... and of course the boys.

"I know! I get it! It's not going to happen. I won't let anything come between me and my family."

Family comes first.

"Always!"

Sid walks towards the door and pulls the cord sharply. The lights go out all at once and he opens the door into the bedroom to darkness. He gets into bed and kisses Mae on the head, her face hidden by a mass of dark red curls.

"I love you, Mae. I'm sorry." He whispers, almost wanting to shout the words so that she could feel the truth in the words. He lies down and pulls the cover over him. He closes his eyes and an image of Valerie Nash flashes before his eyes and he opens them again.

"Shit!" He murmured, knowing that this infatuation was two sided. He turns over and stuffs his hand under his mattress until he can feel his handgun with his fingertips, content now that he knows it's there. He looks over at the digital alarm clock that sits on his bedside table. The red neon numbers pulse back at his drowsy gaze. Listening to Mae's breathing made him forget everything and everyone else. He drifted off with the clock reading 2:13am.

Chapter 15

The screen of Dallas' smart phone displays a photograph of the Texan country music legend *Willie Nelson*, guitar grasped in his hands as he seduces the microphone. The time is overlaid the image showing it to be 2:13am.

"It's getting late, Spider. Are we going to wait for Sniff or what?" Says Dallas as he slides the phone into the pocket of his jeans.

"Fuck him!" Spider growls spitting onto the floor of the parking lot at the rear of a Franken-Burger fast food joint. He leans against the hood of the Corvette that he acquired from the unsuspecting Mr Lennox early that evening, looking cantankerous, his arms crossed tightly like a petulant child. Boris sits on the hood next to him gobbling up the Transylvanian Nightmare combo meal from the cardboard box in the shape of Frankenstein's Monster's head. Chopping on the burger like the rear of a garbage truck, he is babbling some incoherent sentence as Dallas and Spider look at each other with mirrored confused faces.

"What the hell did you just say?" Asks Dallas.

Boris looks at them and stops his relentless gnawing. Cheese, burger, red onion and lettuce hangs out of the corner of his mouth, condiments dripping from the clump and onto his jacket.

He sucks it all in and swallows it down.

"I said, don't you think you were a bit too hard on Sniff?" Says Boris, fingering the sauce stain on his jacket and with the dressing balanced on the tip of his finger it disappears into his mouth.

"What the fuck, man!" Spider squeals yanking out his Glock .18 handgun from the back of his pants and pointing it in Boris' unsuspecting face.

"Whoa!" Dallas yells, holding his hands up as if to stop Spider from going too far.

"Is there a fucking problem here, Boris?" He growls, clenching the handle tightly in his tattooed hand, his thick gold bracelet swinging back and forth. Boris is frozen wide-eyed with his finger still stuck in his mouth, he slowly shakes his head, his shocked expression never altering.

"If you don't like the way I do business then maybe I should just pull the trigger huh?" He shouts waving the gun in his face. Boris' eyes watching every single movement of the barrel.

"What is wrong with you?" Pleads Dallas. Spider shoots him an aggravated stare.

"What d'you mean? 'What's wrong with me?' There is fuck all wrong with me! As far as I'm concerned, I'm the only one functioning normally out of you bunch of cocksuckers!"

"Look man, just put the gun down okay?" Pleads Dallas again.

"Fuck that!" He says and presses the cold steal of the barrel to Boris' forehead.

"Sniff fucked up. Seriously fucked up. I'm not going to let that little douchebag be responsible for bringing The Webheads down, you hear me?"

"Yeah, I hear ya. But please put the gun down. Boris ain't done anything wrong here!" adds Dallas petitioning for Boris' innocence like some defence lawyer.

"Oh, is that right?" Spider says, his head nodding.

"Yeah!" Dallas adds. Boris stares at Dallas with beads of sweat now trickling down his forehead, each one cascading with speed as if they're racing each other. His eyes pleading with Dallas to get him out of this predicament he has found himself in.

"Who is in charge here?" Spider asks, seemingly going off topic a little, but keeping the gun pressed firmly against Boris' moistening skull.

"Well, you are." Dallas answers

"Exactly! I am in charge!" He shouts, saliva bursting from his mouth as veins stand up on his neck with vexation.

"When one of you questions my actions that fucking pisses me off! I make the decisions around here and if you're with me then you will do as you're fucking told!"

"Okay, man. Okay, sure whatever you want. Boris didn't mean anything by it did you Boris?" Dallas asks, and Boris vigorously shakes his head still with his finger clamped between his lips, looking like the missing *Marx Brother*.

Spider begins to calm. Dallas and Spider have been friends since they were children. Dallas knows that he has the power to calm Spider and reel him in when needed. This is one of those times.

"He was only concerned for Sniff, Bro. You did do a fucking number on him back there." Continued Dallas.

"Yeah I know!" Spider agrees, pulling the gun away from Boris' head. Boris whispers a lengthy sigh of relief that was probably felt back in his native homeland of Ukraine. The indent of the barrel sunken into his forehead is deep and red and Boris finally takes his finger out of his mouth.

"I'm sorry boss." He meekly says rubbing his forehead. Spider replays with a nod of his head and now calmly slides the gun back into the rear of his Calvin's for safe keeping.

"I'm done with Sniff. You guys love him so much then he's YOUR problem!" Spider says pointing at Dallas and Boris one by one.

"Okay, sure. We will keep him under control." Agrees Dallas.

"Well, you'd better because if he fucks up again. I'll kill his junkie ass!" Spider scowls, his golden grill glistening under the parking lot street lamps. There is a flurry of musical beeps that rise out of Dallas' pocket. He retrieves his cell phone just as the beeping stops.

"It's a message from Sniff." Dallas says as he softly brushes his thumb on the touchscreen to read the incoming message.

Yo Dal. OMG man, crib crawling wit pigs! I got out. WYA?

"Sniff says, Cops have hit the pad." Dallas informs Spider.

"Shit!" Replies Spider kicking the car tyre.
A twinkling of beeps.

WYA??

"He wants to know where we are?"

"Fuck that shit. Tell him to lay low tonight. We'll meet up tomorrow." Says Spider. Dallas nods and starts to message Sniff back, his fingers rapidly typing on the keys almost robotic knowing exactly where every letter on the small QWERTY layout is, without even really looking.

Ok man, lay low 2nite. Meet up 2morrow.
Dal.

A twinkling of beeps again.

NP. K.

"He said okay." He nestles his cell phone back into his pocket.

"Okay. Let's get rid of this bit of evidence." Spider says approaching Dallas.

"Oh, but it's such a beauty!" groans Boris.

"Gotta be done, man. They'll trace it back to the digs in Bowie Street and back to the meeting in Ventura." Says Spider.

"Now get the gas!" he continues. Boris nods and throws his finished food box into the open window of the car, then walks around to the rear of the car. Dallas whips out a new box of Freebird cigarettes and removes the plastic wrapping. He flicks open the ligand offering Spider a cigarette, he takes one and rests it between his plump lips.

"Do I have to? It's such a nice car!" begs Boris.

"Just do it!" Spider says, cigarette wagging up and down as he speaks. Dallas places a cigarette in his mouth too and with a rapid flick on the lighter, a flame erupts dancing in the night. The pair gather around the flame and the tips of their cigarettes ignite, burning the end into ash. They both inhale and exhale in unison, releasing twin clouds of smoke that dance around them and merge together like two infatuated lovers, before quickly dispersing into the air. Boris pops the trunk and retrieves a 5-gallon gas can, that was hidden under a picnic blanket next to a spare wheel and a foot pump. Reluctantly Boris unscrews the cap and then starts to douse the classic 1992 Corvette ZR-1 with the putrid smelling gasoline. Dallas and Spider enjoy their cigarettes as they watch the gas splash up against the rear window and then on the roof. It immediately rolls down the windscreen, like a thick murky waterfall settling on the hood, seeping into the engine and dripping onto the concrete. Then Boris launches gas into the open passenger window, showering the luxury tan leather seating, that has the initials BL expensively stitched into the headrests.

"That's enough!" Spider declares and Boris immediately stops, then drops the can in through the open window and watches it bounce on the seat. It topples over, and the rest of the contents flows out over the gear lever and hand brake and down onto the plush tan carpet, which soaks it up and quickly turns darker in colour. Spider takes a drag from his cigarette and then flicks the remainder of it towards the car. The stub end hits the side of the door and spins around like a propeller before landing on the driver's seat. The embers glow and then suddenly fizzle out from the dampness of the gasoline. The trio look at each other confused.

"Isn't it supposed to blow up or something?" Boris asks

"That's what happens in the movies." Shrugs Dallas.

"Well, shit!" Spider pulls out his firearm once again and unloads the entire clip at the soggy Corvette. Bullets hit every inch of the car, breaking windows, piercing the doors and sides. The leather interior is ripped apart and the sponge contents vomits from the shredded leather covers. One bullet blows out a tyre and it whistles as the air escapes, but no explosion. Dumbfounded the three just look at each other.

"Boris, go grab that Franken box." Spider says, Boris walks over to the car and retrieves the used packaging from his meal, gasoline had already started to seep into parts of the box. Spider takes it from Boris and holds it out towards Dallas.

"Torch it, Dal!" Spider tells Dallas, who flicks his trusty lighter back into action once again and ignites the corner of the box. Rapidly it burns into life. Spider now holding a ball of roaring flame in his hand quickly relieves himself of the hazardous burden and drops it into the window once again. Instantly the flames fuse with the gasoline creating a destructive union, one that will destroy all in its path. The classic Corvette from the 90's ignites and is smothered in a gyrating cocoon of flame. The trio stand back at a safe distance from the blaze.

"So, what's the plan?" Dallas asks casually puffing on his cigarette.

"This is it. It is time." Spider says calmly, his face bathed in the warm amber glow of the raging inferno in front of him.

"You mean..." Dallas looks at him a little shocked.

"Yeah," interrupts Spider.

"It's time to bring Valentine down!" Spider walks away from the $40,000 bonfire. It explodes as they walk away. Boris and Dallas are jerked and turn to witness flames reaching towards the stars with thick black smoke circling, then consuming the Corvettes carcass and eating it up. Spider did not break his stride or flinch, he struts on as the other two Webheads quicken their pace to catch up with him.

"Tomorrow I fire the first shot in this war. But I'll need some help." Spider continued.

"You know we've got your back boss!" Boris says, Dallas nods in agreement.

"I didn't mean you. If we are going to do this, we will need the help of an unusual ally."

"Who?" Enquires Dallas, who thought he knew what Spider had planned to take Vinnie Valentine's Doomsday crown but obviously he was wrong.

"The leader of La Familia! We need The Coyote!" Spider drops the bombshell as he carries on walking. Dallas and Boris are stopped in their tracks as if their lower half has been devoured by a quagmire. They look at each other in astonishment and both call at the same time, "Are you crazy?"

Chapter 16

2:13am and Thomas wakes up, bolting upright. His breathing is heavy like he had just run a marathon, his white vest sodden through with perspiration as is his hair that is dark with moisture and clinging to his tacky forehead.

"Where am I?" He pants to himself, his muscular chest moving up and down rapidly as he surveys his surroundings. The sweat seeping straight through the cotton and making it transparent and displaying every contour of his lean but muscular physique.

"Oh, now I remember." He wipes the sweat away from his brow, sweeping it sleekly back from his face. As he scans the dingy hotel room, he notices now that he is lying on the floor, lumpy pillow where his head once lay, still embedded with his moist head print. The duvet draped around him, with one damp leg hanging out of the sweaty saddle. He looks at the bed and chortles to himself.

"I guess I'll never get used to beds now."
Years of sleeping on the floor has conditioned his body to where he actually finds this is a more comfortable method of sleeping. He rises to his feet and with hands pressed firmly into his coccyx, he pushes cracking several vertebrae in his spine. Then with a rapid seesaw action of his head, his neck crunches like the

sound of heavy footfall on a pebbled beach. He rubs the scar that slices through his eyebrow again, his trait, we all have them, not even aware he is doing it. He snatches his glasses that had been resting on the bible and slides them into place.

Same dream. Always the same old dream. But, I guess I should be used to it by now, I've been having it for the last 25 years.

He hoists up his watch sitting next to his bible, picking it up carefully in his fingertips by its fine Italian leather strap.

"2:15!" He observes, his weary eyes widening, in his head he felt he'd been asleep for at least a week. Jet lag will do that to a person. Thomas walks again to the window and peers out onto the streets. Not much is happening but even at this time he is surprised that there are still people inhabiting the streets, mostly ladies of the night who are hard at work trying to pull in those few extra bucks before they turn in and call it a night.

That dream. Always so vivid, that night...That cursed night. The night everything changed. The night my Mama left me. The night my Father went too far, too far.

For a while he just stares out of the window, no comments pass his lips nor does anything form in his thoughts. For those moments, he is miles away in an unknown place of sanctuary, somewhere where those dreadful creeping shadows of his past can't hurt him, again a meditation trick, one he has used for years to keep him focused. A place he would tend to visit when he could feel himself getting upset. In his own sort of way, he used this as therapy. He became his very own psychiatrist with only one patient, himself. His eyelids batter together rapidly as if an insect had tried to fly into his eyes, this was just the signal that he was coming back, returning from his happy place as it were, his sanctuary. As he returns, he focuses and sees his reflection in the windowpane. He stares into his own eyes and then there is doubt. Doubt seeping into his psyche like a toxic gas and defenceless to do anything against, it his psyche breathes it in. The poisonous negativity attacks and leaves him asking 'Can I do this?' For what seems like the longest time he stares back at his reflection waiting for an answer, no answer is forthcoming.

"Can I do this?" His voice croaky this time and a lot less confident. His head drops and finds the worn ugly carpet of the $30 a night hotel room looking back up at him. But, before he can say the word he doesn't wish to say, before he truly becomes consumed by the insecurity that is spiralling around inside his head, he hears a voice.

"Why do you doubt yourself, Thomas?" The voice is familiar to him, soft throaty and quiet, as if it is having travelled from a long way away. Thomas continues to look at the carpet, his eyebrows raising as high as they will physically go up his moist forehead. But still he remains silent, he doesn't believe that it is that persona talking to him, it couldn't be.

"Thomas, you must look at your Master when he addresses you!" Says the voice again, this time more direct, more abrupt. Thomas does not need telling a third time and his head springs back up and looks directly into the window again where only moments ago he found his own reflection looking back at him, but not this time. In the pane framed by the dirt and the grime is the face of an ancient Chinese man.

"Sato!" Thomas gasps with a startled reply.

"But, but it can't be you? This is impossible!" He continues, but even in his bewildered and pessimistic state, he still displays the respect to his Master by bringing his right fist up and firmly placing it into the open palm of his left hand. Showing respect with wushu salute.

"I will ask again, Thomas. Why do you doubt yourself?" Grumbles the old horsey voice of Sato.

"I don't know. Maybe I..."

"No! There is no 'Maybe' in the world of the Shaolin!"

"Yes, of course. I doubt my ability. I doubt that I am capable of such a huge undertaking. I doubt I can fulfil my God's wishes and succeed on this crusade."

"Good! You have to release those negative thoughts that you harbour in your mind like the wooden boat."

"The wooden boat?" Thomas asks confused.

"The wooden boat is bound to the dock by thick sturdy rope. The wooden boat belongs to Kâ Róng the harbinger of all that is evil. He fills it with self-pity, self-loathing and cardinal thoughts. When it is full he will entice you onboard, you will be powerless to prevent this, it will be too late. Then he will cut the rope and escort you to Diyu, the realm of the dead. Once there you will rot for eternity with the cargo that you have amassed."

"I see." Nods Thomas.

"To be free of such burden, you must face your fears and not cower away from them. Do not bottle them up, unlike the wine they do not get better with age, no, they get worse! Like chains wrapping around your chest and squeezing until

185

you can no longer breathe. That is why you must embrace the negativity and deal with it. Face what causes you anxiety, face what causes you pain, face the shadows that lie within. Embrace it, grow stronger. Then and only then will you be able to release it."

"And what of the wooden boat?"

"It will then be empty."

"Yes, thank you Master!" Thomas says bowing his head. As Thomas raises his head back up, the image of his Master Sato has vanished leaving only his own reflection. Was Sato even there? Was it a figment of his imagination? Was he dreaming? Or was he speaking to him through a familiar face, a persona that Thomas loves and respects, one he would do anything for? If it was just himself talking to himself, he might not take the advice and again bottle up those negative thoughts and fears. All this goes through Thomas' mind all at once like a bullet piercing his brain.

"Thank you Master. I shall do my best to follow that path. I shall meditate on this." Thomas walks back over to his makeshift bed on the floor and sits down crossing leg over leg and with his back poker straight and his eyes closing, he slides gently back into that place he goes. His breathing slowing, his chest rising and then a long pause before exhaling. The sound of Thomas' breathing is all that can be heard. Even the sound of several gunshots that echo through the alleys of Studd City, like murky water flowing through sewer pipes, doesn't startle him as he drifts. Then a blast, and explosion, coming from the corner of Talbot and Santana does nothing to disturb his heavy musing. In

186

Thomas' mind he is in China and just a small boy again. For a moment he questions himself, *'Why am I back here?'* Then the realisation sinks in that he must go back to the past, back to what he learnt, it must be all fresh in his mind if he is to take on what awaits in the future. Sometimes we must all go back to basics, remember what we were taught and it will help us. Blue. Cornflower blue. A beautiful blue so elegant it was as if it had been applied from palette to canvas. Thomas is still yet to see a sky as blue as the ones that surrounded Mount Lao in Qingdao. Young Thomas had accidentally found himself as a stowaway on a cargo ship to the Shandong Province at the northeast of China. He honestly gave himself up to the Captain and offered to work doing anything that was desired of him. The Captain agreed and Thomas helped with chores. Mostly in the kitchen washing the crew's pots and pans and also helping out with the laundry, washing the crew members grubby clothes and sullied underwear (That part he didn't enjoy), but on the whole he enjoyed his 22 days on the ship. When arriving in the largest city of Shandong, Qingdao, Thomas found himself wandering around the bustling markets. It reminded him of Chinatown back home in Studd City, this made him feel a little easier as it was familiar to him. He told himself to not be scared, this was an adventure, one that a small boy his age could only dream of. So with that in mind, he set off to explore what it had to offer. After a couple of hours walking around the markets, Thomas had had enough of being hassled by vendors cackling at him in a rapid-fire tongue that he didn't understand, having raw fish flapped in his face, being draped in hand embroidered textiles. At one point even a live hen swung into view being held up by her feet as she frantically flapped her wings in an attempt to escape her seemingly ancient toothless custodian. Thomas had grown tired of barging past them and telling them in slowed down English that he had no money, the way we all do when abroad in some foreign country and don't speak the lingo. He managed to make it out of the market and found himself on a gravelled path that stretched out to the horizon which inhabited a large mountain, a combination of stone and foliage made it unlike any mountain he had ever seen or looked at in a book. They'd all been rocky and jagged almost aggressive and sinister but this one looked beautiful. With a rumble in his belly he made his way towards the mountain. It seemed to be days away, if it was even there at all. It was that graceful and charming it couldn't be real, it may all be a dream, but with his instinct telling him to drive forward, he did. 6 hours later and young Thomas was lagging, his movement had become but a shuffling of feet, he resembled a zombie from some low budget gore fest. With nothing in his belly and the sun slowly bidding farewell, he left the path and headed for the cover of woodland where he saw yet another beautiful sight. An enchanting cherry blossom tree frozen in some sort of contorted dance routine. Its curving branches seemed inviting to him, protective like a Mother's hug. He staggered over tired and hungry and collapsed against its broad trunk, slid down the soft grass and soil at its base and fell fast asleep. There is a flash of crimson before Thomas' closed eyes. His face contorts, it's painful, again another flash of crimson so red, so bright and it hurts, it hurts in his head. The pain like a long slender hatpin being plunged through his ear and into the very centre of his brain. He cannot take any more of the pain and he opens his eyes, a trickling of flustered sweat exudes from his damp scalp.

"What was that?" He asks nobody in particular but amazingly gets an answer back. It is muffled and faint but an answer nonetheless, *'Face it!'* is all the voice said. Sato? Maybe... It had to be. Thomas closes his eyes again. There is another painful glare like forked lightning straight between his eyes, he winches but fights the urge to open his eyes this time. The pain stops. The flashes stop and he is standing over the younger version of his sleeping self, safely nestled under the protection of Mother cherry blossom. Thomas smiled, it was a strange surreal feeling to be looking at himself, especially looking at himself over 20 years ago. Then there was a sound, the sound of rustling in the bushes around him. Thomas' head turned on a swivel and the noise of rustling was everywhere, seemingly surrounded. Thomas clenched his fists and instinctively prepared himself for battle, but a thought entered his head.

What good would fighting do me in a dream?

And he was right. The rustling stopped and then there was silence. He looked out into the darkness. He felt eyes burning into him and it made him feel uncomfortable, made him itch almost. Then there was a call, a call of an animal, a bird call. A strange blabbering like a jackhammer yodelling its way through granite. Louder and louder, almost deafening again Thomas winced, but would not allow himself to waken, not this time. The shrill was so much so that he thought his eardrums would

189

explode and blood would burst from his ears like some uncontrollable volcano. But then it stopped and there was silence again and darkness. Thomas took several deep breaths and shouted into the shadowy forest of his dream.

"SHOW YOURSELF!" There was nothing.

"FACE ME!" He shouted again and he heard the blabbering bird shrill again but distant, like the creature had moved away. Then sprinting out of the blackness came a large bird on two long legs, a crane, a red crowned crane. But unlike any crane Thomas had ever seen, its plumage was dark and as black as the shadows it had appeared from. The Crane stopped a few feet from him and settled. It stood there just staring at him, jet black eyes like marbles, he could see his reflection in them. He had never seen his face look so frightened before, scared, scared rigid.

"What do you want?" Thomas asked shuffling backwards to protect his sleeping younger self. Thomas figured that this was some kind of dream demon that had entered his dream to stop him reliving such fond memories and would do so by ingesting Young Thomas. But The Black Crane only had eyes for him. It stretched up on its slender spindled legs and extended his long thick neck. It moved from side to side more like the way a rattlesnake might move before it strikes, and then straightened up to its full height. Thomas' head glanced up at the crane that now towered over him, an intimidating creature of black, only a smudge of crimson streaked on its forehead to distinguish the crane from the dark forest backdrop. It yammered again, so high pitched and gruesome and raised its wings up, spreading them out to their limit, the end feathers quivering as the creature shook. Thomas was terrified of this bird. This gigantic bird now standing around 10 feet tall with its outstretched wingspan making it appear double its original size from when it first appeared out of the bushes. No, cranes in real life weren't this big and definitely not this frightening. The crane stood still like a dark crucifix before making eye contact again with Thomas. Its head weaved its way down to face him with its sharp ice-pick of a beak stabbing its way towards him until it was lingering inches from his face. There was silence again and nothingness, until that horrid ear splitting shrill forced its way down his auditory canal and tore apart Thomas' eardrums again. Then with all the quickness and stealth of a jungle cat, the crane struck, piercing Thomas' flesh with its beak. The attack could look to an outsider as a deranged random assault, but the crane was precise with each puncture. Thomas screamed in agony as The Black Crane repeatedly annihilated him with its deadly mandible dagger. Thomas felt the blood spurting from each wound that the crane administered, spraying out of him and into the darkness like a fluorescent fountain of blood. It shrieks again, it's beak open so wide that Thomas could see his own blood trickling down the animal's throat. Thomas screamed at the top of his lungs, his voice cracking like his brain could no longer take any more of this shrilling, that continued to drill into the very core of his exhausted encephalon. Then suddenly there was silence. Thomas opened his eyes again, now wide-awake sweating profusely and breathing so heavily, he may have been on the verge of a panic attack.

191

"What was that?" He panted, falling back onto his floor bed starring up at the ceiling. Paint peeling away in several places like sunburnt skin and cobwebs smothering every dark corner. His breathing pattern started to return to normal as he wiped the sweat and tears from his eyes then sat bolt upright checking his body for puncture wounds, but there was nothing but his veins protruding from his hot flesh like a bed of worms. Thomas lay back down, his eyes tired. The dream had taken everything out of him and he was completely exhausted. His eyelids vigorously flickered and closed as he fell asleep. He heard the voice of his master again, so very faint and so tender sending a warning.

"Beware The Black Crane."

Chapter 17

The irritating falsetto of Sidney Graham's digital alarm clock wailed. A reaching hand then arm emerged from underneath the duvet and stretched towards the clock, like the crooked branch of a tree. It hovered above the clock before delivering a falling palm that immobilised the displeasing screech. A groan came from underneath the duvet where he lay safely nestled and warm, like a hibernating bear who believes that surely, it's not spring yet? With the sound of the alarm finished, the hand (still placed on top of the alarm clock) fiddled around to find the switch. It found it and flicked it to radio. The sound of five jabbering English girls burst through the small speakers, carrying with it the static that only comes from playing the radio, as the girls reached the line '...*wanna Zigazig ah!*...' Graham grunted with displeasure and immediately switched off the radio. The duvet was thrown back and Graham's eyes winced against the sunlight fighting to break in through the gap in the curtain. His face contorted and forced his eyes open.

"Now you just know that ear-worm is gonna to be with me for the rest of the day!" he looked over to Mae's side of the bed but it is empty. He sighed knowing that now he will have the anticipation building up about how she is going to take his not being home until two in the morning. Not seeing her means he doesn't know what mood she is in.

"Ships that don't even pass in the night." Chortled Graham.

He knew that she has every right to tear him a new asshole and that's what he is afraid of, especially with the amount of guilt he's currently carrying on his back like a clapped-out donkey. He looked at the clock, the glowing red digital numbers 8:02 looked back at him and he pulled back the duvet, his entire body crackling like a bowl of crispy cereal. He lurched towards the ensuite accompanying his travels with "...Really, really, really, really wanna a Zigazig... Oh shut the hell up!"

The heat rose up from the stove and Mae recoiled blowing cold air upwards out of her mouth, as if that would cool things down. Her hand gripping the handle of the frying pan tightly as she poured homemade pancake mixture into it and listened to it hiss like a cockroach as soon as it felt the heat. She caressed the mixture around the pan with a slick rotation of her wrist, something she'd done hundreds, maybe even thousands of times. She hears the heavy plodding footsteps of her husband making his way to wash up, the beams hidden under the ceiling creak.

"Daddy's up!" She says loud enough to be heard over the sizzling breakfast.

"Yes!" Yells an excited Billy thrusting his arms into the air. One hand gripped around a fork that has impaled a half-eaten pancake on it, dripping with syrup.

"Billy! You're getting syrup everywhere!" Mae sighs, shaking her head.

"Whoops, sorry Mommy!" Grins Billy with a mouthful of chewed up pancake. Mae smiles and approaches the kitchen table and slides another pancake on his plate.

"How can I be mad at that little puddum!" winking at him. She turns back to the stove and begins the pancake making process again.

"Todd, put that magazine down and eat your breakfast." Says Mae, in a firm but polite manner.

"Okay, okay!" groans Todd, who places his Pro Wrestling magazine on to the table. The picture on the cover was of a gargantuan looking individual, more like a silverback gorilla than a man, with a mask with a stars and stripes motif. Todd dunks his spoon into his Munchie Balls cereal that are submerged in a bowl half filled with milk, he continues to read his magazine as he shovels the coral into his gaping maw, milk dripping down his chin and onto his red and black flannel shirt.

"I had a dream about Daddy last night." Scoffs Todd, through a mouthful of cereal.

"Was he flying?" Asks his younger brother

"No! Laser brain!" Shouts Todd in that dismissive older brother kind of way.

"I always fly in my dreams." Billy says, holding another piece of dripping sodden pancake in the air on the end of his fork, moving it back and forth pretending it is flying.

"Don't be mean to your brother, Todd!" His mother scolds not even turning around, using that eyes in the back of the head trick that Mothers have.

"Sorry!" Todd groans as the two of them stick their

tongues out at each other, a battle between which looks the grossest, masticated milk and cereal or syrup sodden pancake. Billy squeezes it out through the gap where he lost a tooth two weeks ago and Todd retorts.

"Stop it you two!" Mae says, again using her eyes in the back of her head card.

"So, what was your dream about?" Mae asks.

"Oh yeah! He was wrestling!" he answers plunging another spoonful into his mouth.

"Your Father? Wrestling!" Mae giggles, shaking her head obviously picturing her husband in some skimpy spandex trunks, his freckled torso lathered in baby oil. Then burst out laughing.

"What's so funny?" Asks a bewildered Todd.

"Oh, nothing!" She says composing herself.

"Carry on, I'm listening."

"Yeah, was wrestling against Randy Rogan!"

"Did Daddy win?" Enquired Billy.

"No way! Have you seen the size of Rogan? He's built like a bulldozer!"

"Yeah, but your Daddy is wiry!" giggles Mae again.

"Who's wiry?" Asks Sidney entering the kitchen, trying to undo the knot in his noose like tie.

"Morning Daddy!" calls Billy chomping on another pancake.

"Good morning, Champ! Whoa! It's the Pancake Kid! Keep it in the hole hey buddy?"

"Okay Daddy!"

"Good boy!" says Sidney kissing him on top of his head and ruffling his mop of ginger hair.

"You're wiry. Or so Mom says." Todd tells his Father what they were talking about.

"Oh I am. Your old man is wiry like a fox. Isn't that right Mae?" He says walking past her and pinching her peachy bottom that is hugged so nicely by her fitted denims.

"Behave!" She says, with a smirk on her face. Sidney kisses her on the cheek and moves across the counter top towards the coffee pot, concealing a dark substance that resembles treacle more than coffee.

"Why am I wiry?" He asks pouring himself a mug of coffee, steam ascending towards the ceiling.

"I had a dream about you last night and you were wrestling Randy Rogan." As Todd repeated his dream.

"Is that so? And did your papa bear give him the old Graham Gut buster?" Sidney says while grimacing and growling through his teeth.

"No!" replied Todd

"Oh!" said a rejected Sidney who chugs a mouthful of coffee. Mae starts to laugh again.

"And what do you find so amusing?" Asks Sidney with eyebrows raised and his tie hanging around his neck like a necklace.

"Oh, nothing just had a vision that's all." Giggled Mae.

"Oh yeah?" Sidney asks making his way towards her his hand gripping the mug of hot coffee.

"And what vision would that be?"

197

"A spandex clad ginger God!" she said and then looked at him and burst out laughing. Sidney just stood there as Mae was in fits of hysterics.

"Well." He said and carried on swigging his coffee.

"I'm only teasing. I'm sure you'd make an excellent wrestler!" She said and gave him a kiss on the cheek.

"I sure would!" Growls Sidney slamming his mug down on the counter, coffee sprinkling onto the surface but immediately wiped up by Mae and her trusty cloth. Sidney starts posing and grunting around the kitchen much to the delight of young Billy who cheers him on.

"Yay! Daddy! You're so funny!" Laughs Billy.

"Yeah!" Growls Sidney again.

"Gripper Graham will take on anybody!" He roars and then flexes in several poses worthy of any Mr Universe contestant. Front Double Biceps, Front Lat Spread then turning slightly to a Side Chest pose with toothy grimace, before turning and striking a Back Double Biceps and then spinning on the spot to give them all a look at a popular favourite Most Muscular pose. Mae applauds and whistles at him as Sidney comically wipes pretend sweat from his brow then grabbing his mug again, takes a much-deserved drink after such a performance.

"You said Fuck too." Todd says nonchalantly and Sidney sprays coffee in shock everywhere.

"What?" Shrieks Mae and Sidney in unison, eyes wide and expression hanging, almost gaunt.

"In my dream you said it. What does it mean?" The two parents look at each other, one of those looks that we knew this

198

day would come, but who gets to deal with this one? Rock, paper, scissors perhaps?

"You take this one and I'll do where babies come from." Sidney says leaning over and whispering to Mae out the corner of his mouth. Mae throws the cloth at Sidney hitting him on the face.

"Look honey, that's a grown-up word okay? It's not a very nice word to say, so we don't say it in this household okay?" She says turning back to Sidney trying not to laugh.

"Do you even want any of these pancakes?" She asks Sidney.

"Oh! Erm... no, I'll just have coffee." Sidney squirms, knowing that she had been piling several pancakes onto a plate just for him, she rolls her eyes.

"Charlie!" She calls at the top of her voice and the playful spaniel bursts in through the dog-flap carved into the back door which leads to their garden. Charlie jumps up Sidney for a fuss, groaning something in dog and wagging his tail back and forth like a windscreen wiper try to bat away clumps of snow.

"Hey, boy!" Sidney says and pats him on the head and is met by a woof and then completely ignored when he sees Mae holding a plate of swaying pancakes.

"Here you go, boy. Fill your boots!" She says as she slides the leaning tower of pancakes into his eating bowl. With a vigorous lick of his muzzle with his long flat tongue, he drives his face into a hefty breakfast. Sidney manoeuvres around the table one hand in his pocket, his other gripped around his mug. Brand new shirt with the creases still cutting into it from where it had been folding in the packet, his shoulder holster on homing his Glock .22 and the tightly knotted tie looped around his open collar.

"You couldn't look any more like a cop if you tried!" says Mae shaking her head.

"Let me fix that blasted tie!" She adds approaching him and unknotting it with ease.

"Thanks!" he says with a wink and a smile.

Now is the time when you apologise for being late. And not calling in! And for eye fucking the shit out of Valerie Nash all night. Fuck no! Maybe leave that bit out.

"You could have let me iron that shirt first, Sid! Look at the state of it."

"There wasn't time."

"That's what you always say. Would have only taken five minutes." She flicks up his collar and fastens the button into place, now pressing uncomfortably on his Adam's apple.

"God, it's like having three kids!" Mae groans as she wraps the tie around the collar. Sidney smiles at her lovingly. *If she knew what you had been thinking about doing to Nash, she'd be choking you with that tie round about now.*

"Look Mae, I'm sorry I was late last night...I..."

"You went for a farewell drink with Eric to Lionhearts." she said nonchalantly dropping the tie over and then underneath itself.

Shit! She's onto me! She knows? She has spies, watching me. You haven't done anything! You wanted to though. Shut the fuck up! How?

"How...Err how did you know?" Sidney stutters. She stops tying his tie and looks at him with a confused look on her face, obviously wondering why he is acting so weird.

"You told me you were going out about three weeks ago?"

"Oh? Did I? I don't remember."

"Brain like a sieve!" she says rolling her eyes and continues to tie his tie into the Balthus knot and pushes it into place.

"Then why did you make me dinner?"

"Because Mister Detective..." she says pulling his collar down into place "... I forgot too. Crystal called me and reminded me." She smirked.

Oh, that smile, that smile is why, that cute little smile. That's why you're the one for me.

"I've felt bad all night because I had forgotten to call!" Sidney confesses grabbing her around the waist with one of his arms and kissing her. The playful kiss turns into a sultry passionate one and Sidney lowers the mug down onto the counter and rubs his hand on her stout bottom, before softly caressing her back under her cotton blouse. Proceedings were halted when Mae pulls away and whispers.

"Not now. The kids are here!" And turns to clear the table that is reminiscent of a condiment battlefield with all manner of food and drink spilt on the table like the remains of fallen knights.

"Right boys, time for school!" Mae calls, the boys leave

201

the table in a sudden hustle and bustle and scrapping of chairs on the tiled floor that makes poor Charlie grimace and yowl.

"I best be off to work too." Sidney says grabbing her and planting another succulent kiss on her plump moist lips.

"Goodbye, Detective!" She says.

Sidney walks out towards the hall speaking very loudly so everyone can hear.

"Bye family and Just to reiterate this house is curse free zone okay? I will not allow the dropping of F-Bombs under my roof okay?" He stops in the doorway and waits for a reply. Somewhere in the distance he hears his boys holla in unison "Okay!" then with a wink to Mae he continues to strut towards the front door and then screams "Oh Fuck!" As he falls over Charlie and lands face first on the floor. Charlie totters off grumbling again and behind him he can hear the neighing of hysterical laughter from Mae, he daren't turn around for he would probably laugh too.

"What a great way to start the day! A Fucking Zigazig ah!"

Chapter 18

Thomas finds himself shuffling through the collection of fallen leaves again. It seemed to him that even more had fallen since last night's saunter down memory lane. The weather was fine, in fact it was delightful. The sun was already steadily rising in a cloudless blue sky and it painted the city in a whole new light. With such an exquisite day of weather looming St. Vincent's Square looked beautiful, it looked like it didn't belong in this City. With its dainty architecture and rows of quaint shops and cafés, it could easily be mistaken for a small village somewhere in France or Italy and with the fountain centre piece in full flow it was a magical sight indeed. Thomas stood clutching his weathered case, which was almost completely concealed by his coat and scarf draped over his forearm.

"What a beautiful day!" He said out loud to nobody in particular.

"It certainly is, Father!" came a coarse crocking voice behind him. Thomas turned around to see an old balding man gnawing on a rolled-up cigarette, busily unfolding chairs to set up outside of his café. *The Café Seize*, was shrouded with a white and red striped canopy with its name elegantly caressed across it in a calligraphed black font.

"Oh, good morning! How did you know..." Thomas said

before he was interrupted by a gruff cough from the man. With each cough, the man's cigarette wobbled up and down between his lips like the quiver of a magpie's tail feather, but never once did he remove it, just kept on coughing his guts up.

"I know a dog collar when I see one, kid." Came the wheezy reply when all the hacking had ceased.

"Oh!" Thomas laughed, nodding in agreement.
The old man scratched his armpit and then his portly belly, as cigarette ash flittered to the ground like tiny snowflakes.

"So, are you the new priest? It's been a long time since that place had a priest. Could do with some tender loving care you know? Aren't you a bit young to be a priest? What shall I call you? Do you have a name? My name is Al. Al Dupree. This is my Café, The Café Seize. It's been in my family for years. You don't talk much do you?" Al then began hacking up the contents of whatever mucus was filling his throat for about the next minute or so. Thomas wondered whether he would ever get to introduce himself, then the coughing stopped, and Al spat out a huge blob of phlegm onto the sidewalk and looked at Thomas waiting for him to talk. Thomas saw this as his time to speak.

"My name is Thomas. Thomas Gabriel, well, Father Gabriel now I guess!" He said with a smile and an outstretched hand. Al grabbed his hand with his hefty paw and shook it vigorously up and down.

"Pleased to meet ya!" Thomas was about to continue with the conversation when Al let go of his hand and waddled back towards his chairs that were propped up against the door of the café.

"Probably see ya around then, Father Gabby."

Father Gabby?

Thomas laughed in his head and turned away to gaze at the fountain's beauty again. The sunlight glistened off each little droplet of flowing water, shimmering in its natural splendour. It looked hypnotising by moonlight but by the light of day, it truly was a magnificent sight. Even the cherubs seemed to stand upright and carefree, maybe they too feared what lurks in the corners of this city after dark and cower around the constant flow of the water for protection when night fell. Thomas strolled around the square and over all the misshapen cobbles that burst from the ground in a seemingly uneven pattern of insanity. He gestured with a nod of the head and a good morning for all the shopkeepers that were going about their daily routines. Most were pleasant and reciprocated Thomas' warm pleasantries while some looked at him blankly as if wary of strangers, which Thomas could fully understand. He arrived at the church and immediately gazed up at the steeple that pierced upwards and straight through the tranquil cornflower sky, as if reaching to touch heaven itself. The gothic structure of the building was mesmerising with intricately carved shapes bursting from each corner of the building, amazing still all in one piece. Granted the majority were caked with a layer of damp fleecy moss, which also seeped from the deformed cracks that splintered throughout the stone and split in several directions like the roads on an old map.

Doesn't look in too bad of shape considering how long it's been unmanned.

The church is surrounded by a cast-iron fence, slathered in thick

205

weatherproof black paint that gives it the look of black sticky treacle. Thomas approaches the gate and pushes it open. It squeaks and screeches like a piglet trying to avoid the butchers knife. The high pitch wail causes Thomas to wince with the unpleasant sound grating his eardrums.

"Well, that will definitely need some oil."

"I've been meaning to fix that!" Comes a voice from behind. Thomas turns around to see an elderly black man leaning on a walking stick smiling back at him.

"You must be the new priest?" He says, smiling even more, his gleaming dentures framed by a thick hedge of grey hair, which formed a soft goatee.

"Brand new!" laughed Thomas, holding out his hand.

"You must be Mr. Simmons?"

"I sure am, but you can call me Burt!" replies Burt, softly grasping Thomas' hand.

"And you are?"

"Thomas, Thomas Gabriel!" They grin at each other as they shake hands. Thomas cannot help but smile. Burt just has one of those infectious smiles and such a pleasant aura that one just has to smile. There is an awkward silence as there always is when two new people meet for the first time, and they look at each other almost trying to figure the other out like chess players pondering their next move.

"So, are you the caretaker here?" Thomas asks as he lets go of Burt's hand.

"I certainly am. Have been for the past 37 years now!" Burt says proudly.

"Hasn't been too much to do for the past 7 or 8 years though. Not since Father Timmings passed on. So I try and keep it as clean and tidy and maintained as well as an old codger like me can." He laughs and smiles, showing off those dentures once again. Thomas smiles right back.

"Shall we take a look around?" Thomas asks.

"Of course! Let me give you the guided tour!" Burt says walking through the gate ahead of Thomas who immediately follows. They walk around the church following a narrow gravel path. Thomas looks around at all the shrubbery and foliage that has been wholeheartedly tendered to by Burt to keep it looking as immaculate as it does. They turn the corner to the rear of the quaint church and it's like they have entered a new world entirely. A garden, an almost secret garden, with wooden trellis consumed with clematis flammula (also known as the sweet-scented virgin's bower) climbing up it in a seemingly unsystematic contorted way. Several buds bulge from its vines concealing the pale banana toned flower inside, waiting impatiently for its fall unveiling any day now.

"I've tried to keep myself busy." Burt said almost embarrassed as he unveiled the rows and rows of overturned soil, looking like freshly filled in graves in a cemetery. Thomas looks on with surprise.

"It's an allotment!" Obviously not expecting to see anything like this at the rear of his church.

"Yeah, I'm really sorry. I know I probably shouldn't have done this on church grounds." Burt says bowing his head in awkwardness.

"But, I live in a one room apartment and do so enjoy gardening."

Thomas again smiles and rests an understanding hand on Burt's shoulder.

"It's okay Mr Simmons." Thomas informs him.

"It can be our little secret!" Burt turns to face him and nods showing that contagious smile of his again. Thomas knew that this allotment, this garden was his solitude, his way of escaping whatever hardships he may be facing in life. This small plot of land could be the only thing that was keeping Burt going for all he knew.

"Well, I have just planted some vegetables which should be ready around May or June." Burt pointed a wrinkled finger in the direction of the mounds of dirt.

"Some spring onions, spinach, asparagus, carrots and peas."

"Well, it does say in the good book that God gave us every herb bearing seed, so I guess we're only doing what it tells us too!" Thomas winks at Burt and they laugh at each other. Burt knew that Thomas wasn't the sort to go tattle-tail on him. Burt was excited now and was quick to point out what else was going on in his quaint little haven.

"In the beds around by the fence I've planted some Fritillaria, some Grape Hyacinth and Glory-of-the-Snow. Oh, and Siberian Squill which is a beautiful blue flower, very dainty!"

"Sounds wonderful. I look forward to seeing them in full bloom!" Smiled Thomas, looking around at the mounds of dirt and trying very hard to visualise all the different flowers but failing.

"They will be ready to pop in the spring!" Burt reassures.

"Well, I can't wait!" Thomas glances around and notices a bench sitting flush up against the wall of the church and it was long enough for about three people to use at one time. It was a bit rough around the edges and it was obvious to see that it had been constructed using several different types of wood, maybe even unwanted pieces of furniture. But nevertheless, it was well constructed for what materials the carpenter had to work with.

"Did you make this?" Thomas asked running his hand over the planed and varnished backrest of the bench.

"I did indeed!" Burt said proudly.

"Made it about 15 years ago now. Rufus and I, oh that's Father Timmings, we used to sit out here on warm summer evenings and play chess and drink lemonade, which was freshly made from the lemon tree over there by the tool shed." Burt pointed to the corner of the garden. An old handmade lean-to was hidden behind the lemon tree that is homing lots of not yet ripe lemons in a surprising green colour.

"Yeah, we would really put the world to rights." Burt smiles and stares at the bench obviously lost in a world of reminiscence.

"I miss those days!" sighs Burt, the smile disappearing, his wrinkled face leaving behind a sad look that Thomas didn't care for, he much preferred the smiling Burt.

"Well, Mr Simmons, I guess you'll have to teach me how to play chess then!" Thomas chirps, snapping Burt from his musing and the smile returns once more.

"Yes, I guess I will. That's if you have use for an old codger like me?"

"I don't see any reason why you cannot carry on with your duties. If you would like to stay on, that's okay with me!" smiles Thomas.

"Splendid!" beams Burt.

The two look at each other and it's as though they have known each other for years. At very rare times in everyone's lives, this feeling is felt and an unspoken bond is forged, stronger than any diamond and more precious than any emerald, friendship.

"There is another entrance at the rear." Burt points towards the corner of the church that is hidden in the shade of the hanging shrubbery.

"But let's go back in through the front entrance." Burt says, shuffling back the way they came through the gravel underfoot, his cane jabbing into the haphazard stones and pebbles of various sizes leaving a small crater of where he has been in his wake.

"It will make much more of an impact that way. You'll see the true beauty of the place." Burt retrieves a bundle of keys from his trouser pocket, a multitude of them, more keys on there than there are grapes on a bunch. His withered fingers awkwardly rustles through them as he tries to find the correct key.

"I know what you're thinking, 'Shouldn't he know which blasted key it is after all these years'!" groans Burt.

"But, we've unfortunately had numerous break-ins over

the past few years, so the locks have been changed so many times that I've lost count." This makes Thomas very angry of the lack of disrespect shown by the degenerates in this city, that anyone could even contemplate breaking into such a sacred building, rich with history like St. Vincent's. The keys jingle and jangle magically like breeze passing through dream chimes until finally, Burt grasps the key that is needed to open the front door. The two arrive at the door, concealed in an arched nook. The door is wooden and very thick secured with two thick arrow head T-hinges of black cast-iron. Matching door studs randomly protruding through the hefty wood, varnished in a dark rich mahogany tinge. Burt struggles but with determination manages to stride up the three concrete steps that lead to the entrance. Thomas did think about trying to help him but immediately thought better of it, he already knew that Burt was very independent and the last thing he wanted to do was upset or embarrass him. So Thomas waited for Burt to do it in his own time. Burt shuffled towards the door on the concrete top step. The worn green felt notice board that hung adjacent to the door was empty and had been for some time. Only a few stray rusty tacks stood out, some even had the remanence of old paper around them looking like torn petals surrounding a corroded floret. Suddenly Burt stopped in his tracks.

"Those hoodlums!" He sneered. Thomas quickly moved forward and stood on the bottom step.

"Is there something wrong, Mr Simmons?" He enquires.

"The door is open. They've been here again!" He almost grows in frustration, his elderly fist grips his cane tightly as he gives it a little shake out of aggravation.

"Mr Simmons, let me go in first. If they're still in there I..." Thomas says walking up the next step, but is interrupted by a snapping Burt.

"No, son! I was in Nam! I've dealt with worse than anything these louses could dish out!" Thomas admired his pride and his bravery, but he still felt the need to protect him from whatever lay in wait for them behind the door. Suddenly the door swings open, violently striking the stone wall inside the church. Two scruffy looking delinquents come charging out of the church and barge into Burt, knocking him down the steps but luckily into the waiting arms of Thomas, whose reactions quickly stop Burt from hitting the deck.

"Get out of the way you fucking fossil!" One of them yells as they hurtle down the steps and across the gravelled path towards the gate.

"Why you..." Shouts Burt, but is immediately interrupted by a concerned Thomas.

"I've got you! Are you okay?"

"Those little shitheads!" He growls then realises he is in the company of a priest and grows a little embarrassed. His plump cheeks glowing with creased wrinkles running through them they looked like two dried prunes.

"I am so sorry for using that kind of language around you, Father!" Thomas smiles as he props Burt back up onto the top step and allows him to secure his cane onto the ground.

"That's okay, Mr Simmons. It was justified." Burt straightens his olive green knitted cardigan back into place.

"Thank you, Son. You really saved me from taking a nasty spill." He thumps his left thigh with his fist and complains.

"This shrapnel plays havoc with my balance."

"You complaining again you old buzzard?" Comes the gravelly tones of a man that must smoke more than 20 a day.

"Every time I'm here you're always fucking whinging about something!" The hooded figure exits the shadows of the doorway and waltzes out of the church.

"You? I might have known it would be you!" Growls Burt again like a grumpy old bear who has woken up too early from hibernation. The face of Sniff can now be seen as he comes into the daylight. His drooping eyes flicker and his whole face winces like a vampire being caught in the sunlight. Dried blood from last night's antics stain his face, his once slender nose a little swollen and misshapen.

"Who are you?" Thomas demands, trying to move in front of Burt who stands his ground face to face with Sniff. Sniff slots a wad of bills into his baggy sweatpants pocket and retrieves a cigarette from the same pocket. He smiles a horrid jagged grin, his teeth worn in shades of black and yellow like a bruised banana.

"Who's this, old man? Your new boyfriend?" He scoffs, clamping the cigarette between his chapped lips.

"You son of a..." Burt grimaces and his body stiffens as he clutches his cane tightly. He raises it into the air with the intent to lash out with it, but he is now held back by Thomas.

"You son of a? Well, that's a strange name!" Sniff laughs as he flicks his lighter and it softly burns into the end of his cigarette. He then takes a long drag and blows it into Burt's face. Thomas can take no more of this and forces himself past Burt with no hesitation and stares down at the hooded reaper like figure of Sniff.

"I don't know who you think you are, but you are trespassing in my church. Now leave before I..." Thomas' fists clench and his nose twitches causing his glasses to judder on the bridge. Sniff smiles for a second time, again displaying that horrendous cavern of cavities.

"What are you going to do about it, Father?" And then blows more cigarette smoke into Thomas' face. The sickening vapours burrow into his nostrils and down the back of his throat causing him to cough. His glasses mist up and his eyes begin to water, but he fights it all back as not to show any weakness. Thomas' can feel his blood boiling in his body like a pressure cooker, his hands are now ridiculously pale from being balled up so tightly.

"Why, you..." Thomas grimaces and then is interrupted by a calming voice of reason.

"Leave the maggot, Son. He's not worth you losing your job over!" comes the soothing gruffness of Burt's voice, accompanied by a tender hand on the shoulder which is calming.

"So, what's it going to be, Father?" Sniff enquires. Sniff appears arrogant and tough for the simple fact that he knows that a priest is never going to get physical and even a weak ass like Sniff could take an elderly man. Thomas calms and can feel his blood pressure dropping back to normal, his heart rate levelling off.

"Leave now, or I will call the police!" he says.

"I'm going, I'm going. No need to get your panties all twisted, man!" And with that he barges past Thomas and down the steps towards the gate. Even just the thought of Sniff nudging him and not being able to do something makes Thomas' blood begin to simmer again. He turns to watch Sniff walk away. Then, Burt's touch is on his shoulder again and it immediately levels out, like someone took the pot off the gas.

Burt, I think you are going to be good for me. That piece of the puzzle that I have always been missing.

"Let it go." Burt says, and Thomas nods in agreement, just as Sniff walks through the gate and turns back to shout.

"Thanks for leaving the door unlocked for us, old man. It saved me breaking the lock this time!" and shuffled away laughing to himself. They look at each other and then both move forward to investigate the door. Sniff was right, there was no sign of forced entry. Burt had indeed forgot to lock the door.

"Oh, I can't believe it! I am so sorry! What must you think of me?" Burt murmurs shuffling inside the church, the sound of the cane poking at the floor changed as the concrete flooring was replaced by tiles, and with each prod of the cane came an echo. Burt continues to shuffle along the tiled flooring and takes a seat on the back row of the procession of pews lined up in twin rows running the length of the nave.

"I can't believe I did that. I'm getting so forgetful in my old age!" Burt sighs shaking his head. He rubs his head ruffling the tight grey curls that recede from his wrinkled forehead. Thomas sits down beside him.

"It's okay, Mr Simmons. It happens to the best of us! You can't beat yourself up over something like this." Burt begins to cry. He turns to Thomas, tears dripping from the bulging bags that hang under his eyes. Thomas automatically wraps a caring arm gently around his hunched shoulders.

"Please don't get upset about it!" Burt with his drooping eyes murmurs "I've been like this for the past couple of years, you know forgetting stuff. Ever since... ever since I lost her. I lost my Doris." Burt sobs, his head sinking into his shaking hands. Thomas' heart melts. He squeezes him tightly but says nothing, Thomas just lets Burt work it out of his system. The sound of Burt's weeping reverberates around the church bounding off the stone walls and arched ceiling. After a few minutes, Burt stops and tries to compose himself.

"Whatever must you think of me!" Thomas gently rubs his back.

"It's okay, Mr Simmons. It's okay!" he answers. Burt then turns to him wiping his sore moist eyes with a handkerchief he has retrieved from his trouser pocket.

"Please call me Burt!" he sniffles, flashing that contagious smile again if only for a moment. Thomas smiles nodding in agreement.

"Okay Burt, of course." There is a moment of silence again as Burt dabs at his eyes, then the silence is broken by Burt blowing his bulbous dripping nose into his handkerchief, the sound filling the nave like a ships foghorn on a murky night. Burt arches his backside off the hard-wooden pew and pulls out his wallet, tan and worn with bits of paper sprouting out of it like foliage on a corsage. He opens it up and reveals a torn and creased old photograph of his wife. A beaming smile that was not unlike Burt's. She wore a large straw hat, holding up a glass with some kind of turquoise coloured cocktail in it, overflowing with skewered exotic fruits and topped with a pink parasol.

"That was taken in Hawaii about five or six years ago. The life and soul of the party, Ha! Yeah, that was my Doris." Burt sniffs handing the photograph to Thomas. He smiles and then asks the $64,000 Question.

"How erm... how did she die?"

"Cancer."

"Oh!" Thomas mutters softly, immediately able to comprehend that Burt has been through hell.

"Yeah, it started off in her pancreas and God bless her, she was a fighter and she beat it! But, it came back a second time and once it had spread through her lymph nodes, there was no fighting it." Burt took the photograph of Doris back and just stared at it.

"It's just so difficult to put it into words how hard it is, how heart breaking it is to lose the person you have loved all your life. To wake up on that first morning without her almost tore me apart. Trying to go about doing your daily routine and she's not there..." Tears start to cascade down his face again, merging into the grooves of his worn face.

"...She was my best friend, my soul mate. I know it sounds cliché, but she was my everything. She was my world!" Thomas rubs Burt's shoulders trying to fight back the spume of tears manifesting in his own eyes. He knows that there is nothing he can say, and although he lost his mother at an early age, he could never understand, it is a different love and a different type of loss. Thomas had never loved, not really. He had never been in one place long enough apart from a fleeting romance with Maria, a girl he met in Paris years ago now. So long ago.

"It really is hard to explain, unless you've had to deal with it." Burt said sliding the photograph back into his wallet. Thomas nods in agreement.

"It is made harder for people who don't have any family. We never had any children so there is no one there to share the grief. Nobody to pick you up when you're down, when you hit rock bottom. All you can do is pick yourself up or just stay down." Burt wipes the moisture from his face and stares forward at a gigantic gothic style crucifix rising up on the altar, with the depiction of Jesus Christ at the crucifixion secured on it. His slender face hanging down and to the side, wearing a mask of sadness and despondency, and a crown of the sharpest thorns.

"I mean I have a sister, she's a little younger than me, Agatha. But she has her own family and besides she lives in New York, so we rarely see each other. She came to the funeral and stayed a few days, we talk on the phone but it's not the same as having that someone to share your thoughts with. That someone to tell 'I'm having a crappy day today, I'm gonna need your help on this one' and for them to just tell you things are going to be alright!" He turns to Thomas with those sweet puppy dog eyes with almost a deep yearning in them asking for help, asking Thomas for help. Thomas could see this.

218

"Burt, I want you to know that I will always be here for you whatever you need." Thomas says losing the battle to fight back those tears and then they come. In two unhurried trickles they come, like sprinters being filmed in slow motion. Neck and neck as they reach the finish line together and then fall from the tip of his chin.

"That's very kind of you son, but I don't want you to make promises you can't keep. We don't know each other and... although I do feel like I could tell you anything..."

"No Burt, I'm not just saying it for the sake of it or just because of what my job is. I feel your pain and I want to help you!"

"That's nice of you, but you don't owe me anything Thomas!"

"Don't owe you anything? Take a look around this place, Burt!" Thomas stands up and steps into the aisle. He looks up at the beautifully arched ceiling and then to the gorgeous intricately constructed stained-glass windows that gather up on either side of the building.

"Look at this place!" He said stretching his arms out either side of him and turning around on the spot.

"From the polished pews, the gleaming candlesticks, to the spotless carpet. You have kept this place alive, Burt." Thomas walks back over to Burt and helps him to his feet.

"Without you, this place would have surely fell into ruin, become vandalised and forgotten."

"I guess." Murmurs a modest Burt. The two stroll down the aisle towards the altar.

219

"Without you being the glue to hold St. Vincent's together I wouldn't have a job. I wouldn't be here talking to you now!"

"I appreciate that, Thomas. But I was only doing my job!"

"And I for one am very grateful that you have!" They reach the altar and look up at the towering depiction of Jesus.

"I can promise you that I will be there for you, Burt. I'm a true believer that we are all pawns in God's plan. We have been brought together for a reason. I feel the connection. I believe that we could both be what the other has been missing in life!" Thomas turns to Burt and holds out his hand.

"I will be there for you, Burt. If you'll be there for me?" Burt smirks and nods in agreement and shakes Thomas firmly by the hand.

"Now that's settled, shall we continue with the tour?" Thomas asks.

"Yes, of course! There is a back room with a small kitchen and bathroom left to see on this floor and then two stories above it. Two small bedrooms and then a very tiny attic space."

"Sounds wonderful!" Thomas says again looking around and taking in the beauty of the church, his church.

"Can I ask what those guys were doing here?" Enquires Thomas as they move towards the private quarters.

"They deal drugs usually!" sighs Burt.

"That's disgusting! How could they? And in a place of God too!"

"You don't have to tell me, Son! I usually have to clean up after them! But today it doesn't look like they've made too much mess." Burt opens the door to the private area and there in the middle of the room is a large umber pile of human faeces. The horrendous smell hits their nostrils causing them to both recoil in unison.

"I spoke too soon!" sighs Burt. Thomas starts to cackle and then laugh hysterically. Burt looks at him as if he's insane.

"What has gotten into you? What's so funny?" Burt asks. Thomas composes himself before turning to a bemused looking Burt.   "This is just the sort of stuff that I've come to clean up in this city!"

"Well, you're in luck, kid. There's plenty of this stuff floating around here!" Burt grins.

Chapter 19

Detective Graham saunters through the seemingly always hectic main office of his floor in the SCPD's central precinct situated in the Jones area of the city. He swerves several erratic and flustered officers that pass in front of him, but it doesn't stop momentum and he carries right on towards his office. As he dodges, ducks and dives to reach his destination like he is in some crazy living assault course, he greets everyone with a pleasant salutation, most of which falling on deaf ears that are too focussed in what they are doing to have time for pleasantries. He almost reaches the door to his office when a line of officers' shuffle past. Graham is kept waiting like a motorist stuck waiting at a railroad crossing as a freight train shunts past with a seemingly never-ending line of carriages bringing up the rear. *Jesus! C'mon guys! I want to get in my office, sit down and have a shit cup of Joe. Is that too much to ask?* Thinks Graham to himself but on the outside, he smiles and nods at everyone as they pass. Officer's Nash and Carruthers approach and Graham's Adam's apple plummets down to his gut before surging all the way back up, like a yoyo, topping it all off with a gulping sound. Nash is gripping a folder to her bosom and Carruthers is talking away at a hundred miles an hour (as usual). Nash spots Graham and her face automatically lights up. She passes, fluttering her eyelashes at him and he returns a nervous looking smile, which is accompanied by two side orders of sweat blushing cheeks and trickling beads of sweat from his receding auburn hairline. She passes and Graham cannot help but follow her with his doe like eyes, again hypnotised by the sensual swaying of her backside which he sensed was definitely enhanced for his eyes only. With the train passed on, Graham exhaled deeply and quickly scuttling into his office, closing the door behind him.

"Man, I can't go on seeing her every day! I feel like I'm a kid in high school again!" He says taking off his jacket and hanging it up on the peg behind the door.

"It's Daisy Snitsky in 8th grade all over again!" He sinks down into his chair and slowly swivels around on it like a child would. He comes to a halt in front of the window, almost halted in his tracks by such a beautiful bright fall day. Rays of sunlight sliced through the city and ricocheted off the windows of the buildings opposite causing a brightness so dazzling, Graham couldn't gaze into it without fear of being blinded. He squinted to instinctively protect his eyes.

"Wow! What a beautiful day it is out there." He gasped. The sunlight is quickly replaced by the reflection of that beautiful cornflower blue sky. Graham shakes his head in the disbelief that he had missed that natural beauty of mother nature in all her glory while he was stuck in traffic. It is quite obvious that he has other things on his mind. Graham sits in silence gazing out of the window and leans back in his chair closing his eyes. The heat from the sun on his face is soothing but doesn't stop the cogs in his mind from turning. He sees

223

everything clearly in his head, it's a race, a marathon, he's running at a pace that is as fast as he can go. In front of him are a large bunch of low lives and cutthroats, faceless members of the Doomsday Gang all rhythmically chanting 'Doomsday, Doomsday!' with each stride. Way out in the lead is Vinnie Valentine, still smoking his cigar as he effortlessly saunters on and calls 'You'll never catch me, Copper!' Before laughing loudly in that obnoxious mocking guffaw. Graham tries to quicken his pace but he cannot go any faster. He looks to his left and level with him is Mae and the boys. He smiles. *Keeping the pace with their old man.*

He looks to his right and his good friend and partner Freeman is there, going stride for stride with him, with him all the way. 'Keep going, Sid. Keep going!' Then he happens to look over his shoulder and Nash is there bringing up the rear. Her dark hair tied back in a ponytail which swishes back and forth like the tail of an Elegant steed. Sweat kissing her olive skin as it cascades down her neck and disappears into her cleavage. Graham quickly turns back around to face the front. Valentine and The Doomsday Gang are way off in the distance now, only a trail of smoke from Valentine's cigar can be seen bursting into the air like a steam train hurtling into the distance. Mae and the boys have moved up further in front 'Mae?' He calls through wheezing gasps, but she doesn't reply. He turns left and Freeman is still there. He turns back and Nash is right on his tail. She winks at him playfully which makes his head snap back into a forward position and Mae and the boys are moving ever further away.

"No!" He calls and erupts from his chair panting and

sweating profusely. He stands up slamming the palms of his hands on the desk gasping for air. He shakes his head.

"No, I can't, and I won't jeopardise everything just for some fun! Even though...even though..." He collapses back into his chair, "...I want too!" he murmurs shamefully.

The door opens and Detective Freeman appears.

"Jesus Christ, Sid! You look like you've just gone an hour with Barbie Butkus!" Laughs Freeman leaning on the doorframe and crossing his arms in anticipation of the yarn that his partner is no doubt going to spin.

"What? Barbie who?" Graham says a little confused.

"She's a porn star you fucking happily married man you!" He laughs again as he enters the room and closes the door behind him.

"Now, what's up Sid?" He asks in a less juvenile manner.

"Just dozed off and had a dream, well a nightmare I guess. Can we talk about this later, Rich?"

"Sure!" replies Freeman

"Thanks."

"But, why the fuck you 'dozing off' at 10 in the morning?" Chortles Freeman again.

"It's 10 o'clock?" Shrieks Graham

"Yeah!" Laughs Freeman

"We should have been to see Rogers in forensics at 9:30!"

"I know. That's where I've been waiting for your sorry ass! Now come on you old bastard."

Graham grabs a worn shirt that lay discarded on top of a filling cabinet and wiped his face on it, to relinquish it of sweat. He recoiled from the smell of the shirt that should have been part of last weeks laundry and throws it back where it once lay, to fester some more.

"Come on, let's go!" Graham says heading for the door. Freeman opens the door for him and bows down flamboyantly ushering him through with his free hand.

"After you, Detective!" mocks Freeman.

"Don't be an ass, Rich!" comes the reply, and the two walk through the main office towards the elevator.

"Oh, Detective Graham!" Comes the call from Sergeant Richards, like the squawking of a crow that drills into Grahams ears and causes him to cringe, but not just because of its annoying tone but because of the annoying creature that the sounds escapes from. The two detectives ignore the squall (as they usually do) and carry on towards the elevator. They slightly quickened their pace until the sound again reverberated through their eardrums.

"Oh, Detectives!" They sigh in unison and stop in their tracks and all at once Staff Sergeant Richards is there again fiddling with his glasses and flipping through page after page of his notebook.

"What is it now, Richards?" Groans Graham.

"Oh, well you know last night when I..." he starts but is interrupted straight away by Graham.

"Yes, Yes, Richards I remember, but can you get on with it. We have places to be!"

"Oh, yes, well of course. I'm not the sort to beat about

the bush you know!"

Graham and Freeman glance at each other and Freeman, rolls his eyes impatiently, which Richards sees and turns his nose up as he looks back at the contents of his notebook.

"Yes, well, Lieutenant Rogers from downstairs in forensics left a message about your meeting this morning."

Graham closes his eyes as if to talk himself out of saying something he would later regret.

"Well, he wondered if you were still going to be meeting with him as the appointment was agreed on for..." He pauses as he flicks the page up to read what is underneath on the next page.

"...9:30am." He stares up at Graham through his thick spectacles as Graham opens his eyes and applies the fakest smile he could muster, the sort of smile donned by politicians during public speaking engagements. He is just about to answer Richards when Richards starts to talk again.

"And it is now..." Looking down at his state of the art digital watch (water resistant to 1,640 feet, a fact he told everyone in the office about thirty times when he received it from his mother for his birthday).

"...10:11am precisely."

"I know that Richards! That is where we are going now and we would have been there by now if you hadn't have engaged us in this useless fucking conversation and wasted our fucking time!" Graham growled through gritted teeth. Richards looked back at him agog and even Freeman looked a little shocked.

"Now! If there's nothing else, my partner and I would like to get on with our day. Okay with you?" Graham asks. Richards doesn't answer.

"Splendid!" Graham shrieks, the word smothered with sarcasm, as he heads off towards the elevator. Freeman quickly follows leaving Richards in their wake stunned to the spot. The two Detectives saunter into the elevator just as the doors close and stand there in silence for a moment as Graham selects the button emblazoned with a large B, denoting that they are on their way to the basement.

"Little rough on him back there weren't you Sid?" Asks Freeman, his words breaking the monotony of their silence and the droning sound of the elevator mechanics that grinds together as it takes them to their destination. Graham lets out a sigh and rubs the palm of his hand over his still slightly moist face.

"I know, I know!" he says quietly, the sentence wrapped in one big package of guilt and tied up nicely with a ribbon of regret.

"Is there something wrong, Sid? Look man, you know I'm always here for you right?" Freeman asks solemnly.

"I know, Rich. I appreciate that I really do. I've just got a lot of things going on in my head at the moment."

The elevator slows and prattles away with its own little language as if to say, 'we're here now'. Then a high pitch chime lets them know that they have reached their floor and the doors open, the lift seems to exhale in relief that its strenuous journey is now over. The two get out in silence and walk along a slender corridor, closed in by office doors on either side of them. They continue in silence towards the double doors at the end of the corridor. Several officers and people in lab technician coats pass and morning pleasantries are shared between them and the detectives and then again silence. Only the sound of their leather soled brogues rapping in unison on the hard-tiled flooring.

"Well, do you want to talk about it?" Freeman enquires as they reach the double doors that they push open and they carry on moving down another identical corridor, the doors swinging slowly back into place in their wake.

"A part of me does and there is a part of me that wants to bury it and try and forget about it all."

They stop in front of another set of double doors and Graham turns to Freeman.

"Can we talk about this later?"

"Hey, sure Sid, look whenever you're ready."

"Thanks. Now let's go and see if Rogers has anything for us."

They push open the double doors into a brightly lit room congested with desks that are homing all manner of computers and equipment. Officers in lab coats can be seen focusing on whatever task they have that morning, totally consumed by their job in hand, immune to the detective's arrival. The two of them stand there for a minute or two awkwardly, completely unacknowledged by the busy technicians that obviously find what they are looking at in their microscopes or what is on their computer screens more important.

"Detectives!" They hear echoing from the far corner of the room. They both look over and see Lieutenant Rogers in a

229

lab coat and purple latex gloves waving them over with a head strap magnifying glass secured to his head. They acknowledge him and make their way over to him.

"Hey Roger! What have you got for us?" Asks Graham.

"Good Morning Detective! Hello again Detective Freeman!" nods the eccentric Lieutenant with a big smile and still the magnifying head strap over his eyes, the lens making his eyes look like two large bulging bubbles about ready to burst.

"Boy, do I have got some goodies for you this morning!" he says rubbing his latex covered hands together vigorously like a greedy shopkeeper hoping to get his latest customers money. As he does this with his hands, the latex stroking together makes an amusing sound like flatulence, causing Freeman to snigger. Graham turns to him and rolls his eyes at him and Freeman straightens his quivering lip.

"So, what have we got, Rogers?" Graham asks.
Rogers takes off the head strap magnifying glass and places it on his desk before planting himself onto his wheeled stool and pushes himself backwards across the gleaming tiled floor towards his computer.

"Step into my office gentlemen!" he says as he glides across the floor. Rogers flicks off the gloves and discards them into a waiting waste paper basket underneath his desk in a cloud of powder that is left from the interior of the gloves. They fall and lay at the top of a pile of other discarded and no longer needed latex gloves.

"Right! Let's do this!" He calls, clapping his hands together creating another cloud of powder that remains on his hands. He viciously attacks the computers keyboard jabbing away at the keys in quick succession and up comes a report on the screen. He quickly scans down the screen holding the arrow key accompanied by a whistling noise by Rogers.

"We checked the blood and it belonged to..." he pauses theatrically.

"...drum roll please..." Which he does with his mouth before erupting into a cymbal noise.

"...Mister Joseph Webb. AKA Spider!" he swivels on the chair to face the detectives with a huge grin on his face.

"Our old friend!" says Freeman.

"Well, that settles it. The Doomsday Gang were definitely there last night then?" He says turning to Sid, who looks deep in thought, now fully in detective mode.

"Yeah, but why was Spider's blood at the scene?" Graham questions.

"Maybe he upset someone?"

"Could be." Graham nods slightly through squinted eyes.

"Yeah, it doesn't do to cross Valentine!" adds Rogers.

"Still nothing to make an arrest on though." Admits Graham.

"Yeah, what we going to arrest him on? Bleeding!" Scoffs Freeman.

"Wait, I've got more!" Rogers smiles spinning on his stool and scooting it over to a pile of files lying in disarray on his desk.

"We cast the tyre track that you guys found at the scene." He says opening the file and showing it to them. Graham takes it and peruses it. Photographs of the tyre track and casted track stare back at him.

"It's likely it belongs to an early 90's sports car. Clay Thompson seems to think it's to a Chevrolet Corvette. He's a car guy."

"Could it be a ZR1? Cherry red Corvette?" Asks Graham.

"Maybe!" Shrugs Rogers.

"1992?"

"It's possible. Sure!" Agrees Rogers.

"You know something I don't, Sid?" Enquires a perplexed Freeman.

"Richards was babbling on last night about Bret Lennox's stolen car." Says Graham turning to face him.

"Of course!" Freeman says nodding profusely.

"Wait a minute! THE Bret Lennox?" Asks Rogers wide-eyed.

"Yes!" Says Graham

"Oh, Man! I loved him in the Maple Falls Massacre movies!" grins Rogers excitedly.

"Yeah, he is great in those isn't he?" Agrees Freeman.

"Focus please gentlemen!" Snaps Graham closing the file and tapping it on the desk as he thinks.

"Why would the tyre tracks to Bret Lennox's car be at a Doomsday Gang meeting in Ventura?"

"Well, I shouldn't have thought that Lennox had any connections to The Doomsday Gang." Scoffs Freeman.

"You never know. They are largest distributors of cocaine in Studd City and you know some of these Hollywood types like the odd toot on the snow train." Rogers says followed by a loud tooting noise.

"That is true. But I very much doubt that he would be invited to a gang meeting. Valentine likes to keep those get togethers hush hush. No, Lennox reported that it was stolen from outside Pinewood High in Butterworth. I'd go out on a limb and say that it was stolen by a Doomsday Gang member who then had a little joyride over to Ventura to show it off to his buddies." States Graham.

"So, could it be Spider?" Asks Freeman.

"It could be. We know he was there... Hey, if we can find that car and a print we've got him for grand theft auto. At least that will be one of the fuckers off the street!" Says Graham buzzing now with the inevitable chase that will soon commence.

"Oh, there were traces of Stardust found at the scene too." Adds Rogers.

"I believe that Valentine doesn't deal that type of cocaine?"

"No, he doesn't. We believe that that particular drug is coming out of Mexico, through who though, we don't know yet." Adds Freeman. "And Valentine always deals with Eduardo Colón in Venezuela."

"Colón is old school. Good old Cocaine for him, no trimmings, no gimmicks!" agrees Graham.

"So why would there be Stardust there then do you think?" Enquires Rogers, who has stopped swirling around on his stool now and looks more serious but enjoying watching the detectives at work.

"It could be that one of the gang members likes a little sparkle in his coke." says Graham

"And go behind Valentine's back? Rather him than me!" Freeman says shaking his head.

"Maybe it was Spider that had been partaking in it? It would make sense. He deals a bit of Stardust, Valentine and..."

"Whammo!" Freeman interrupts. "He gives Spider a little smack on the wrist and tells him he's been a naughty boy"

"My thoughts exactly, Rich!" nods Graham.
Rogers sits agog, fascinated by the two detectives.

"You two should have your own TV series you know. GRAHAM & FREEMAN! On the trail of..."

"Okay, Rogers calm down!" intervenes Graham before Rogers can lay out the first episode of this brand new police drama.

"What is the last known address you have for Spider?" Asks Graham. Rogers swivels on his stool to face the computer.

"Let's see... Here we are. 55 Adonis Street, Apartment C, Ventura."

"Right. Let's go and pay Spider a visit!" says Graham slamming the file on the desk.

Chapter 20

The fall sun was now high in the sky and spraying down its warm beams on the placid waters of the Hennig River. The reflection bright and blinding as it ricochets off each rolling ripple as it flows underneath the Ventura Bridge. The sunbeams burst through the ribcage of iron girders that shrouds Ventura Bridge in its gargantuan lenticular truss design, creating shadows that slice vertically and horizontally as if the traffic below is imprisoned. An exquisite Ivory coloured 1965 Shelby GT350 Mustang, charges across the Ventura Bridge, weaving in and out of the busy midday traffic like a superstar running back on his way to making a touchdown. The engine thunders away, reverberating everything that surrounds it like all classic muscle cars do, almost purring and growling like some sleek jungle cat. You would think with the sound of its roaring engine and squealing tyres any other sound would be lost and consumed by it, but that is not the case here. The musical talents of the Notorious one bellowing through its customised speakers were turned up to the maximum and the words of the Brooklyn native rapper, emanated for all the fellow bridge users to hear, whether they wanted to or not. Spider's tattooed arm draped out of the window, his hand moving with each lyric that is spouted from his musical hero, feeling each word and gesturing along with the song. Spider knows how to pick a car when he 'acquires' one and this one is no exception An absolute beauty, the owner will be livid and if he's got any sense, will be on his knees right about now praying that Spider doesn't do what he did to the Corvette the night before. He grips the solid wood steering wheel, it's urethane clear coat covering lets it shine in the sunlight as the speedometer that can be seen through it shows the car moving rapidly towards 8okm/h. Going at this pace the two mile bridge would take no time to cross, but that isn't taking into account other drivers, drivers that actually stay within the confines of the law and stick to the speed limit. The speedometer has to slow rapidly to 50km/h and Spider is not happy.

"Fuck this shit!" He growls. He is now sandwiched in by a steady flow of traffic. He tries to squeeze out of a gap and around the car in front but there is no way the car will get through and the driver to his right lets him know with a long blast of his horn.

"Ah, fuck you man!" Roars Spider.

Like an annoyed petulant child, he rests his temple on his fist that is now leaning on the open window. The music continues to surge from the speakers, but Spider begins to zone out from the ballad of his all time favourite rapper to the constant bellowing of car horns, and even to the traffic in front of him that now moves ever so slowly and methodical like the lurch of a three-toed sloth. A dangerous time and place to indulge in a spot of wool-gathering.

What the fuck are you doing? You must be all kinds of crazy, man! You're fucked up is what you are!

"Damn right I am!" He murmurs.

What makes you think you are going to just roll up in La Familia's turf? They'll fucking kill you!

"Fuck that shit. Nobody's gonna take me down!"

Then you are one deluded mother fucker. You hear me? Yo Joseph! You in there? I don't think you are. No! There is no way you're fucking in there.

"Yeah, I'm here. I'm switched on player. I am on top of this, believe me!"

You dumb ass.

"For real! This is how it's gonna go down."

The traffic trundles along and Spider is completely lost in his own world, battling against his own conscience as if trying to persuade himself that this is actually a good idea.

"I'm gonna drive my ass through Santa Raza until I reach that shit-hole trailer park those La Familia pussies call home. I'm gonna slide out this Mustang just as cool as *Samuel L. Jackson!*"

Ha! You ain't no Samuel L. Jackson! You're having delusions of grandeur and shit.

"I'll stroll past those pansy assed momma's boys and swagger straight on up to The Coyote's fuckin' trailer and beat that door till he brings his ugly Mexican ass out to talk to me like a man."

BEEEEEEEP!

Spider is immediately snapped from his daze, realising he has almost veered into the next lane and subsequently almost into the 10-ton tanker that was rolling on past. Spider grasps the wheel with both hands and steadies the braying Mustang as if it were a real stallion and he had once again taken control of the reigns. He blew out a heavy sigh of relief when he returned to the safety of his own lane and put his eyes back on the road. Several songs had been played and Spider's favourite was no longer on the radio, instead the airwaves were filled with the drowning of a man's voice advertising used cars. Spider turned off the radio and settled back into focussing on the road ahead. The traffic starts to move a little quicker now and the end of the bridge was insight. He could see Forge City up ahead through the metallic frame of the tall truss bridge. The Mustang exits the bridge and turns left into the area known as Santa Raza, which is well known to everyone as La Familia territory. The Mustang's engine growls as if acting as a deterrent to any degenerates that might fancy their chances, like a lion warning off any would be pretenders to his throne. Santa Raza is a Latino community, hence why The Coyote made his base there and any one of these pedestrians could be a La Familia loyalist or a snitch. It wouldn't do for them to spot Spider as they wouldn't think twice about plugging him right where he sat. Spider figured that by rolling straight up to The Coyote, he would be curious enough to at least let him have his say, but if someone spotted him, that would all be dashed and so would the element of surprise. For his own safety he closed the window and was now hidden by the tinted glass. He also wasn't going to go speeding around the neighbourhood, he knew that would draw attention to himself, so he stuck to the speed limits and followed the traffic as it trundled along South Street.

HA! You're seriously one stupid asshole! You're thinking in your head, our head! That you're gonna be all inconspicuous and shit. Damn it Bro you're in a mother fucking bright white Mustang! Mother fucking muscle car. Why didn't you just steal some old ass Honda or something. Shit!

"I like nice ass cars that's why. A man can still have high standards. Even if he's a thief."

The Mustang takes a left onto Eve Street and continues following the trail of traffic that trudges along in front.

You really think you're going to come out in once piece after this?

"Yeah, or I wouldn't fucking be doing it would I?"

Chill. I'm only your conscious, sheesh!

"It's about time they woke up and smelt the coffee. I'm the fucking top dog! Not Valentine! Not anyone else in The Doomsday for that matter! Not even The Coyote! After this, everyone is going to know that! Everybody is going to be bowing down to me when I take my rightful spot at the top of the mother fucking mountain." He turns the radio back on and before his conscience can give him more advice (that might see him backing out of this suicidal exploit), he aggressively twists the volume knob to its maximum, draining out any unwanted banter from mister moral sense. As another personal favourite of his erupts through the speakers, he joins in with his ugly gravelly tone duetting with the voice on the radio about how they both share their love for California. With a loud voice and an even louder radio he turns off South Street and onto Corazón Avenue and rolls towards his destination. Small ramshackle one story

239

houses line up on either side of the road, crooked and beaten down. They resembled soldiers standing to attention, but in the form of maybe an army of the dead, or the undead. To see a property with glass in its windows was rare. Most were cracked, shattered or in some cases covered by splintering boards of wood or compressed cardboard boxes. Lawns were left to grow wild and free and some even homed the smouldered remains of bonfires. Another right turn into Girasol Lane. More of the same scenery as the mustang rolls through and then a quick left turn onto Trinity Lane and heading towards Santa Raza's trailer park. Spider kills the radio and a nervously shaking foot loosens pressure on the accelerator, the pace slow and steady now. Groups of Latino males who are gathered together in random places on the sidewalk glare at the Mustang, like it was a UFO, for all intents and purposes they're probably right. No-one from The Doomsday Gang has set foot in Forge City since '89. When then gang general 'Little' Georgie Wells rode into town like some mysterious cowboy in some vintage western, and walked straight up to a very young and arrogant Eduardo Gonzalez and punched him square in the face. Broke The Coyote's nose in his own backyard. Legend has it that all the other generals tried to talk 'Little' Georgie out of going, but The Coyote had shot Georgie's son just a few days prior and junior didn't make it. Apparently, George had tears in his eyes as he stood there and watched as Gonzalez swung a machete in his direction. Georgie's head was found floating in the Hennig River a few weeks later with a note balled up and stuffed in his mouth. After the note was dried out the words 'Fuck You Doomsday' were clear. Georgie's body was never retrieved, if you believe the rumour and innuendo, The Coyote and pack of wild dogs, La Familia, ate it.

"No fucking mongrel is going to be gnawing on my fine black ass. I ain't no ones chew toy!"

Spider scowls as he reminds himself of the tale of Georgie Wells. He stops about 100 yards from the entrance to the trailer park. At the entrance, a scruffy looking Mexican male is sitting on a torn up driver's seat from a car, throwing a red rubber ball down the sidewalk for a flea bitten pit bull terrier that immediately gives chase after it. The dog catches it on its fifth or sixth bounce and gnaws on it with its sharp maulers, thick white slobber smothering the ball and he flicks it in all directions as it playfully tussles with the ball in his jaws. The man whistles sharply and the dog trots back towards him, obviously hoping the ritual will continue. Spider looks in the rear-view mirror and notices that the crowds that he had seen along the street had now joined together and were closing in together. Obviously to get a closer look at the mysterious stranger that has just rolled into town.

"Fuck!" Spider says adjusting the mirror.

"Just what I fucking needed. An audience!"

He stalls a few minutes longer waiting for the guard at the entrance to wipe off the excess dog drool from the ball on his tatty military shirt.

"Let's at least get rid of the fucking mutt." Spider says to himself. There was no reply from his conscience this time. His inner monologue had no useful words of encouragement now. Spider was on his own. The ball is thrown again down the sidewalk.

"Here's the pitch!" Spider whispers and starts to drive on towards the trailer park.

The guard sees the Mustang coming and frowns. Obviously he is not expecting anyone, so he climbs to his feet and now the handle of a handgun can be seen protruding from the waistband of his trousers. He grips the handle with his dirty hand that is covered in slobber and holds his hand up, gesturing for Spider to stop the car. Spider ignores him and accelerates slightly whizzing past the shocked guard. He pulls out the gun and fires it into the air, it is followed up by a loud scream of something in Spanish and he is quickly joined by the gathered gaggle of gang members that had been so curious about the mustang only minutes earlier. A look in his rear view mirror and he can see the angry rabble giving chase, led by the guard with the gun and now flanked by the pit bull complete with a slobber soaked ball clamped in its jaws. As Spider whizzed by several dilapidated trailer homes, most of which have children playing outside (That should all probably be at school about now), watching on and are joined by their families who surge out of their homes in droves to see what all the commotion is. Spider switches his attentions back to what's in front of him just in time to be met by a clothesline that is congested with someone's underwear. A very large pair of soaking wet panties splats against the windscreen, which causes Spider to lose control for a second.

"Shit! Those are some huge panties!" he yells as he activates the wipers to bat away the unwanted undergarments that had attacked the windscreen. The car drags the clothesline filled with the once clean underwear across the gravel and dust that makes up the through road. A large lady wearing nothing but a stained housecoat charges from her trailer giving chase after her laundry. Her massive bulk jiggles up and down as she tries to keep up, her gigantic drooping breast spills from the confines of the housecoat and propels itself in every direction before she trips and falls face first into unforgiving gravel. The Mustang slides around a tight corner, dust being pushed up into the air from the rapidly spinning back wheels, and then drives on again. Spider notices the large trailer at the bottom of the park straight ahead and he has a welcoming committee waiting for him.

"Here we go!" He says turning off the radio and slowing down completely until he comes to a halt about 200 yards away from his destination. In front of him is a large trailer, a lot nicer than all the others in the park, with a large satellite dish pitched outside. One of those old school dishes that get you all those extra channels that you never ever watch. Cuddled up closely to the trailer is a 1964 Chevrolet Impala Lowrider convertible custom, sitting so close to the group its wheels can hardly be seen. A flamboyant metallic paint job in glistening turquoise violently interrupted by burning flame design that flows over the bonnet of the car and along the side consuming both doors. This also means that The Coyote is home as he goes nowhere without his precious Alexa. Spider peers through the windscreen at a familiar pack standing in front of him. Members of The Coyote's elite, the top dogs if you will. Sitting in a wheelchair nestled up to a white plastic garden table playing dominos was El Perro (which means The Old Dog), the oldest of the group and

Gonzalez's father figure and confidant. He doesn't partake in much nowadays as he is confined to a wheelchair, but he is happy enough to just sit and play dominoes all day. The Old Dog doesn't acknowledge the Mustang and carries on with his game adjacent to another old timer, (Spider didn't recognise the other old man). Spider's eyes wander and then focus on the two tall slender individuals, Ricardo and Raul, The Rivera Brothers. A set of twins that have become affectionately known as Romulus and Remus. Romulus the taller of the two with long silky black hair and Remus the stockier with a shaved head and a thick black moustache. Both identically dressed in sky blue velour tracksuits, each wringing wooden baseball bats in their hands. Standing in the middle of the two towering twins is Brian Torres, who is also known as The Dingo. The right hand man to The Coyote and a complete psychopath, he lives and breathes for violence. He has been known to curb stomp those foolish enough to try to start altercations with him. He would gladly murder you where you stand and actually enjoy doing it, but like any trained dog, only when his master commands it. Dingo scowls, raging like a boiling pot of vegetables. The only thing right now uglier than him, is his thick black mohawk style haircut that rises from his large cranium. Spider takes a deep breath and looks at the handgun sitting on the passenger seat of the stolen Mustang. For several seconds the two just glare at each other then Spider turns away, knowing that if they see him with a firearm he could be taken down before he has even had the chance to explain why he is there. He opens the door and steps out onto the gravel. Striding from the Mustang he slams the door behind him and stands there for a moment just as the charging rabble arrive out of breath and panting, even the dog collapses on the floor and starts to gnaw on his ball. Does Spider stand there to let everyone see who it is? To make a statement? Or is it fear that freezes him to the spot? Maybe all of these reasons. Spider starts to walk slowly towards Dingo, Romulus and Remus with one thought playing over and over in his head on a loop like an old faulty record player.

I'm Dead.

As he approaches them, his mouth becomes dry and lump a clogs up his swallow reflex, the gravel can be heard being crushed under foot and that is the only sound. The sun is at its highest for the day and it beats down on him like a man condemned.

I'm Dead.

Like a scene from a *Spaghetti Western* he saunters towards them, sweat cascading from underneath his dreadlocks and dampening his forehead. He daren't wipe his brow. He had come this far and to show any kind of weakness now would sign his death warrant, that's if it hadn't already been signed.

I'm Dead.

The gaggle of La Familia loyalists had been shuffling forwards behind him but keeping a safe distance and Spider took a quick look over his shoulder to see if they were there and they were, but as he kept walking they all stopped by the Mustang. The guard jumped into the Mustang and powered up the engine once more. The roar of the steel stallion made Spider jump slightly but he carried on walking hoping that Dingo didn't see it. The

Mustang was then reversed out of the situation and taken to who knows where.

I'm Dead.

Dingo didn't see the slight jump of the approaching Spider that caused his tattooed body to be smothered with thousands of tiny little goose bumps. But he did reach around behind his back and retrieve his hand gun that was using the combination of his jeans waistband and the crack of his hairy ass as a useful holster.

I'm Dead.

Dingo revealed the handgun and held it out in front of him, aiming it straight at Spider. Spider stopped. Was he going to stop then anyway? Had he gone as far as he was going to go or was it fear that halted him in his tracks. The gravel crunched under his sneakers for the last time. He took a deep breath again.

Fuck it. I'm dead anyway he thought, and started walking towards them again. Dingo looked at the twins in disbelief and they returned their own bafflement with a matching pair of shrugging shoulders. With Spider about twenty yards from them Dingo shouted, "You loco, man?" In his thick Spanish accent. Spider stopped again and they just stared at each other. Spider gazed at the twins and the old timers playing dominoes. El Perro looked up from his game to make eye contact with Spider then rubbed his ageing fingertips across his greying moustache before looking back at the game.

"I'm unarmed." Spider says holding his hands up in the air. Dingo angrily ploughed straight towards him, his gun pointed out in front until it was inches from Spider's nose.

"Did I tell you, that you could speak, man?" He growls at him. Spider doesn't answer and tries to remain cool but the loaded Desert Eagle being waved around in front of his face, was making it difficult for him.

"What the fuck you want? You wanna die huh? Is that it? You gotta death wish, man?" Dingo asks.

"I want to speak to The Coyote!" Spider says staring through Dingo and trying not to make eye contact with any of them.

"No fucking way man!" Romulus and Remus circle him trapping him in a triangle of terror.

"Where are your homies, Spider?" Dingo asks. Spider makes eye contact on hearing his own name and Dingo smiles at him showing off a few gold nuggets imbedded into his gums.

"Oh yeah, man! I know who you are. But I wanna know what the fuck you want with The Coyote! And why the fuck you think you can come here on our turf like some big shot and not think you ain't gonna get leaded!" Dingo screams in his face, spit flying out and hitting Spider on his sweat sodden cheeks. Spider's nose begins to crease in at the corners and he can feel himself getting hot.

"I said I wanna speak with The Coyote! Not The Chihuahua!" Spider growls.
Dingo presses the gun into Spider's temple and screams at him again.

"What the fuck, man! Oh, you're dead!"
Dingo pulls back the hammer and presses it again into the face of Spider. Spider has had enough and swats away the gun

247

knocking the desert eagle into the gravel. The twins immediately move in to strike Spider with their bats, but Dingo calls them off.

"No!"

They stop in mid swing.

"Are you..." Romulus starts "...sure?" And Remus finishes. A trait that they both do all the time.

"Oh yeah! This fucker is gonna get the special treatment, homes!" Dingo smiles again as his hand disappears behind his back once again, this time flicking the catch of a tan leather holster hanging from his belt that is home to 'Rosalita', his 20" bowie knife. As he reveals it, the blade glistens in the sunlight, the reflection blinding Spider who has to squint to even see Dingo now.

"I told you I'm unarmed! You stupid fuck!" Spider says as Dingo dances around in front of him throwing the knife from hand to hand.

"What you say, man? You disrespecting me?"

"Dice him, Dingo..." mocks Romulus.

"...Just like Georgie Wells!" Finishes Remus.

Dingo signals to Remus who swings like *Babe Ruth* and unleashes a mighty blow with the bat to Spider's thigh. The sound of the solid wooden striking his thigh is a loud dull thud, like the sound of a heavyweight boxer slugging a sand filled punchbag. Spider falls to his knees wincing in pain. He grits his plated teeth tightly and only a groan escapes through the gaps. Small dust clouds erupt around his knees now stained by the gravel as he winces with pain.

"Fuck!" Screams Spider.

"Look! You stupid fuck, I want to see your boss. I have a proposition for him!"

Dingo grabs a handful of his dreadlocks and holds the point of the blade in front of his eyeball.

"Maybe I will pop your fucking eyeballs out! Or cut your tongue out man!" They all laugh, mocking the grounded and powerless Spider. Dingo pulls him closer and puts the blade to Spider's throat the blade scraping upwards against the stubble growing from his throat, before resting on his Adam's apple. Spider daren't swallow.

"Or maybe I'll just cut your fucking black head off!" Dingo whispers in a tone that would send shivers down your spine.

I'm Dead.

"Dingo!" His name is called and it echoes around the trailer park. To Spider it seemed to hang around in the air forever as the knife was unpleasantly still pressed against his throat.

"Let him go!" came the voice again.

"What?" Dingo yelled pulling the knife away from Spider's throat. Spider swallowed and swallowed heavily and finally breathed out. He felt like he hadn't even taken a breath since Rosalita made her grand entrance. Dingo let go of Spider and span on the spot like an ice skater to face the voice, the sound of gravel scratching underneath his heavy steel toe capped boots.

"What are you talking about, man?" Dingo yells angrily. The Coyote exits his luxury trailer. Casually sauntering down the foldout steps to the entrance of his one-story palace. He stands there in the sunlight wearing only a pair of baggy jeans and slip on sandals, his olive-skinned torso is lean but in good shape for a man of almost fifty, and smothered in tattoos, too many to even comprehend counting. He squints to see through the sun's rays that are streaming down like sharp shards obscuring his view of the situation. He glances over at El Perro who looks up and the two exchange words in their native tongue and then The Coyote nods, El Perro concentrates again on his game of dominoes. The Coyote retrieves a white vest that is hanging from his waist band and slips it on before shuffling through the gravel towards them. The sunlight bounces off his bald head and unattractive face tattoo's splice his features, from far away they look like scars.

"Why can't I take this culeras head, man?" Dingo shrieks angrily at his boss who continues to take his time to get to them.

"Because I said so!" He calmly replies.

Behind Spider there is a buzz of excitement from the group, just the sight of The Coyote is enough to make his followers excitable. He arrives and holds up a palm to his followers and smiles at them, his crooked grin framed by a black goatee beard, flicked with tufts of grey. Dingo approaches him as if to try to talk some sense into his leader, but before he can utter a word, The Coyote covers Dingo's mouth with the palm of his hand and shushes him like one would a noisy toddler.

"Cool it, amigo. I said no!"

The Coyote looks at the grounded Spider up and down and then glances over at the twins.

"Raul. Give me the bat!" The Coyote demands holding

250

out his hand. Remus approaches and hands his boss the bat.

"Gracias!" he says taking the bat and then looks at Spider right in his eyes. Spider's head is again filled with dread and he remembers the tale of 'Little' Georgie Wells again.

I'm Dead.

But The Coyote turns to Remus who is still standing next to him.

"You hit him?" he asks and Remus gestures with a nod of his head. The Coyote lifts up the bat and raps him on the top of his head with it, not overly hard or aggressive more playful, like clip around the ear of mama when you've been bad. But nevertheless, the hollow sound was loud and carried. Remus rubbed his head and was handed back the bat before falling back into the ranks behind the packs leader. The Coyote looks at Spider and stares at him through those squinting beady eyes, as if he is trying to work out a mathematical equation on a school chalkboard. He turns to look at El Perro who looks up from his dominoes long enough to give him the slightest of nods again, what it means though is anybody's guess but The Coyote gestures back with several little nods.

"Can you stand up?" The Coyote asks Spider.

Spider is a little taken by surprise but with wide eyes replies as he climbs to his feet disturbing the gravel again, he replies "Yeah."

"You're Spider, huh?" The Coyote asks looking him up and down.

"Yeah."

"I've heard of you. You fuck up a lot of my boys back at Ripley Beach that time."

"Gotta do what you gotta do."

"Ain't that the truth!" The Coyote replies smiling almost laughing softly to himself.

"You know I am sitting back in my trailer and I hear all this commotion out here. Loud engines and shouting! Then I hear this one starting up like some fucking wild animal!" gesturing with a flick of his head in Dingo's direction who now looks beetroot red and about ready to kill somebody, anybody.

"First of all, I want to apologise for your uncivilised greeting. They don't get many visitors." said The Coyote.

"It's cool. I would've probably done the same as The Chihuahua!" Spider replies.

"Mother fucking culera!" Shrieks Dingo who goes to charge at Spider, but he is held back by Romulus and Remus. The Coyote looks at Spider and smiles then punches Spider straight in the face. There is a crack, probably his nose breaking and Spider is rocked on the spot and then grabs his nose.

"Fuck!" He growls.

"Now, I don't want you to take my welcome for weakness, but you start insulting La Familia and there will be consequences." Said The Coyote.

"You understand?"

Spider straightens back up and nods, blood gushing from both his nostrils like water leaving a pair of pillar sink taps.

"El Perro informs me that you must have ironclad balls in your sack to do what you have just done. So, I guess I'm curious as to why you have come here, alone and unarmed! You must be really brave or really fucking stupid, man! I mean I

252

presume you've heard the stories of the last Doomsday member that came here?" Spider nods wiping away the constant flow of blood with the back of his hand.

"Good! Then that saves me the trouble of peeling the scab off that old wound. Anyway, that was a long time ago and I have changed. Oh, don't get me wrong! I'm probably still going to kill you... and it probably will be by beheading as it's traditional. But, nowadays I at least would like to listen to your story first." The Coyote smiles a sadistic smile as he awaits Spider's answer. As Spider is about to open his mouth a figure appears in the doorway of the trailer and stops him before he can even start. The figure is a beautiful Latino girl, probably in her early 20's, her skin bronzed and black flowing hair that cascaded down her back in a loose natural curls. The Coyote turns to see what has stopped Spider and he smiles.

"Ah I see!" he chuckles.

"She is enough to stop any man in his tracks, no?"
She flicks her hair away from her face to reveal perfect beauty but not innocence, her eyes had seen things and she had done things, you could tell from her eyes she was not to be trusted. Dressed only in a large men's shirt (presumably The Coyote's) and hardly buttoned up to show off her long slender legs and voluptuous breasts, she flirted with the doorframe leaning up it with her sizeably but perfectly sized rear. With the sun shining down on her and that gentle fall breeze rearing its head again she was perfection, or as close to perfection as you could physically get. Spider is almost hypnotised by her until The Coyote comes close to him and whispers in his ear.

253

"That's mine. And if you don't stop staring at her I'm going to cut those gigantic balls of yours off and hand them to her to wear as earrings. You get me?" Spider immediately looks at The Coyote.

"Are you going to be done soon Eduardo or what?" She calls impatiently.

"In a minute!" The Coyote shouts back.

"Fucking hurry up already!" she shrieks.

"Jacqueline! Go back inside!" The Coyote shouts, his patience wavering.

"Fuck you!" She shouts before disappearing back into the trailer, the shirt catching the wind as she turned on the spot and unveiling her peach like bottom. Just for a second but a moment that will stay inside Spider's memory banks until the day he dies, which could be in about three minutes if The Coyote doesn't buy what he is selling.

"Ha! She is fiery no? I am thinking you like your women fiery too huh? Yeah you do, I can tell. So please carry on!" The Coyote asks looking at his watch and folding his arms, in a 'This better be good' stance.

"There ain't that much to tell you really. I just have a way of getting something to you that you desperately want." Spider announces and is met by laughter by The Coyote.

"What makes you think you have anything that I want? I have everything I need, man! I live in fucking luxury, I have all the blow I could ever wish for. I have the love and support of all these wonderful people!" He gestures to the rabble of trailer park residents that seems to have gotten bigger and they all cheer and shout encouraging remarks in Spanish to him.

"I have my pride and joy in my little Alexa and I get to bang the shit out of that bitch in there every single night!" He laughs out loud and for a moment seems to stand in the sunlight bathing in his own admiration. "Yeah, man, I don't know what you think I want but I have everything I need right here." He clicks his fingers in Dingo's direction whose eyes widen, and a dreadful sadistic look consumes his face knowing that he will get his wish and that showtime is upon us. He hands The Coyote Rosalita who spins it around by its wooden handle that is strangled by dirty electrical tape.

"Get on your knees, Spider."

"Look, man I have..." Spider pleads but is interrupted by a screaming Coyote.

"I said get on your fucking knees!" He twirls the machete loosely in his grip the sun reflects off the pristine blade. It is quite apparent that Dingo takes great care of Rosalita the way that The Coyote does his customer Impala, Alexa.

"Your domestic dogs, they like to play with their food, yes?" The Coyote asks still swinging the machete around like he's a martial arts expert in some old *Bruce Lee* movie.

"But we are wild dogs my friend and play time is over!" He holds up the machete and Spider loses him in the sunlight, just his silhouette can be made out, reminding Spider of a scene from *The Texas Chainsaw Massacre*.

I'm Dead.

He brings down the machete with so much force that it whistles through the air, almost splicing it.

"Valentine!" Calls out Spider, his eyes almost closed awaiting the impact that never comes. He opens his eyes and The Coyote is standing over him and Rosalita is hovering about three inches above his perspiring scalp.

The Coyote tilts his head to the side, ironically looking like a canine when they are confused about something.

"What?"

"Valentine! I can give you Valentine."

Chapter 21

Thomas' young brow seeped with perspiration as his dainty hands, smooth and unworked, gripped the jagged granite that formed majestic Mount Lao. The Chinese sun was sweltering but he was making good time and was anxious to reach the very top. Climbing around an awkward protrusion of rock, Thomas lost his footing. His tattered sneakers with little to no tread on the soles were obviously not designed for rock climbing, if indeed any actual sport at all. He managed to grip a thick root that snaked out between a crevice in the mountain and stop himself from falling to his death. His heart skipped a beat and then began rapidly thumping away like a war drum. He then made the mistake of following the cascading pieces of granite that became dislodged by his inexperienced tread. His eyes widened like china saucers as it gazed below and fear set in, more sweat came gushing from his hairline, now dark and sodden as he clambered to find his footing again. He finally did after anxiously swinging from the root like an unconvincing *Tarzan,* hanging there and scraping at the rock face with his feet trying desperately to find a nook to home his toes. When he was safe he took a minute or two to try and control his breathing and heart rate, the last thing he wanted was a panic attack, not here, not stuck up a mountain. There was really no way of getting back down, not for someone as unexperienced at climbing as him, so the only way out of this was to carry on climbing. Well, there was another way out of this, but that would involve Thomas plummeting to his death and he would rather not think about that option. Thomas reached a point where the mountain levelled off and he could see foliage and a valley sandwiched between two other rock faces that split off and went on their own way bursting towards the sky. Thomas thought about climbing one of these twins but then decided against it and chose the safer option which was the valley. He trekked through the trees, plants and all manner of foliage that lay ahead amazed that any of it could grow at all, all the way up here, where rocky spear heads pierced the cornflower canvas that hung above. As he went deeper into the valley he could feel a natural change within the ground. It was much softer underneath, soil, thick and stodgy underfoot took the place of the solid uneven granite. He'd also noticed that the last mile or so he had walked had begun to slope and with the quagmire of earth beneath his useless sneakers, he had started to find it quite difficult to keep his balance and stay upright. Then there was the distant sound that he couldn't quite make out, it reminded him of television when there was no more programming on the chancel and the hissing white noise would strike filling the screen with a frenzied snowstorm. Yes, the ground had indeed started to slope, which he found out the hard way when he slipped and went sliding down an embankment, one that seemed to appear from nowhere because the drop was obscured by a herd of oversized elephant ear plants. Thomas hurtled down the bank which was accompanied by a terrified bloodcurdling scream, until he finally hit water. Much to his surprise and relief, Thomas had been saved by the softest of landings. He burst from the water to catch his breath and wipe his face and hair free of as much water as he could, while he bobbed up and down like a lonely weather buoy stranded out in the middle of the ocean. He looked around taking in his surroundings and noticed he was in a small lagoon filled with the clearest water he had ever seen. As the excess water left his ears and he could hear properly again, the sound of the white noise attacked him once more. It was then he realised that the sound was being emitted by a heavenly waterfall that poured into the lagoon over a hanging fringe of jagged rock. In awe, Thomas turned around to take it all in. It's as if he were some famous explorer and had stumbled upon a secret realm that nobody else had ever set foot on. The waterfall, the lagoon, the shrubbery foliage and trees that surrounded it amazed Thomas, it was for intent and purposes his. His own little world. He liked the seclusion of it all, the greenery made him feel safe like he was enclosed in some strange snow globe. When he had finally taken it in as much as his young brain could, he swam to the nearest bank. He removed his clothes and lay them over some protruding branches to dry and then as naked as the day he was born, he ran and dived back into the crystal-clear waters. At first Thomas giggled to himself finding that he was bathing naked without the protection or confines of bathroom walls, but soon loosened up when he told himself that he was alone and in a secret lagoon halfway up the Laoshan Mountain that stood near the coast of south eastern China. He laughed to himself before diving under the clear waters leaving his bare rear end to emerge on the top of the water, like some strange looking air breathing sea mammal, before disappearing under the water altogether leaving a trail of bursting bubbles in his wake. After what felt like hours splashing around he lay back on top of the water. His feet slowly kicking away underneath to keep him afloat as he looked up at the sun that hung above him in what he thought was his own little piece of heaven. All was quiet, apart from the constant falling of water which had become very therapeutic to Thomas' ears as he began to doze, closing his eyes and thinking for a moment how free he was. Then he heard the breaking of a twig from somewhere out in the congestion of foliage that surrounded him. Thomas' muse evaporated and he bolted up in a flailing of arms and an eruption of lagoon water. Thomas looked around nervously, listening for the sound again like we all do when we hear some unexplained sound in the witching hour, and tell ourselves if we hear the same sound again then it isn't a psychotic killer in your house waiting to sneak in and slit your throat. He waits but he doesn't hear the sound again and he then tries to reason with himself telling himself, it was maybe an animal or bird but knowing deep down it wasn't. Holding his breath, he floated in the middle of the lagoon slowly turning 360 degrees to see if he could see anything. He couldn't.

"Hello?" He called. The sound of his voice echoed around him several times before fading away into the trees. There was no reply and if Thomas was being honest, he didn't suppose there would be one.

"Hello?" He called again, same response of his own voice

echoing back at him.

"Is there anyone there?"

Nothing. Thomas pushed his wet hair that had flopped and clung to his face out of his eyes and started to make for the bank where his clothes were still drying in a sharp shard of sunlight. He quickly exited the waters and dithered a little as he grabbed his still slightly damp red hooded sweatshirt and began to dry himself off with it,. Still he kept his head on a swivel obviously not convinced that what he heard was just wildlife. When he was dry enough he quickly slid into his underpants and then threw on his faded and worn jeans that had now doubled in weight having not completely dried out. Thomas didn't care, he was scared and although his time at this beautiful lagoon had been magical, the enchantment had been ruined by whatever lay in wait behind those trees. He quickly put on his t-shirt and then looked around again, now he was clothed again he didn't feel as vulnerable. Then not being able to see anything or hear anything, he sat himself down on a rock and started to slide his clammy socks on.

"When are you going to grow up Thomas?" He said out loud.   "You can't always be scared of everything you know!"

"This is true!" came a voice in a Chinese accent from behind him. Thomas' head span round and he fell off the rock with half a wet sneaker balancing on his toes. Sitting crossed legged on large rock next to the waterfall was a small bald boy around Thomas' age, maybe a couple of years younger than him. He was fully garbed in saffron robes and a long wooden pole lay across his lap.

261

"Who are you?" The boy asked in broken English, his head tilting to one side with a bewildered expression on his innocent face.

"I'm... erm... Thomas. My name is Thomas." He spluttered and stuttered in his flabbergasted state.

"I see." The boy nodded.

"Why are you here, Thomas?"

"I... well it's a long story actually!" he replied getting to his feet and sinking his foot into his wayward sneaker.

"All stories can be as long or as short as you want to make them!" the boy smiles.

"Well, that is what my father says."

"I guess you're right!" Thomas smiled back, which abruptly left his face and was replaced with the strawberry brushed cheeks of embarrassment when he realised that this little guy had seen his scrawny little ass naked.

"How long have you been there?" He added finding it very difficult to look him in the eye.

"Since bottom stick out of water." Came the reply. Thomas' face glowed vibrantly, as red as a cars brake light and accompanied it with the only reply he could muster.

"Oh!"

"Can I ask who you are?" Thomas asks.

"I am Lo Cho Xing. But please be calling me Xing." he says bowing his head respectfully.

There is an awkward silence for a moment as the two just stare at each other, each waiting for the other to speak.

"Tell me why are you here? No one is ever coming here."

Xing asks. Thomas kneels and ties his damp shoelaces into bows securing them onto his feet.

"I really don't know" Thomas says.

"I have only ended up in your country by chance and I thought I would explore"

"Why do you climb Mount Laoshan? It is very dangerous to do so for you I think?"

"Yeah, it was a little."

"Lots of questions there will be for you I feel." Xing says before springing to his feet as agile as a cat.

"Come. You follow me?" he adds as he starts to climb up the rock face.

"Questions from who?" Thomas calls grabbing his sweatshirt and tying it around his waist.

"You see, you see!" Xing replies already reaching the top and patiently waiting for Thomas to again try his luck at rock climbing. After several minutes of Thomas struggling, Xing breaks the silence.

"I think you is in much need of practice."

"No kidding!" Thomas murmurs as he drags himself up to the top. Xing helps him get to his feet and Thomas' eyes immediately widen, and his jaw hangs accompanied by the only word that was fitting for such an occasion.

"Wow!" As standing not 200 yards away from him, was a beautifully exquisite Buddhist temple.

A trickling stream lay next to where they stood at the edge of the waterfall. The stream snaking past them through the greenest grass that Thomas had ever laid eyes on, each strand seemingly dancing its own private dance in the subtle licking of the breeze. The air was so fresh that it hurt Thomas' chest at first, he imagined this is what it might feel like when a paramedic administered oxygen to a patient. The sky was so full of life it was like an acrylic painting on a huge canvas, every shade of blue seemed to blend before his eyes and every contour of cloud stood out, he had to fight to resist the urge to try to reach out and touch one. And that golden glow from the sun that shone down and gently kissed the ancient temple that stood majestically and invitingly hidden in an alcove of Mount Lao. As far as Thomas was concerned, it was that magnificent it could be heaven itself.

"Come, Thomas. You follow me!" Xing's words tugged him out from his reverie and he walked alongside Xing through the quivering waves of grass.

"Is this your home, Xing?" Thomas asked, his head still on a swivel taking in all the natural delights that came into view.

"Yes, I live here with my father and the other monks."

"Monks?"

"Yes, this is a monastery of the Shaolin."

They reach the large wooden doors, the chunky planks smothered in a vibrant red paint.

"Please come inside." Xing pushes one of the two gigantic doors open and bows his head while gesturing with his staff to go in. Thomas is a little apprehensive but feels a strange urge inside himself to go in, call it curiosity or the natural inquisitive nature of the human being. Maybe it was fate prodding at him to go in. He walked through the doorway almost in slow motion in awe by what captivated his eyes, things he had never seen before, things that no-one living on the streets of Studd City could ever experience. Again, that luxuriousness of mother nature's carpet, so green, so bright and then sprouting up from the ground were dozens of immaculately trimmed bonsai trees of all sizes. What appeared to be solid golden buddha statutes decorated the main building of the temple. Around the grounds were several monks going about their daily chores, all dressed in the saffron garbs identical to what Xing was wearing. One monk was pruning the largest of the bonsai trees that stood in the middle of a splendid piece of garden. He methodically snipped at the dead branches in varying intervals with sudden sharp flicks. Some monks were rhythmically swiping brooms across the stone slabbed area surrounding the temple itself, so in time was their movements it could easily have been mistaken for a dance routine. Xing lead Thomas down a pebbled path towards the temple. He glanced at the monks who returned the glance with a slight nod of their heads, as much intrigue in their gaze as he had in his. Then as they arrive at some steps, Thomas stopped dead in his tracks and for the second time since climbing up that rock face, his jaw swung open and plummeted like some elevator car that's cables had been cut.

"Are you okay, Thomas?" Xing asked. Thomas couldn't answer, he just pointed to where his gawk was fixated. There were several long wooden poles as thick as utility poles bursting from the ground towards the sky, all at varying heights but all of them about 8 feet tall. On the tallest one in the centre, at around 14 feet in the air was a monk standing on one leg like a sleeping flamingo, with his arms stretched out either side of him holding wooden buckets, each one filled with water. The monk did not spill a drop, nor did he move even in the slight thrust of the constant breeze.

"Oh, does that impress you?" Xing asks.

Thomas nods slowly, his mouth still wide open.

"How long will he stay up there like that?" Thomas asks.

"Until his mind is free." Xing answers nonchalantly almost shrugging as if it were a day to day occurrence, which for him it was of course. The pair walked up the steps towards the main temple. In one open room Thomas noticed several monks sat crossed legged on the gleaming maple wood flooring that had evidently been lovingly cared for to keep it in such pristine fashion. Thomas was so busy watching row upon row of monks deep in meditation that he hadn't noticed an old figure shuffle towards them. Xing respectfully bowed as Thomas still gawped at the congregation of meditating monks.

"This is Thomas, Father. I found him bathing in the lagoon." Xing said.

"Hello, Thomas." Thomas turned to see Xing's father, the master of the temple, Lo Cho Sato. Thomas focused on the man's ancient face and overly long moustache and beard that dangled freely from his chin.

"H-Hello, Sir!"

"You may call me Sato!"

"Sato."

"Now, you must get out of those wet clothes or you will get a fever I fear."

"Yeah, I guess."

"And tell me what brings you here, Thomas?"

Thomas. Thomas. Thomas. Thomas. Thomas.

The word seemed to echo in his head for the longest time and then his vision blurred before returning in the brightest of light that blinded him.

"Thomas?"

"Master Sato?" Thomas grumbled in an almost drowsy state.

"Who?" Came the reply.

Thomas' vision returns and Burt is standing in front of him holding two cups of coffee in his hands with a puzzled look on his face.

"I think you've been dreaming, Thomas!" he chuckles, that grand smile rearing its irresistible head once again. Thomas smiled back, checking his surroundings and realising he was sitting on the bench in the church's quaint little garden. The sun rays bouncing off the lemons on the lemon tree and illuminating them into life like Christmas lights some misshapen tree.

"I must have dropped off there for a while." Thomas said almost embarrassed.

"It happens to the best of us." Burt said handing him the coffee in its cardboard container with a plastic lid, steam rising out of the small hole in it.

"Thanks, Burt!" Thomas said attempting to sip the hot coffee from the cup and failing. Burt sat next to him on the bench to a chorus of arthritic creaks.

"You didn't have to buy the coffee, Burt."

"It's the least I can do after you spent the last couple of

hours scrubbing crap off the carpet!" Burt realised he had just said what some could consider a curse word and immediately apologised.   "Oh, forgive my language, Thomas."

"It's okay!" laughed Thomas.

"You don't need to apologise."

They sat for a while saying nothing at all just taking in the afternoon sun and trying to sip up the scalding coffee.

"It's beautiful out here isn't it?" Burt said.

"It is. It's almost as if we are in another country or another place altogether!"

"Yeah! You're not wrong. I think that's what I like about it." There was another pause and then silence. Both maybe wishing they were somewhere else, not due to the company you understand, just the reminiscence of the conversation that took them somewhere else.

"Well," Burt said pulling himself to his feet again accompanied by the creaking cacophony.

"I best be getting home!"

"Oh!" Thomas said politely joining him standing.

"Do you have to go?"

"I'm afraid so!" Burt said smiling.

"But I'll be back to see how you are getting on tomorrow. If it's okay with you that is?"

"Of course, Burt. You will always be welcome." The two said their goodbyes and Burt tottered off down the path and out through the gate. Thomas sat back down on the bench and drank his coffee thinking to himself that even in the worst place and the worst situation you can always find that escapism. In China it had been the lagoon, now it was the garden.

> To carry many rocks on ones back,
> without stopping to rest is foolish.
> Solitude is needed by all,
> or the rocks will break ones back.

- Master Lo Cho Sato

Chapter 22

Detective Graham angrily kicks a soda can across the sidewalk outside the broken down apartment complex on Adonis Street, deep in the bowels of Ventura, Doomsday country. The half crunched aluminium *Koko Pop* can bounces in such an unorthodox way as it heads towards the curb, leaving behind it a slight trail of pineapple and orange soda in its wake as it falls off the edge of the curb and ends its journey a couple of yards in the road.

"Goddamn it!" Growls Graham out of annoyance and aggravation, the reaction of a man under stress and feeling the pressure.

"Calm down, Sid!" said Freeman.

"It was a hundred to one shot that they were going to be here anyway." Graham walks over to his Ford Squire and abruptly drops his keister on the bonnet. The suspension breathes in heavily under the sudden impact before breathing back out again having got over the initial shock of being used as a space hopper. Graham sighed long and hard.

"I'm getting sick of this shit, Rich!"

"C'mon Sid! You really expected them to all just be sitting around waiting for us to turn up?" scoffs Freeman joining him on the bonnet of their old faithful steed.

"No! Of course I didn't!"

"You used to love the chase! 'The thrill of the chase' you used to say and 'It feels like you've earned it'. What happened partner? Where's your head at?"

"What do you mean?" Graham enquires defensively.

"I don't know what you mean?"

"Your head's not in the game and you know it!" Freeman pressures him but Graham replies by looking elsewhere and remains silent. Graham gazes around the street at anything and everything apart from looking in Freeman's eyes. There is silence between the two and sensing that Graham isn't going to talk any time soon, Freeman tries again.

"Is everything okay at home?"

"What makes you say that?" Graham answers defensively again his head spinning to look at Freeman.

"Why wouldn't everything be okay at home? The Boys are doing well, and Mae is great. I couldn't ask for a better wife than her!"

"Okay, okay calm down. I only want to know what's wrong. I am your best friend after all!"

"I know. I'm sorry. I know you're just looking out for me. But really, she is great and we are great, both of us together!" rambles Graham.

"Sid, I never asked about Mae. Are you trying to convince yourself of something here?"

"I..." Graham interrupts himself with a huge sigh, the kind of deep and long sort of sigh that you do before you let out a hidden secret or let a skeleton escape from the confines of the closet.

"It's Nash!" The fear of being judged could be read on Graham's face as if it had been stamped on his forehead for the world to see.

"What about her?" Asks Freeman.

"She has a thing for me..."

"Well, yeah, everybody knows that? So..." Freeman waits for Graham to go somewhere with his statement then his eyebrows climb up his forehead when he realises.

"Oh! You like her too?"

Graham nods and then bows his head in shame like someone in the box on trial for a crime they know they have committed.

"Shit!" Freeman replies.

Again, there is a pause as Freeman searches for his next sentence.   "Do you... erm, you know... Love her?"

"No! No of course not... I..." he sighs again.

"Rich, I don't know. I don't know whether it's a lust thing or just because she's taken an interest in me and I feel flattered... I just don't know!"

"No wonder your head's been so messed up lately! Obviously, you're feeling guilty I take it?"

"Yes, extremely! I'm actually dreaming about the situation now! It's driving me nuts!"

"That's understandable, but you have nothing to feel guilty about, Sid! Fuck, you haven't done anything! You haven't acted on it or... Shit, Sid... You haven't have you?"

"Rich! C'mon!"

"I know, I know man, I'm sorry that was a shitty thing to

say. Of course you haven't!"

Graham turns to Freeman and for the first time makes eye contact with him, his droopy ageing eyelids sank and Freeman could see what was in his eyes.

"Oh Shit, Sid! You want to, don't you?"

"I feel so terrible. I feel like a right bastard!"

"That's why you feel so guilty then I guess."

"Yeah!"

The two stay there on the bonnet of the run-down Ford Squire taking in their surroundings. Not that there is much to look at in Ventura, ironically there are probably more eyes watching them. Doomsday eyes. Freeman places a cigarette between his lips and lights it, he offers the half empty packet of Freebird's to Graham. Graham declines.

"Trying to give it up!"

"So where to now?" Freeman asks

"Well, Spider is long gone from here. They probably don't even use this place anymore."

"It might be worth trying to track down some of his cronies. Check out some of their usual haunts and see if we don't get lucky."

"You might be onto something there, Rich. Best thing we can do as we don't have any other leads to go on."

"Hey, you know where they've been spotted now and again?" Freeman says, a wry smile sneaking around the cigarette protruding from his plump lips.

"And where would that be?"

"Perfect Java!" he winks before blowing a long and large

cloud of smoke into the air.

Graham smiles and then begins to laugh.

"Okay. But you're buying!"

Chapter 23

The sun starts to descend behind the crooked landscape of Studd City's concrete jungle. The dark shards of metal, glass and granite burst towards the heavens casting a jagged silhouette on a velvety sky of glowing amethyst. Thomas totters around the main hall of St Vincent's Church, his footsteps carry in the empty hall. The sound drifting up towards the high majestic ceiling becoming lost and then being replaced by the almost identical sound of the next footstep. He takes in his new surroundings, his new home. The evening light of the sunset bursts through the long slender stained glass windows, bathing him in a glorious spectrum of colour. He smiled to himself enjoying a moment of quiet solitude and looked up at the large statue of Jesus Christ consuming the altar.

"I imagine you've seen some action in here over the years huh?" He walks over to the organ hidden in the corner under a bombardment of bronze piping sprouting out like various length chimneys. He slid his fingertips gently over the ivories, disturbing the thick layer of dust that had accumulated over its years of inactivity. Underneath the grime, the off-white keys can be seen like the nicotine stained teeth of a heavy smoker, once pearly whites now discoloured after such flagrant neglect.

"I guess Burt forgot to clean the organ." Thomas chuckled to himself. He plunged several keys down, the ugly out of tune sound was cringeworthy and exploded from the pipes filling the air with years of dust that had nestled there. The soot like cloud flowed over his head before evaporating into nothingness. He walked towards the backroom which would be his living quarters, where he would be spending a lot of his down time, and the place he'd spent scrubbing human faeces off the carpet earlier in the day. As he entered the backroom his nose suddenly contorted with the unpleasant odour from Sniff's stool that still lingered in the air. He walked on through the small room that homed a worn sofa pointed at an old television set that no longer had a screen. A small square table with two mismatched chairs slid underneath it, a small window hung over the tired old sink in the petit kitchenette, which was made up of three cupboards, a small refrigerator and outdated stove. In the opposite corner was a fatigued leather armchair with an upright lamp sprouting from behind it, a spot perfect for reading Thomas thought to himself. He tiptoed around the large damp patch in the middle of the carpet and picked up a can of air freshener that had been discarded of on the sofa. Thomas unleashed the contents of the can into the air and around the vicinity of the patch. Finally, Thomas could breathe again and instead of the stale damp aroma of human faeces, his nostrils were treated to a combination of lavender and vanilla. A formidable duo that worked well in tandem to neutralise those foul odours, well at least that's what it said on the side of the can. Thomas made his way through a small corridor. A door in front of him that lead to the rear of the church was locked and double bolted. The bolts looked clean and new as Thomas looked at them realising that they'd obviously had to have been replaced due to a break in no doubt. On closer inspection it was clear that the door had been forced before. There was splintered shards of wood hanging off the door frame where it would have been kicked in. He shook his head in despair at a world where not even a church was sacred anymore. Turning to his left he was met by a staircase leading straight up with no turns or deviations. As he made his way up, he heard the rail. It rocked in his grip and plaster fell from around the brackets that held it to the wall. He made his way gingerly as not to pull the thing away from the wall. Under his footsteps each stair squeaked like the shrill of a snared rodent, the fact that there was no carpet laid down only helped to amplify this grating caterwaul. When he reached the first floor, behind him was another staircase that led to the attic space. To his left was the bathroom and a tiny box room. He turned right and walked towards a door, which would be his new bedroom. The doorknob wobbled as he turned it and flaking fragments of paint fell off the door as he opened it to the sound of a wailing hinge.

"Not that I'm used to living in luxury, but I'm definitely going to have to get in touch with the clergy to get this place fixed up a little."

His room was generous in size and more than adequate for his needs. A double bed frame topped with a mattress sits underneath a large circular window. It was peculiar to see a window of such shape these days, but Thomas found it pleasant and thought that a window of such size would let in a considerable amount of light. Thomas's suitcase was already on the bed, having been brought up and left earlier. The floor like the rest of the upstairs did not have the luxury of any carpet. He approaches the window to find out what view will be in store for him every morning. Unfortunately, he is not amused by the sight of The Devine Tower dominating the cityscape. Making matters worse the fact that evening is rapidly approaching the neon on the tower's sign have been lit and the word DEVINE shimmers at him, irritation in pulsating red neon, like a beacon of arrogance.

"Just great! Just what I wanted to wake up to every morning!" he sighs.

"But, I guess that's enough to give me motivation to change this city each day."

As the sun had now cowered behind the gargantuan structures, he flicked the light switch on and the single lightbulb that hung from the centre of the room, flickered sporadically before settling. Thomas looks around now with the light helping to illuminate his new dwelling place and notices an old wooden dresser. Equipped with four sets of drawers and crowned with a mirror albeit congested with a layer of dust. He approaches it and wipes his hand across the mirror, ploughing through the dust so he can see his reflection. He undoes his clerical collar and rubs the area around his neck and throat, which had become reddish from where the uncomfortable collar had dug into his flesh.

"I don't think I'll ever get used to these things!" he said as he began to unbutton the rest of his shirt. He looked around to see if there was anything else to survey. There were no pictures or points of interest hung on the wall, but you could see the remains of where several had once been in various sized pale squares, which only really displayed how dismal the paint work now looked, in it's now grimy sand coloured tone. A wooden crucifix hung on the wall, its shape was very gothic with each end forming a small sharp arrowhead. In the corner was a rickety looking wardrobe. He approached it and opened it up to find a single rail (probably holding the thing together he thought), homing several misshaped wire coat hangers and above that was a shelf, with a pillow and duvet rolled up.

"Well, at least that will keep me warm until I get the chance to buy some new bedding."

Thomas dragged the duvet out of the wardrobe and as it unravelled, a strong smell of damp collided with his nostrils making him wince. Leaving it to fall into a heap on the floor, the pillow followed with the same outcome. Mould could be seen on the pillow and duvet cover, with hideous eczema like patches that had seeped into the cotton. Thomas gave up and walked towards the bed and his case, discarding his shirt on the bed on arrival. Now topless he stretched his back and neck,. The sound of several bone's cracking made it sound like the inner workings and cogs of a clock, crunching together to help drive the hands around its face. His stomach grouched and complained, reminding him that he had had nothing to eat all day.

"Okay, we'll feed you soon. Be patient!"

He unclipped the arches on his elderly travel case, that was tattooed like a sailor's arm with all the ports it had visited, from Asia to Europe. He opened it up and Thomas laughed to himself thinking that this is the first thing he'd opened that hadn't creaked since arriving here, it was said in jest, but he was probably right. He let the case lid fall onto the bed, opening it up to reveal the contents. He travelled light as he always had, he never needed much. He had very little in his possession for his tenure at the temple in Mount Lao all those years ago. Training as a Shaolin monk and living at that time a Buddhist existence, there was no need for any material possessions of any kind. Again in more recent years travelling through Europe and settling in Rome where he had spent the last seven years studying the Catholic religion and becoming a priest. So living out of a suitcase had been the norm for him for much of his adult life. The first item to be removed was his Bible which he placed on the small nightstand. Then a small leather toiletry bag, homing all the usual things, toothpaste, toothbrush, comb, aftershave, shampoo, deodorant etc. Followed by several pairs of white underpants, all of them rolled up like burritos, done so to obviously make the most of the space when packing. Then several pairs of socks were popped out and rolled around the bed before settling huddled together. Two clerical shirts came next which he lay on the bed and two pairs of black smart trousers, identical to the ones he was currently wearing. Then came various other clothes as well as a vibrant pair of neon pink running shoes, the tread worn down quite a bit from excessive use. A black hooded sweatshirt came next which he put on after feeling a draft blow in from somewhere as the sky outside was consumed by darkness and the temperature dropped. He smiled as he looked down at his keepsake, an old cigar box, brandished with the brand called Talbot. So old that they didn't even make that brand anymore. He remembered back when the captain of the cargo ship gave it to him to keep his dimes and nickels in that he had luckily won playing pontoon with the crew. He opened it up and sitting on top was the only photograph he owned of his mother, quite possibly the only one of his mother in existence. He smiled and gave it a kiss before placing it on top of his bible. Underneath there were some odds and ends and bric-a-brac, things that he had picked up on his travels that meant nothing to anyone else but him. Then curiously a piece of red silk like material that he lifted out and held in his hands, softly stroking it with his thumbs. He let it unravel revealing a sash. A long red sash that was almost see-through which would have been used to go around a Shaolin monk's waist. This one had very special sentiment to Thomas, it once belonged to his Kung Fu master. Master Sato. As his eyes closed he was immediately back in China, on the magnificent Mount Laoshan and standing in front of Master Sato on a crisp winters day. A 24-year-old Thomas draped in the saffron garbs of the Shaolin, his shorn down to the very skin and trying to hold back the tears that have manifested and are hanging on his lashes, trying but failing.

"You have worked so hard for twelve years, Thomas. Given your heart and soul and dedicated your life to the Shaolin art." Sato said with almost a croak in his voice.

"I can ask no more of you and I can teach you nothing else."

"But, I have so much to learn!" Thomas whines trying so desperately to keep those tears at bay and not feel the embarrassment of crying in front of his master. The man that had become the father figure that he had yearned for all these years.

"So much to learn about life, yes! But about Kung Fu and the ways of the Shaolin? No! There is nothing more I can give you, Thomas."

"I... But, I don't want to go, Master!" He sobs.

"Where will I go? What will I do?"

"That is something you must discover for yourself. I cannot teach you this." The inevitable happens and the eyelid dam can hold now more. The banks burst and the tears fall. In a rare show of compassion, Sato rests his old wrinkled hand on his shoulder and gently squeezes it. Thomas looks up in shock and sadness with tears trickling down his cheeks. He knew that for a Shaolin master to show this kind of sentiment to a student was unheard of, even his son Xing rarely felt such tenderness.

"Let the tears come, Thomas. This is good, this is important for the mind and the body."

"But, I don't want to show weakness!" Thomas said abruptly, annoyed at himself.

"Especially in front of you master."

"Do not mistake love for weakness. Your heart is heavy because your time here is over. You have shown love to me, to my son and to the others, but more importantly you have shown

282

love for what you do. Love is not weakness. In fact, love is the most powerful force in the world."

Thomas stands in front of his mentor, now a man, weeping.

"I just don't know what I will do!"

"That is the fear. Fear is the force that holds people back, preventing them from reaching their full potential. Every human being on this planet is given gifts, something they can do better than anyone else, but it is that fear that obstructs them. They then go on and live their lives unknowing of what they were fully capable of. Then they die and are forgotten, never leaving the mark on this world that they were destined to leave. That is why you must learn to control the fear. Focus the love you have, the passion inside you. You have a good heart Thomas, a kind heart and you have much love to give. To where you focus that love is in your hands. I have taught you the ancient ways of the Shaolin and maybe that will help you on your journey maybe it will not. But If you ever need to call upon it, it will be there."

"I feel so lost, master." Thomas sniffs, wiping the droplets away from his moist cheeks with the back of his hand.

"In time you will find your way."

"But, I don't want to leave!"

There is a silent pause between the two and all that can be heard is the harsh winter breeze swiping across the mountain. A flash of red slices through the grey sky that is congested with clouds, looking like used cotton wool balls. It catches Sato's eye, a Rose-finch flutters around above their heads, it's dainty wings vigorously pulsating up and down, seemingly trying with all its intestinal fortitude to keep its plump torso airborne. Sato watches it through its irregular flying pattern through the squinted eyes of concentration. Sato slowly lifts his arm up into the air and positions his hand to mimic a tree branch, inviting the Rose-finch to rest its weary feathers for a while. It lands on the palm of his hand and pitter-patters around on its dainty digits, before ruffling through its luscious wine coloured feathers with its stubby beak, paying no attention to Sato or even the sobbing Thomas.

"You see the bird Thomas?" Thomas looks up and replies with a nod of his head.

"The bird is nurtured and loved from the moment it hatches. It spends time being cared for and taught their way of life, but when it is time for the bird to leave the nest it leaves. The bird must fly, that is the nature of the creature. When it is time, it is time."

"But this is different!"

"There is no difference, Thomas. It is overcoming the fear that is felt by all, even by the bird. Surely even the bird when perched on the edge of its nest for the first time feels that fear. Do you not think that the bird feels the same apprehension that you feel now?" The Rose-finch flies away and disappears into the dark clouds.

"Of course it does, but the instinct that is instilled in it knows that it must take the leap if it is to build its own legacy, to live its own life, to follow its destiny. They must take that first step and fly."

"I guess you're right." Thomas groans.

"Yes!" Nods Sato.

"The bird flies but never returns to the nest. Your time here has come to an end and now it is you that must spread your wings."

Thomas begins to cry again.

"You have been my greatest student, Thomas!"

Thomas looked up in astonishment, knowing exactly what an honour his master's statement was.

"I...I don't know what to say!" Thomas stutters.

"It is true. For years I have trained many monks that have excelled in the art of the Shaolin, but you have surpassed all that have come before you and maybe there will never be anyone that will match your ability and integrity!"

"I am truly honoured, Master. But surely you've over exaggerated my capabilities?" question Thomas bowing respectively before his master.

"I have nothing to gain from such gestures. Your abilities even outshine that of my own son Xing. That is why he has become bitter towards you, his jealousy consumes him and that is his burden to carry."

Thomas wipes his eyes again and stands up straight, beaming with pride.

"Then I thank you for all that you have done for me, Master!"

"I have a gift for you, Thomas!" Sato started to untie the red sash that was wrapped around his waist. He holds it in his hands and pulls it through his fingertips.

"This was given to me by my master, Master Xi, on his death bed. Then I was his only student and he was like a father to me... Maybe you may feel the same way about me?" Thomas smiled bashfully towards his master.

"He gave me this because he said that I had nothing else to learn about Kung Fu. He told me that he had been suffering with an illness for several years and that it was his time to go, but out of respect for me he forced himself to hold on so that he could give me everything he could."

Sato fell silent for a moment, closing his eyes having obviously taken that time to reminisce about his master. Several moments passed until he spoke again.

"That is why I want you to have this!" Sato hands him the sash. Thomas' face shows his shock, wide eyed and jaw hung.

"I can't accept this, Master!"

"To hand it back now would disrespect me. Besides you have earned this, Thomas. Take it, it is yours."

Thomas grasps the sash in his hands running his fingers over the thin soft material. A smashing sound erupts somewhere down in the church hall and the clouds of Thomas' daydream disband.

"What was that?"

Another crash erupts accompanied by a chorus of boisterous yammering and laughter. Thomas drops the sash back into his open case and with a spring in his step, was out the door and on his way down the stairs. When arriving in the back room Thomas slowed down and was very cautious. He realised now that the front door had not been locked and anybody or anything could be waiting for him in the church hall. Thomas was intelligent enough to know to take his time and use the element of surprise to his advantage.

"Where is that old fuck?" came the call from shrieking a voice that echoed and carried in the huge hall. Thomas peaked around the door and peered into the hall. Sniff, Boris and Dallas were in the hall. Dallas lay on a pew with his leather cowboy boots hanging over the side into the aisle, while cigarette smoke climbs up from his nose and mouth into the air.

"I thought you said that old guy would be here?" asks Dallas.

"He usually is. Old fuck has nothing else to do!" replies Sniff who walks towards one end of the pew.

"He forgot to lock the door again too, saves me breaking in." chuckles Sniff.

"This is really boring just hanging around this place!" scoffs Boris standing adjacent to Sniff at the other end of the long thick wooden pew. They both grab an end each and topple it backwards creating a humongous crash again, echoing through the hall. With closer inspection from Thomas he could see several other pews lying on their backs.

"Fuck you, man!" seethes Sniff.

"This is my pad! I pretty much own this fucking place."

"Who cares! You sleep in a fucking church, who gives a shit!" comes the nonchalant response by Dallas.

"Okay, okay. As soon as they get here with my stash we'll party and then head out." Said Sniff.

"Yes, but it means hanging around here and this place gives me the creeps!" moans Boris looking around at the pictures depicted in the stained glass windows and carved cherubs that top the pillars. Obviously getting the feeling he is being watched by them and more eerily being judged by them.

"You pussy!" Laughs Sniff shuffling over the altar.

"Ah, Fuck you!" Growls Boris and sits down on one of the pews. Thomas looks on and weighs up his options. To stay put or to act. If he acts then he will have to do it under cover, it would be foolish to show his hand in what he had planned at such an early stage. He takes off his glasses and puts them down on top of a nearby bookcase that homed only a dozen dust coated novels. Behind the door stood an old broom. Thomas grasped it firmly and putting his foot firmly on the broom end to steady it, he twisted the handle out of its threaded hole. Now with a makeshift staff in his hands, he swivels it around in his hands effortlessly like a drum major leading a marching band. He moves quietly back to the door and examines the situation yet again.

"You guys are such a bore, you know that?" Sniff moans.

"I'll show you how to have fun!"

Sniff approaches the thick stone font that cradles a shallow pool of holy water.

"This needs topping up!" Sniff unzips his jeans and pulls out his small withered penis and he swings it back and forth in his nicotine stained fingertips and laughing like a braying donkey. Dallas and Boris watch on and laugh through matching cringes painted on both of their faces.

"Oh, Jesus!" Dallas cries. On hearing Dallas' statement, Sniff turns to the large statue of Jesus Christ's crucifixion and shakes his flaccid penis in its direction while sticking his tongue out at it. Laughter erupts from them all in the hall. Sniff turns around again and starts to urinate in the font, the warm stream trickles out and mixes with the blessed water while steam bellows upwards.

"Oh that feels good!" he groans. Hysterical laughter fills the hall again. Anger bubbles up inside Thomas at the utter disgraceful and disrespectful attitude that this creature, Sniff seems to excrete. Thomas pulls his hood up and notices a large bank of switches on the wall next to him, controlling all the lights in the main hall.

"I've seen enough!" Thomas whispers almost smiling. He swipes his palm across the switches, all the lights go out in the church hall simultaneously.

"What the hell?" Dallas says bolting upright. Silence falls and all that can be heard is the sporadic sound of urine dripping from Sniff's puckered foreskin as it falls into the font. The church now dimly lit by a handful of candles still alight, the hall becomes immediately caressed by shadows that dominate the room. The dancing flames rising from the candles, flicker in a draft.

"I don't like this!" Boris murmurs in a shaking east European voice.

"It's probably just a power cut." Says Dallas, trying to convince himself more than anything.

"It's probably that old fuck messing with us!" adds Sniff, still frozen hanging over the font with his hand gripping his penis. Suddenly the candles go out and the hall is now lit by only streetlights outside, barely illuminating anything through the long slender stained glass.

"Okay, what the fuck is going on?" Dallas shouts, his voice bouncing around like a ping pong ball in the vast hall.

"Everyone get together!" calls Dallas sensing something is not quite right. Boris joins him at the foot of the altar steps, both of them looking round frantically. Sniff remains where he is like an explicit water feature.

"Sniff! Put your fucking dick away and get over here!" Dallas shouts. Sniff quickly conceals his shrinking manhood and quickly zips up his zipper, trying not to catch himself in the process. He joins them and the three of them huddle back to back, their eyes rapidly flitting back and forth across the dark corners of the church.

"Did you see that?" Boris points into a dark corner behind a pillar.

"What? What was it?" shrieks Sniff.

"I didn't see anything!" Dallas yells, denial in his voice.

"There!" Boris points to another pillar.

"There it is again!"

"Tool up!" Dallas whispers while retrieving his handgun from the waistband of his jeans. Sniff pulls out a flick knife from his jacket pocket and Boris picks up a heavy brass candelabra. The candles falling from it and to the floor as he grasps it in both his hands horizontally across his chest. Only the sound of a breeze that whistles through the hall can be heard.

"Leave!" comes the bellowing voice of Thomas. The word carries around the hall and makes the trio of degenerates jump out of their skin.

"Who's gonna make us? Show yourself!" Calls Dallas into the darkness. There is no reply.

"Where the fuck is he, man?" snivels Sniff.

"Show your fucking self or I swear I'll fucking shoot you!" Calls Dallas again. There was no reply again. A dark silhouette darts past Dallas' peripheral vision and he reacts by shooting nervously into the darkness. For a split second the flash of the gunfire illuminates the hall and Thomas can be seen, his identity kept secret by the hood that shrouds his face. The bullet whistles behind by a few feet and clips a large stone pillar, chipping a piece of it off.

"I saw him! Fire again!" Yells Boris.

"And waist all the ammo? Fucking idiot!" Dallas snaps.

"I'll fire when he's close enough."

"Is this close enough?" whispers Thomas appearing right next to Dallas. They all jump out of their skin as Thomas uses his makeshift staff to knock the gun from his shaking grip. The gun rotates into the air and when the gun hits the ground it is triggered again. Another shot is fired, another bullet soars into the darkness and hits something somewhere.

"What the fuck!" Dallas shouts, taking a swipe with his balled up right fist at Thomas who easily dodges it and thwacks the tip of the staff across the bridge of his nose with a very ugly sounding crack. It splits the skin and blood seeps from the wound, the force of the strike also causing his nostrils to leak too.

"Shit! My fucking nose!" he groans grabbing his face with both hands.

"What happened?" yells Boris.

"My fucking nose!" Dallas yells back.

"Oh shit, man! Where is he, man?" Warbles Sniff, the flick knife wobbling about in his sweaty grip.

"I'm right here!" whispers Thomas again, appearing next to Boris who is startled. He takes an almighty swing with the candelabra, but Thomas is nimble and quick and he ducks under that candlestick! Boris' momentum causes him to spin on the spot leaving him open for Thomas to sweep his legs from underneath him effortlessly with his staff. Boris hits the deck, unleashing a tirade of Ukrainian curse words.

"Oh shit! Oh shit! Oh fucking shit!" shakes Sniff, his eyes darting right to left until Thomas appears in front of him, shrouded in darkness and mystery.

"I think it's time you left." He whispered.

"Fuck you!" Sniff yells and lunges, jabbing the blade in Thomas' vicinity, to no avail. With two twists of his staff he whips it across Sniff's wrist causing him to drop the blade. He then windmills it into Sniff's groin, immediately dropping him to his knees in a high pitch groan, cupping his tender testicles firmly in his hands.

"Fuck this shit!" cries Dallas as he makes for the door, quickly followed by Boris, both high tailing it down the aisle. Sniff starts to follow them, crouched over like the Hunchback of

Notre Dame still clutching his throbbing privates. As Dallas and Boris exit the church they pass two skinny looking males, gaunt faces with dark circles dragging from their eyelids and with a look of absolute astonishment on their faces having witnessed what this mysterious hooded figure has just done. One of them gripping a screwed up brown paper bag in his hand.

Thomas looks up at them.

"Are you next?" he enquires and gets his answer by two identical vigorous shaking heads just as they turn and fled. Thomas then quickly moves to block Sniff's slow retreat.

"This church is off limits!" he growls. Sniff quivers.

"Okay, okay, man whatever you want!"

Thomas lifts the staff in the air as if he is going to deliver another blow which causes Sniff to cower and hide his face. Thomas uses this time to drift quietly behind a pillar and when Sniff realises that the blow isn't coming, he emerges from his shell like a reluctant tortoise. When he sees that the mysterious avenger has disappeared he bolts down the aisle and out the door. Thomas appears from behind the pillar and swivelling the staff in his hands stops it by jamming it to the floor with one hand and holding it firmly in his grip. He pulls back the hood and smiles.

"Well, that's shaken a bit of rust off."

Chapter 24

In an unknown safe house in Forge City, Spider sits in the dark, his face illuminated only by the glow of his cell phone screen. He scrolls nonchalantly through his contacts, stroking his finger downwards on the touch sensitive screen until he reaches the name he requires, Dallas. He selects the bright green icon that has a phone shaped pictured emblazoned on it and the screen indicates that it is calling. Spider lifts the cell phone up and rests it against his ear. The light from the phone's screen shines on the black widow tattoo that is etched on his neck, surrounded by a contorting cobweb that disappears down his neck.

"Yo, it's me!" Spider says, his grill gleaming in the lament glow.

"Fuck, Spider! Where the fuck have you been all week?" Dallas answers vexed but a little relieved.

"Been fucking worried about you bro!"

"Gee calm down, mom!" sniggers Spider.

"We thought those La Familia bitches had done you in."

"Nah, man, I'm cool!"

"So, where are you?"

"Forge."

"What?" yells Dallas, so loud that Spider winces and pulls the phone away from his ear.

"Fuck! Chill, Dal! Jesus!"

"Why the hell are you in Forge? You're gonna get plugged!"

"Nah, man. No way. I've been laying low while I sorted everything out.""

"You mean he's in?" Dallas enquires a sense of disbelief in his voice.

"Damn right he is."

"Well shit me! I don't believe it!"

"I know right. I thought they were gonna fuck me up man, but nah he was cool when I told him my plan."

"So, we going ahead with it?"

"Yeah."

"When?"

"Soon. Just lie low for a few days and I'll be in touch. No need to draw any unnecessary attention to us, you get me?"

"Yeah, sure no problem."

"That means keeping that douche bag Sniff on a short fucking leash!" snarls Spider. Just speaking Sniff's name makes his blood boil.

"I don't want him fucking this up for me or else I'll cut his maggot dick off!"

"Yeah... About him..." Dallas murmurs tactfully.

"What the fuck's he done now?"

"Well, he took us to the church the other night for a deal."

"Yeah?"

"Well, it didn't go to plan."

"What'd ya mean?"

"Someone was there and he...Well he fucked us up. Some fucking Bruce Lee shit, man!"

"Fuck! Any ideas who it was?"

"No idea. It was too dark. Church is off limits now though bro. I tell ya I don't want to mess with that guy again."

"Shit!"

"Sniff said he overheard the old guy caretaker talking to a priest too, so looks like it's reopening."

"Yeah man, steer clear of that place. We have more important shit to concentrate on anyway."

"Yeah, sure. But that's the thing, since that happened we haven't seen Sniff since."

"Fuck! I swear one of these days I'm gonna..." Spider growls, almost losing it but after a few seconds manages to get his anger under control.

"...Just find the dumb fuck and then keep him under wraps, yeah?"

"I'll find him, bro."

"No problem. What'd you want me to say if any Generals start asking questions?"

"Tell them I'm visiting a sick aunt or some bullshit. I don't know, make some shit up!"

"Yeah, sure."

"Just be cool man and I'll be in touch soon. Laters."

"See ya!" Spider ends the call and switches off the phone.

Chapter 25

Vinnie Valentine stirs restlessly in his expensive leather armchair, lost in a cloud of dark cigar smoke that rises around him. He sits staring into the glowing amber flames of a raging fire that flickers in the confines of a huge ostentatious solid marble fireplace, that protrudes from his designer wallpapered walls in his luxury apartment in The Borough. The Doomsday Gang boss who has everything he could ever wish for, is uncharacteristically quiet and solemn on this cold fall evening. Gazing into the gyrating flames, rubbing against each other like two lovers entwined in sensual pleasure.

"You seem very quiet tonight, Vin?" The sweet voice of his wife, never loosing that unmistakable Brooklyn accent, cuts through the orange glowing muse that has consumed him.

"Huh?" Valentine replies, not really hearing the words but recognising her voice. He places the half used cigar into the solid glass ashtray that sits balanced on the arm of the chair.

"I said, you're quiet." She says again pouring eighty-year-old whiskey from the fine cut glass decanter into two hefty whiskey glasses.

"You seem distracted." She continued as she handed him a glass and sat adjacent to him in a matching leather armchair. The leather squeaking under her weight.

"So, you wanna tell me what's wrong Vin?" She asks.

Her bulbous lips wrap around the rim of the glass. Taking a small sip, she leaves her mark with a suitable shade of rose lipstick.

"I don't know what it is. Just got a feeling you know?" he answers looking at her sipping his whiskey, swilling it around the inside of his mouth. He takes the time to appreciate the age of the drink.

"You and your feelings." She says with an almost dismissing roll of her heavily made up eyes.

"Hey!" he snaps, not appreciating the look on her face. "Don't disrespect me, Sophia! Remember I'm the reason you're able to live this life!" he angrily jams the chunky cigar into his mouth and takes a drag on it.

"Yeah you are! But maybe you're the one that needs to take a look around and realise what they've got. Not me!" she growls, not getting angry, but a vexed tone in her voice is enough to get her point across.

"What're you talking about woman?"

"You with your moping around like you have the world on your shoulders. You've got everything you ever wanted! You're more powerful than your Father (God rest his soul)..." crossing her heart with her fingers and looking up to the ceiling. "...ever was! You have built a vast fortune..."

"Which you like to squander!" Valentine intervenes playfully.

"That's what I'm here for!" Sophia replies winking at him.

"And don't interrupt me when I'm on a roll." Valentine holds his hand up gesturing an unspoken apology.

"Yeah honey, the power, the wealth, family, respect. You have it all!" She chugs down the rest of her whiskey in one gulp like some veteran barfly and rises slowly and provocatively out of the chair, the leather hissing in her wake. She's dressed in an oriental dressing gown in the finest silk with fabulous embroidered dragons depicted on it.

"Plus, you have me." She's smirks. Her middle aged and heavily made up face wrinkles but there are still flickers of the feisty attractive woman she used to be, before the excessive drinking and cocaine use had taken its toll on her looks.

"I sure do!" smirks Valentine, sipping on his whiskey again. He leans back in his chair and surveys what stands before him.

"I guess I'm stressed out a little that's all."

"Oh, poor baby!" She says pulling at her gown causing it to gape and expose the round curve of her implanted breast.

"I know something that is scientifically proven to be beneficial for stress relief." She says biting her plump bottom lip while rubbing her fingers down the front of her torso and then slowly untying the gown's belt.

"You don't say!" smiles Valentine.

"Very beneficial!" She opens her gown unveiling her body, the beautiful body of a woman in her late 40's. The protruding surgically enhanced breasts look out of place on her worn olive skin that is riddled with cellulite and stretch marks, caused in no small part to the trifecta of Valentine offspring that

300

she has mothered. She drops the gown to the Arabian style rug that dominates the fireplace area and stands proud of her body, of her tiger stripes and so she should. The vibrant glow of the fire licking her with its warm lambent caresses, bathing every exquisite curve of her body. Like an Amazonian warrior she wears the scars with honour and her husband loves that about her.

"Well, please do tell." He says in his gravelly tone. She approaches him and he arches up from his seat to meet and kiss her, but with her hand, gently pushes him back into his seat. She grabs his kneecaps and opens his legs and slowly kneels in between them, remembering to keep eye contact with him as she lowers herself into her desired position.

"Oh!" Valentine says smirking.

"I think I know this technique." Playfully her eyelids flicker at him, reflecting the open fire's flames that dance and burn in her eyes. She unbuckles his belt and unzips his trousers, her hand disappears into his underpants and unveils his girth. He closes his eyes, his head settling back into the indent of his chair which fits perfectly.

"I feel better already!" he says exhaling heavily.

"Oh no you don't!" she says grabbing his manhood firmly, enough to cause Valentine's eyes to open.

"Whoa!" he chortles.

"Okay, you're the boss!"

"You better believe it!" she says loosening her grip and then slowly massaging her hand up and down his penis.

"Maybe I should tell everyone who really controls things at the top of The Doomsday ladder?"

"Don't push your luck!" She tightens her grip again in unison with her biting down on her bottom lip. He closes his eyes and groans, suddenly finding himself in that bizarre plain between pleasure and pain.

"Okay. First thing tomorrow morning I hand everything over to you!" They both chuckle and she increases the speed of her caressing hand.

"I'm being serious though. I want you to lie back, close your eyes, relax and tell me about what's on your mind."

"Really?"

"Yes! 'Really!'. Vera says it helps George."

"Jesus Fucking Christ Sophia! You're talking about our sex life to that nosey..." She interrupts him.

"No, of course not. She was telling me down at the salon that he was having a tough time with his job and while during fellatio it helped him get things off his chest."

"I bet it did!" barked Valentine.

"I'm being serious!" she scowls at him still vigorously massaging his penis in her hand like a seasoned professional.

"Okay, okay!"

"Now, close your eyes and tell me all about it." She says as she starts to lick her tongue up and down his rising shaft.

"The problem is these peons that I have following me."

"Those 'peons' as you call them are doing all the heavy lifting for you!" she says slurping with a mouthful of saliva.

"You shouldn't forget about the little people." She adds before continuing.

"Fuck the little people! I haven't got where I am now thinking about the little people. They're merely pawns in my game."

"That's all very well," She stops, his erect penis now gripped in her hand.

"I know how you feel about it, but you can't let them know that or you've lost them." Valentine places his hand on the top of her head and pushes her back down to carry on with this new experimental stress relieving procedure.

"I know that!" he adds, taking a swig of his whiskey. Sophia sinks her maw around his penis and begins to slowly suck. He groans with pleasure and softly caresses her long dark hair, pushing it back away from her face so he can watch her while she pleasures him.

"It's just lately I've noticed some dissension in the ranks. I've heard rumbles about certain people in the group and I fear there may be an uprising from these few bad apples. It may cause a mutiny." His wife doesn't answer, seemingly totally engrossed in what she is doing.

"You hear me?" He scoffs.

"Huh, huh!" She agrees, looking at him with those hazel eyes framed heavily with lilac eyeshadow and fluttering those dark eyelashes, thick with too much mascara.

"I thought I'd made my feelings clear to the main antagoniser and I've given the little prick enough warnings, but he continues to cause trouble. I'm going to have to kill the fuck!" he groans with delight.

"Tho gill'im!" she mumbles, her mouth filled, but luckily Valentine understands what she is saying and obviously doesn't want her to stop again.

"Yeah, shame he's such an arrogant prick, he'd have had a bright future as a general if he didn't have such a high opinion of himself." He pushes her head down firmly and she takes all of him, until it lodges itself into the back of her throat causing her to gag. He smiles at her as she frowns at him, he loosens his grip on her head and she carries on.

"And to make matters worse, Twitch informs me that he's gone AWOL. Even his cronies don't know where he is! Well, allegedly!" He groans again, closing his eyes and grabbing her long thick hair tightly in his large ape like hand. His other hand grabs the arm of the chair leaving clawing indents into the old leather.

"Faster!" he moans, she vigorously increases the speed and incorporates her hand into her flawless technique, moving it up and down simultaneously with her mouth.

"My gut tells me he's planning something... I guess... I'll just have... to... wait...Oh... God!" he ejaculates into her mouth and she slows her motion, caressing him slower. She rises and swallows deep and hard.

"You should always go with your gut instinct, honey. You know that." She says wiping the excess semen away from her lips.

"Yeah I know. Do you think I'm being paranoid?" he asks breathing slightly heavy.

"Honey..." She takes the whiskey glass out of his hand and takes a sip washing it around her mouth.

"In your position you've every right to be paranoid. There are always leeches out there who want to get what they can from the people at the top. I guess you've got to accept that."

"They're all fucking leeches! All of them! Can't trust any of them... Well, apart from Twitch."

She climbs onto his lap, her body naked and every curve lit by the light of the raging flames, she cuddles and kisses him.

"That maybe so, but they're the worker ants in this colony and without them the queen cannot live in the luxury she is accustomed to!" she smiles at him kissing him on his square stubbled jaw.

"My queen!" he chuckles caressing her cheek with the back of his hand.

"You do what you feel you have to, honey. If you need to squash an ant to get the others to fall in line, then so be it."

"I love you, my queen!" He says and the two embrace, kissing passionately.

Chapter 26

The sun had not even risen in Studd City and Thomas had already been awake for an hour. Thomas, garbed in dark gym shorts and a vest, sat quietly in an impressive box splits position. Only the sound of his deep breathing could be heard in his newly decorated sleeping quarters. Fresh magnolia paint coating the once dreary walls and on the wall, hung the only photograph of his mother, framed elegantly in a place for all to see.

A week has passed since I first arrived back in Studd City. I have become very settled here. The church is starting to feel like home to me and I can't speak more highly of the clergy and how quickly they got this place back into a liveable condition.

With sweat shining over Thomas' ripped physique, he manoeuvres himself into a position known to some as the prone cobra. Lying on his front and lifting his upper body off the now newly carpeted floor, he contracts his abdominal area and arches up his head, neck and upper torso to help strengthen his core.

I've really gotten to know Burt and if I'm really honest, I've come to love him. How could you not? He's such a loving and caring individual with such a kind heart and what a wicked sense of humour. Makes me smile just thinking about him, he just has that effect on you. I don't want to jinx things but... he could be that piece of my jigsaw that I've always been missing. Sato was always there for me and he taught me so much, he made a man out of me, but he has Xing. Xing is his son and I'm not and that's something I can never change. Besides I need to be cared for. I need that arm around my shoulder when I'm low and to tell me everything will be alright. That wasn't Sato's style. He very rarely showed any living emotion. Positive mental attitude was what he instilled in me and he helped by nurturing me that way through his knowledge of Shaolin and the Buddhist religion. But loving he wasn't and I guess I need that. Guess I always have.

A swivel of his body and he was on his back. His body as straight as an arrow, he began to do the next part of his training regime, leg raises. He tightened his core and lifted his legs up into the air, his bare feet pointing towards the ceiling. His moist quadriceps contorting and bulging under the thin layer of skin under each repetition.

I've yet to make that important first step out into the dark underworld that I had promised I would. Not because of fear but I knew I was not ready to begin my crusade. I wasn't ready to fight yet. That time with those goons in the church hall was not good timing but my hand was forced and soI had to act. And I'm glad I did because I haven't had any trouble from anyone since. The time has given me chance to train and really focus on getting physically and mentally prepared for such a huge undertaking. I have my daily routine down to a tee now.

Thomas starts to roll around the room, tight short forward rolls using the momentum to move straight up to his feet. He kept the

307

rolls short due to the lack of space, which also helped him with his spatial awareness.

My day starts at 5am where I start with twenty minutes of breathing meditation to calm me and clear my mind. Followed by ten minutes of breath of fire breathing to charge me up for the training ahead. I keep to quick deep diaphragmatic breathing, two to three breaths per second. Then shaking to raise the core temperature, starting with hands, then arms, then legs, then the whole body. It's not easy to train in such a small area, it's not ideal but I have been able to modify and manipulate a routine that works perfectly for small or confined spaces. When I was training in my chosen field as a Priest, my room was no bigger than a jail cell. It was there that I was really under pressure due to space constructions. But because I couldn't have anyone knowing what I was doing, I had to do it in my room. So my room today is huge compared to that.

Thomas finds his feet again, shaking off his limbs and loosening up those warm muscles. Grabbing a towel, he wipes away excess sweat from his brow and groom around his face and neck, then discards it onto the bed.

When I start my night job as protector of people as a crusader, I guess you could say a vigilante, 5am starts maybe a little optimistic. I very much doubt that I'll be raring to go at that time in the morning after a night of patrolling, apprehending and more than likely, fighting. I am in no way in denial that I will meet all sorts of characters that will be thirsty for my blood and if my chosen name becomes the thing of legend, then surely many that which to take my scalp.

He slumps onto the edge of the bed and after some blind rummaging underneath, retrieves his vibrant luminous running shoes that wouldn't look out of place on an Olympic sprinter. He pulled on some thick white sport socks and slotted his feet into the sneakers.

I'll go for a run and explore the city some more. I can easily move in and out of the back streets and build up a mental picture of the place. A mental blueprint if you will, the element of surprise will be my friend and also quick getaways will be useful. And of course, sometimes maybe a place to hide? I'm not that arrogant to believe I won't be outnumbered from time to time or even...hurt! So, a safe place to lay low will be a Godsend.

He quickly ties his laces and grabs his black hooded jacket making his way downstairs. Halfway down the stairs he is halted in mid stride by the sound of something being dropped in living quarters.

What was that?

The sound was something metallic being banged or dropped, maybe a tin?

It's those cockroaches again! They've come back!

Thomas creeps down the stairs and turns into the corridor. Light illuminates the end of the short corridor indicating someone is in the living quarters.

Maybe I am arrogant. Arrogant to believe things will be that easy. Of course they've come back. It's what they do.

Edging forward slowly with caution, he bounds forward ready to fight. His stance is sharp and his limbs are tense and stretched out resembling that of a bird, a crane to be exact, one of the ancient Kung Fu animal fighting styles. He is met by immediate relief and drops his guard returning to a normal stance. Standing at the kitchenette, Burt puts a tea bag from an old square tin into a mug and was in mid pour with the kettle when... "Burt!" Thomas chortles shaking his head.

"I thought you were a burglar!"

"Oh, good morning, son!" Burt says turning around to greet him with that infectious smile of his.

"I was just going to make you a cup of Joe."

"You startled me. Why are you here so early?" Thomas enquires.

"I didn't sleep too well last night. Some nights are hard and I still miss Doris I guess. The loneliness is the hardest." He sighs adding a touch of milk to his tea and flicking the spoon around the cup rapidly in an anticlockwise turn until turning the desired colour.

"Oh!" Thomas' heart sank and he felt for Burt.

"So I thought I'd come on over and annoy you!" he beamed.

"So do you want some coffee?"

"No, Burt actually I'm just heading out for my morning run. But I won't be long, you're more than welcome to stay?"

"Yeah sure, I'll set the chess board up for your return."

"Sounds great, Burt!" Thomas smiles and heads for the door.

"You really going out in those things?" Burt laughs pointing at his overly bright running shoes.

"Yeah? Why?"

"Bit out there aren't they?"

"I guess so!" Thomas laughs.

"See you soon!" heading out into a city that was still half asleep, rubbing its eyes and scratching at its unwanted erection. Thomas keeps a steady pace moving out of Montreal, pushing against the gentle fall breeze.

The beauty of running at this time of day is that there aren't many people around. Mainly deliverymen bringing stock to cafe's and food stores, helping them get a head start on their daily chores.

His brightly coloured running shoes fell on the sidewalk firmly with each stride, but hardly made a noise. Thomas was very light on his feet and seemed to glide across the sidewalk.

I can take a detour through the back streets of Hope where I can really flex those parkour muscles. Then through to the park, a couple of laps of that and head back to the church. Maybe even stop off at Perfect Java and grab Burt a doughnut.

A smile caresses his lips as he crosses the road on the corner of 24th street and heads into Hope.

I can't help but smile when I think of him. What a great man he is. Maybe I'll take him out to dinner tonight? See if we can get a table at Nunzio's. It would be nice to listen to some of his Vietnam war stories again.

He slows down and keeps his head on a swivel, seeing if there is anyone around paying attention to him. There's hardly anyone around and those that are going about their business totally oblivious to the jogging priest. He pulls his hood up and turns quickly into an alleyway. He increases his speed and lets rip like a majestic cheetah striding across the plains on the tail of a frantic impala. He steams straight at a large metal dumpster and leaps at it without even a second thought, landing neatly on the lid without so much as a wobble. He does not pause and slow his stride at all before springing up into the air and grabbing the bottom rung of a metal ladder hanging from a zigzagging fire escape. His grip is loose and his hands are only there to guide his body. Using the momentum, he swings like an Olympic gymnast on the uneven bars and jettisons himself into the air feet first before letting go of the rung rotating in the air and landing back down onto his feet and continuing to run. He leaps over trash cans that stand in his way, then somersaults over yet more trash cans topped with trash bags swelling with garbage. He lands low and forward rolls on the dirty floor, before moving up back to his feet and carrying on.

I don't think there is anything more therapeutic than being out in the fresh air alone with your thoughts and just running. I feel so free.

A high steel fence blocks his way but with a quick adjustment of his body, he leaps at one of the walls that the fence is secured to and almost runs up the wall before springing and twisting his body, clearing the fence and lands on the other side of it. He stops for a second, controlling his breathing which was understandably heavy and then just like that, he's off again. Driving forward he bounds up a fire escape heading towards the roof of the building. On the roof Thomas really opens up what he can do. Full speed across the gravelled flooring and bounding, jumping and twisting over various obstacles that stand in his way. He skids to a halt and stands looking out at the city. HIs eyes naturally drawn to the gigantic neon letters that top the Devine Tower.

Something keeps pulling me to that place. Something deep down inside my gut pinches me every time I see that place. But could a place like that really be responsible for the hardships that this city faces every day? Granted, Devine Incorporated have destroyed a portion of the city for their own financial gain, but that's just business isn't it? No, the real ones dragging this place down into the mire are these gangs. Especially this Doomsday Gang! Those are the ones I'll have to bring down first.

The sun rises and paints the sky with its vibrant fiery palette. Thomas takes the time to look on one of God's greatest creations, the sunrise.

Chapter 27

Burt Simmons shuffles along the sidewalk towards Perfect Java. His cane ricocheting off the hard and uneven slabs that lay underfoot. Fellow locals all know Burt and shower him with pleasantries, he throws them a nod or a smile and those further afield a wave. His head was up and down so much he resembled a nodding dog toy, like his head was bouncing around on a spring. He passed Hawtrey's news stand and the two shook hands exchanging pleasantries. Burt purchased a copy of the city's number one grossing newspaper, The Studd.

"See ya later, Charlie!" he says leaving the newsstand and a smiling Charlie. Again, Burt loving he has the knack of making people smile. Burt shuffled into Perfect Java's diner and made for a gap in the long counter that was congested with several customers enjoying various breakfast combinations, some just sipping on steaming hot coffee out of oversized mugs. Waitress Jessica again scuttles around back and forth behind the counter like a bluebottle in a field of manure, unable to settle at one place. Her cheeks were blushed with the crimson tint of aggravation and exasperation, while her father, as always, stood at the far corner of the counter under the hanging television with his cronies giving their unprofessional and probably unwanted opinions on the local sports teams. Jessica makes eye contact with Burt. Her brow rippled under a wave of fluster, her eyes shouted for help, but her mouth said, 'I'll be right with you, Mr Simmons!' while balancing coffee cups and plates of bagels and other delicious breakfast pastries. Burt fired back with a pleasant smile and a wink.

"I'm in no rush, Jess. You do what you got to do, honey." She smiles back at him before dishing out the crockery she's juggling like some awkward vaudeville routine. Burt is spotted by Keith whose face lights up.

"Ah Burt! Come and join us!" he calls gesturing for him to come over with a wave of his hand. Burt makes his way through the very busy diner. A part of him really thinks that Keith should be helping his daughter, instead of examining the defeat of the Studd City Sharks to the Sanctuary City Talons in last night's PBFL's game.

"Hi Keith!"

"Hey, Burt! Just watching the highlights from last night's game."

"Bit busy in here this morning. Think Jess could do with a hand?"

"Breakfast rush." Keith dismisses Burt's plea to help his daughter with the mass of customers. Turning back to the screen nonchalantly, joining in with his cronies all fixated on the screen like a trance has taken hold.

"Sharks lose again I take it?"

"Yeah!" barks a scowling Keith.

"I lost Goddamn money on those pussies again!"

"Maybe you should stop wasting your money!" Burt chuckles.

"Ha! You're probably right."

"They've not been the same team since they lost Reed."

"Yeah, you're right. Damn what a player he was!" Keith shakes his head seemingly reminiscing, maybe playing a best of Desmond Reed montage in his head. Then suddenly, he was snapped back to his conversation with Burt.

"Yeah, that scandal really hurt us. We've never recovered from that."

"WE sure haven't!" Burt chuckled to himself. It always made him laugh when these guys talked about US and WE like they were part of the team.

"He still wasn't the player his old man was!" Burt states propping himself up on one of the empty bar stools with some difficulty, the shrapnel in his thigh the reason for the difficulty in its movement.

"You're damn right, Burt!" Agrees Keith who was immediately surrounded by a group of nodding heads, his fellow sport cronies which was accompanied with a grumble of agreement.

"Did I ever tell you about the time I saw 'Big' Bubba nail that 95 yard touchdown pass to Cottingham? Was back in '79 and..." Burt stopped listening. He liked Keith and he liked sports but there was more to life than that and yes, he had heard this tale of the titans before, only about fifty times before. Burt's gaze was drawn to Jess, hoping that she was ready to serve him, and he could go about his business. But the queue had seemingly some how gotten longer and she was still bouncing around behind the counter like a hyperactive ping pong ball. He looked around at the busy diner, some usual faces were there, faces who he didn't know but saw them every day. The pretty librarian sunk into her usual booth, cappuccino fixed in one hand and a good book in the other. The two detectives on an early dose of black coffee and doughnuts, they've usually been on an all-night stakeout and this is either their supper or they're just waking up and this is their breakfast. Hard to tell some days as they always look haggard and tired. His gaze pans past the window, illuminated with the neon Perfect Java sign flickering in bright pink. A young girl of East Asian persuasion with her hood pulled up over her head had her dirty face pressed up against the window, her breath fogging up the glass, hunger etched into her young face.

Poor girl. I can almost hear the grumbling of her stomach from here. I often get her a little something, if she sticks around long enough that is. She's quite skittish.

His focus stops at the booth straight in front of him and his eyes widen in their wrinkly sockets. He immediately turns back to face Keith, whose lips are still moving but his eyes are fixated on the television. The booth that now resides behind him, homed his arch nemesis Sniff and other Webheads, Dallas and Boris. They hadn't noticed him, and he was lucky for he knew if Sniff saw him, he would make his life a misery as usual. But being the inquisitive old so and so that he is, he couldn't help but hone in and listen to their conversation.

"So, what are we supposed to fucking do now? Just sit around and wait for him to tell us when we can take a shit?" Sniff whines like a petulant child rolling tobacco into blanks.

"You have somewhere better to be?" Boris asks, his mouth full of morning bagel.

"I'm sitting on a shit load of Stardust I need to get rid of!"   "What? You're still dealing that shit? Spider told you that if Valentine finds out that you're dealing with The Vixen, then you're dead! Fuck! We'll all be dead just being associated with your retarded ass!" Dallas says taking a sip of scalding hot coffee.

"Calm your ass, cowboy! I haven't dealt with her since Spider fucked up my face. You think I'm that stupid that I want that to happen again?" Sniff states.
Dallas stops himself from taking another sip.

"You really want me to answer that?" he smirks.

"Fuck you!" Seethes Sniff saluting Dallas with a nicotine stained middle finger. Boris and Dallas erupt in laughter, bagel crumbs escape from Boris' chomping maw.

"Boris! Jesus, Man! You're spitting all over us!" Dallas blasts, picking several chewed up pieces of bagel out of his mug that have found themselves floating on the dark hot surface.

"Sorry!" Boris blushes.

"Anyway, Sniff! If you hadn't of fucked things up with the church, you'd have got rid of that stash weeks ago!" Dallas scalds and on hearing the church mentioned, Burt's eyebrows raise on his crinkled-up forehead, which now resembles the creases in an old sweater. They had his undivided attention.

318

"That wasn't my fault! I didn't know that guy was going to be there did I?" he pleaded, his words falling on deaf ears.

"Well, I'm not going back there again!" Dallas states.

"Me neither!" adds Boris.

"No way am I looking for another ass kicking from a mysterious..." Dallas continues but is interrupted by Boris.

"I still think it was a phantom!" he says spitting yet more crumbs everywhere.

"Yeah Boris, a phantom that knows Karate!" Sniff scoffs.

"Do you have any better ideas of his identity?" Dallas asks sarcastically, already knowing that Sniff doesn't have a clue.

"I don't know!" shrugs Sniff, his attention returning to his cigarette rolling.

"There you go then. It could be haunted a place that old!" Dallas adds.

"Yeah!" Boris nods in agreement.

"Fuck sake!" Sniff shakes his head and then a strange look caresses his uneven face that looks like the texture of an ancient treasure map.

"Maybe it was the priest?"

Dallas and Boris look at him and then look at each other and all of them burst out laughing knowing the absurdity of the statement. Burt looked shocked, his mouth gaping in awe.

Thomas?

Unfortunately for Burt, the sight of his face just excited Keith more, who obviously thought that Burt was listening to his football stories, that he actually started another.

"And then there was that epic try in '83..." but Burt stopped listening again and he tuned in to Webheads radio once more.

"So, where is he? Did he say?" Asked Boris.

"No idea! Somewhere in Forge, but that's all I know." Says Dallas.

"He said he'd let me know when it was go time."

"So, we're really going ahead with this?" gulps Boris out of fear and swallowing his bagel.

"Yeah, this is it!"

"I can't believe he got The Coyote on side, man! That guy is a lunatic!" said Sniff, his tacky blackish tongue sliding across his cigarette paper sealing it in place.

"Well, who else hates Valentine as much as Spider. It's the only way we're gonna bring him down. He'll never see it coming! But until then we have to wait. I got the feeling it may be a week or so." Said Dallas.

"What will be a week or so?" came the voice of Detective Graham who had just joined them at their booth. Burt looked slyly over his shoulder and saw Detective's Graham and Freeman standing over them.

"Oh shit Detective, nothing. Just chewing the fat that's all!" Dallas said smiling at the Detectives.

"That so?" nods Graham sliding next to Boris in the booth as Freeman stood next to Dallas to stop any escape the Texan might be planning. Sniff was trapped, sandwiched by Dallas and the diner window, so he isn't even bothered, he just carried on rolling his cigarettes.

"We've been looking for you guys." Graham states ripping a chunk out of Boris' bagel and launching it into his mouth.

"Oh yeah? Well, I don't know why, we ain't done nothing!"

"Yeah, I know." Graham chews.

"We know you haven't been up to much lately because we caught up with a friend of yours." Freeman added.

"Oh yeah? Who's that then?" Dallas asks.

"Jack 'Twitch' Thompson. You know Jack, right?" Freeman asks but is met by a table full of shaking heads.

"Never heard of him." Dallas adds.

"Oh really!" Says Graham.

"Well he knows you. You know what he said about you guys?"

"Surprise me!"

"Nothing." Graham smiles.

"Nothing?" asks Boris confused.

"Yeah nothing, comrade! He said that you guys had been off the radar for a while, haven't been putting much in the Doomsday piggy bank lately. He said you guys hadn't even been in touch to pick up your stash." Graham stated.

"New leaf." Shrugged Dallas.

The two Detectives laughed.

"Yeah sure!" Freeman nodded sarcastically.

"They reckon you guys are planning something." He added.

"Oh really? Like what?" Dallas enquires sipping on his coffee, trying hard not to make eye contact with them. He knew that these guys were like living breathing lie detectors and would know by just the wrong twitch of an eye.

"He doesn't know, just a theory Valentine has, I hear." Graham says.

"Well, like I said we ain't up to anything, we've just been chillin'."

"Oh, I know you haven't been up to anything! I told Twitch that didn't I Rich?" Graham says looking over at Freeman who answers with a simple "Yep!" Graham looks back at Dallas.

"I know because what the hell could you four fuckwits pull off? You guys couldn't pull your own dicks! Especially that nut sack over there!" gesturing at Sniff who doesn't even look up.

"We all know that Spider pulls your strings. Heck I bet you guys can't even take a shit without his say so!"
Sniff sniggers, thinking back to his earlier Spider's shit approval statement.

"Something funny pencil neck?" Growls Graham.

"Nothing." Murmurs Sniff.

"Like what's floating around in your head! I'm gonna ask you guys this once and once only. Where is Spider?"

"We honestly don't know." Dallas chortles to himself looking Graham in the eyes for the first time in the conversation.

"Lying piece of shit!" Freeman says nudging Dallas' head with the palm of his hand.

"No, Rich!" Graham grins.

"He's actually telling the truth. Aren't ya?"

"Yep!" Dallas smiles back.

"Well then, we'll let you boys enjoy the rest of your breakfast." Graham says rising from his seat and turns to leave before pounding his fists down on the table, making Boris jump out of his pale Eastern European skin and spilling Dallas' coffee in the process.

"If you hear from Spider tell him we would like a little chat!" and with a sadistic smile, Graham grabs a handful of the cigarettes Sniff had been rolling and crunches them up in his grip.

"Don't fuck with me, boys!" he whispers.

"If I find out that you guys know where he is and you don't tell me, well, you'll be going to Skelter with him!" he lets go of the cigarettes and the broken and bent butts fall onto the table, useless.

"See ya around!" Graham says and the Detectives leave.

The three huddle together and the voices can no longer be heard by Burt, he zones back into Keith's conversation.

"...and boy what a tackle that was! Must have been '75... No wait I'm wrong it was '77..."

"Mister Simmons!" calls Jess, her face flustered and her brow carrying a thin layer of sweat but a smile awaits him, and he can see the breakfast rush is over.

"I'd love to stay and chat Keith, but I've gotta get moving."

"Hey, no problem, Burt! Always nice to have a trip down nostalgia boulevard with a fellow sports nut." He grins an

323

uneven smile topped by his paintbrush like moustache, thick and streaked with various shades of grey.

"Yeah!" smiles Burt and as he turns to face Jess he adds, "It was actually '79."

"Was it really?" questions Keith, creases of confusion furrowing across his bald head as his old cogs turn rapidly inside.

"Yep! It was the year The Sharks won the Premier Bowl."

"Of course it was!" laughed Keith clapping his hands together and turning to his cronies.

"Does he know his football or what!"

"Sorry about your wait, Mr Simmons. What can I get ya this morning?" Jess asks.

"Well, to start with you can call me Burt! I keep telling you that!" he winks.

"Mr Simmons was my Father."

"Okay, I'm sorry." She smiles.

"What can I get ya, Burt?"

"Two coffees to go. One black, one with cream and sugar."

"Sure!" she turns to the mass of coffee making machinery that stands behind her, steam rising from parts of it and making all kinds of noises like an asthmatic steam train.

"Oh, and I'll take one of your custard filled doughnuts too please."

"No problem!" she says while the coffee slurps into a takeout cup, the Perfect Java logo printed around it.

"Oh wait!" he says which gets her attention and he turns to face him. Burt turns to the window, but the little homeless teen has gone, leaving behind just a face print on the glass.

"Will there be anything else?"

"Oh! Sorry Jess! No, not today."

"Okay. There you go!" she says with a smile sliding the cardboard cup holder towards him with the two hot coffees slotted in place and the doughnut hidden in a paper bag on top of the remaining open sections. Burt retrieves his wallet and fingers the notes between his stubby fingertips. Jess leans over and puts her hands gently on top of his and whispers.

"This is on the house!" she winks at him and smiles a gentle smile, before calling out to another waiting customer.

"What can I get ya?"

What a lovely girl.

Burt makes for the exit and starts his trip back to the church.

Well, Thomas what have you been up to. We do indeed have lots to talk about.

Chapter 28

The Graham's bedroom curtains drawn in the middle of the day could be classified as suspicious. Maybe Detective Graham was working very late and he was treating himself to an overlong sleep. Maybe Mae was feeling under the weather and wrapped up in the bedcovers? Or it could be possible that there had sadly been a bereavement in the family and as it has become accustomed, they have drawn the curtains to indicate that they are grieving and do not wish to be disturbed. None of these explanations are true. As the midday sunlight slices through the gap in the curtains, it casts a spotlight on the bedroom's proceedings. The thick duvet cover is draped over several quivering lumps and bumps, like a living breathing mountain range. The cover is thrown back to reveal Sidney Graham and his wife entwined in the sensual vines of amore. Their naked bodies writhing rhythmically together in unison like a bow drawing across the strings of a violin, creating their own intimate music. Their naked skin is moist with perspiration from the sweat that seeps from their pores. Mae groans with pleasure as Sid thrusts vigorously, her legs wrapping themselves around his bare backside constricting like a python not wanting him to escape, (not that he would want to). She sinks her fingers into his freckle covered back so firmly that it leaves behind red indentations on his pale flesh. Sid grunts as his pelvis thrusts away like a piston, the couple wearing very different expressions. Mae's eyes closed, her head tipped back and buried in a cavern of soft duck feathers that are homed in the pillow, she bites her bottom lip and groans with excitement. Sid stares at her face, his eyes wide open, concentration stamped on his face as sweat drips down his brow. He pants heavily trying with all his might to continue a charade that seemed like a great idea when he returned home early from work (for a change) around twenty minutes ago.

C'mon you bastard. Don't you go limp on me now!

He pushes again, trying to focus and keep it going but who is he kidding? He's done, it isn't going to happen.

"Oh, fuck it!" Shouts Sid as he pulls his retreating penis from his wife's eager moist orifice. He kneels on the bed his head dropping in embarrassment, his flaccid penis flopping onto his thigh, exhausted and lifeless.

"What's wrong?" Mae asks, concern forcing its way through her stammered breathing.

"I... I can't... I'm just having a bit of trouble." He says sheepishly, like a cloud of embarrassment and guilt is raining down on him. Mae sits up kneeling adjacent to him and plants a caring and tender hand on his thigh.

"Do you want to talk about it?"

"No!" he snaps, still unable to look at her. Mae recoils from the venomous strike, feeling a little useless and vulnerable herself now. She wraps her arms around her drooping breasts. Immediately Sid wishes he could take that back, he looks at her for the first time with sorrow in his eyes.

"I'm sorry, Mae. I didn't mean to shout." He taps her hand and holds it tightly and this time looks her straight in her eyes, the first time he's really been able to do that for weeks.

"This isn't your fault. None of it!"

"It's okay, Sid. This doesn't make you any less of a man in my eyes." Mae smiles tenderly stroking his cheek with her hand. He smiles too and kisses her hand.

"You're a wonderful woman Mae and I don't deserve you." A tear wells up in his eye and blurs his vision before he quickly wipes it away with the back of his hand.

"What are you talking about?"

"You deserve better than me. You're better off without me!"

"Don't be silly! What kind of talk is that?" she shakes her head dismissing his outlandish statements.

"Look I've been..." But Mae interrupts him by leaning towards him and kissing him softly, before kneeling back down.

"You're not listening to me, Mae!"

"What are you trying to say?"

"I... don't know."

"Look I'm sure this happens to every guy sometime or another. It's no big deal."

"No big deal!"

"Okay, I didn't mean to put it like that. That wasn't very tactful, I'm sorry. But I just mean, it doesn't bother me, it doesn't make me love you any less."

"Mae...I..."

"Look it's okay, you've been under a lot of stress lately. I understand the pressure you're under at work. I get it!"

"No, it's not that, I..."

Tell her that you think you've fallen for someone else you fucking pussy!

"I... I think I'm..."

A coward! That's what you are!

She caresses his thighs and kisses him again, the rough bristles of his beard do little to halt Mae's advances, besides he's had the goatee for about 15 years now, so she's used to it. Sid gently pushes her away.

"Mae, please I need to tell you this!"

She kneels looking at him through confused and concerned eyes, naked as the day she was born. Her pale sweaty skin glistens in the light that peeks in through the gaping curtain like some peeping Tom.

"Okay!" she answers waiting patiently on what her husband has to say.

"I'm all ears." Her cascading red hair as never looked so full and luscious. She looked so innocent, yet so animalistic and wild, raw, her hand continued to gently rub his hairy thigh as Sid stared at her.

Look at her. She looks absolutely beautiful. What an amazing woman she is! And you want to throw all that away? You want to fuck that all up don't ya? Idiot! Her innocence is beautiful it truly is, but you can see in her eyes she wants to finish where you left off. She so desperately wants to make love. And you pick this moment when she is open to you and vulnerable,

naked of everything not just clothes. And you want to tell her
that you want to trade her in for a newer model with less miles
on the clock and a better chassis. That you want to fuck Valerie
Nash.

"I think I want..."

You'll destroy her.

"To have another go by the look of things!" She interrupts with a playful wide eyed expression on her face.

Sid looks down to see his erect penis now towering out of his auburn nest of pubic hair, ready willing and able.

Where did that come from? Did that happen because of Mae or
because I was thinking of...

"Oh..." he says surprising himself. But before he can say another word she leans in again and passionately kisses him, her hand gripping his manhood firmly. The two become enthralled in an animalistic show of passion. They claw at each other, Sid grabbing at her breast and gnawing at her neck as she vigorously rubs his penis. As they passionately kiss each other, she straddles him and rapidly gyrates on him, arching her back to allow Sid to grasp her breasts with his hands and lose his face in between them, kissing and sucking her firm nipples and then licking them with his tongue and moving up the slender arch of her swan like neck, then into wet tongue lead kisses. She arches again and pushes against him faster and faster, and now groaning and moaning in ecstasy as she reaches the pinnacle of orgasmic pleasure. She shrieks and slows her gyrating down, but she still wants him, continuing to kiss him again passionately.

"Oh, Sid... Oh God, that was amazing!" she pants, still riding him slowly now and she kisses him around his neck.

"I don't think I can come." He says also breathing heavily. She climbs off him and starts to rub his penis again with her grip tighter this time and kisses him, her eyes open staring into his.

"Just concentrate on me." She says still working his penis.

They stare at each other and Sid feels his penis throbbing in her sweaty palm and for a moment closes his eyes, he opens them again and sees Valerie in front of him, his eyes grow wide and she kisses him. He closes his eyes again and opens them to see Mae again, her hand rubbing faster and faster up and down his shaft.

"Okay... I think I can..." He says and again he sees Valerie, he closes his eyes once more and shakes away the vision. Mae lets go and turns around kneeling on all fours in front of him, knowing that this particular sexual position was his favourite and obviously hoping it will get the job done. She arches her lower back to push her bottom towards him, he caresses her pale bouncy cheeks with his hand. She then turns to look at him over her shoulder and it's Valerie's face again.

"You can do it, Detective."

Without a second thought he ploughs into her and after several rapid thrusts he ejaculates in a roar of aggressive euphoria.

You fucking bastard!

Chapter 29

The city park is situated in the centre of Studd City, with entrances and exits to it from various places such as Hays Pier, Napoli, St. Patricks, Royale and Butterworth. Also, within a stones throw of several El Rail stops including a main station in Alexandrea which can connect to the neighbouring Forge City, using the coast to coast bridge that spans the whole of the Hennig River and leads into Forge's central station, Monsoon.

It was a lovely summery afternoon, which for this time of year was very unexpected but by the mass of people that were there, they found it thoroughly enjoyable. The luscious, freshly cut grass looked extraordinarily green for the fall, and trees that did keep their leaves throughout this time of year looked majestic and thriving in the warm glow of the sun. It's amazing how something so delightful and colourful could be found in such a mundane cluster of concrete and glass in dreary shades of grey. Small children even frolicked about in the park's quaint pond, splashing around and making the most of this Indian summer. Lurking in the shade of a gigantic elm are three familiar faces, but look out of place in such an idyllic and picturesque setting. Sniff lies on the grass, hood up to conceal his greasy matted hair and even greasier looking complexion as several rings of smoke leave his foul-smelling maw rising into the sky, like smoke signals in some old western movie. Dallas sits up against the trunk of the elm, eyes closed and enjoying taking in the weather, even chewing on a bit of grass, maybe reminiscing of a childhood spent in the warm climate of his home, Texas. Boris looks glum, trying his best to hide from the suns warm affections, but trying to keep his mind occupied by sucking on an orange and pineapple flavoured *Koko Pop* drink. The sound of him slurping up through the straw like a plumber unblocking a drain had started to grate on Dallas.

"Can you give it a rest with that, Boris?" Dallas groans.

"What?" Answers the ever deluded Boris.

"For fuck sake, man!" Dallas seethes, an eye opening up and cutting in his direction.

"You sound like you're in a Goddamn Barbie Butkus movie!"

"I don't know what you mean?" Boris says looking on confused.

"He means you sound like you're sucking a dick!" Sniff grunts before sniggering.

"Fuck you both!" Grumbles Boris, now reluctant to go back to his cool beverage. He looks at it and tries to slowly and quietly suck on the straw, but again comes that gross wet slurp and then the quick chirp of 'Suck a dick!' From Sniff, every time he tries until Boris gives up and disposes of the cup emblazoned with the Franken-Burger logo on it onto the floor. Dallas and Sniff laugh at him and he grumbles something in his native tongue and leans up the tree petulantly looking in the other direction.

"I tell you one thing..." Sniff starts "...Spider's time keeping doesn't get any better" A shadow is cast over Dallas and Sniff along with a familiar voice.

"Oh yeah? I'm fucking early according to my watch"
They look up to see Spider standing before them. His dreadlocked hair uncharacteristically tied back and a Studd City Sharks baseball cap sitting on his head along with a pair of sunglasses.

"Spider!" Calls Dallas rising from his resting place at the base of the elm and greeting him with a touch of the knuckles.

"Okay, okay, quieten it down, bro!" Spider shushes the excitable Dallas who had obviously missed his best friend.

"Incognito you know?" he adds lowering his sunglasses and winking at him.
Boris quickly joins them, but Sniff remains exactly where he is.

"Where have you been, Spider?" Boris asks, a mixture of concern and annoyance in his voice.

"Cool it big man, I'm here now that's all that matters." The two touch knuckles.

"What have you been up to, Boris?"

"Sucking dick." Sniff adds.

"Fuck you!" Boris snaps back.
Spider scowls over at Sniff, who hasn't even bothered to get up to meet their leader, and Spider nonchalantly greets him with "Sniff!" Sniff holds his hand up in the air and waves before returning to his ring blowing. Spider can feel the anger train raging up the tracks towards his brain, but he is able to derail it momentarily knowing that he has more important things on his

mind now.

I'll deal with you another time you fucking piss ant!

"So, what's going on? When is this shit going down? Did you see The Coyote? Did they fuck with you?" All at once everything oozes out of Dallas' mouth like misshapen beef passing through a meat grinder, spewing out at Spider's feet.

"Okay man, calm down!" Spider says trying to control the conversation.

"Yo, The Coyote is a slick mother fucker, man, but he's cool."

"So, is he in?" Boris asks.

"You bet your fucking life he's in!" Smiles Spider.

"He fucking hates Valentine with a passion! He would do anything to see the old bastard go down."

"So, they were cool with you?" Dallas adds, trying not to sound too concerned about his friend's wellbeing but failing miserably.

"Yeah man! No problem!" He nonchalantly starts before becoming a little more cordial.

"Well... you know they fucked with me a little to start with, you know?" he laughs trying to sound like he was cool with it all.

"But I expected as much, you know? Besides when he heard that I want to give him Valentine's head, he was putty in my hands, bro!"

"So, everything is cool?" Dallas asked

"Yeah, it's cool! We even talked about working with each other when I'm in charge. You know, ending all that gang

335

warfare bullshit. If we work together we can make more than Valentine ever dreamed of man, I tell ya!"

"Yeah!" laughs Sniff, "Like that's gonna happen!"
Spider seethes and for a second, he can feel the wheels on that anger train starting to slowly grind on the rail again.

"You got something to say?" He growls at Sniff.

"Only that The Coyote won't work with you!" He laughs again "He won't work with any Doomsdayers! As soon as that fucker has seen Big Vinnie fall, he'll take us out too! It'll be all out war!"

"Fuck you, Sniff!" Spider growls at him.

"You've never met the guy, what the fuck would you know about it? I know what I know! Okay?"

"Yeah man, whatever you say. I'm cool with anything you wanna do anyways." Sniff says as yet more smoke rings leave his mouth and evaporate. Spider shakes his head and turns his attention back to Boris and Dallas.

"Anyway, he's in. All I have to do is set it up." Says Spider.

"We have a week to come up with a plan to lure the old bastard into the trap!"

"Where we gonna do this?" Boris asks.

"It's gonna go down at Ventura Bridge."

"Easy for La Familia to make their grand unexpected entrance I guess." Dallas nods.

"You got it, Dal. We reel him in and when he thinks he has got the upper hand, WHAMMO! Here comes the cavalry. It can't fail!"

"What if you can't lure old Vinnie?" Sniff adds.

Just the sound of his voice grinds so many of Spider's gears now, a part of him wishing he hadn't stopped hitting him that night.

"That won't be a problem. The guy's ego is so big that if I confront him and challenge him then he'll have to. He'll want to make an example of me and show his followers what a big man he is."

"And what if The Coyote does turns on us?" Dallas enquires.

"Well, if that happens, and I don't think it will!" cutting seething eyes in Sniff's direction for putting the thought in everyone's head.

"I guess we will have to deal with it. Boris! You'll be in charge with watching our backs after it kicks off."

"No problem!" agrees Boris.

"I gotta go. Still trying to stay low, you know?"

"Yeah, don't we know it. We've had the pigs sniffing round after you." Dallas informs him.

"Why?"

"That stolen car!"

"Ah shit, yeah, definitely have to stay low then. Don't want to get picked up now, it would ruin everything."

"Twitch has been asking where you are too. I think he smells a rat." Boris adds.

"Oh, fuck him! Tell him my mother is sick or something!" Spider says slipping his sunglasses back on .

"I'll be in touch."

And with that they all go their separate ways into the

wonderment of the sunny day, maybe the last good weather Studd will see this year. Sniff is left alone on the grass, staring up at the sky through a Marijuana fuelled haze.

"Suck a dick."

Chapter 30

Joyous laughter bursts out from table number seven and carries through Nunzio's restaurant, on a busy night, not full but busy all the same. Thomas and Burt sit at the table, their faces aching from all the laughing as they tuck into their delicious spaghetti and meatballs. Momma's recipe still being used all these years later, it's always in such demand, it would be a shame if the recipe and its secret died with Nunzio. The dull old lighting paints them in an amber light giving them both a metallic look to them, almost like two robots. Table seven sits against the wall with the 8 x 10's of Sean Connery, Christopher Lee, Tim Curry, Margaret Rutherford and Gene Kelly, all staring at the pair consuming their meal.

"Sergeant Blackman made him march with one boot for the rest of the week!"

"You do make me laugh, Burt. You really do!" chuckles Thomas wiping his teary eyes with his napkin.

"I just say it like I see it!" he replies, chuckling to himself. His demeanour changes suddenly and he looks sad, the kind of sadness you see on a scalded dog or a child who has just dropped their ice-cream on the floor. Thomas' heart always rose into his throat when he saw that look on Burt's old weathered face.

"It wasn't all confetti and rainbows though, I wish it was. I saw one of my best friends die out there. Not just die...be blown up! Those type of things stay with you forever, even with how hard you try to shake them, they're still there lingering like a bad smell."

"I understand, Burt." Thomas says in a sincere caring tone.

"Do you?" Burt bites a little.

"I don't think you can ever understand something like that unless you have seen it first hand, unless you have lived it!"

"The mind can be cruel. Like a sponge that soaks up all the hurt, the pain, the danger and suffering. Soaks it all up and then sits there refusing to be rung out."

Burt looks up at Thomas and they make eye contact. Burt can see in his eyes that he knows. He knows what Burt feels, he too has seen the dark dastardly deeds of man. Thomas carries on.

"No matter how hard you wring out that sponge, you can never get it completely dry can you? Meaning you can never forget, you can never truly move on, it's always just... there."

"Very true, Thomas. Very true. That is exactly how I feel. But how do you... What things could your young eyes have possibly seen to make an analogy like that?"

As Thomas' head drops slightly as he pushes a large rotund meatball around in the sauce with his fork. Burt immediately tries to take back his prying questioning.

"Oh, Thomas, I am sorry. I should not pry into your affairs. Please just forget I ever said anything." Thomas smiles at him and there is a moment of awkward silence, the sort that rears its ugly head between two young teenagers on a first date. The silence seems to go on for several minutes but in fact only 30 seconds had passed in reality, but the sound of Nunzio shouting something in Italian comes booming from the kitchen. A cascade of quiet chuckling sweeps over the restaurant, all the customers knowing what a character the owner is.

"When I was a child, my father used to beat me." Announces Thomas. Burt closes his eyes and inside his old heart cracks a little. Thomas' words are like a small metal hammer tapping away at a block of toffee. Burt's eyes open glazed with a thin layer of moisture, he slowly places his knife and fork on the table and listens intently at what Thomas has to say, he had Burt's undivided attention.

"I...I..." Thomas tries.

"It's okay, Thomas. You don't have to do this."

"No, I want to, Burt!"

"Very well. In your own time."

"We lived in a broken down trailer, my mother, father and me. My father had lost his job and was angry at the man, everything was the fault of the man, never his fault! I would love to say that my father was a nice guy when he didn't have a drink inside him. I would love to tell you that we played all manner of games and had some many joyful times until he lost his job and he hit the bottle. I would love to say that, but it would be a lie. I can honestly never remember a time when he didn't have alcohol in his system."

"The devils brew, Thomas. It never leads to anything good!" Burt said.

"He beat me for anything and everything. I was damned if I did and damned if I didn't. A part of me wishes that I had rebelled a little and got under his skin, heck, if I was going to get a beating anyway I might as well do something to make it worthwhile right? But I was...I'm not like that, I could never bring myself to do anything, besides I was terrified of him. Terrified of my own father." Thomas shakes his head still not being able to believe that a child could grow up in such an environment. In such a world where a child doesn't have the love and affection of his father. Thomas removed his glasses and rubbed the tip of his finger across the scar on his eyebrow.

"You see this?" Thomas asks and is met by a nod from Burt.   "He did this to me on my fifth birthday because I spilt his beer!"
Burt shakes his head in disbelief, his nose wrinkling a little in anger but calms himself.

"And what about your Mama? How did she cope?" Burt asked.

"She didn't. He beat her too. Actually, she took worse beatings than me because she used to stand up for me and try and go toe to toe with him. I guess she wasn't very bright in that regard. Even when she was pregnant he still beat her. The man has no conscience."

"What happened to them?"

"My mama is dead..."

"Did he..." Burt reluctantly manages, not really able to bring himself to ask the full sentence.

"No... well, in a roundabout way I guess you could say he

did. He drove her to it. She had started to take drugs to obviously block everything out. Nothing too full on, just prescription pills but I don't suppose that could have been good for the baby growing inside her. She locked herself in the bathroom one night after one particular blazing row that left her with a split lip. Sadly, she took an overdose and died on the bathroom floor."

"Oh, that is terrible!" Burt sighed.

"I found her lying there and even at such a young age I knew to call for an ambulance. That is memory that I would love to forget... seeing her lying there like that...dead!"

"And what about the baby?"

"I was told that they gave her a Caesarean, but it was too late, there was nothing they could do. Was a boy too!" He smiled.

"Would have been nice to have had a little brother."

"That's such a tragic story Thomas, I'm so very sorry."

"Oh, if only that were the end of it, Burt!"

Nunzio shuffles over to their table.

"Hey, Burt! Haven't seen you in a while!" He grins slapping Burt on the back and almost causing him to have an extreme closeup of his spaghetti and meatballs.

"Hi, Nunzio! How's it going?"

"Bene, Bene!" Nunzio nods in his thick Italian accent.

"Business is ticking over you know?"

"That's good!" Burt smiles.

"Who's your friend?" Nunzio asks grinning at Thomas.

"Thomas, Father Thomas Gabriel!" Thomas smiles and

puts his hand out for Nunzio to shake it which he does in a rugged vigorous handshake, and a grip that could choke a chicken.

"Hey, you must be the new priest up at St. Vincent's, Yeah?"

"Yes, I am!"

"Bene, Bene, I'll have to come down and catch a Sunday sermon. I haven't been to church since I lost my Rosa. The big man upstairs hasn't been in my good books you see!"

"Well, if you ever want someone to come and talk too about it, my door is always open." Thomas adds.

"Hey, thanks Father! You know I just might do that!" he beams.

"You, enjoying your meal?"

"Oh yes!" Thomas nods.

"Bene! Momma's secret recipe!" He says winking before laughing and moving on to the next table.

"What a character that Nunzio is!" Grins Burt.

"He sure is!" agrees Thomas goring his last meatball with his fork and slotting it into his mouth. Silence shrouds the table again as they both finish chewing.

"Death is a hard thing to get over, no matter how hard we try. Try to move on, try to forget. You can't. Not a day goes by that I don't think about Doris." Burt says.

"I think that's healthy though Burt. It's better than bottling things up. Remembering the good times and talking about those happy memories brings the pleasant thoughts to the forefront of your mind. It trains your brain that when you think

344

of the person that you have lost, instead of being sad and feeling down, you have replaced it with a happy memory."

"What are you, a shrink?" Burt laughs.

"It sounds like you've had some counselling yourself there."

"Well yeah, kind of."

"Oh, I am sorry I don't mean that to come out like that. I'm not making fun of you!"

"No not at all! Had a lot of counselling as a child for what I had seen when I was put into the orphanage, but I've also had a very good teacher that has taught me the importance of mindfulness which I have learnt to almost master through meditation!"

"Almost?"

"It's quite tough to put a positive spin on some of the things I've seen." Thomas laughs.

"Yeah, I'll give it a try when I start thinking about Doris. Don't know whether it will rid me of those ghosts from back in Vietnam, but I'll give it a shot."

Thomas smiles at him.

"Do you want dessert?" Burt asks.

"No, I shouldn't. I had that doughnut you brought me earlier. Have too many of those and it stops becoming a treat!"

"Too true!" Burt laughs in agreement. Burt holds his hand up and gestures to the waiter who just happens to be passing. The waiter nods at him and heads towards the cash register.

"It's been a lovely meal, Burt."

The waiter brings over the bill on a silver platter and places it on the table.

"Your bill gentlemen. Thank you and I hope you enjoyed your meal." The waiter said in a pleasant but robotic way, he'd probably said that about fifty times today. He is thanked by Burt and Thomas and the waiter leaves to give them the privacy while sorting out the money for the bill. Burt dives into the inner pocket of his tweed sports jacket looking for his wallet.

"No, Burt!"

"What?"

"I'm paying for this!" Thomas insists revealing his own wallet and sifting through various values of dollar bills.

"No, I've got it, it's fine."

"No Burt, I insist on paying. You've helped me enough and this is my way of saying thank you for making me feel so welcome on returning... I mean on coming to Studd City." Thomas blushes knowing that he has let slip something that he may not have wanted to and Burt who is a smart old fox knows. Thomas looks into his wallet to not make eye contact with Burt and places the money with a decent sized tip on the platter and stands.

"How about we go back to the church for a quick game of chess?"

"You're on, Thomas!"

They walk out in silence, buy giving gestures of goodbyes to the waiter and Nunzio. Outside the warm day has turned into a nice evening and still holding onto that unexpected warmth as long as it can. The two walk slowly together down the sidewalk until

Burt speaks. Thomas is adamant that he is going to ask about him being in Studd City before, but he doesn't.

"So, what happened to your father?" Burt asks.

"Oh!" Thomas replies taken aback and not expecting that particular question.

"He's in prison."

"Best place for him!" Burt seethes, "Oh, no offence!"

"None taken, that's exactly where he deserves to be."

"What is he in for? Neglect? Grievous bodily harm?"

"Murder!" Thomas says. This stops Burt in his tracks.

"Murder?"

They carry on walking again

"A care worker came around to the trailer one day to take me. She had a legal document to take me away and he was going to be arrested for the violence. She came with the sheriff and my father did not want to go quietly. He was of course loaded up and he hit the sheriff in the nose and drove a cork screw into her throat. She died right there in front of me."

"I don't know what to say, Thomas!" Burt shakes his head, "The things you have seen. You must be haunted everyday!"

"I try not to be. Like I say the meditation and mindfulness helps. Plus having something to focus on helps a lot, like the goal I want to achieve while being here in Studd City."

"Which is?"

"Helping the people of this city by embracing the word of God and rebuilding this community that has been bullied for way too long."

"I see!" Burt grins, "Nothing to do with beating up Doomsday Gang members then?"

Thomas' eyes grow wide and he looks at Burt who winks at him.

"I don't know what you mean, Burt!" Thomas lies.

"Yes you do. I heard our mutual friend discussing what had happened to them the last time they stopped by the church."

"I...Oh no!" Thomas' head dropped, was the game up before it had even started?

"Don't worry they don't know it was you. So, what do you have planned then? They mention some kind of martial art was used. Karate?"

"Kung Fu. Shaolin Kung Fu."

"Impressive!" Burt nods, "So, you want to be some kind of neighbourhood watchman or something?"

"I guess!" Thomas laughs, "Something like that."

"Okay!" Burt agrees.

"You're not going to call the clergy and have me removed?"

"The way I see it by ridding our streets of those cockroaches is a public service and something the big man upstairs would agree on I'm sure."

"I won't get you involved in it Burt, I promise."

"Like hell you won't! I'm in!"

"What?"

"You heard me. I want in on this! It's about time someone stood up and made a stand for this city."

"I don't know what to say Burt!"

"You can start by telling me the whole story. The true story!"

"What do you mean?"

"I mean about your 'Return' to Studd City." Burt smiles that award-winning smile.

Chapter 31

The illuminating glow of Studd City's red light district stands by its name bathing all that pass through it in sickly vibrant neon. Roma had always been the boil on the backside of Studd City, that area that people don't like to admit is there. But it is there, boy is it ever and oh how it's grown. Unfortunately, with Studd City falling out of favour, seemingly with every other state in the United States, nobody wanted to come there anymore and ironically Studd City became the boil on the backside of America, no longer having anything to offer, saw it fall into decay. That's when crime started to increase and the downward spiral span out of control. Things looked bleak until Billionaire entrepreneur and property tycoon, Robert Devine arrived in Studd City. His cash injection was just what the city needed, but unfortunately the finances only seem to be flowing in a certain direction and the places that really needed it are being overlooked and falling into ruin. Roma's despicable lifestyle had spread like leprosy with more gentleman's clubs, massage parlours and adult cinemas popping up like toadstools, and causing its cancer to infect brother and sister areas. In a way, Roma cannot be blamed for it as it is just mirroring the society in which it inhabits, a scab will always grow on a wound. One of the most popular clubs in Roma is called 'Masquerades' which if you believe the online reviews, is apparently 'a classy and refined establishment with the best Burlesque experience in Studd City'. The place is owned and managed by the very hands, on Beatrix Roux. Her stage name is Maîtresse Masquerade.

On this particular evening the club has a very important guest, one that is on the guest list of every club in Studd City, Vinnie Valentine. In the alley at the rear exit of the club is parked a majestic classic 1969 Cadillac painted in a luscious black, shinning like the texture of treacle. The personal licence plate reading VV1 in chunky embossed letters, screaming out that this is Valentine's pride and joy. Ironically it is parked right underneath a no parking sign, but because of who he is, Maîtresse Masquerade allows him to park his princess there, no questions asked. In the constant neon flash of lights, a figure passes quickly and quietly around to the front of the Cadillac. As the scarlet letters of Masquerades pulse again the figure is revealed to be Spider. He takes out a flick knife and activates the blade. It gleams pinkish in the light and smiles a devilish smile like an unruly child who is up to no good.

"No turning back now." He says to himself, "It's about time you fucking got yours Valentine!"

He takes the knife and without a second thought, he slashes it across the car's hood. The blade slices through the paintwork exposing its ugliness, the hard-rugged metal shell that hides beneath its expensive paint job. With several vigorous flicks of his wrist and accompanied by a hideous soundtrack of metallic carving, Spider's name appeared on the hood of Valentine's prize 1969 Cadillac.

"Now that's a fucking work of art right there!" Spider smiles "Some Rembrandt shit!" He slots the blade safely back into its pearl handle and slides it back into the deep pocket of his baggy jeans. He looks at his handy work, suddenly his face is brushed with contemplation, has he made a mistake? Does he think he has gone too far? No, he is merely conspiring with his conscience to do yet more dark deeds.

"I think it's too dark!" he says delving into his rear pocket and retrieving a can of spray paint, A bright pristine white.

"Need to brighten this sum bitch up!" He vigorously shakes the can, probably mirroring what is happening across the road at the XXX cinema as horny delinquents pleasure themselves to some sordid explicit porno on the large screen. Covering his nose and mouth with his bandanna with one hand he unleashes the contents of the can in the direction of the vintage automobile. His penmanship is poor, not that his calligraphy with the flick knife was any better, but this was juvenile. The words 'Pussy', 'Asshole' and 'Fag' find their way onto the once luscious paintwork, smudging and dripping as Spider quickly goes into a tirade of violent blasts with the can, before discarding it into the floor. The metallic sound of the can as it bounces on the concrete floor and rolls into a corner, was not what he needed for it draws the attention of the doorman standing at the edge of the alleyway, policing the front entrance of the club. Out the corner of his eye, Spider notices the silhouette of a large male block out the lights from the street.

"Shit!" he whispers to himself and ducks down behind the car. Luckily, it's dark in the alleyway with lots of shadows to hide oneself. The doorman walks a few steps slowly into the alleyway and is bathed in the glow for a moment of the club's neon sign, revealing an intimidating sight indeed. A large man stands in a black suit with a black turtleneck sweater worn underneath, but the most startling thing about this doorman was that he was wearing a latex gimp mask tightly gripping his misshapen skull. This wasn't compulsive to wear, it was not part of his uniform, he just always wore it and nobody but Maîtresse Masquerade knew his true identity. He was known to all as Plugg.

"Who's there?" Plugg called into the darkness, the neon light bouncing off his latex clad dome and the mouthpiece zip glistening and twinkling like a mouthful of stars. He is met by silence. The darkness shrouded the car enough that Plugg could not see any of the damage done to the car, all he could see was the rear metal bumper and the slender tail lights flashing at him in the flickering sequence of the neon sign.

"Anybody there?" Plugg calls again taking a few steps towards the car.

"Fuck!" Spider whispers ultimately knowing that if he got any closer he would surely see the word pussy in bright white spray paint staring back at him. Quietly and slowly Spider retrieves his flick knife from his pocket again and activates the blade. The sound isn't loud but enough to intrigue Plugg to come ever closer.

"If anyone is there you better get your ass out here now, or else you're gonna get fucked up!" Plugg shouts, pulling open his suit jacket and retrieving a hidden prison card style baton that with a flick of his wrist, is doubled in size. Spider thinks for a moment and does something he's never going to be proud of but needs must.

"Meow!" Spider cries gently.

Plugg immediately stops frozen like a statue and then he hears the call of a cat again.

"Meow!" Plugg smirks and turns on the spot and heads back down to the front of the club.

"Fucking cat!"

Spider breathes a heavy sigh of relief and lowers the knife.

"Remind me never to tell anyone about that. Fucks sake!"

He rises to his feet and surveys his handy work, but he's still not finished. Taking the knife in his hand like some horror movie slasher, he drives it into one of the front tyres, cutting downwards like the head of the household carving the turkey on the day of thanks. The pressured air escapes in a wheeze like the breathing of an elderly man attached to an oxygen tank. He makes his way around the car and slashes away at the rubber of each tyre. Slowly the car drops as if the life had all but left it and it had given up. Spider had won, he had defeated the 1969 Cadillac and humiliated it in the process.

"One more thing!" Spider grins, his golden grill twinkling in the neon and picking up the spray can again. He sprayed a dot in the centre of the windshield and then sprayed around it with a circle and then again, another circle, creating a target on the glass. Misshapen and not really perfect circles but it resembled a target nonetheless.

"Now, I wait." He ascends the fire escape, stopping around three flights up the four story building that stood adjacent to the rear exit of Masquerades. A rucksack waited for him, which he had placed there before hand. He placed the spray can and his bandanna into it and takes out a chunk of brick, half the size of a full brick, jagged and uneven where it had been broken in two. He checked the weight of the hefty lump in his hand and then playfully tossed it into the air a few times catching it each time like a pitcher awaiting the signal from the crouching catcher to launch a curve ball or a splitter. He took a folded up piece of paper out of his bag and wrapped it around the lump of brick, then secured it with a thick rubber band before placing it down on the metal grill platform where it sat next to his sickeningly white brand new Jordan's. He then swiftly retrieved his cell phone to look at the time. The time flashed up on the touchscreen as 23:45.

"He'll be leaving soon. He's always back home to Sophia by Midnight. Fucking fat cunt under the thumb!" he sneered. He stashed his cell phone into the rucksack and zipped it up before slipping it onto his person. He picked up the brick and waited.

Too late for second thoughts now. Don't even think it. You fucking hear me nigger? This fucking asshole deserves everything he's got coming. No buts man! Don't even think of his family. Don't even think that. Would he? Would he fuck! He wouldn't even give it a second thought. He'd fuck you up and laugh about it, even fucking brag to his mother fucking friends about the shit he did. I guaran-damn-tee that he bragged how he had you on your knees spitting up blood a few months ago. For real! You bet your fucking black ass he did. Shouted it out from the rooftops no doubt. And don't forget taking a lion's share. A huge fucking beast of a lion's share from all our hard work. Dangerous fucking work! All the while he sits in his ivory palace and counts the profits. Well, fuck him! Treating me like I'm a piece of shit! A nothing, a nobody. Well, I ain't a fucking nobody and it's time to step up and prove to everyone what you already know! One day you're gonna run this city. That day might as well come sooner than later.

The back door of the club opened and out trudged Vinnie Valentine, being the filling for a Chapman sandwich. He was wearing a black Dolce and Gabbana three piece and looked like the 24.5 million dollars that he was worth. His booming laughter filled the alleyway rise to meet the hidden Spider, he couldn't hide the fact that it shook him and he swallowed hard. Valentine was at the tail end of some joke that Spider doubted that the twins understood, they just laughed along with the man the city called 'The Thunder'.

"...And I said two grand and it's yours!" Valentine scoffed puffing out great clouds of grey cigar smoke from his grinning maw.

"That's a good one boss!" laughed Big Ben.

"Yeah, real funny, boss!" seconded Little Ben. Both of them went overboard with the laughter and Valentine's face dropped and chewed on the end of his moist cigar.

"Okay, don't hurt yourselves!" he added before setting eyes on his beloved Cadillac. His eyes grew as wide as saucers, the Chapman twin's mouths stretched even wider in shock. Valentine crushed his cigar in his large chunky hand, not even showing the effects that the embers could have on the palm of his hand. He breathed out almost like a bull contemplating goring through some poor matador and his face changed colour rapidly from red, to purple, to blue and back through again like a camouflaging chameleon.

"MY FUCKING CAR!" he bellowed.

Spider thought for a moment that it actually rattled the fire escape he was standing on and he actually gripped the safety rail just in case.

"What the fuck happened to my car?" Valentine booms.

The Chapman twins look at Valentine and shrug. This is not the answer Valentine wants.

"What the hell do you mean..." mimicking their nonchalant shrugs while pulling a dumbfounded facial expression.

They look at each other and shrug again.

"Jesus Christ! You two must be the two stupidest retards walking this planet! Why do I keep you two around?"

They shrug again.

"For fuck's sake!" he looks up to the heavens, closing his eyes "Help me, Poppa! Help me!"

He rubs his head and then approaches his beloved car, shaking his head.

"What the actual fuck! Where were you guys?"

"W-we were with you, boss!" answered Big Ben, the eldest twin (by a whole six minutes. He was the brains of the operation).

"Well, you shouldn't have been! One of you should've been watching the car! You were no doubt watching all those titties bouncing around in there!"

"They are nice titties though, boss!" adds Little Ben, giggling a little until an irate Valentine grabs him by the lapels of his jacket and pulls him in close. Burning his eyeballs with his Cuban cigar breath like some seriously pissed off dragon.

"I know they're nice titties, Ben! I know that! They're all nice titties! I like them all! Big titties, little titties, medium-sized titties, fake titties, freckled titties, round titties, saggy titties, pale titties, chocolate titties, Asian titties, flat titties and huge, gigantic, Sasquatch titties! I fucking love them all Goddamn it!" There is a pause as Valentine breathes in and out heavily and rapidly until Big Ben breaks the silence.

"Me too, boss!" Valentine sighs and lets go of Little Ben's jacket.

"What do I pay you for? Seriously!"
The lump of brick wrapped in a creased and ripped piece of scrap paper descends at speed towards the car. Valentine hears it whistling through the air and turns just as it hits the mark, a perfect bullseye, right into the windshield, severely cracking and splintering the glass, ironically creating a cobweb effect on the windshield. The brick bounces off the cracked glass and rolls onto the floor, coming to a complete stop at Valentine's feet. The sound of the thud and splitting glass was almost deafening but amazingly Valentine did not flinch. The same could not be said for his bodyguards, who almost wet their pants. Little Ben may have a little. They all looked up to see a figure shrouded in

shadow bolt up the remaining stairs to the roof and then he was gone.

"YEAH, YOU RUN YOU FUCK! YOU'RE FUCKING DEAD WHEN I CATCH YOU. YOU HEAR ME?" Valentine blasts.

He bends down and picks up the lump of brick, ripping the rubber band off it with ease and then removes the paper that was now almost shredded from the impact. He drops the brick to the ground with another dull thud. He is about to read the note when Plugg comes plodding up the alleyway, baton in hand again.

"What's going on?" he asks.

"Where the fuck were you butt plug?" he spits venomously at Plugg.

"Oh shit!" Plugg says in shock after seeing the car, rubbing a rough hand over the squeaky latex mask.

"Oh shit indeed!" Valentine replies, "Did you not hear anything?"

Now, Plugg may like being dominated by oversized hairy men and enjoy the taking and the giving of penetrative anal sex, he may also enjoy being trodden on by his mistress in her six inch stiletto heels, until he bleeds. But he's no fool. He knows that depending on what he says in the next few seconds will make the difference on where he spends tonight. In the warm grip of whoever he takes home from the club or the cold murky waters of the Hennig River with a new pair of shoes. He lies.

"I didn't hear anything, Mr Valentine. I swear!" underneath his gimp mask the moisture soaks his forehead and it squeaks with every rippling movement of his worried brow.

"I'm not surprised you can't hear anything with that stupid fucking thing on your head! Fucking Fag Freak!" Valentine growls before turning his attentions back to the note and opening it. He stares at the note. His face twitches with several emotions, anger takes hold and his face burns red as though his head may just explode, but then goes blank. He returns to his normal look of arrogance before grinning, at first humorous and then an angry grimace. He screws the note up and drops it to the floor as he quietly growls one name. A name that has been a pain in his ass for too long.

"Spider!"

Chapter 32

Thomas bounds across the Studd City skyline clad in black garbs. The hood of his dark sweatshirt acting again as his safety net, masking his identity from anyone he may come into contact with. Each stride is accompanied by a flash of extravagant fluorescent pink, his footwear definitely not cut out for a job as a vigilante. He bounds and jumps over gaps between buildings like he'd done it a thousand times before. He had of course, but in Paris, London, Moscow and Rome. That was where he modified what he had learnt through his Shaolin Kung Fu training and added to his repertoire by perfecting Parkour: the art of free running. He was a natural and all those cities were his playground. But Studd City he was still finding his way around. Tonight is another patrol night, helping him to get to know the city, to learn every curve of her, every nook and every cranny. Getting to know her like a young courting couple making out for the first time, exploring each other with enthusiasm and uncovering those little secrets that makes her who she is.

Almost a week of patrols under my belt and still I'm going strong. I'm learning more about the city and finding it easier to find my way around. Sure, I was here for years as a child, but that was down there. The place looks a lot different from up here.

He stops on the edge of a building and looks up at the Devine Tower. The large sign stands bold and strong with arrogance.

I don't like that place and I don't like what it stands for. I won't say I don't like the owner, Robert Devine as I've never actually met him. But, I don't like what he's doing. I hate to say it but that building is helping me with my bearings around here, because the monstrosity is so big you can see it from pretty much anywhere in the city. So, it really does help the orienteering of this vast place.

He jumps off the edge of the building without a second thought for his safety or wellbeing. He grabs onto a fire escape with his gloved hand and swings himself up onto the rail before jumping to a window ledge, tiptoeing across its narrowness and then gripping the ledge above and pulling himself up onto another rooftop. He charges across again, vaulting everything in his path. Some jumps he adds elaborate spins and turns too, purely for his own pleasure and amusement. Only scratching the surface of what he is capable of.

I've had a few little scuffles. Minor league stuff really. But good to scrape off some more of that rust. I've stopped a handful of robberies, muggings and one guy trying to drown a sack of kittens. I don't know what is wrong with this world I really don't. I've took a few shots and dished a lot out. But, so far so good!

He comes to a halt again and looks over another ledge. Below him is the large bulky structure of the el train rail and in the distance the rattling of the 21:20 from Griffin to Alexandrea. It's late.

And here's a little trick I've picked up.

The train comes shunting along at a decent speed, but as it had only just departed from the Griffin station, it hadn't picked up too much pace just yet and Thomas knew this. He also knew that jumping onto the roof of a train that was moving at full force would probably not end well. As it passes beneath him Thomas leaps and safely lands in a three point stance. The commuters inside probably not even taking any notice of the large thud that on the train's roof, as busy train passengers very rarely take notice of anything around them.

It's definitely a quicker way to get around the city. Even though it's a tad loud. Okay, it's deafening! But it serves the purpose. I kind of feel guilty for all the free rides I'm going to be taking at Studd City's Metro Rail expense. Maybe I will make a yearly anonymous donation to them.

He holds on to the roof as it picks up speed. Its old wheels crunch along the rusty iron rails underneath it, sparks spitting out from the impact as it makes for Alexandrea.

I get chance to have a breather. Zone out a little and think. The best thing I could have done was open up to Burt. Well, I say, 'open up' but that old walrus figured it out himself.

He can't help but smile to himself, Burt having that contagious effect on him once again.

But he's had some great ideas and has been very positive about the whole ordeal. Having someone to share it all with is a huge positive. Doing this alone could break a person.

The train whistles towards its destination blowing his hood off his head, his brown hair flopping around and blowing in the current. Luckily for him there is nobody around to see him.

Maybe having a hood is out.

The train takes a turn and there is an uncomfortable ruckus of metal on metal colliding, ear churning, but then starts to slow down as it enters Alexandrea. Thomas stands as it slows, still remembering to keep his stance wide and strong. He pulls his hood back into place and it shrouds his face again. He readies himself and leaps to a nearby ledge and quickly makes his way down the face of the building using protruding ledges and worn moist drainpipes, before disappearing into an alleyway.

Yeah, *Burt will really be helpful to my crusade. Experienced first aider from his days in Vietnam. Hoping that I'm not going to need to call on him for anything like that very often but I'm also not stupid to believe I won't get hurt. And I'll need his expertise.*

He bursts through the alleyway and leaps over a sleeping stray dog, that has wrapped its bony flea bitten carcass around the base of a trash can. The dog's ears prick up and it lifts its head to look to see what it was that just vaulted over him, but Thomas had long gone and with a grumble the dog drops its head and goes back to sleep.

He has also told me that he served as a RTO (Radio Telephone Operator) and had to lug around 20 pounds of FM receiver/ Transmitter equipment through Vietnamese swamps and jungles. As well as keeping a look out for Charlie.

Up a fire escape, off the fire escape and over a fence and away again. As Thomas ponders random thoughts.

I wonder what this big secret it is he has to show me at the church. The plot thickens. And I wonder whether I'll ever beat him at chess.

The scream of a woman in distress echoes through the alleyway and bursts his thought bubble in mid sentence. Without a second thought Thomas sets off in the direction of the scream, determination etched in his face.

Sarah Daniels thought it would be a good idea to take a shortcut on her way home from the library. It wasn't. As she cut through the alley between Fuji's Noodles and Sika's Samoan Snack Shack, she passed a gentleman that sat in a heap on an armchair of damp cardboard boxes and garbage bags. His weight had caused them to split along and vomited up leftovers and rotting banana skins. His head hung between his knees hiding from the outside world. Sarah looked at him and at first felt afraid and instinctively gripped her handbag tightly, cringing at the sight of the filth and waste that surrounded him like a moat around a castle. Then when she looked closer at him sitting there downtrodden and filthy. She felt sorry for him and pulled out a dollar bill from her purse and offered it to him.

"Here you go!" She said meekly, but the homeless man didn't reply and kept his head sunk between his hole infested jeans.

"Sir?" she tried again to get his attention. For a split second she entertained the thought that maybe he was dead, but at closer inspection she could see that he was breathing, his shoulders rising with each slow breath.

"I'll just leave it here for you." She said smiling, as she placed the dollar bill on the floor at his feet, Lincoln side up. She continued a. her way when further into the alley she heard the man speak, his tone gravelly and bitter.

"What the fuck is this?"

She turned startled by the voice, it frightened her, but what scared her more was the look in his eyes as he peered out from his shadowy nook, like the head of a tortoise peeping out of its dark shell.

"You think I want your money?" he seethed and rose to his feet starting to shuffle towards her, like some festering zombie rising from its grave and going in search of fresh brains.

"I'm sorry, sir!" She stammered, "I thought you..."

"WAS BEGGING!" he shouted, spittle exploding from his yellow decaying maulers.

"I'm sorry if I offended you..."

"Did I ask for your fucking money?" he asked shuffling closer. She had frozen now, scared for her life and her body would now only allow her the odd step backwards. Her heels scraping the uneven concrete as she did.

"I don't want your money..." he said now wearing a hideous smile that would haunt her for the rest of her days. She found herself up against a wall and now she no longer had a view of the street. Now she realised why he was smiling. He knew and she knew, she was trapped. Cornered like some defenceless animal, cowering with fear and moisture building up in her eyes.

"No, I don't want your money lady!" his voice now lowering to a whisper. His face now so close to hers, his breath emitting some putrid odour that she was sure smelt worse than the contents of the oozing garbage bag he was sitting on.

"W-what do you want?" she managed to squeeze out of her tightening throat. He immediately grabbed her arms, his grip strong, too strong, no point in fighting against it.

"I want your pussy!" he growled and flicked a moist tongue around his chapped lips. Sarah screamed. A scream that came from the pit of her stomach. He didn't like that, and he threw her to the floor.

"Shut the fuck up you cunt!" he growls "We can do this two ways..." and he produces a large kitchen knife.

"With or without?"
She swallows deep as he unbuttons his denims and removes his penis, blemished with some kind of chaffing rash. She sees her own terrified reflection in the blade and her fear rises, as does his penis. He swoops down to his knees, kneeling in front of her toying with the knife, toying with her, enjoying the power and control he has over her. He grabs her tights and rips them away, they surrender and easily come apart, leaving her exposed and a way in for him.

"Oh, you smell so good...like strawberries!" he says smelling the inside of her thigh and rubbing his rough chapped hands up her leg until it disappears under her tight pencil skirt.

"No... Please don't do this!" she snivels.

"Shut up!" he shouts grabbing her by the throat and squeezing her face until it starts to turn violet. Tears stream down her cheeks and she feels angry but not at him, at herself. She thought she was stronger than this, she thought that she'd escaped being manhandled by men but somehow she always manages to be taken advantage of. As her body is starved of oxygen, she feels an unwanted hand tearing the buttons from her blouse and groping at her breasts, violently freeing them of their safe haven, flashes of her former husband assaulting her in their small kitchen many years ago. Hitting her, slapping her, choking her, fucking her... Tears glistening on her cheeks as she is made to gag and choke on her ex husbands large penis. Slipping into unconsciousness, her complexion turns blue now. His hand grabbing at her panties, tearing, ripping, fully exposed now. She thinks now of Dennis, her boyfriend of three months, probably at the apartment waiting for her to come home and make supper. He's not like her ex, or so she tells herself. He only hit her once, when she spilt salad cream on his designer shirt. Oh, and the time she forgot to record the game. And was there another time? The man takes his hand from around her throat and she gasps, the damage has been done and he has killed her spirit and any fight that was in her as gone. She lies there just happy to be breathing and she sees him rubbing his penis in his grimy hand. He spits on the end of his penis, the spittle dribbling down it and becoming lost in his grip. He smears it around the glans, lubricating it ready for entry. Sarah almost vomits, it burns in her throat as it ascends, but she can't allow him the satisfaction, so she swallows it back down and lies back and awaits the inevitable. The Inevitable that never came. She sees a trash can lid gliding through the air at some speed, like a frisbee being thrown for a dog to fetch. It hits the man in his face and knocks him backwards onto the cold unforgiving concrete, his legs flaying into the air with his jeans in a scrunch around his ankles.

"What the fuck!" he bellows trying to get to his feet and pull his jeans up. A difficult task for a flustered man with an erect penis.

"I don't think that's appropriate language to use in front of lady. Do you?" Asks Thomas stepping out of the shadows. His identity concealed by hood and shadow, smoke and mirrors.
The man stares at him trying to button his jeans, with a knife in one hand and flaying penis refusing to be put back away.

"Oh, you just wait you bastard! You just fucking wait!"
Sarah realises this is her time to escape and sits up wrapping her tattered blouse around her exposed bosom. But a part of her wants to watch to see what happens.

"Miss? You are free to go. Go on get yourself home." Thomas says gently smiling at her, his mouth the only part of his face visible. She smiles back and starts to get to her feet. One shoe off and her tights hanging from her in disarray. But the man stops her in her tracks.

"You're not going anywhere! We've got unfinished business!" he seethes. She stands on the spot and does not move a muscle. How could his words make her freeze so? But she is terrified.

"Leave the lady alone!" Thomas growls.

"What about you then?" the man asks "You look like a pussy! And I loves me some pussy!" he points the knife in his direction.

"You smell like a pussy too!" he charges at Thomas and swipes his knife at him with relentless hate. Thomas dodges every thrust seemingly with ease, looking for the right time, the right opening to make his move. The knife slices through Thomas' left shoulder.

Lucky.

Thomas grimaces and blood seeps from the wound.

Lucky for me it's just a flesh wound. Got to end this now. But he's flailing that thing around like he's an out of control windmill.

Thomas waits for the next thrust and he steps into it. The thrusting arm passing by his ribcage and Thomas locks the man's arm in his, trapping it. Thomas jerks his arm forcefully upwards and twists his body. Something snaps in the man's arm, if he is lucky it will only be tendons. The knife falls from his hand and hits the floor. The man screams and sets off running, cradling his limp arm as he disappears out onto the street. Thomas is about to turn and leave but is met by Sarah.

"You're bleeding!" she says softly.

"It's nothing, just a flesh wound. Are you okay?"

"Yeah...well I think so. My throat hurts, and I feel like I need a bath."

"Get yourself a taxi and go home."

"Yeah."

"Don't go walking through alleys at this time of night. Not around here, it's not safe."

"Yeah, I guess you're right. Who are you?"

"Just call me your guardian angel!" he smiles.

"And don't forget your bag." He adds.

She turns to pick up her handbag that lies discarded on the floor.

"Well, I can't thank you enough for saving my..." As she stands back up and turns around he has gone.

"...life."

She stands all alone looking around for a few seconds before slotting her foot into her heeled shoe and hurrying off towards the street. Thomas stands in the shadows of a different alleyway watching Sarah call for a cab.

"She's beautiful!" he says under his breath.

"She sure is!" comes a voice from behind, a startled Thomas spins around ready to fight again, but is met by an elderly homeless man. He too is shrouded by a hood, but for other reasons. Society has deemed him to grotesque for their eyes, so he hides his heavily scarred face as well as he can.

"Who..." Thomas starts but is interrupted by the shrouded man.

"I was going to ask you the same question."

There is a silent pause between the two and nobody speaks until the shrouded man laughs.

"I'm only messing with you, kid. Ah, the taxi's here!"

Thomas turns to see Sarah slide into the backseat of the cab and watches it drive away.

"She's safe now, kid." His voice is odd, almost muffled like he is chewing a toffee while speaking, "You did good" he says turning around slowly to his shopping trolley that is crammed with all sorts, a rolled up sleeping bag sitting on top that is tied with a piece of string.

"You saw that?" Thomas asks.

"Oh yeah I saw!" chortles the man, rummaging around in his shopping trolley and pulling out a half empty bottle of *Koko Pop* soda.

"That poor girl! It's a good job you were there to go *Hong Kong Phooey* on his ass. I'd have stepped in and showed that guy what for, but bad hip you know?" he takes a swig from the bottle emptying it, and as he tips his head backwards to get the last drops of soda, his face can be seen which takes Thomas by surprise. The Man's face looks like it's been passed through a meat tenderiser, twice. He wipes his mouth with the sleeve of his dirty threadbare overcoat and turns to face Thomas smiling a smile with more gaps than teeth, under a severe cleft pallet scar that appears to have been made by hand and not left through a needed operation since birth.

"So, who are you?" Thomas asks.

"My name is Elliot, well it used to be. Around these parts these days I'm known to all as Vermin."

"Vernon?"

"No, Ver-min! Because of my beautiful good looks!" he smiles again and two protruding front teeth poke out making him resemble a rodent.

"Yeah, it's the teeth, I think... Reminds them of a rat I guess. And because of this little guy!" he whistles and his shopping trolley begins to rattle when out pops a large brown sewer rat. Thomas grimaces.

"Yeah, that's the look Kasper always gets, bless him. He's nearly as ugly as me!" he roars laughing and Kasper runs up his arm and perches himself on his shoulder.

"You still haven't told me your name, kid." Vermin questions, unravelling the string around his sleeping bag.

"I... I can't tell you."

"Ooh a secret. Oh well, I'll find out sooner or later. I always do. Don't I Kasper?"
He is met with a squeak from Kasper and Vermin strokes him.

"Clever boy!"

"What do you mean, you'll find out?"

"I am the eyes and the ears of this fine city my friend. Nothing happens here without me knowing about it!" he unravels his sleeping bag onto the floor settling down for the night.

"I've been watching you for the past few weeks you know?"

"You have?" Thomas says startled.

"Yep!" he says sliding down the wall slowly and sitting onto his sleeping bag.

"First I thought you were nuts, but then I realised what you're doing, well planning to do."

"Look, I don't know what you're talking about."

"Sure you do, kid. You don't have to play games with me. I respect your mission, it's gonna be tough to bring them all down. Yeah, real tough! I knew a man who tried once...Years ago now...He failed."

Thomas looked on at him like a deer stuck in the soft lemon glow of headlights.

"How..." Thomas stumbles but is intercepted again before he can manage a sentence.

"The eyes and the ears kid. The eyes and the ears!" slowly lifting his head and winking at him with a glazed and useless right eye and revealing more of his misshapen face.

"Look, I better be going." Thomas says a little shocked and startled.

"Yeah kid, sure! Make sure you get that wound seen to. Only looks like a flesh wound though, so you should be fine. I'll see you around."

Thomas leaves. Kasper scurries down and sits in Vermin's lap. He strokes his matted fur and smiles an uneven smile, but a smile of love nonetheless.

"Shall I let you into a secret Kasper?"

Kasper tilts his head and squeaks, then seemingly just ignores him and starts washing himself.

"That guy... He's the new priest at St. Vincent's."

Kasper stops washing and tilts his head, squeaking again.

"How do I know?" he smiles looking out at the busy night street flying by the alleyway entry.

"The eyes and ears Kasper my dear boy! The eyes and the ears!"

Chapter 33

Burt shuffles down the aisle of the empty church hall. The impact of his walking stick echoes through the emptiness with each step, sounding like the ticking of a grandfather clock. He retrieves the church keys from his pocket, jangling together as he sieves through them to find the correct key for the front entrance.

"Time to call it a night!" Burt says as he slots the key into the lock. As he locks the door, there is knock on it. Burt is taken aback and his first thought is that it's Sniff and his band of coked up hoodlums. Unfortunately in Studd City, if someone knocks on your door at this time of night, it's usually bad news. Sometimes the best (and safest) thing to do is just ignore it and hope they go away. The door is gently rapped on again. Burt readies himself by holding his walking cane aloft.

"Whose there?" He asks.

"Oh, hi... This is Detective Graham of the SCPD." comes the muffled response from the other side of the thick door. Burt lowers the cane, a look of confusion on his face that suddenly changes to concern.

Thomas! Something has happened to Thomas!

Burt unlocks the door as Detective Graham greets him with a friendly smile, hands tucked into his pockets looking very melancholy. Not the look a member of the Police Department usually wears for a 'bad news' visit.

"Is there s-s-something wrong, Detective?" Burt's asks through a stuttering worried reply.

"What? Oh no, nothing!" Graham smiles putting Burt at ease.

"I've been meaning to visit for a while, but I haven't had the chance."

"Oh, I see!"

"I was in the neighbourhood and I saw the lights on and thought there's no time like the present."

Burt looks at him and manages a forced smile, knowing that Thomas is out on patrol and he'd have to think up a convincing lie on the church's priest's whereabouts, and think it up quick.

"Could I come in?" Graham asks, Burt unknowingly blocking the entrance.

"Oh, I am sorry, Detective!" moving away from the door and welcoming him in.

"I haven't been in here for a while." Graham says looking around the church, reminiscing of past visits to the place "It still looks the same!" he smiles.

They walk together up the aisle towards the altar.

"We do try to keep it all looking nice and inviting." Says Burt, still intrigued as to why the Detective is here.

"I hear that there is a new sheriff in town too!"

"Sorry?"

"A new priest?" Graham asks.

"Oh, yes! That would be Father Gabriel."

"Is Father Gabriel here? I'd like to meet him. I need to talk to him, well, erm need to have him listen to me." He looks over at the confessional, slightly embarrassed.

"Oh, I see!" Burt says, thinking on his feet now, "If you want to go and wait in there I'll go and get him."

"Thanks, Mister...?"

"Simmons, Burt Simmons!" Burt answers and the two shake hands.

"I've seen you around all these years and never knew your name." He smiles.

The two go their separate ways. Graham walks towards the confessional and Burt makes his way into the back room.

Okay now think you old buzzard. You can't tell him Thomas isn't here now, it'll sound suspicious. And where else would a priest be at ten o'clock at night! Okay, wait until he's settled in there and go and sit in there with him. He won't see me and all I have to do is listen. I know I probably shouldn't do it and I'm sure I shouldn't be listening to people spilling their guts and sins. And will they get forgiveness on their sins if it's not told to a man of the cloth? Oh I don't know what to do now.

Burt thinks about the matter for as long as he can.

No! You've got to do it. You've got to cover for Thomas.

Burt is about to go back out when Thomas stumbles in through the back door.

"Oh, Thomas I'm so glad you're back!"

"So am I Burt, believe me!"

"Detective Graham of the SCPD is waiting for you in the confessional!"

377

"Okay, I'd better slip in there quickly then. And make sure he leaves before I come out, I can't let him see me like this!" They both walk out and make their way towards the large beautifully carved confessional booth. Two thick velvet curtains hang from each booth, one of them is pulled around fully to conceal the sinner, which happens to be Detective Sidney Graham in this instance, giving him his privacy.

"Remember, make sure he leaves before I come out, Burt." Thomas whispers.

"Okay!" Replies Burt, then he stops, grabbing hold of Thomas' arm stopping him in his tracks.

"Thomas! You're wounded? You're bleeding!" he says, trying to keep his voice low.

"I'm okay, Burt. It's only a flesh wound."

"But you need to have that looked at immediately!"

"Let me get through this and we'll take a look at it." He smiles at Burt placing his hand on his shoulder, he can see the worry on Burt's face. Thomas slips into the other booth and slides the curtain shut before sitting down. He opens a small window in the wall between them revealing a crosshatched formation of wood, making it very difficult to see who is in either booth.

"Forgive me Father, for I have sinned. It's been...I...can't remember how long it's been, Father!" Graham says.

"It's okay. Please continue." Thomas says.

"Well, I haven't sinned as such... I mean I haven't acted but I have thought about it." Graham stutters, finding himself sweating profusely.

378

"Carnal thoughts?"

"Yes, yes I guess they are."

"Please continue. I'm listening."

"There is this woman and I've been having... I've been fantasising about her. A lot! She likes me and she's been flirting with me and I...I feel...I don't actually know how I feel to be perfectly honest with you, Father."

"I see. It's not unnatural to feel lustful thoughts towards the opposite sex. We are but human beings with needs. Have you thought about asking this woman to go out on a date? Maybe get to know her and..."

"No, you don't understand, Father!" Graham interrupts "I apologise for cutting you off, but that's the thing, I can't ask her out, I can't go out with her. I can't do any of those things!"

"Why not?"

"Because I'm a married man." Graham murmurs. Shame and guilt shrouding him in the little booth, it makes him feel claustrophobic.

"Oh, I see!"

"And I have two children."

"Then that makes it a bit awkward doesn't it?"

"Yeah! Just a little!" Graham chuckles.

"Are you happy at home? What is your home life like?"

"Well, that's just it, there is nothing wrong with my home life or my marriage. Obviously we have our moments. A lot of that is because I'm a co... Because of my job. I work long, unsociable hours and sometimes I have to put the needs of my job before my family and I know that makes me sound like a real jerk, but the job is... Well, let's just say it's a very important one. Sometimes life and death!"

"Do you suffer a lot of guilt over this? Do you feel like you're neglecting them?"

"Yeah! Yeah I do. My wife makes me feel really guilty, you know when I miss meals or that important sports game my eldest is in. I mean you can't get those moments back can you?"

"Unfortunately not!"

"And I guess then I feel that my boys will grow up messed up and be bitter towards me for missing these moments that are important to them. I just hope they understand that my job is... I'm making excuses now. Maybe I need a career change?"

"I don't think you have to be so drastic. You obviously like your job and are good at it, that is why you feel so torn. If it's a job where you can save lives, then this city is indebted to you. I would say maybe look into your time management and work something out with your work timetable and your home life. I'm sure that an events calendar could be attained from your children's school so you could plan your timetable at work around it accordingly."

"Yeah! Yeah that's a really good idea! That could work. Thanks!"

Suddenly Burt's hand appears through the curtain of Thomas' booth holding an ice pack. Thomas turns and smiles taking the ice pack and he holds it on his injured arm, acting as a temporary treatment until after the Detective has left.

"And what of your wife? You said she makes you feel guilty?"

"Yeah... Well, she doesn't mean it, she will snap at me and be pissed at me... Oh! Please forgive my language. If I'm late, or can't make an appointment, or have to cancel plans or whatever. I can see why, I'd be annoyed to. But she knew when we got together what she was letting herself in for, she knew I was a... She knew the job could be a pain in the rear."

"Maybe you're taking her reactions and taking them out of context?"

"What do you mean?"

"Because you are already feeling guilt from not being able to be there for said event and if you then cancel or show up late then you're already mad at yourself already, so whatever comment she makes about the situation you're going to react, and this is what may cause the arguments."

"Okay, I can see where you're coming from. How would I go about changing that?"

"That's basically just brain training and stop beating yourself up. Like you said, she knows what the job entails and you're coming home waiting for the argument, when you need to tell yourself it's out of your hands, if you can't do anything about the said situation then don't worry about it. Naturally she may be annoyed if plans have changed so just go in and let her say her piece. She just wants to vent, just wants to get it off her chest."

"Yeah, I can see that, yeah!"

"Let her say what she has to and then give her a hug and show her some affection and then make time for each other. How is your sex life?"

"It's good when we have it. But I'm working so many long hours and she's looking after the kids all day, so a lot of the time when it's actually time to climb in between the sheets, we're both just too exhausted to do anything!"

"Again, this could be a time management subject. As you need to find time for the family you must also find some time for each other. To love each other, connect with each other and be intimate."

"Yes, again that makes total sense!"

"Now, about this other woman..."

"Well, she's not 'the other woman' I mean we haven't done anything together, nothing at all!" Graham snaps back feeling like Thomas is maybe attacking him.

"I'm on your side here. Remember I'm here to listen and give you guidance if I can."

"I'm sorry for reacting like that, Father."

"It's okay. What thoughts have you had about her?"

"Well, I've pictured her in... Erm...intimate scenarios. Weird dreams and now, I'm not proud of this but I made love to my wife a few days ago and I pictured her face!" Graham grimaces like a child waiting to get an ear lashing from the headmaster.

"What weird dreams?"

"Oh!" Graham was surprised that Thomas didn't shoot him down for thinking of another woman while having sex with his wife.   "Well, in a marathon and I'm running, she's behind me and she starts gaining on me as my wife and

382

boys take off in front and no matter how hard I push, I can't catch them and then Nash...Erm she is almost by my side."

"You're confused, torn between her and your family. She is chasing you and making the advances to you, you're not making them to her, but you like the attention, most men would! It's stroking your ego and so far you have managed to keep your head on straight and keep her at bay. You fear that if you lie with this other woman then you will not only lose your wife, but your children too, your whole family! You know that's an incredible amount to lose, that is your world!"

Graham starts to well up a little and he starts to become emotional, knowing that everything Thomas has just said is the truth, that's exactly how he feels.

"Yes, Father...that is all true but, what do I do?"

"Do you see this woman at your place of work?"

"Yes."

"I believe that this is the issue. You see her every day and every day she flirts with you and gives you this attention that caters to your ego. Because your sex life is not as frequent as maybe it once was, you are left with an abundance of sexual frustration. I think that is why you're finding yourself having these thoughts, these feelings."

"Wow...okay!"

"If you and your wife can make time for each other intimately on a regular basis, then you're urges will go there and you won't be looking for a surrogate to absorb your libido."

"Holy shit!"

383

Thomas fights trying not to laugh and as he shakes he grabs his flesh wound in pain.

"Oh! Father I'm so sorry. It's just all that makes so much sense! Thank you so much for this!" Graham says quickly getting to his feet, already backing out of the booth.

"I've gotta go. I'm going to make love to my wife!" he bellows as he leaves the confessional and strides down the aisle and out of the door. Burt shuffles quickly behind him and locks the door behind him, then walks back up the aisle. Thomas exits the confessional grasping the ice pack to his arm, shaking his head and laughing.

"I think I like that guy." Thomas laughs.

"Did he just say what I think he said?" Burt asks approaching at his top speed, which isn't fast by any stretch.

"He did!" laughs Thomas.

"What did you two talk about?"

"Ah, you know I can't talk about it, Burt. What happens in the booth, stays in the booth!"

"Well, let's check that arm of yours."
Thomas removes his sweatshirt revealing a black vest. The blade had sliced his flesh and luckily had stopped bleeding now. Burt wipes away the excess blood with his handkerchief to get a better look at the wound. He pinches the flesh together on either side and Thomas winces.

"Ouch!"

"You big baby! I've seen worse bee stings, kid!" he says winking at him "Nothing some superglue can't fix."

"Superglue?"

"That's how we did it back in Nam, kid. We can't really take you to the hospital and get you stitched up can we? They'll ask questions. They'll want to know why a priest has a two inch gash across his arm!"

"Okay, okay you're the boss!"

Burt steps back and looks him up and down.

"What's wrong?" Thomas asks.

"You'll definitely need a better outfit than that. And those horrible looking things on your feet will have to go!"

"What's the matter with them?"

"Rule number one of vigilantism, don't wear fluorescent sneakers. You look like you've trodden in a *My Little Pony*!"

They both laugh and Burt starts to waddle towards the organ hidden in a draft ridden cranny of the hall.

"I'll make you something. I'm quite handy with a needle and thread!" Burt says, stopping halted by a moment of pondering.

"I think Doris' old sewing machine is lying around somewhere?" he says out loud, "I'll have a look for it when I go home." Burt carries on towards the organ and Thomas follows.

"Where are you going, Burt?"

"I told you I had a surprise for you that may be of some use to the campaign."

They reach the organ and Thomas looks at it a little bemused.

"What, you're going to show me your hidden talent as a *Liberace* tribute?" Thomas laughs.

"Taught him everything he knew!" Burt says sarcastically.

The large organ is pillared by two templar knights carved in stone, embracing long slender shields. The shield on the left with a crucifix chiselled into it. The one on the right is etched painstakingly detailed as the Key of Solomon.

"I wanted to introduce you to these two gentlemen." Burt points at the statues of the knights. Thomas looks at them and then back at Burt, confusion plastered across his face.

"I'm confused Burt."

"Watch!" Burt says, and he starts to pull all the stops out on the organ. As he pulls out the stop marked mute and there is a rumble coming from the wall behind the organ. Amazingly the Knight holding the shield with the crucifix slides away opening a narrow entrance. Thomas' jaw drops and he stares wide eyed at what he has just seen taking place in front of him.

"Okay, what just happened?"
Burt laughs.

"Follow me!" Burt said retrieving the church keys and activating a keyring torch he headed through the narrow gap.

"Be careful of the steps, they're quite steep." Burt warned.

"Steps! There are steps?" Thomas says shaking his head in disbelief.

"This is like something out of *The Cat and the Canary*!" Thomas follows Burt who stands at the top of a narrow stairwell, a surrounding cocoon of stone, damp and claustrophobic. Burt tentatively makes his way down the steps with Thomas close behind shadowing Burt to keep him safe. The glow of the keyring struggles to illuminate the darkness. Thomas retrieves his cell phone and turns the backlight on, which helps immensely to guide their way down to a secret underground room. Thomas shines the light around unveiling a room from another time. The low ceiling at around eight feet in height at its highest in the open area in the centre of what you would call a cellar. Wall, floor and ceiling all stone.

"What is this place?" Thomas asks in awe, slowly shining the light around like he's a living breathing lighthouse.
"Pretty neat isn't it?" Says Burt.

"Your predecessor, Father Timmings let me in on this little secret years ago. It hasn't been used for about eighty years!"

"Amazing! But what was it used for?"

"It was used to hide alcohol during prohibition." Burt says pointing to one side of the cellar that had low archways concealing old beer kegs and barrels. Old wooden crates and boxes sit piled on top of each other, balanced in strange teetering towers like a giant game of *Jenga*.

"Father Timmings told me that a priest called Father Hubble used to store them here, hiding them from the law for mafia boss, Tiny Lorenzo."

"Tiny Lorenzo?"

"Yeah, this was way before The Valentine family took over. He was a... I don't know what the politically correct term is for them these days... Little Person?" Burt shrugs a little embarrassed at his ignorance.

"I believe that is correct. And he was head of a mafia family?"

"He sure was. A nasty piece of work by all accounts. Died in a shootout at the lighthouse in North Peak."

Thomas walks around and looks inside the crates, they're all empty then moves the kegs, which are also light and empty. Smothered in dust and cobwebs, Thomas wipes his hand on his trousers.

"You won't find anything in there, Thomas. It's all long gone."

"The Police confiscated it all I presume?"

"No, that old dog Father Hubble continued to sell it to people when the Lorenzo Gang was wiped out. He must have been a character!"

"So it would seem. So who knows about this place?"

"Well, that's the thing. You and I are the only people alive that know about it. The authorities never found it and The Lorenzo Gang were the only ones back then that knew about it and they got wiped out in the early 30's. And obviously Father Hubble who passed the secret onto Father Timmings. But they're all gone so nobody knows about this place but us. Heck, it's not even on the blueprints for this place because I've seen them."

"That's incredible! What an exclusive club we are part of!"

The light cuts through another dark crevice of the cellar and comes across a door.

"Look, there's a door!" Thomas approaches it. As he wipes dust away from it, it is thick metal and cold to touch, underneath it is abused by a gruesome layer of rust. The key remains in the lock but both lock and key have also fell victim to the rust, becoming suffocated by it so much that they key will not even budge when Thomas attempts to turn it.

"Where does it go?" Thomas asks.

"To the sewers I believe. That would have been how they brought the goods in I'd imagine."

"This is a cool place!" Thomas says taking it all in.

"That's why I wanted to show you this place. We can use this as the nerve centre for your campaign."

"Really! You think it will work?"

"It's perfect! Nobody knows about it. There is an entrance to the sewers, so you can come and go unnoticed, so you won't have to enter the church via street level."

"Yeah, that's true!"

"Plus there is enough space for you to do your training. Plus, we could run some electric down here and I could get to know how to use that laptop contraption you've brought. Maybe I'll be able to help that way and stay in contact with you when you're out in the field."

Thomas smiles at Burt, the light of the phone bouncing off his teeth.

"You've thought of everything haven't you Burt? Are you sure you don't want to be the one out in the field?"

"I wish I could, Thomas. If I was thirty years younger I'd be out there with you!"

"Well, it looks like we've got some hard graft ahead of us if we want to get this place anywhere near what you've envisioned, Burt."

Burt smiles and squeezes Thomas' shoulder, Thomas winces.

"Have faith, Thomas!" says Burt, then he realises Thomas looks in pain, he loosens his grip.

"That was your bad arm wasn't it?"

Thomas nods and squeezes out a comical murmur.

"Yep!"

The two stand in the damp and dark, lit only by a white light rising up and elevating their shadows on the ceiling. Their laughter echoes through the cellar and into the empty hall above.

Chapter 34

Burt stands in yet another snaking queue at the busy diner, Perfect Java. The normal arrangement of the owner Keith watching sports with his friends at the corner of the counter, ignoring everything else around him. While his daughter Jess, runs around trying to serve everyone. They say that when a chicken is beheaded that its body still functions and runs around in a random unorthodox manner. Burt thought that Jess' daily routine would mirror this perfectly. But Burt is in no rush for his coffee and besides, he is far enough away from Keith without the fear of being dragged into yet another tedious debate about sports. Burt lets his gaze wander around the diner, mostly met by a sea of people's heads bobbing up and down restlessly in front of him.

I've patched up Thomas and have made a start on his new uniform. He's going to love it. I just know he is. I'll have a wander around the flea market when I've finished here and see if I can pick up some other little knick-knacks he can use.

Burt stretches out his back, his bones crunch like a key being turned in a rusty lock.

It was nice of Thomas to let me stay over last night. But that spare bed is very uncomfortable. But it's still nice to have the company instead of sitting up all night thinking about how much I miss Doris. Yeah, the nights are definitely the hardest. It's amazing how I still sleep on the same side of the bed and don't crease her side. Some nights I forget and I make two mugs of hot chocolate, it's not until I place it on her nightstand that I realise she's not there. She's not there.

Burt's eyes start to fill up. They usually do when he thinks of her and most nights they empty as he stares aimlessly at their photo album, propped up in bed, the occasional gaze to see if she will magically manifest beside him, curlers in her chalky hair, glowing nose and cheeks from the routine face pack. But, she's not there.

He collects himself and thinks about other things.

Of course he needs a name. But what? I think something biblical would be fitting. Yes, it should be something that parallels what he stands for in his everyday life. All he wants to do is see justice done. Yes, he has one hell of a campaign ahead of him, a crusade almost... A Crusader... The Justice Crusader... No that's not right... He wishes to help make this city safe for its inhabitants, looking over them like a guardian angel... Guardian of Justice...I've got it! The Angel of Justice!

Burt laughs to himself and claps his hands together, very pleased with himself. The man standing in front of him in the queue turns around and gives him a look as though he's thinking, 'Great, I always get stuck next to the nut!' Burt isn't deterred that's made him happy and now he knows just how to make Thomas' uniform come to life. The queue shuffles along again slowly like a chain gang waiting in line to be given their slop and scraps. He then hears a familiar voice join him at the back of the queue. It's Sniff. Burt hopes that Sniff won't recognise him. Sniff talks obnoxiously loud on his cell phone behind him. Burt turns slightly and he can see Sniff's reflection in the large metallic industrial coffee maker behind the counter. Sniff is paying no attention to who is around him, he's actually looking out of the window, hood up, index finger up his nostril. Burt is thankful because he really doesn't like this guy. He is scum of the earth, ironically Sniff would probably agree with Burt's perception of him. But then Sniff says something that pricks his interest.

"It's going down tonight, bro!" Sniff says.

Burt can't hear what the person on the other end of the conversation is saying but he listens intently.

"No, dick! I just said I can't drop it off tonight…I know, but I can't! Fuck! Will you listen!"

Sniff lowers his voice now, he's stupid but maybe not that stupid, but Burt can still hear.

"Look man if I tell, you can't say shit to anyone! Okay… You fucking promise, asshole! Okay, it's happening tonight, it's all going down at the Ventura Bridge at midnight. Yeah, straight up! Spider is gonna fucking slug Valentine. No BS man, I'm telling ya! He's got back up and everything! Big Vinnie's going down!" Sniff laughs and then looks at the contents of his nose oozing out onto the tip of his finger. Sage coloured mucus mixing with the dirt under his nails on a canvas of nicotine yellow stained canvas of his skin. He wipes the booger on his pants, already heavily besmirched in a plethora of unidentifiable stains, most disturbingly the majority around his crotch area.

"Yeah... I know, fucked up shit you know. Yeah, yeah, he figures he's gonna rule the roost, you know? Maybe! I just look out for me bro you know that. Got my own Stardust deal with The Vixen anyway. Yeah that's right man, I hear ya!"

He cackles like a braying donkey before it turns into a mucus lined cough, rising up out of his throat and out into the diner.

"What's taking so fucking long, man!" He shouts at the top of his voice. It's enough to make Burt jump and almost enough to straighten the creases in his wrinkled skin and the knot in his stomach tightens. He not only detests this man, but he is scared of him too. He's so out of left field, that makes him dangerous and unpredictable.

"HEY!" Keith shouts across the busy diner of customers trying not to make eye contact with Sniff.

"Any more of that language and you're out of here! You hear me?"

Sniff shrugs and goes back to his phone call.

"Fucking hell man, you're one pushy son of a bitch! Okay man I can get it you by 10 tonight. What? No I can't party, not tonight...I've just told you why! You fucked up? Yeah thought so! You want an 8ball? Yeah cool, later man." He hangs up the cell phone and yells again at the top of his lungs.

"This place is fucking bullshit man! Bitch is too slow!" Sniff heads for the door when Keith fires back.

"Get the hell outta here you low life!"

"Why don't you fucking help the bitch out instead watching the tube, man!"

Sniff barges out and Keith is left red faced through the sudden adrenaline rush and a pinch of embarrassment. Burt couldn't help but agree with Sniff. Probably the first and last time they would ever agree on something.

Chapter 35

Thomas finishes his weekly sermon and the disappointing turnout leaves through the main door. Thomas stands at the altar behind the bulky wooden podium and sighing, shuffles his notes back into order. The last of the congregation leave and the heavy duty door is closed behind them. The thud echoes through the now empty church hall.

Another disappointing house but we did get three more than last week. I guess that can be seen as a small victory. Slow build Thomas, just keep telling yourself it's a slow build. They will come.

He steps down the altar and walks towards his private quarters.

Yes, it's still early days. The people of this city haven't been given anything from the city for the last decade so why should they have faith? Why should they have any hope? Any hope in change. They have been trodden down like grapes to make wine. Wine for the rich and powerful while they have been left to fester in the bottom of the barrel.

Thomas pulls off his pristine chasuble and drapes it over his arm, then slips off the stole and lies it on top of his chasuble. He winces slightly, his wound still hurting with certain movements of his arm.

The sad thing is that they don't want to leave the barrel now. The barrel has become their safe haven, it is what they have come to know. And once people are set in their ways it is hard to show them a new direction. They have been duped before, their trust is not given away that easily. You can hold your hand out to them, tell them you will help them out of the barrel, but they will look at you through sceptical eyes. Trust needs to be earned, and I shall earn that trust. If I can rid the streets of the filth then I can show them that they don't have to live in fear.

He walks into the solitude of the backroom and is greeted by the arrival of Burt, carrying a large laundry bag, swelling with enigma.

"Oh, hi Burt! I didn't see you come in." Thomas says laying his chasuble and stole over the back of the armchair and begins to untie his cincture, adding that to the increasing pile of sermon apparel.

"I snuck in during prayer." Burt replies, placing the bag of intrigue onto the coffee table next to the chessboard that has the remains of an earlier game still in progress.

"Oh, I see!" says Thomas removing the bag off over his head and laying that neatly across the chair too, them now standing in his everyday Priest dress he adjusts his hair with a firm swipe through his hand and adjusts his glasses.

"I have a surprise for you, Burt" Thomas smiles then spotting the bag, looks intrigued.

"What have you got in the bag, Burt?"

"Ah, I too have a surprise for you!"

"And what's that?" Thomas asks trying to peek inside the bag like a snooping child at Christmas.

"No peeking Thomas! I actually have some news for you too. Some very important news as well as these goodies."

"Really? Do tell!" Thomas says intrigue gripping him.

"No, I insist you go first!" Says Burt.

"Okay!" Thomas replies, "Follow me!"

They walk back out of the room and into the hall crossing towards the organ, which shields the secret entrance to the cellar.

"I've found a name!"

"You have?"

"Yes!" He smiles pointing at the two nights guarding the precious secret.

"Do you know what that symbol is on the knights' shield?" Burt shakes his head "Can't say that I do, no!"

"That is the Key of Solomon..."

"The Vatican City key?" Burt asks, nodding having heard the name now.

"Yes! And because of my connection to the place and seeing this key, I took it as a sign... I will be going by the name of Vatican!"

"Hey, that works!" Burt says smiling.

"I came up with something too, but yours is better than mine." He laughs.

"Go on, tell me?"

"Well, it's The Angel of Justice, but..."

"That's fantastic, Burt! Hey maybe I'll have them both! There aren't any rules are there?" He laughs.

"Let me check the vigilante rulebook!" mocks Burt.

"Vatican, The Angel of Justice!" Thomas grins "I like that." His mind wanders off somewhere for a moment, probably into some childhood fantasy of himself as Vatican standing majestically with his hands on his hips, cape blowing in the wind.

"So do you want to know what I've got in the bag or do you want the important news I have locked away in my old brain?"

"Save the news, I want to know what goodies you've brought me?" Thomas laughs as they both walk back towards the backroom.

"You're like a child!" laughs Burt.

They reach the backroom and for privacy, Burt shuts the door to the church. He rummages around in the bag.

"I've put together some items that may be of benefit to you while you're out on the field. Some of these things are only for starters, we can get new things as we can afford them, or I can update them as we go along."

"Update them?"

"If you want any designs adding to things or little touches like that. I am a dab hand with a needle and thread. Doris was too, I think that's where I learnt a lot of it from."

"I can't wait!" Thomas says excitedly.

"I'll save my creation until last, but first of all, I'll reveal what I found today down at the flea market!"

"The flea market?"

"It's amazing the things you can find there, Thomas. Like these!" Burt unveils a pair of black leather motorcycle boots.

"You are a size Eleven aren't you?"

"Yes! Oh Burt they're great!" He takes one and surveys it. "Hey they're surprisingly light!"

"Wait, there's more!" As Burt retrieves a pair of black leather motor cross gloves, the hard plastic across the knuckles were slightly scraped but other than, that they were in perfect condition.

"Scraped a little, but they look durable and the grip looks good too."

"They'll be fine!" Thomas says, sliding one on to try it, clenching his gloved hand into a fist and then opening it again.

"Then there's this for any little items you'll need with you out there." He pulls out a police style utility belt, black in colouring with several pouches attached to it and fixed together with a plastic buckle clip.

"Of course! I haven't even thought about that! What type of things do you suggest, Burt?"

"Oh, I don't know... maybe any weapons that you devise, first aid kit, a small tool kit perhaps? A torch, tape recorder? Oh, and this may sound ridiculous, but something to eat?"

"Sure, I'll take a lunchbox and a thermos!" laughs Thomas.

"I'm being serious! Energy bar and energy drink. You never know when you'd need something like that."

"I'm only teasing, Burt. It makes perfect sense."

"Then there is this little beauty that I thought could come in handy!" Burt shows him a small earpiece that resembled an earring aid.

"A hands-free cell phone ear piece! You don't see these around much these days!"

"I guess not, that's why I found it for next to nothing at the flea market!"

"Well, I will definitely need my hands free and it will be useful to stay in touch with you."

Burt stops rummaging and looks up at Thomas who is investigating his new belt.

"Now this is the pièce de résistance...I won't be mad if you don't like it and I can always change it to something else. But I thought of you and your crusade..."

He lifts out a padded set of hockey shoulder pads and attached to the front and back was long slender pieces of white fabric trimmed with a red seam. In the centre of the torso sits a lovingly embroidered crucifix, the very same shape as the one on the stone knight's shield, in a luscious vibrant red, it gave it the look of a Knight's Templar surcoat.

"I don't know what to say!" Thomas says in awe and a little in love with the design. He takes it in his hands and caresses the emblem, his emblem! Like a blind man reading braille, taking in every painstakingly sewn stitch by his friend. Realising the care and hard work that had gone into it. Knowing all this, Thomas would have said he liked it even if he didn't, but he did. He loved it.

"Well, is it okay?" Burt nervously asks.

401

"It's more than okay, Burt. It's perfect!" and with that, Thomas hugs him. Burt was caught off guard but hugs him back, an embracing of friendship. An affectionate show of emotions that they both appreciated and needed.

"I am glad!" Burt says smiling.

"Now for the important information I have for you." Thomas looks again at his new uniform enamoured with it and is only half listening to Burt. Rubbing his fingers over the crucifix again and again.

"There is to be a meeting between The Doomsday Gang and Vinnie Valentine!" Thomas' ears prick up and now Burt has his undivided attention.

"I overheard that cockroach, that Sniff!" Burt scowls at the very mention of his name, almost feeling sickly violated by saying it himself "He was talking to someone on his cell phone about some meeting"

"With Valentine?" Thomas asks.

"Yes, I believe that someone Sniff knows is going to try and kill Valentine. I presume one of his little gaggle must be fed up of being treated like dogs and are fighting back."

"But it would put a bunch of key Doomsday Gang members all in one place at one time." Thomas says thinking it all over.

"Exactly! Right for the pickings. And if someone were to discreetly contact the authorities! We'd have them!" Burt smiles.

"Make sure it's Detective Graham you inform...I like him, he's one of the good guys. I figure a sting like this would be a huge feather in his cap!"

"And of course you'd be there to help if need be."

"Sure... I think I should get there first, survey the situation and then contact you to give you the green light to contact Graham." They both nod at each other.

"I mean it wouldn't make sense to just have the cops waiting for them. They'd run and then that would be a chance wasted."

"Agreed!"

"So, when does this little get together take place?"

"Tonight!"

"Tonight? Doesn't give us much time to prepare..."

"You're already prepared Thomas. You need this to show you how prepared you are."

"I hope you're right!"

"I'm sure of it, I have faith in you."

"Whereabouts will it be hosted?"

"Ventura Bridge, at midnight!"

"Right. Then it's on!" Burt rummages in his bag again and pulls out some boot polish and a rag and sits down and starts polishing Thomas' boots.

"Well, we best make a start then!" He dabs his rag into the black oasis and starts to vigorously rub it against the leather. Thomas looks at him and smiles. He pictured him in the army doing this with his military issue size eights as he is perched on the corner of some cast iron bed, drenched head to foot in military green. Then he looks at him now and down at his black loafers and they are shimmering his own reflection back at him. He still maintains that perfection today in everyday life.

What a guy!

"Unfortunately, I wasn't able to find you anything to mask your face." Burt says busily massaging the polish into the leather in circular motions.

"Maybe you could try the internet? I'm sure you'd be able to find something on there? I hear they have just about everything on there!"

"Yeah, with what I have in mind a fancy dress website might be the answer. Doesn't help us tonight though." Thomas ponders.

"No." Burt agrees focusing on what he is doing.

Thomas smiles as an idea forms in his head. He dips his fingers into the boot polish and removing his glasses. He swipes it across his eyes blacking out much of the upper part of his face.

"How about this?"

Burt looks up and smiles.

"Well, that should do it kid!"

Several emotions stampede across his gut like wild bison, but none of that can wipe the smile from Thomas' face.

Chapter 36

A cold frigid wind swept across the Ventura Bridge like a spine-chilling apparition. Fall was finally coming to an end and winter was being ushered in by this wintry gale that forced its way in from the Gulf of Alaska. A battered Ford Crown Victoria caressed with streaks of rust like racing stripes, sits askew on the bridge. Adjacent to the dilapidated jalopy stands Spider and his fellow Webheads; Dallas, Sniff and Boris, all huddled together like a colony of penguins, shivering in the late night wintry breeze. A combination of cigarette smoke and vapours of cold breath rise into the night air, intertwined in a forbidden bachata, cavorting together before disappearing. The gang is looking jittery, handguns on show in their waistband holsters. Their hands quivering a little as they hover over the handles, knowing that they will be using them tonight. It could all get ugly. Spider is the only one that doesn't seem fazed by the whole ordeal. The man who has the most to lose out of them all, the man who has put it all on the line and if it all goes wrong... it's his head served up on a silver platter. So if anyone should be nervous about tonight it's him, but he isn't, not on the outside anyway. His exterior is tough like the shell of a coconut, hard and tough to penetrate, but on the inside he must be bubbling like a cauldron of emotions.

"It's almost midnight!" Stutters Boris.

"I don't like this. Not one bit!"

"Oh, stop being a fucking pussy, Boris!" Dallas snaps.

"What? You mean you're not nervous at all?"

"I could be gunned down by an angry mob boss and left to rot on an ugly ass bridge! In the cold! In the middle of the fucking night! And you ask me if I'm nervous?"

"There is no need for sarcasm!" Boris scoffs.

"You two need to chill the fuck out!" Sniff intervenes, being the voice of reason, which is surprisingly out of character.

"Look, Spider has this all under control. Right Spider?" Sniff continues. They all turn to look at Spider like he is the messiah, waiting for his words to soothe their apprehensive state. Spider takes a long drag of his cigarette and blows the smoke out of the corner of his mouth and nods.

"It's cool!" Spider says nonchalantly.

"See!" Sniff adds.

"'It's cool!' Seriously is that all you have to say on the matter?" Dallas yelps, his voice carrying around the deserted bridge. In the daytime the only road that joins Studd City to Forge City is crowded with traffic, but not at this time of night. Nobody wants to be out this late in either city, not if they've got any sense.

"Take it easy, Dal!" Spider says trying to reassure him.

"Take it easy he says? I'm shitting in my fucking Calvin's here! Fuck! Boris, this all your fault!"

"How is this my fault?" He argues.

406

"I thought I had myself under control until you started yapping."

"Guys, Fuck!" Shouts Sniff, "Spider said he has this under control, then he's got it under control, okay?"

"I hate to agree with Sniff! I mean fuck! That's rarer than the burger meat that Gilbert Carino sells on the corner of Finkle and Reeves!"

They all let out a chuckle.

"But, he is right! I have it all under control."

The headlights of a brand new Lincoln Navigator bathes the quivering cluster as it rolls towards them.

"He's here!" Sniff says.

There is an immediate discarding of cigarettes, all at different stages of their life spans, all not yet finished, but discarded nonetheless. The large black boulder of a machine stops maybe fifty yards away from them and for a moment, just sits there seemingly watching them, stalking them like a lioness stalks a zebra. Unlike the lioness the bulky SUV is not hiding in the shards of sunburnt African grass, no, it is there in plain sight bathed in moonlight, illuminated like an actor on stage being lit up by the spotlight. It wants to be seen. But these zebra, as skittish as they are will not run, not tonight.

Thomas' footsteps explode on the damp concrete of the Ventura docks. He picks up a thundering pace as he heads towards the daunting iron structure that lies prone up ahead, like the bones of a slain dragon with its hollowed out ribcage of iron girders acting as a coliseum for the evenings brutal gladiatorial contest.

His uniform fits him well and would not have looked out of place galloping over the Holy Land to do battle. His ivory surcoat ripples in the wind revealing his lycra fitted apparel that he uses so regularly when running. His gloved hand grips the broom handle he used as a Bo staff to fend off the delinquents that invaded the church just a month prior.

This makeshift Bo staff isn't ideal. It's awkward to manoeuvre while I'm running. I don't really need it, but Burt insisted I take something. So how do I say no to him?

He fights against the wintry gale, the piercing current biting his face. His cheeks chaffing under the bombardment staining his jowl in scarlet blemish. He looks up at the gargantuan structure that seems to be moving under the spell of the enchanting first moon of the winter. He reduces his speed but not out of need, it is apprehension and fear that slows him to a gentle lollop.

Suddenly I feel sick, my gut is doing a loop the loop. This is big! I've been preparing for this for months and now the time has finally come I'm terrified. Sure, this isn't my first rodeo, but I've handled nothing like this. Just the anticipation of what could happen to me tonight is frightening.

He stops running and walks slowly towards the bridge. He staggers and leans on a nearby bollard. It steadies him and a thought burrows its way deep into his mind like a drilling rig drill piercing his skull, exposing his brain to something he never thought he would think possible.

I could die tonight.

Violently he vomits. The discharge slaps the floor, a pool of watery gruel disperses on the uneven docks.

I've dealt with all manner of depraved individuals. Thieves, rapists, murderers and sometimes gangs, sometimes up to 8 at a time.

But this is different. I'm walking into a potential war zone with nowhere to hide. This could be it.

He slinks down against the bollard, almost draping himself on top of it. His breathing pattern becoming heavy and his chest tight as though his torso was in the clutches of a man-eating python, constricting with each struggling breath. Anxiety attacks.

I don't think I can do this.

He drops to his knees and struggles to control his breathing. The python tightens its coils once more.

"I'm alone!" he gasps, his heart rate speeds up rapidly, beating so hard. He fears it may explode from the safety of its cage and end up in a quivering heap on the damp dockyard floor next to the puddle of broth like vomit that sits casually fermenting.

Oh the fear! The fear of being alone is so strong it clouds my judgement. Alone...not just now, not just here and now in this crazy crusade I find myself on but in life. Fear of being alone, forever alone.

He grasps at his thighs tightly trying to control himself, trying to remember his breathing training, his mediation, but it's all cloudy.

I can't focus. Cloudy...dark clouds obstruct my vision. Almost black. The Blackness...The Black... The Black Crane!

A violent and aggressive vision strikes at him and brings him out of his haze.

"Burt!" he pants. Slowly his breathing returns to some kind of normality.

"I still have Burt!"

He activates his ear piece and hears the dialling tone softly bleeping in his ear.

"Thomas? I mean Vatican! Is everything okay?" Burt asks, with obvious trepidation in his voice.

"Burt! I'm here..."

"Good, good! I was starting to get worried."

"I...I don't think I can do this!" Thomas says, swallowing deep and tasting that burning sensation left over from the vomit, that taste that feels like a snail has left its slimy trail in your gullet. There is a pause. Burt knows how difficult this must be for Thomas and before Burt can say anything, Thomas speaks again.

"I'm scared Burt!" Battling his own ego to even say the sentence, but he trusts Burt.

"That's understandable!" Burt says softly, "I'm all the way back here and I'm chomping on my fingernails!"

This time it is Burt that is met by silence.

"Listen, open the rear pouch of your utility belt."

"But...why?" Thomas asks a little confused.

"I slipped something in there for you. Something that may help you in moments of self doubt."

Blindly he reaches around and detaches the press stud and opens the pouch. He delves in and grabs something soft, some kind of fabric. He takes it out and immediately on seeing it, he wells up with emotion. He holds in his hands the crimson silk sash that was a gift from his mentor, Master Sato.

"I know how much that means to you. Sato believes in you. I believe in you!"

He clenches the sash in his hands and buries his boot polished brow into its soft caress, smelling it, smelling Sato, the temple, Xing, the mountain, China itself. Smells trigger memories. His face emerges from the sanctuary of his dear master's crimson sash. He smiles as if by the power of positivity and support had wiped away the anxiety in one fell swoop. Again, his polish sodden brow wrinkles in that sure look of determination.

"Thank you Burt!"

"Go get'em champ!" Burt says and even though Thomas could not see him, he could hear the smile in his voice. And how can he disobey that smile?

"Vatican out." He says, confident and gruff. A complete three sixty to the warbling voice that meekly stuttered and almost called 'I quit' just minutes ago. The line went dead and somewhere Burt is smiling and fist pumping the air. Vatican slowly folds up the sash and places it back into his pouch at the rear of his utility belt. He takes a deep breath, possibly the deepest breath he has ever taken, his chest expanding with the cold night air. He looks over at the cold uninviting Hennig River that laps up against the side of the docks. He sees his reflection and for a moment in the ripples he could have sworn that he saw Sato looking back at him. Then with a quick turn, he headed up towards the bridge. He made quick work of the concrete slope

411

that connected Ventura Bridge to the docks. On arrival he could see two cars and a cluster of bodies. He crept along the edge of the bridge and kept himself concealed in-between the iron girders and the shadows, until he was adjacent to Spider and his group. He crouched down and took in another breath of that fresh sharp air and waited and watched what was about to unfold.

Chapter 37

Detective Graham sits at his desk and yawns. He stretches his arms out above his head and leans back into his office chair. His desk clustered with mugshots of several familiar faces. He stands up and collects all the mugshots up into his hands shuffling them a little as he does so, like a magician with a gigantic pack of playing cards. He walks over to his large cork board, yawning as he does so, and starts to pin the mugshots to the board. Familiar faces of Joseph Webb AKA Spider, is pinned up first and then below his, Boris Volkov, Danny Orton AKA Dallas and Sylvester Jones AKA Sniff, follow in quick succession. Then on the other side of the board he pins up Jack Thompson AKA Twitch, George Ramsbottom AKA Grill, Elvis Valentine and The Chapman twins. He then adds some more under a header entitled 'Possible Associates'. He holds up a photograph cut from a sports magazine of Desmond Reed AKA Dee Zee. He's tired and not paying attention as he jabs the pin into his finger. He growls and pins up the photograph with a blood stained pin. He immediately slots his finger into his mouth and sucks it gently. He takes it out and looks at the tiny hole in his throbbing finger and wonders for a second that how can something so small hurt so much. He ignores the constant throbbing and wipes the excess blood onto his trousers. The next photograph to go up is a candid shot of 'The Cats Whiskers' club owner Charles Samuels. Then he looks down into his hand as one mugshot remains. Vincent 'The Thunder' Valentine. He stares at it and sneers, creasing the photo up at each side where his grip bites into it. Blood from his finger trickles down across the image of Valentine's arrogant smug face. The phone rings and causes Graham to jump.

"Jesus!" He cries walking over to the desk and slamming the mugshot of Valentine down on to it. He lets the phone ring as he looks up at the clock and sees just how late it is.

"This must be Mae to tell me my dinner is in the dog again!" He picks up the receiver and readies himself for an ear lashing from his wife.

"Look Mae, I'm really sorry I lost track of time again..." There is no reply from the other end.

"Hello?" He asks.

"Is this Graham?" A muffled voice crackles on the other end of a bad line.

"Erm yes, this is Detective Graham. Who is this?"

"Never mind who I am. I'm not important, not anymore?"

"Sorry?" Graham asks confused

"Listen to me. It's all about to kick off at Ventura Bridge!"

"What is? What are you talking about?"

"Just shut up and listen for a minute, Sid!"

"Wait a minute how'd you know..."

"Pipe down!" The caller yells before lowering his voice

again.   "You're wasting valuable time!"

"Okay, okay I'm listening, just spit it out already!"

"Ventura Bridge is about to be turned into a war zone!"

"What?"

"You wanna catch The Doomsday? You wanna catch Valentine? They're all going to be there and it isn't going be pretty."

"How do you know all of this?" Graham demands.

"The eyes and the ears, my friend!" The caller hangs up and Graham is met by the annoyance of the dull drawn out dialling tone.

"Fuck!" he cries and bursts out of his office.

The phone begins to ring again. It rings, and rings and rings.

Chapter 38

The large bungling Chapman twins exit the vehicle and glance over at the small assembly of Webheads. One of them opens the rear door and a thick cloud of cigar smoke escapes into the cold night air. There is the sound of heavy and expensive shoes connecting with the bridge's tarmac and out saunters Vinnie Valentine. He eye fucks the hell out of Spider and doesn't even give the other members of his pitiful gang the respect or consideration of so much as a glance. Valentine chews on the end of the cigar as lumps of ash fall from its smouldering tip and he smiles.

"So, you wanted to see me about something, kid?" He starts to walk up towards them, casually without a care in the world.

Spider's stomach turns and knots itself like the bow on a Christmas present, but he can't show that. He can't show weakness.

"Too fuck'in right!" Spider sneers.

Valentine mocks him with his booming laughter that echoes and seems to surround them, smothering them.

"You know for that shit you pulled with my car I should just kill you now." Valentine grins as he stops right in front of him. Spider has to look up to the towering Valentine that

416

appears to have blocked out the moons glow and suddenly bathed Spider in shadow.

"Go for it!" Spider says, spreading his arms out either side as if to show his back up behind him. Valentine glances at them all and smiles again.

"Cute!" he gnaws again on his cigar.

"I see you brought your cavalry with you. I can smell the shit in their pants from here."

"Fuck you!" Spider sneers again puffing out his chest in a lame attempt to be as big as Valentine.

"No, I think it'll be me that will be fucking you with my foot straight up your black ass!"

"Fuck you, you wop!" Spider bites back.

They growl at each other and then Valentine starts laughing again.

"Oh don't worry, it's not a race thing. To me it doesn't matter what colour you are, if you get in my way I will slaughter you!"

There is a pause as Valentine calls to the Chapman Twins who simultaneously join him either side.

"Now, I can only presume that you are not happy with how I'm running things and that you and your little faggots think that you can do better?"

"We couldn't do much worse!" scoffs Sniff.

"Ah the brains of the operation speaks! Don't think I don't know what game you have been playing too Jones! Dealing your own shit! Well, Vixen's shit!"

Spider turns to Sniff and frowns at him.

"Oh you didn't know he was still doing that?" Valentine asks sarcastically.

"How can you have people watch your back if you can't trust them, kid?"

"I trust them!" he snaps.

"Then more fool you. To create an empire, you have got to have the respect and the support of those behind you. My men would gladly lie on their swords for me. Would your men do the same?" Valentine scans them all jittery and nervous.

"I don't think they would. Especially not that dribbling pile of dog shit!" He says pointing a chunky cigar in Sniffs direction.

"Look, they got my back. They believe in the same things I do!"

"And what do you believe?" Valentine asks.

"That you're a selfish motherfucker who makes your followers do all the dirty work for you, while you just count all the money that's rolling in! And we are sick of it! We are the ones taking all the fucking risks and we get shit!"

"And you want to be the leader of this operation?"

"Damn fucking straight! And I would do a fucking better job at it than your fat ass!"

Spider can't believe he just said that, his adrenaline has kicked in now and there is no turning back.

"Yes, a fair and just leader! Giving a fair share of the profits to the people." Valentine mocks.

"Yeah! Yeah motherfucker that's right!"

"Sure you would." He smiles, "D'you smell that boys?" Valentine turns to ask The twins who both look back at him with vacant stares.

"Smell what, Boss?" Little Ben asks.

Valentine rolls his eyes.

"Bullshit, boys, bullshit! Let me tell you what would happen. You'd start off with a fair slice of pie for everyone, then you'd become greedy and want more. So you take more and become selfish. Then you can have what you want. Cars, houses, women anything you want. You going to pass all that up, so you can give some lowlife runner a fair share of the profits? I don't think so. Then you get paranoid that people want your money! That's how it works, that's how it always works. And you see my paranoia told me that it was you and look where we are now."

They stare at each other, a deathly gaze of fuck you versus fuck you.

Vatican looks on peering through the shadows. His heart beating at full pelt in his chest, his chest breathing rapidly and heavily again causing the red crucifix on his chest to rise and fall.

The adrenaline rush is unbelievable! It reminds me a lot of a medieval battle with the two leaders meeting on the battlefield before the mayhem ensues. But they were the days when men were warriors! And fought sword to sword. Hand to hand. Battles weren't won with bullets! I fear blood will be spilt here tonight.

Valentine looks down at Spider, who in fairness has not backed down or moved a muscle from the daunting presence of Vinnie

Valentine, and somewhere deep inside he respects that. He would never say it, but he does.

"So you've got your two balls and a dick behind you trembling in their sneakers, with their Glock's hanging out of their pants. You think that intimidates me?"

"There is still more of us than you. Still more bullets to fill your ass with. Besides Tweedle Dee and Tweedle Dum there probably don't even know how to take a piss, let alone fire a gun!" Spider fires back.

"Fuck you, maggot!" Growls Big Ben.

"Easy, boys!" Says Valentine, "You're right. They aren't very good when it comes to shooting."

The Chapman Twins look at him disheartened and both murmur "Boss?" At the same time.

"That is why I have to give them these!" Valentine continues and with that, The Chapman twins unveil matching UZI sub machine guns. The Webheads eyes grow wide at the sight of the game changers.

"Yeah, it doesn't matter if you can't hit a donkey's ass with a banjo with these beauties. They'll just spread through anything they're aimed at. Which on this occasion, happens to be you!"

Just then a couple of cars slowly approach and park up next to Valentine's brand new Lincoln Navigator. Out steps Twitch Thompson, Dee Zee, Cheshire Charles, Grill and a handful of Doomsday Gang members all armed and raring to get involved.

"Oh, and here is my cavalry." Valentine smiles, taking a large drag on his cigar he puffs the smoke into Spider's face. Spider's stomach curdles from the sickening smell of smoke that clogs his airways and he unleashes a vicious cough. Clutching his knees, he coughs and yaks. All he can hear is the thundering laughter of Valentine, looming over him like a storm cloud.

"You know something, kid? You've shown you have some balls and I respect that. That really pains me to say but I do I respect that you have stood up for what you believe in (Even if it's wrong) and came here to face me tonight. So because I'm such a soft centred old fool, I feel I owe you something. Hell, in about five minutes time you're going to be as dead as roadkill, so I think you deserve a free shot." Valentine drops his cigar to the roads and treads on it with his extortionately priced Italian loafers. Ash, smouldering embers and smoke disperse from underneath his heavy foot.

"Go on. Take your best shot. I owe you that much." Valentine says placing his hands behind his back and leaning forward, leaving his large square chin out in no man's land to be hit like a high striker at the annual state fair. Spider turns to his crew and mouths the words 'Where are they?' And suddenly Spider feels like he's been double-crossed. It doesn't appear that La Familia will be coming, and they are doomed.

I'm dead.

Vatican watches on shrouded by the bridge's gigantic frame. His fist clenches as anger whizzes through his veins. He wants to make his move, but his brain is telling him no, even though his heart is saying yes.

Anyone can see that this Valentine is a bully. And I do hate bullies! Met a few of them through my life. Ricky Landell and his friends at the orphanage, Light-fingered Larry on these

421

very streets when I was homeless and of course the biggest tormentor of them all, my father. Father? That's a laugh... Dwayne!

He calms himself gripping his staff with both hands and tightly squeezes it, as though it were a wet towel and he were wringing out all the moisture. This was another technique he had learnt from Sato, to put those feelings into an inanimate object. It works, he is calm again.

I know this Spider is no saint, far from it. But he needs to do something here before it becomes a bloodbath. It's almost as if he's stalling for something. Waiting for something to happen. But what?

Spider rises out of the cloud of cigar smoke that orbits him like the rings of Saturn. Something has changed. His face wears a different expression, an expression of someone that no longer gives a fuck. The face of a man with nothing less to lose. He stands up straight and balling a fist, he pulls back his arm the way that you'd pull back and hold the launcher on a pinball machine, holding it before letting it fly furiously into the game. Spider strikes and his fist snaps violently into the solid square jaw of Valentine's skull. The force of the impact sounds like the gunshot of a faraway hunter's rifle and it rocks Valentine, visibly to all that his eyes roll back in his head as his head is harshly whipped back. There is complete silence as everyone looks on wide eyed and open mouthed, none of them can compute what has just taken place. Not even Spider. He's definitely earned Valentine's respect now, hasn't he? Blood trickles out of the corner of Valentine's mouth and he checks for blood gently patting away with his chunky finger tips.

"You've got one hell of a punch, kid." Valentine declares. Then he smiles a sadistic, horrible and unnervingly lecherous looking smile. His rows of teeth now stained with blood making them appear pink.

"But, I'm still standing and that was your free shot." Valentine rises back from his slouch after taking such a shot, a punch that had years of pent-up aggression behind it. He stands tall and his large intimidating frame looms over Spider once more. He unbuttons his suit jacket and lets it fall behind him, immediately caught by Big Ben standing on his right hand side. Then undoing his cuffs of his shirt, he rolls them up to reveal his large hairy apelike forearms, resembling *Popeye's* but without the homemade stick and poke anchor tattoos.

"Now! It's my turn!" Seethes Valentine, hissing little pink blood bubbles through his clenched teeth. Now if the sound of Spider's fist connecting with Valentine's jaw was like the sound of a far-off hunter's rifle, then this in comparison was like a shotgun going off right next to your ear. Valentine's huge mitt smothers Spider's face as it drives into his nose causing it to explode in a Vesuvius of blood and mucus. Spider drops to the floor in a heap, his head spinning around like an out of control Ferris wheel on high speed. The faces of the spectators seem to whiz past his eyes several times in quick succession. Spider tries to get back to his feet but is welcomed to consciousness with another fist to the face, left eye socket, immediate welt. Then another into the side of his temple, head ringing like an alarm bell, eyes rolling back in his head like a slot machine. Jackpot! Collect your winnings. Dallas and Boris suddenly attempt to move in and help Spider, at least to his feet but adjacent to them are the Chapman twins and they are ready with their Submachine guns aiming at them.

"Stay the fuck back assholes!" Little Ben growls and they do, slowly with hands up in peace they do. What else could they do. Valentine repeatedly rains down on him with hailstorm from the Gods, until suddenly he stops. He stands over Spider's kneeling carcass that gently sways in the cold breeze like a wilting flower. Valentine's breathing pattern heavy now, even Valentine has had enough, out of practice maybe? His clenched fists saturated with Spider's blood that in the moonlight, appears dark, almost black.

"You know something," He pauses to catch his breath, "I really did think you had a future with us. You could have been the one to take over when I was done. You have more sense than my idiot of a son, I could have made that happen."
Spider looks up at him through swelling eyes and grins a cracked smile, without diamonds and a golden grill but replaced by bloodied gums.

"Now you tell me!" he scoffs.

"Your trouble is your fucking attitude! If you'd have just knuckled down and shown me what you were capable of, this time next year you'd have been eating from the top table. But now...well, there is no next year for you!" He holds out his blood stained right hand and Big Ben hands him a Desert Eagle.50, its silver barrel glistening in the soft light of the moon. He cocks the gun and Spider rises kneeling up straight, he knows his time on this earth is over so he wants to go out like a man and he awaits the final playing piece to make its move. He points the gun directly at Spider's face, he closes his eyes and waits.

Do something Thomas! Help him! But, what can I do? To go in now would be suicide! A distraction! You can make a distraction and save this guy's life!

Valentine spits some blood out of his mouth before gripping the handle of the gun just how he wants it.

"Fool me once shame on you, fool me twice shame on me. But try and fuck me in the ass like a dirty fucking whore, then fuck you!" He growls and with that he adjusts his aim and fires sending a bullet hurtling towards the unsuspecting Sniff that cuts through his thigh like shit through a goose. Again that dumbfounded look is sweeps across everyone's faces, including Vatican who was about to make a move. Sniff cries out in pain and collapses next to the car grabbing at his leg. Boris kneels next to him acting as a useless nursemaid.

"That's for dealing Stardust to my customers, asshole!" Valentine growls waving the gun in his direction, before turning his attentions back to Spider again.

"Now, where was I..." he says pointing the gun his Spider's face again.

There is a gunshot and both Valentine and Spider look at the gun in confusion. The shot did not come from his gun.

"Boss..." Whimpers Little Ben from behind him. He

turns around to see blood stream down his egg like cranium, from a hole in his forehead.

"Ben?" Valentine says in shock, and the large barrel chested twin that was born a whole six minutes after his brother falls to the floor, dead.

"No!" shouts Big Ben and kneels down to the body of his dead twin brother who had shared everything together, a womb, an apartment, eerily a girlfriend and some would even say a brain. He lifts him up and cries over his dead bulking mass. But before anyone else can act, two retarded looking Dodge pick up trucks hurtle onto the scene from behind Spider's Webheads, coming from the Forge City side. The back of the open pick up trucks are filled with La Familia members all brandishing various guns and firing them in every direction like raging Native Americans.

"Take cover!" Valentine yells and heads for the safety of the Ford Navigator, diving into the backseat. La Familia's trucks come screeching and skidding to a halt and The Coyote jumps down with two handguns in his hands and gives the call.

"Kill this Doomsday cagar!" And they all unload their weapons at the Doomsday Gang who quickly take cover behind their vehicles. Dallas scrambles towards Spider and helps him to his feet and makes for the safety of their car. Boris does the same dragging a screaming Sniff with him.

"Are you okay, man?" Dallas asks Spider who is coming around now. He nods wiping the blood from his potholed face.

"I'm fucking fantastic, Dal!"

They both laugh.

"You are a fucking legend, man! Can't believe you took all that punishment from him!" Dallas says shaking his head. The Coyote joins them.

"Are you fuckers gonna help us or what?" Grinning a crooked grin with the devil in his eyes like some mad man.

"What took you so long ass hole?" Spider laughs.

"Gotta make an entrance, man!" He laughs before bolting up and leaning over the car firing bullets into the Doomsday's cars, screaming obscenities in Spanish.

Vatican watches on helpless. Moments ago he was about to act to save a man's life who was about to be executed. He could not have sat idly by and do nothing as that happened. Now he looks on at a war.

What can I do? Nothing. There is nothing I can do.

Guns erupt just tens of yards away like a vicious scene from a movie set in WWII. Bullets ricochet off cars, pierce windows, and turn the bodies of the cars into Swiss cheese. Members of each gang are gunned down with multiple hits creating fountains of blood that spray into the air and then falls to the floor with the fresh corpse that it just abandoned.

The itch in my gut to act is incredible. My heart screaming at me to do something. Anything! But I can't. I am not frozen with fear. Not now, I am way passed that. I have no body armour. Nothing to protect me but my wits and a Bo staff...Well a broom handle. Lives are being lost before my very eyes and I can do nothing. Maybe the authorities will be here soon and I can help round up any stragglers trying to leave the party

427

early. It's all I can do.

Bullets rebound off the iron girders that Vatican hides behind and realises just how close to the action he actually is.

Note to self, body armour.

Behind the wheel of the once Ford Crown Victoria, Sniff leans up against it wincing in pain as Boris wraps a makeshift torque out of the sleeve of his shirt.

"Oh fuck! Boris give it to me straight! Am I gonna die or what?" Sniff snivels.

"Don't be a pussy! You'll be fine, just stay down." Boris answers and then pulls out his gun and adds to the relentless deafening cry of gunfire.

Vinnie Valentine sits in the back of the brand new SUV that is being pebble-dashed by an onslaught of bullets on his cell phone to his wife.

"It doesn't look good...I know, I know...The fucker had it all planned out, was a set up all along...yeah...yeah...he had some help from the Fucking Coyote! I know... You don't need to tell me that! The little fucking turncoat!"

The tinted windshield explodes and he drops behind the front seat only to see the rear windshield go too and shower him in shards of brown glass.

"I know...I gotta get out of here! I'm gonna make a move...I love you too." He hangs up the cell phone and opens the door and calls to Big Ben who is emptying his UZI in an emotional tirade towards those that have just taken his brother's life.

"We've gotta get out of here, Ben! C'mon now!" He bellows.

Ben jumps into the driver's seat and tries to start the car but is met by a bombardment of bullets and takes one in the shoulder. He ducks down behind the steering wheel.

"Are you okay, Ben?"

"Yeah, Boss. Just tagged my shoulder!"

"We gotta get out of here!"

"I'll try, Boss. But gotta wait for those bullets to stop."

"I got news for ya! They ain't gonna be stopping any time soon. Now floor it!"

Big Ben turns the ignition and barges straight forward into the remains of the Webheads broken Crown Victoria. They become under fire as Big Ben ducks down again for his own safety, bullets exploding all around him as his tries to reverse out of the danger zone, but the front fender of the navigator has become caught on the rear wheel arch of the Victoria.

"Get us the fuck out of here, Ben!" Shouts Valentine.

In the distance the sound of sirens can be heard screaming like banshees in the night, heading to the carnage under glows of blue and red.

"Good old, Burt!" Vatican tells himself. No need for silence now, nobody would hear him if he wailed at the top of his lungs. A beep tickles his eardrum indicating an incoming call. He activates the earpiece and hears Burt's soft husky voice under the serenade of bullets.

"Vatican...is everything okay?"

"Well, I'm fine Burt. But it's really kicked off here!"

"As long as you are safe."

"I couldn't jump into this even if I wanted too! I'd be tenderised in seconds. Well done on tipping off Graham. I can hear them, they're on their way and they're going to catch them all in the act."

"I wish I could take credit, but I couldn't get through to him. Somebody else must have beat me to it!"

The SCPD arrive on the scene, various vehicles and riot vans hurtle onto the bridge. Detective Graham bursts from a police car which is driven by Officer Wilson. Clad in riot gear, the police dive into position and ready their weapons. Graham with a megaphone in hand makes himself heard over the thunderous bullet orchestra.

"This is the SCPD! Drop your weapons immediately!" Comes the distorted cry of Detective Graham's shrieking megaphone. Some of the Doomsday gang turn their attention to the Police and start to fire at them. Graham dives behind the squad car where he is met by Detective Freeman.

"I take it they're not gonna come quietly, Sid?"
He says light-heartedly.

"That's a negative, Rich!" Smiles Graham, "Just like the old days, huh?"
Eric Stone arrives in his SWAT gear.

"What's the plan, Detective?"

"Give'em hell, Eric!" Graham shouts.
Stone jogs back over to his unit and they unleash their firepower back at them.

Big Ben relentlessly tries to reverse the SUV, the rear wheels spinning in a cloud of burning rubber.

The Coyote and Spider suddenly approach the car with guns aimed at the backseat both smiling as Vinnie Valentine meets their gaze. Stranded and helpless, for the first time the stone faced brute looks scared. Terrified. His two arch nemesis' closing in on him with several bullets with his name on.

"Ben!" He calls desperately.

"Get me the fuck out of here now!"

"Time to say adios, Vinnie." Calls the Coyote smiling and Spider with his face unrecognisable smiles a grin with more tongue than teeth. They aim and their arms are steady. Valentine looks into the barrels of the guns like they're the eyes of the grim reaper. The navigator viciously rips away from the vicinity and backs into the bridge, just yards away from where Vatican is standing. If the girders weren't there, then he would have been dead. Ben struggles to turn the hefty vehicle away from the assault but he does. Spider and Coyote start to fire relentlessly at the fleeing vehicle and pierce the shell again but luckily for Valentine he remains unscathed.

"I fucking love you Ben!" He calls as they make their way speeding past his own and towards the police.

"Now let's get the hell out..." The Navigator's tyres blow out, a police spike strip lay in wait for them like a pit viper emerging from a bed of dried leaves. It strikes and rips the tyres to shreds. The sound of the tyres exploding was almost as loud as the roar of battle all-around them. Ben loses control and the day old SUV skids and crashes into the bridge coming to a

431

complete halt. Big Ben's unconscious bulk is draped over the wheel, that has bent and under the impact of his weight, probably broken some of his ribs in retaliation. Graham leads the charge towards the crash site with him Officer's Nash, Wilson and Jameson. Graham swings open the rear door to find a shaken and disorientated Vinnie Valentine in front of him.

"Fucking Jackpot!" Graham smiles.

"You've got nothing on me, Detective!" Valentine snarls.

"Oh yeah? We'll see! Jameson, Nash cuff him and read him his rights!" Jameson moves in with the handcuffs and Valentine launches a fist into his face, destroying his nose. Nash pulls out her gun and points in Valentine's face.

"Assault of an officer and resisting arrest! I think we have something on you now asshole!" She snarls at him like the feisty little firecracker she is. It's enough to give Graham an immediate erection, but he manages to keep the stallion in the corral.

"Good job, Nash!" he smiles at her as other officers arrive, "You guys get these two outta here. And somebody get Jameson a handkerchief!"

"Wilson! Go to the bridge entrance and get Phillips to make sure there is a barricade in place before one of them tries to run again."

"Okay, sir!" Wilson answers stuttering nervously. Graham can see this and places a hand on his shoulder and adds, "You're doing great kid!" and smiles that fatherly smile of reassurance that everyone needs from time to time.

"Thanks, sir!"

Graham turns his attentions to Nash.

"Nash, I need you to get in touch with FCPD and get them to block off their side of the bridge and move in behind the assailants. Then we got'em!"

"Yes, sir!" she says professionally but with that little fleck in her eye that sparkles at him when she looks into his eyes. Graham turns around to see Wilson standing staring at him like a new born baby fawn that has staggered onto a busy road. A hand clasped around his neck.

"Wilson? Wilson are you okay, kid?" Graham calls. Wilson takes his hand away from his neck and blood spumes out of the carotid artery. He looks at his hand that is smothered in the warmth of thick red blood.

"Oh shit! No!" Graham murmurs to himself and Wilson falls to the floor. He runs over to his prone body, his life fading rapidly, and he kneels by him pulling his scrawny body onto his lap. He firmly grasps his hand on the wound. He knows there is nothing he can do so he holds him in his arms, as Robert Wilson's eyes go grey and barren like two empty pools.

Sniff pulls himself into the front seat of the busted up Ford Victoria and attempts to start the engine, repeatedly turning it over until something clicks.

"I've had enough of this shit! I'm out of here!" He grizzles, snot and tears running down his gaunt features. Boris and Dallas appear at the windows.

"What are you doing, Sniff?" Dallas calls in between firing his handgun at Doomsday and Police.

"Thought I'd take a road trip! Wanna join me? We can

433

be like the fucking Griswolds!" He screams incoherently.

"I'm in!" Says Boris and climbs in the passenger seat.

"What are you guys doing?"

"Saving our ass, Dal! Now come on!" Boris yells.

"What about Spider?" Dallas says climbing in the backseat and dodging the assault of flailing bullets.

"We'll pick him up." Boris adds.

Finally the engine kicks in and Sniff floors it straight passed the Doomsday Gang.

"Sniff! What about Spider?" Dallas yells.

"Fuck him! We're going to mother fucking Wally World!" Sniff screams speeding passed the Police and straight through the gap in the unfinished barriers.

Eric Stone unleashes a frenzy of bullets at the fleeing vehicle that sprays the driver's door. The vehicle serves uncontrollably, Sniff is hit. Boris grapes the wheel and manoeuvres it straight again and they speed away. Spider stands watching on as his friends have abandoned him.

"The fucking bastards!" He seethes. Suddenly another car bursts passed him, and he dives and rolls out of its way to see The Doomsday generals making a getaway heading towards Forge City. Spider stands in the middle of the battlefield, gun in hand and looks around to see La Familia still unloading on the Doomsday cannon fodder that remains. There is no one of any real importance and they fire back as well as firing at police. Like a soldier just standing in the middle of no man's land. Suddenly a stream of light descends, illuminating him on the blood stained asphalt. He looks up and a rapid sweeping of blustery current

434

surrounds him, his dreadlocks quiver and move like the head of gorgons that is alive with a scalp of snakes, his clothes flutter and move too with the current. The feeling that he is standing in the innards of a tornado.

"Am I dead?" Spider asks himself as he stands almost lost in a trance, "Is this death? I felt nothing? Was I shot? I...I don't remember..."

Vatican watches on, confused at the sight of Spider just standing there lost.

I could take him down now. The shower of gunfire is not as overwhelming as before. But the Police... my cover would surely be blown then...

The light and current passes over Spider and he sees that it is a FCPD helicopter hovering over the battlefield bathing it in bright white light.

"What the fuck am I doing? I've gotta get out of here!" He says and looking up at the large iron girder structure, he runs towards it away from the firefight. He hears the voice of The Coyote call, something about being a pussy and leaving, but he carries on going and jumps up onto the girders and starts to climb up the structure. Vatican sees Spider making his escape. To where? Who knows! But nobody has seemed to notice him in all the confusion. Vatican gives chase.

Now we are talking.

The Coyote spots them and frowns in a mixture of confusion and wonderment.

"They're Fucking Loco man. Let's get out of here!" he calls and the remaining La Familia climb on to the back of the pick up trucks and make their escape. But their way is suddenly lit by more spotlights than they can count, blinding them and haunting them in their tracks as FCPD's finest are waiting for them.

Spider reaches the top of the structure and starts to run across the platform heading for the top, towards Forge City. Vatican arrives right on his tail giving chase. He made up ground with ease, this is his speciality, this is what he does best.

"Give it up, Spider!" Vatican calls rapidly approaching.

"What the fuck?" Spider shrieks. He turns and aims his gun over his shoulder and fires a few shots that rebound off the iron platform below Vatican's feet.

"Fuck you! Whoever you are." He screams and takes off faster. Vatican increases speed too.

Down on the bridge the last of the Doomsday Gang are being taken into custody and Detective Graham stands next to Detective Freeman. A cigarette quivering in his blood stained grip as Freeman lights it for him. They hear gunshots from above and they both look upward to see two men running on top of the bridges structure.

"Jesus H. Christ!" Graham murmurs and then shouts at the top of his voice, "Someone get me the chopper on those two idiots!"

Spider runs out of bullets and throws the gun at Vatican. It hits the girder just as he strides forward, and he steps on it, slipping on it and losing his balance, he falls off the main platform to another below. The helicopter circles bathing light at Spider who replies with a middle finger salute, smiling thinking that he has lost Vatican. Vatican passes through under a beam below him and comes out in front of Spider, blocking his escape route.

"It's game over, Spider!"

"Who the fuck are you? And what has this got to do with you asshole?"

"Maybe I'm your guardian angel?"

"Maybe you can just go and fuck off and get out of my way!" Spider launches at Vatican and a fight ensues. Spider's style is animalistic with real aggression, this makes him unpredictable with the possibility of fighting dirty. Vatican dodges his offence, blocking each ruthless attack with his staff. Staying defensive for now, unsure footing now could lead to his demise. The helicopter spasmodically circles them, occasionally bathing them with light. Graham on the ground communicates with the helicopter with a squad car radio receiver in his bloodied hand.

"This is Detective Graham of the SCPD. What the hell is going on up there?"

"Two guys fighting up here, Detective. One is dressed up like some sort of Knights Templar!"

"A Knight's Templar?" He says turning to Freeman.

"Like Sean Connery in Prince of Thieves."

"What the fuck?" He says before asking the pilot another question, "Why can't you keep that Goddamn light on them?"

"The wind is not our friend up here, sir. I'm having

trouble keeping her hovering as it is!"

Vatican's foot trips on a protruding bolt and Spider smashes him in the face with a few shots before running again. Vatican rises and launches the staff like a javelin that hits Spider right in the middle of his back knocking him over and rolling off the top of the bridge.

"No!" Vatican calls and runs to the edge where Spider fell but is met by a stiff kick in the face as a hanging spider ascends back onto the bridge.

"It's over, Spider. Give yourself up. They have Valentine. That's what you wanted wasn't it?"

"I wanted to be in fucking charge! I wanted to run things!" He's tired and beaten, almost emotional, his shoulders hunch and he looks defeated.

"I might as well just jump!"

"Now don't do anything we will both regret!"

"I could not give a flying fuck about your regrets, man! Don't even know who you are? I know you're fucking crazy though!"

The helicopter comes around again, closer this time, almost close to touch. The megaphone erupts from the helicopter but the combination of distortion, wind and propellers drown it out so it's impossible to hear what they are saying.

"You're going to jail, Spider. Might as well make this easy on yourself."

"Valentine will kill my ass!"

"They will be obligated to protect you. They'll put you in a different prison, I promise."

"You don't know him, he'll get to me. Guys got fucking connections. I'm dead now no matter what."

"Don't say that!"

"You seem like a nice guy... a real nice..." He head butts Vatican in the head and then with nothing left to lose, a tired Spider does the unthinkable and jumps off the bridge, grabbing hold of the helicopter landing skid which sends the helicopter into a spin.

"So long sucker!" Spider calls as he hangs from the rotating helicopter. Suddenly spider's eyes grow wide and Vatican can see he's losing his grip.

"He's down!" Freeman screams from the bridge pointing upwards as Spider plummets towards the Hennig River. He disappeared with a splash into the freezing dark waters.

"Where is the other guy?" Graham calls to the pilot. The helicopter circles the bridge several times, shining its beam in between the girders.

"That's a negative, Detective, He's gone!"

"I want somebody up there looking for this crusader, now! And I want some frogs in that river pronto! Drain the bastard if you have to!"

Chapter 39

Vatican could still hear the propellers of the police helicopter cutting through the cold air, but the sound was muffled. Occasionally he saw the searchlight saunter past him so he would stop and then when it had passed, he would move again. Slowly working his way back down the bridge, upside down like a sloth, gripping the girders from underneath. He heard the muffled voices above him of police officers surveying the scene atop the bridge, looking for any clues to who the mysterious man on the bridge was, they found nothing. Even the staff found its way into the Hennig River along with Spider. Vatican left nothing behind. Finally, Vatican reached a sturdy thick steel cable, he climbed onto it gripping himself around it the way a Koala grips the gum tree. He surveys what is left below. The tarmac is splattered with the blood of the fallen. Some of the fallen still lie in a heap, their lifeless corpses covered by dark shrouds. Some are shepherded on gurneys, dressed head to toe in black bags into the back of vans, unceremoniously piled in on top of one another, the start of a very long few days for the coroners. He slides down to the bridge edge, still hidden by the girders and looks down at the lights flitting around the surface of the Hennig River. He manages to bide his time and then scale down the concrete slope he first came up earlier that night, that seemed like days ago now. Ducking and diving behind several random police officers at the dockyards edge, he found himself in an empty abandoned warehouse where he collapses on his back on the dirty concrete. He gazed up through the broken skylights and the moon shone down on his exhausted body as he lay lifeless letting that damp cold breeze lap at his face. Vatican closes his eyes and he thinks of all that have fallen, many of which will not find their way into heaven and maybe the majority don't even deserve too. He rises and kneels, looking again skyward. They were still human beings, still fathers, brothers, sons, uncles and maybe even grandfathers. So he does the only thing he can, the only thing he has left in his power to do. He prays for them.

Revelation 12:7-11

Now war arose in heaven, Michael and his angels fighting against the dragon. And the dragon and his angels fought back, but he was defeated, and there was no longer any place for them in heaven. And the great dragon was thrown down, that ancient serpent, who is called the devil and Satan, the deceiver of the whole world—he was thrown down to the earth, and his angels were thrown down with him. And I heard a loud voice in heaven, saying, Now the salvation and the power and the kingdom of our God and the authority of his Christ have come, for the accuser of our brothers has been thrown down, who accuses them day and night before our God. And they have conquered him by the blood of the Lamb and by the word of their testimony, for they loved not their lives even unto death.

- The Holy Bible

Chapter 40

The red neon of the sign atop of The Devine Tower bathes the penthouse apartment below in a soft subtle shade of salmon, the colour of an expensive rosé wine. A wall of windows on one side of the luxury apartment arrogantly displays the best view of Studd City, in this gargantuan glass shard there is no hiding for The Devine tower sees all. Groans of female pleasure carries over the delicate sound of Frederic Chopin's Nocturne op. 9, No.1 in an alluring B-flat minor. It seems to waltz around the opulent open plan suite, caressing all the fine art and modern art with its tender sensual tones. Then the groans and moans of a woman on the verge of climax drown out the piano. Robert Devine erratically pounds away at his personal assistant, Michelle Hardy, as she groans restlessly on all fours, her head buried in the soft satin sheets of his large super king sized bed. Her pale ripe bottom pointed upwards almost yearning for more of Devine's aggressive thrusting. He tips his head back, his black wet hair flicking sweat down his back as he looks up to the ceiling, a mirror image of what takes place on the bed pleases his eyes and he smiles watching as she squirms and wriggles pleasantly under his masterful strokes. He wipes the sweat from his long slender facial features and moves in closer to her, his hand snaking around her thighs until he finds her sodden vulva.

His skeletal fingers manoeuvre as if they were the fingers of Chopin himself and locates her clitoris and strokes it gently. She gasps and arches her pelvis, her buttocks clenching together in relish as he continues to penetrate her and gently rub with his fingertips. He kisses her back and shoulder and smiles an arrogant grin as he speeds up the process of fingering the imaginary ivories until she explodes in an exasperating shriek of delight, her voice echoing around the apartment long and loud. Devine kneels up still thrusting his manhood inside her and now becoming one with the music. His toned slender body swaying in time as it reaches his favourite part of the piece. Michelle cries relentlessly with each barrage of her boss's penis. Devine's face changes to a look of annoyance at the sound of her caterwauling.

"Shut up, this is my favourite part." And with that he shoves her head down into the covers where it stays, the sheets muffling the sounds of her pleasure. Devine grinds to the music writhing with it as if he were conducting it with his body until he loses control and ejaculates. She collapses into a heap onto the bed, breathing heavily, her breasts glistening with sweat, the same sweat that mats her long strawberry blonde hair over her panting face.

"That was amazing!" She squeals.

Devine smiles and stands up wiping his pulsating penis on the satin sheets that lie in disarray. Suddenly his penthouse is filled with the brightest of light that obviously obtains Devine's attention.

"What is it?" Michelle says sitting up on the bed.

"Go to sleep!" he snaps.

444

"But..." she attempts to say something but is met by a glance that was unpleasant and almost scary, something in his eyes, something unnatural. She knows to do as she is told and lies back down. The light disappears for a few seconds but then is back again, lighting even the darkest nooks of his penthouse. A Helicopter hurtles past heading towards Ventura Bridge. Robert Devine strides towards the glass that fills one side of the penthouse and stands gazing at the extravagant light show that illuminates the bridge like it's opening night at the big top. He stares out of the window and his face contorts with an unpleasant look as though he'd smelt something decomposing under his flaring nostrils. Wearing a look on his face now as if he knows that a seed has just been planted that could grow up to be a beanstalk and entwine itself around everything he had built and squeeze until there is nothing left. A red tint flickers in his eye, only for a second, but that could have just been a trick of the light.

The Angel of Justice will return in...

VATICAN RETRIBUTION

Visit the website www.djbwriter.co.uk

Follow author Daniel J.Barnes on social media
@DJBWriter on Facebook, Instagram & Twitter.

Proud to be part of the Eighty3 Design family.
For all your website and graphic design needs.

www.eighty3.co.uk

Printed in Great Britain
by Amazon